A JACK BY ANY OTHER NAME

Also by Lesley L. Smith

Temporal Dreams
Neutrino Warning
Kat Cubed
Reality Alternatives
Conservation of Luck

The Space Operetta Series:
Book 1: *A Jack By Any Other Name*
Book 2: *A Jack In The Dark*
Book 3*: A Jack For All Seasons*

The Quantum Cop Series:
Book 1: *The Quantum Cop*
Book 2: *Quantum Murder*
Book 3*: Quantum Mayhem*

A Jack by Any Other Name

By Lesley L. Smith

Quarky Media

Boulder Colorado

A Jack by Any Other Name
Published by Quarky Media, PO Box 3332, Boulder, CO 80307
www.quarkymedia.com

Copyright © 2017 Lesley L. Smith

ISBN: 978-0-9973131-2-3 (ebook)
ISBN: 978-0-9973131-3-0 (print)

A JACK BY ANY OTHER NAME

Chapter One

"Mr. Jones, we need you to kill a man." The stranger glanced around nervously. A crowded restaurant was no place for such talk, even though people often thought it was. The high noise level only gave limited privacy. And, to be fair, although every table was occupied in this dining establishment, the thick carpeting and tablecloths effectively muted the clink of silverware and hum of conversations.

I shook my head. "You are mistaken, sir. I'm not an assassin. Killing is more of a hobby with me." I was a musician, a singer. And I wasn't even on duty right now. I was home on Earth for some much-needed R & R. This guy shouldn't be bothering me while I was on holiday. To give him credit, though, I was an excellent assassin, in addition to being an excellent singer.

"The only thing you should be doing here is eating," I said. "Have you had dinner? Would you like to join my wife and me? We've finished this lovely bottle of wine, but we can order another."

He leaned over the table. "I'm not here to eat." His rumpled twentieth-century-style suit didn't exactly inspire confidence. It was doubtful he had the judgment or the funds to call for a hit.

"Oh, come now," I said. "I insist." He had irked me by interrupting an evening with a delightful damsel--my wife and first officer. He either needed to go away or calm down and eat with us.

Or maybe I'd have to kill him after all. It does not do to encourage bad manners; one should retaliate urbanely but firmly.

Where was the lovely Gina? She'd gone off to the washroom a while ago. She should have returned by now. I stood up to get a better look at the rear of the restaurant. Was she on her way back to our table even now? Sadly, there was no sign of my lady.

As I sat down at the romantic table for two, a small dark spot appeared on the stranger's tie and quickly started leaking red fluid. He looked startled and tried to say something, but only blood came out of his mouth. He collapsed on the floor. It all happened quite quickly.

And then I felt something push me into the table. Pain radiated from my back and coursed throughout my body. That was not part of the plan.

I realized that, apparently, the rumple-suited stranger wasn't the only one who'd been shot.

What a bother.

"Mr. Jones? Jack?" a woman said.

I opened my eyes. I lay in bed surrounded by white walls, white sheets, beeping equipment and a beautiful woman in a white uniform. "Where am I?" I asked. "What happened?"

"My name is Sophia." She leaned over me a bit, giving me a view of cornflower blue eyes and perfectly even pearly-white teeth. "You're on Earth in a Duplication Center. I'm sorry to say you were murdered." She added gently, "You were shot."

I jerked back, and my body responded sluggishly. "What? Clearly, I'm alive. I'm not murdered. What are you talking about?"

"I don't know many details about the crime." She pushed a blonde curl behind her ear. "I'm a duplication engineer. Your original body was murdered, but we cloned it and downloaded your memories. Unfortunately, the last thirty-two years of your memories were lost, deleted." She shook her head. "It's unusual. It very nearly was a true murder."

Murdered. A new body. I couldn't talk for a moment. Finally, I said, "Thirty-two years of memories? What year is it? How old am I?"

"It's twenty-ninety-five."

Twenty-ninety-five? Bizarre. I remembered it being twenty-sixty-three.

"You were fifty years old." She had a great bedside manner, very calm, and seemed truly concerned about me. I felt safe. And it didn't hurt that she was one of the best-looking women I'd ever met.

Wait. "Fifty?" I didn't remember being fifty, forty, or thirty, for that matter. And I didn't feel fifty. I held up my arm and looked at it. I flexed. It looked the way it always looked, didn't it? I stared. It did look kind of flabby and pale.

"Your new body is eighteen years old, and you have eighteen years of memories, so you feel eighteen. For all intents and purposes, you're eighteen." She smiled at me. She had a nice smile. Dimples. I had no idea what fifty-year-old me would have thought, but I liked dimples. This woman was very hot--all athletic curves and bouncy blonde curls. This me thought he'd like to get to know her better. A lot better.

"Sophia, huh?"

She nodded.

"*Shall I compare thee to a summer's day? Thou art more lovely and more temperate....*"

She interrupted me with a giggle and then said, "Let's focus on your recovery for now. Can you sit up?"

I tried to sit, but my muscles were still too weak. It was weird to think this was a new body. It seemed like my regular body.

"We'll try again later, Jack," she said.

I searched my memories, but they seemed to be all there, my childhood and teen years. Unfortunately, I even remembered my parents' deaths years ago (cancer and cancer). And I'd never had any siblings. I was alone.

I guessed if I had no recollection of my later life, I wouldn't know it was missing, right? "I don't understand. I know I recorded my memories regularly--at least for the eighteen years I remember. I assume I kept recording. How could someone get to them? And who cloned me?" Cloning was very expensive. "Am I rich?" Please say yes.

"The Terran Cultural Committee paid," she said. "You must be important to them."

Why was I important to the TCC? The TCC traded Terran culture and technologies for alien culture and technologies and also kept an eye on Terran citizens and colonies throughout the galaxy.

If they cloned me, presumably, the fifty-year-old me was important. Would the eighteen-year-old me be? What if I wasn't?

9

Did they ever repossess cloned bodies?

I had another disturbing thought: I'd lived a lifetime and didn't know anything about myself. "Who am I, er, who was I?"

She touched her holo-pad. "The data says Jack Jones was the captain and lead vocalist of the TCC's premiere spaceship, the *Shakespeare*, before his murder." She glanced at me. "You basically flew around the galaxy and sang."

I did love singing and music, so that part sounded good. Exploring the galaxy sounded good, too. Being the captain also sounded good. Huh. Yay, me.

"Did they catch my murderer? Who was it? Why'd they murder me? What happened to him, her or it?"

"I don't have that information. Sorry." She threw me another glance. "It, ah, also says here you have a wife, Gina Gomez, and she's your first officer."

"A wife? I don't remember any wife." Family! Maybe she could tell me what was going on. Maybe she could comfort me in my time of need. "Please call this Gina woman." I hoped she was hot.

Sophia looked at her pad again. "Uh, actually, the TCC says you're not supposed to contact your wife. When you wake up, we're supposed to contact a Noah Anderson from TCC." She scrunched up her nose; it was adorable. "I already called him. Sorry. He's on his way."

I felt an urge to reassure Sophia. I reached for her hand and massaged it gently with my fingers. "It's okay."

She showed me her dimples again. Beautiful.

Whatever happened, I didn't want to forget her. "Hey, I bet memory recording has advanced a lot in the thirty years I've forgotten."

She nodded.

"You don't happen to have any spare gear lying around, do you?"

She bit her lip. "Well..."

I gazed into her eyes; they were beautiful, the color of a Terran sky right before sunset.

"I guess that would be okay. We do have a lot of tech here. I'll find something for you."

"Thanks." That was one mission accomplished. I wasn't

going to lose my memories again if I could help it. I was going to record my memories every day, and hopefully, they wouldn't get lost or deleted this time. Hey, I could do it every morning right after I brushed my teeth.

I settled back into the bed. Maybe this Noah guy would have some answers for me.

In the meantime, maybe I could research my murder and my pre-murder life and the TCC and the *Shakespeare*. "Can I borrow your pad while I wait?"

A seemingly bigger-than-life-sized version of a man stood next to my bed. He looked like a mountain--or a bear, a shaggy gray-haired bear. Did bears get gray fur?

Was this the murderer here to finish the job? I flinched.

"What's wrong?" the man said. "Oh, right, you don't recognize me. I'm Noah." He searched my face.

My face must not have given him the expression he sought. "Noah Anderson."

I shrugged. "Okay."

"I'm here from TCC."

"Good," I said. "Maybe you can tell me what the hell's going on?"

He sat down surprisingly gingerly on the edge of the bed. It creaked. "You got shot, buddy."

"I know that."

He held up his hands. "Okay, okay. Don't get your panties in a bunch."

Panties? Did men wear panties in this era? Or was this guy an asshole? My fists involuntarily clenched, but I didn't have the muscle tone to keep it up. Shit. I deflated.

"Who are you? Who shot me and why? Did they catch him? Why did TCC bring me back? What happened to my memory recordings?"

He shifted, and the bed rocked. "We're not getting off on the right foot here. I'm Noah. I'm your best friend. I'm sorry you got shot. I'm sorry your recordings were lost. We're still trying to figure out what happened. We don't know who or what shot you. We don't know if it was some kind of anti-TCC plot or if it was personal, or both. We're investigating."

"Anti-TCC plot? That doesn't make sense. Neither does personal. I thought I was a singer. Who hates singers?"

He leaned towards me and whispered, "The *Shakespeare* doesn't just spread Earth's culture around the galaxy. Really, the TCC is a bunch of spies. And you, of all the spies on a ship chock-full of spies, you were the biggest spy of them all."

Wow. "Really?" A spy? That didn't sound right. I didn't feel spy-y.

"Jack?" Noah asked. "Did you hear me? You were a spy."

"I heard you," I said slowly. "Am I still a spy?"

"That's a good question." He rubbed chin.

"New topic," I said. "You've had a month to find my killer." I'd read the news reports about my murder. "Did you get him? If not, any leads? And most importantly, am I still in danger?"

"We didn't get him." He shook his head. "We're not even sure the murderer was a 'him.' We haven't made progress on your murder or the mystery man who died after accosting you in the restaurant."

"No progress?" That seemed hard to believe. Was it possible they didn't want to solve my murder? That wasn't right. I shook my head. "Why not? Crimes should be easier to solve on Earth, not harder."

"Our best operative was out of commission, for one thing."

"Meaning what?" I asked.

He gave me an odd look.

Huh. "I'm the best operative?"

"Yeah," he said.

That was at least a little gratifying. On the other hand, how good could I be if I got murdered?

He paused for a moment, looking around the room. "At least you were."

"What am I now?"

"That's the question, isn't it? Since we haven't solved the murder, we don't know if you're still in danger or not. My gut tells me you are. What do you think?"

I surveyed my gut. It did not feel good. "My gut tells me I'm screwed."

"You always did have a good gut." He smiled a grim smile that didn't reach his eyes. Frankly, it was a bit scary. This guy

12

was my best friend? He seemed like he could break somebody in two if they looked at him wrong.

"We'd like you to go back on the *Shakespeare* and try to draw out the killers," he said. "What do you think?"

"What? 'Draw out'?" I'm embarrassed to say my voice squeaked. "You want me to be bait?"

"I keep forgetting you're not the old Jack." Noah grabbed my arm and then dropped it.

It flopped down on the bed.

"But you're definitely not him. You're not in very good shape. Your cloning was kind of a rush job."

Rush job? What did that mean?

He continued. "The *Shakespeare*'s leaving in a couple of weeks."

I tried to control the squeakiness in my voice. "I understand you all have made a large investment in me, and I really want to find my murderer or murderers." I took a deep breath. "I'm willing to go on the ship. But can't I go incognito or something?" I didn't want people shooting at me right off the bat.

He considered. "That's a good idea. But..."

"But what?" Squeak. Damn.

"Your singing voice is pretty distinctive."

I really, really didn't want to be a singing sitting duck. "Uh, what about if I'm Jack's son? I could have inherited his voice, right?"

Noah tilted his head. "Yeah. Not a bad idea, not bad at all. That could work."

Over the next two weeks, I was a good boy and did my physical therapy and voice training. TCC brought in several brutal therapists and kept me busy morning, noon, and night.

I did record my memories every day right around toothbrush time.

In the wee hours, I researched my old life and the *Shakespeare*.

Everything ached, but I was getting my muscle tone back, and I could sing pretty well. The squeakiness went away, at least.

Nurse Sophia, excuse me, dupe engineer Sophia seemed

dazzled by my voice. She somehow managed to be hanging around every time I worked with my vocal coach. What was it about women and singers? Whatever it was, I liked it.

Her friendly, delighted smile always brightened my day.

One night near the end of my stay at the dupe facility, she approached me. "You know, you were the most famous singer of your generation. Sentient species all over the galaxy sing your praises." She grinned and looked at me expectantly. "Pun intended."

I grinned back at her. I was tired of being treated like a piece of meat to be therapied into submission. It was nice to be appreciated, and she was awfully hot. I wanted to be treated like an actual person. I wanted Sophia to treat me like a man.

"You like me," I said. "Your beautiful smile was one of the first things I saw when I woke up."

"I thought you were cute." She pointed at me playfully. Another beautiful smile lit her face as she turned away to attend to her other duties.

"Maybe you could show me some of Jack's old performances?" I called after her as she walked away. I'd seen a lot of them already, but I figured it'd be extra fun watching them with her.

The better I felt, the more pissed about my situation I was. You couldn't just kill me and get away with it. The only bright spot was Sophia.

Once I was mostly recovered, in preparation for our new mission, the TCC booked my crew and me at a place in North America called Red Rocks. Our manager claimed I was still too weak to participate in any theater or dancing, so I was to do musical interludes--whatever they were. I insisted my dupe engineer accompany me--for my health, of course.

It turned out the venue was beautiful, a natural amphitheater made of red sandstone. We were to perform out in the open under the stars. I was psyched.

Noah had told me I had singing and spy skills, but I had a strong feeling that enticing women with my voice was my greatest skill. I was about to find out.

Sophia waited with me backstage before the show. I had

high hopes for our after-show festivities.

In the meantime, I was going to meet Old Jack's wife, Gina, in person for the first time, so I was a little nervous. What did you say to a wife you'd never met? She might not even know I'd been cloned. Awkward.

She showed up, very curvaceous, arm in arm, with another crew member, a Carter Nillion, at the last possible moment. Carter was also a good-looking guy, maybe not as good-looking as me, but not bad. They were both very attractive for old people. What were they--forty? The way they hung off each other, I assumed they were together.

"Greetings, Gina, Carter," I said with a flourish. "*The course of true love never did run smooth.*" Getting murdered definitely interfered with love's course.

I'd been in a lot of shows as a teenager and had been known for quoting the bard. When I studied the old version of me, he'd kept it up. Yay, Jack.

This version of me didn't know Gina and Carter, but if I had, I'd be guessing they were nauseated from the expressions on their faces.

"Who are you?" Carter asked.

"Yeah, who the hell are you?" She leaned toward me and glowered.

I stepped back, and Sophia squeezed my hand. I glanced at her, and she showed me those delectable dimples and nodded encouragingly.

Gina was intimidating. I was married to this? "I'm, uh, a new member of the troupe, Jack Jones Junior, at your service." I bowed with a flourish. I was good at flourishes.

Carter's mouth fell open.

Gina's skin seemed to pale under its chocolatey hue. "Jack didn't have a son."

"Yes, he did," I said.

"No," she said. "Who's the mother? No. I would've known."

"Uh, he didn't know about me." I just thought of that. Brilliant. It would explain why I didn't know much about the last thirty years of Old Jack.

Of course, it probably made me less bait-y. But as far as I was concerned, that was a good thing.

15

Gina narrowed her eyes at me. "Did Jack tell you about what we did in the mud springs of planet Geryon 876 d?"

I didn't react. I had no idea what they did in the mud springs. I knew what I hoped they'd, we'd, done in the mud springs...

"With those three native girls?" she added.

Maybe Gina wasn't as bad as she seemed. I smiled. "Sounds fun, but sorry. Never met him. But I do look forward to working with you and becoming friends." My smile grew. "And hearing your stories about the mud springs on Geryon 876 d, of course."

It was big of me to befriend my ex-wife, who clearly had hooked up with another guy, but then, I was big. Even murder couldn't keep me down!

Yeah, I was a little amped up about the show.

Gina and Carter exchanged a look.

"We're not working together," Gina said. "I'm the captain. I approve all the crew. I didn't approve you."

"I work for TCC." I waved my arm around backstage. They'd set all this up, after all. "I'm in this show, and I'm in the crew."

"But..." Gina looked around backstage. The crew was treating me like I was supposed to be here. Because I was. I was practically the star of the show. Hadn't they put this whole thing together for me?

Carter finally said, "Nice to meet you, I guess. Your dad was a good man, a good friend." And yet Carter hooked up with his wife so soon? It had only been about a month since I'd been shot. I'd have to keep an eye on this guy.

He poked Gina with his elbow. So far, he wasn't looking too nefarious.

"Yes," Gina said. "Nice to meet you."

"So, gosh, Jack hasn't had a chance to introduce me yet," Sophia said. "I'm Sophia Olsson. It's so nice to meet you."

Gina and Carter introduced themselves to her politely.

"And what's your relationship with Jack Junior here?" Gina asked.

"Nurse?" Carter smirked.

"Oh, we're lovers," Sophia said. We hadn't done it yet, but that boded even better for our after-show festivities. "He's wonderful." She leaned up and planted a juicy kiss right on my

16

lips.

My eighteen-year-old body responded enthusiastically. The kiss must be a promise of coming attractions. I really liked Sophia. She was my favorite homo sapien. Of course, she was one of the only homo sapiens I knew, but still...

"How old are you, young lady?" Gina asked.

Sophia smiled at her. "Twenty-five."

Carter coughed. "Standard Terran years? Wow. You're practically a baby."

"Thank you," Sophia said, and then, I could swear, she batted her eyelashes.

My former first and second officers didn't look happy. Ha. Yay, Sophia.

One of the stagehands came up to us. "There you are. We need to do sound checks. And Costume has been looking all over for you guys. You two go over there." He pointed Gina and Carter towards Costumes, and they followed his directions.

"You--" he pointed at me "--come onstage."

"Can I come?" Sophia asked.

"Whatever," he said.

As we walked onstage, Sophia said, "I'm proud of you, Jack. Was it difficult seeing Gina with Carter? How long were you together?"

I'd been investigating myself. "Decades." But she didn't want to hear about that. Buck up, Jack. I tried to smile. "Well, *the play's the thing...*"

"Why do you keep talking like that?"

I blew out a breath. "I'm trying to fit in. That's how Old Jack acted."

She smiled at me. She had an adorable smile. "That sounds like a lot of work. Seems to me that being murdered is a good excuse to let Old Jack go."

She made a good point, and I was still feeling that kiss. "Your wish is my command. So, Sophia, I appreciate all your help. I appreciate you. What do you say, after the show, you come back to my hotel room?"

"I thought you'd never ask." Hello, dimples. "But forget the hotel. You're coming home to stay with me."

17

The sound check and the costume fitting passed in a blur.

I felt excited but nervous, too. According to the biography of Jack Jones, he'd, or rather I'd, given hundreds of concerts over the years. So, why was I nervous? Maybe there was something wrong with this body?

If it hadn't been for Sophia at my side, I would have been a wreck. But she kept smiling at me, flashing her dimples, nodding, holding my hand or rubbing my arm.

After what seemed like forever, it was finally time for me to go on.

"I'll just sit here," Sophia said, planting herself delicately on a stool in the wings.

As I walked onstage, I looked out into the crowd, and it was packed, with people--mostly homo sapiens--sitting shoulder to shoulder on the sandstone benches under the stars. Clouds scudded by, alternately hiding and revealing the moon. The breeze was warm and lovely, not unlike Sophia. I glanced at her.

She waved charmingly.

When the music started, the sound was so amazing I turned around to check if an orchestra had snuck in when I wasn't paying attention.

They had.

Where did they come from? There must have been thirty musicians dressed all in black, sitting in folding chairs, reading music from black stands. They sounded wonderful. I loved live music; the human energy was exhilarating.

The lead violin gave me a look like 'quit staring.'

"Ready, Jack?" the guy talking in my earbud asked. "There's sheet music on the stand, there."

I nodded. I needed the music. Supposedly Old Jack never needed the music.

As I listened to the notes melding together, I lost myself. The only thing that mattered was the melodies, the chords, and the harmonies. The soul-transporting beauty.

My part started in the next measure. I breathed in deeply.

Chapter Two

Everything faded away except the music.

I was swept away by waves of munificent grace. My voice was an instrument, full and rich, embodying the symphonic sounds. I didn't have to strain to reach the highest or lowest notes. It was as if the music flowed through me from the collective souls of humanity's past directly to the souls in the audience.

As the last note faded away, I became aware of the spotlights shining in my eyes. I squinted and looked out into the audience, ready for the adulation that was my due.

They didn't move or make a sound. Several had their mouths hanging open. Some women had tears on their cheeks.

Why didn't they clap? Had Earth society changed so much in the thirty years I'd forgotten?

Well, whatever. I knew I did a great job. I gave them a small smile and bowed.

I turned to walk offstage.

Sophia jumped off her stool, her cheeks wet. She, at least, beamed at me.

As I walked toward her, she ran right at me and jumped into my arms.

Then, as if a spell was broken, the audience leaped to its feet and started clapping. Thunderous waves of applause broke over us. That was more like it.

Sophia whispered in my ear, "That was amazing. You may be the best singer in the history of the human race."

I knew I was good, very good, but even I had to admit that was a bit much. "Thanks, Sophia. That's kind of you." I carried her across the stage and set her down in the wings.

There, Gina and Carter were waiting to go on for their next scene.

"Wasn't Jack amazing?" Sophia asked them.

"Eh." Carter shrugged, face red.

"Not bad," Gina said. But, as I walked away, I could swear I saw her wipe a tear from the corner of her eye.

The rest of the show was pretty typical, from what I could tell. I got standing ovations for each of my sets.

Finally, at the end of the night, when the last scene had been staged, and the last note played, the crowd jumped to its feet, chanting, "Jack! Jack! Jack!"

But my voice was shot.

"You have to do an encore," Sophia said.

"Jack! Jack! Jack!"

I didn't want to give the crowd less than they deserved, less than my best.

The conductor stared at me, holding up his baton as if saying, 'What now?'

I had an epiphany. I walked onto the stage and approached the conductor, mic off. "What about the Terran world anthem? You guys know that, don't you?" That must still exist.

"Are you sure?" he asked.

"Yeah." I stepped to the front of the stage as the musicians played the first famous notes. Mic on: "Please join me, everyone." Mic off.

For a few minutes, everyone in the auditorium and everyone around the world watching on holo-view were united in Terran pride. If there'd been any military skirmishes on the planet, I'm sure they would have been put on hold.

Afterward, as the last notes faded away, the crowd cheered and clapped. "Jack! Jack! Jack!"

"Do another encore," Sophia said. She'd run onto the stage again. I'm not entirely sure she grasped the concept of a stage and how it was supposed to be for performers.

"I honestly can't."

"Aw."

"Jack! Jack! Jack!"

"I'm worn out," I said. "And we're shipping out tomorrow."

Via my earbud, the manager said, "Another encore, Jack?"

I shook my head. Mic on. "Thanks for coming, everyone. Good night!"

They turned up the house lights. The crowd started filing out.

On stage, musicians, men and women alike, mobbed me.

"Buy you a drink, Jack?"

"Want some company, Jack?"

"Great show, Jack."

"Want more company, Jack?"

"Want even more company, Jack?"

Sophia clutched my arm as the musicians threatened to separate us.

"Thank you all very much for your kind offers," I said. "But I have a previous engagement."

Reluctantly, the crowd parted. It was probably a grave disappointment for them, but they'd get over it. Eventually.

"I hope you're not too tired," Sophia said.

"Never fear, my dear. I'll persevere." I grinned. "You're my favorite, by far, Dupe Engineer. For a night with you, I'd crawl light-years."

She grinned back. "Goody."

As we found our limousine, people still clamoring around us, I couldn't help noticing Gina and Carter slip away unlauded. I didn't gloat--or, if I did, it was a very modest amount. "The man that hath no music in himself, nor is not moved with concord of sweet sounds, is fit for treasons, stratagems, and spoils."

I had to hand it to Sophia. She was as hot in the sack as she looked. She even taught me a few things I'm pretty sure hadn't been legal the last time I remembered having sex.

I was surprised to realize when I was supposed to report to the ship, I didn't want to leave Sophia behind. We had a real connection, and she was the only person this version of me knew.

"Thanks, Soph." I nuzzled her neck.

She turned and smiled at me. "I understand you have to leave Earth, and you have to be free to do your work, but *parting is such sweet sorrow.*"

Yes, it was. Something caught in my throat. "Can, er, can I

see you next time I'm on Earth?"

She nodded, eyes bright.

I whispered, "Then, *I shall say good night till it be morrow.*"

When I got to the ship, I didn't remember anything about it. Supposedly, I'd served here for years. I'd hoped familiar surroundings might jar something loose, but no go.

The ship itself was pretty amazing. At a kilometer long, it seemed huge; there were fifty decks. The interior design was surprising; virtually everything was covered with decoration or ornamentation: tapestries, props, and elaborate theatrical scenes painted on all the walls, as you might imagine Shakespeare's plays figured prominently. It felt like being backstage at a big historical theatre.

When I got to the bridge to talk to Captain Gomez to get my new assignment (which I was sure was important), an ensign made me turn around and go to the cargo hold.

I managed to find the cargo hold, but it was full of boxes and crates and not full of people giving out assignments. Even here, the walls had some dramatic murals. I liked murals. "Hello? Is anyone here?" I called out. "Ensign Jones reporting for duty."

A guy about my age, well-built, with tan skin, walked out from behind some crates and said, "Hey. You Jones?"

Was this guy my boss? "Uh, yes, sir. Ensign Jones reporting for duty. I guess I'm to get my assignment from you."

He pulled out his fon while looking me up and down. "How old are you, kid?"

Who was he to imply I was too young? He looked about twenty himself. "Old enough," I said. And, actually, he wasn't bad looking; he had a kind of healthy glow about him.

He chuckled. "Fair enough." He punched some keys on his fon. "You're in luck, kid. You're only here in cargo part-time. Your primary assignment is performing." He glanced up at me. "Featured performer." He glanced back at his fon. "Vocal training, dance, theatrical fighting." He smirked. What did that mean? "And way down at the bottom of the list, cargo bay, assisting me."

If I'd remembered being captain, I'm sure I would have been seething at the demotion to the cargo bay. But since I didn't remember, I was just excited to be on a spaceship.

On the other hand, it sounded like I'd have a bunch of bosses, and this guy was just one of many. Crap. I didn't like bosses. "Who are you again?"

"Daniel Martinez. Hold up your fon, and I'll send you your work schedule."

I did as he asked and glanced at the resulting schedule. My duties in the cargo bay weren't too onerous, mostly loading or unloading cargo, go figure, when we were on a planet.

"Ready to get to work?" He put his fon away and got some gloves out of his pocket.

"Yes, sir."

He chuckled again. "You don't have to call me sir. Save that for the officers. We're pretty easygoing down here."

Gloves. Now that would have been a good idea.

"You want to borrow my extra gloves?" Daniel asked, reaching into his pocket. "You must be new. First tour?" He held out another pair of gloves.

"Thanks." I took the gloves. What to say? Probably not *The quality of mercy is not strained, it droppeth as the gentle rain from heaven upon the place beneath. It is twice blest: It blesseth him that gives and him that takes.*

"Jones? You okay?"

"Yeah. Thanks." I put on the gloves; they fit like, well, you know. I liked this Daniel guy.

"So, what do you hear about our captain?" he asked. "I heard she's a platinum-plated bitch. She's got that first officer, Nillion, wrapped around her little finger."

Why would I be married to a bitch? I didn't understand Old Jack at all. "I guess I haven't heard much of anything. I'm new." Speaking of new, I was in the market for some new friends, some friends who didn't know Old Jack. This tour would last forever without friends. "Dude."

Daniel burst out laughing. "Dude? What century are you from?"

Ugh. Apparently, dude had stopped being popular sometime in the last thirty years. "Heh, heh. Gotcha. Joke."

"Stick with me," Daniel said. "I'll show you the ropes."

I needed some rope-showing. "Thanks."

Daniel was staring at me. "You know, you look a little

23

familiar."

Ugh. The moment of truth was here already. But I liked Daniel; I didn't want him to associate the platinum-plated bitch and whatever other dirt he had on Old Jack with me. "I'm the old Captain Jack Jones' son. People say I kind of look like him. But I'm here to pay my dues. I don't want any special treatment." Actually, I'd love some special treatment--if it was of the good variety and not of the murdery variety.

"So, uh, Captain Gomez is your mom? Sorry." He tried to backpedal like he was swimming away from a tsunami.

"No, no relation to Captain Gomez. My, uh, dad had a fling."

"Oh." Awkward. "Sorry to hear about your dad's murder."

I shrugged. "Thanks. We didn't know each other. Never met him."

"Okay," he said.

We went to work.

There was a lot of cargo to load and secure in the hold.

A lot.

I was very bored with moving boxes from one spot to another by the time my fon rang. "Yeah."

"Jack! Buddy!" The small hologram of Noah said. "I'm here. Meet me in your cabin?"

"What cabin? Where?"

"Who's that you're talking to?" Daniel asked, squinting at the tiny hologram.

I shrugged. "Some officer. He wants me to report to him."

"Typical," Daniel said. "I'll catch up with you later. Dude." He snickered as he turned back to his cargo containers.

Noah gave me directions to a cabin on deck thirty.

When I got there, that bear-looking guy stood in the corridor. "Hurry up. We don't want people to see us."

"Why not? So, go in. What's stopping you?"

"You are, Jack." He pointed at the locking mechanism, and when I didn't get clued in quickly enough, he pressed my hand against the pad.

The door snicked open, releasing a puff of stale air. I took a step forward.

"Wait." Noah put his hand out to stop me.

"I thought you were in a hurry," I said.

He pulled a metal device out of his jacket pocket, flipped a switch, and pointed it inside the open doorway. Nothing happened.

"I guess it's okay," he said and darted inside. He moved fast for such a big guy. "Come on."

"What was that all about?" I stepped inside, and he closed the door behind us.

"We don't know who murdered you, and your room hasn't been disturbed."

"What? You think they left a trap for me? For a month?"

"Maybe." He sat his large bulk on the edge of the cluttered desk.

"What do you want? For all I know, you're the murderer here to finish the job."

Chapter Three

In my cabin Noah shook his big head at me, gray hair flopping. "If I wanted to murder you, I could have easily done it in the dupe facility." He stared at me.

Gulp.

"I'm not sure I even believe all this spy stuff," I said. "Prove it."

He shrugged. "How? It's secret. Either you think I'm a credible source, or you don't."

That was convenient, if very annoying. "If I was the chief spy, what am I now?"

"That's a good question, Jack," he said, his voice more serious. "What kind of work assignment did you get when you reported for duty?"

"Performing and training and…." I scowled and looked down at the carpeting. "I had to go work in the cargo bay."

Noah suppressed a guffaw with difficulty. "Sorry, buddy. But at least it's low profile. You'll probably stay under the killers' radar longer."

I gulped. Staying under the radar sounded good, very good. He made a good point. I would stay under the killers' radar stuck in the cargo bay. And did I have any other skills, spy-type skills? Not that I knew of. "Did you have me assigned to the cargo bay?"

He smiled but shook his head. "Must be TCC."

"Are you going to continue the investigation on Earth after we leave?" I asked.

"Of course," he said. "I don't know what new leads we'll get, but I promise to personally follow up."

That was a little reassuring, but I still felt like I was flailing around here on the ship, and I wanted to conduct my own investigation. "I want to investigate here."

"Not a bad idea. You might turn something up." He politely left unsaid that Old Jack would surely turn something up. "I can give you all the official top-secret files we have on your career and your murder." He held up his fon.

"What about the security footage from the restaurant where the murder occurred?"

"Yeah," he said.

I held up my fon, and he transferred the data. But was the data he gave me reliable? I'd have to scrutinize it and decide for myself. I could already see that being an investigator basically meant not trusting anyone.

"You know, I have my own personal, unofficial resources and files, too," he said. "Most spies do."

"So, what? You're bragging?" He was getting on my nerves surprisingly quickly for someone I didn't know. Could that mean I did remember him on some level, subconsciously or something?

"Maybe you have some data hidden somewhere, too. Like here in your cabin. You might even have some cached memories here."

That was a very interesting idea. I pulled out the drawer in the small desk. No memories. No obvious murder-relevant clues.

Noah levered up his bulk. "Well, I said what I came to say. Good luck, buddy."

I was overcome with a moment of self-pity. My situation sucked; I didn't know what was going on or whom I could trust. I didn't have a family or even any friends that I remembered. "Were you telling the truth? Were we buddies?"

Noah grabbed me for a big bear hug on his way to the door. "You poor bastard." We hugged for a few seconds, and then he let me go. "We're going to figure this out. Don't worry." He paused in the doorway and looked back at me. "Check that. Worry. Watch your back until we catch the bastards."

As he left, I nodded, more confused than ever. Were Noah and I friends? Could I trust him? All I knew for sure was I needed more information.

So this was my cabin. I had at least two hundred square feet all to myself, with a bed, desk, closet, chair and tiny attached bathroom with toilet, sink and shower. It was luxurious. Had I picked out the furnishings personally? Or were they standard issue? I blew out a breath of air. Who knew? Not me.

On the wall over the desk hung some framed 3-D photos. There were several featuring an old but surprisingly happy-looking me with Gina. I shook my head. I couldn't figure out that relationship. She seemed like a bitch. She must be crazy-good in the sack--that was the only thing that made sense.

That made me think of Sophia for a moment. I missed her already. Heck, we were still in orbit. I decided to call her. It took her a long time to answer, and when she did, she sounded out of breath.

"Jack?" she said. "Are you all right? How did you hear about the explosion so quickly?"

"Explosion?" I asked. Oh no! "What explosion? Are you all right?" My heart felt like it was the thing that was exploding.

"The explosion isn't why you're calling?" she asked.

"Please slow down and tell me if you're okay, and then tell me about the explosion," I said, trying to speak calmly. I wanted to rush to her, hold her in my arms, and comfort her.

"My apartment blew up early this morning," she said. "They don't know what the cause was yet. I would have been there..." She paused. "I would have been there, but I couldn't sleep, I missed you, so I went to work very early." Her voice petered out.

"Thank God you're okay!" Surely apartment explosions weren't that common in this day and age. "Do you need a new place to stay? Do you need some money?" Did I even have any money? "Can I do anything for you?"

"You already have," she said. "It's nice to hear your voice."

"It's nice to hear your voice, too," I said. "I really care about you, Sophia. I'm very glad you didn't blow up."

"Thanks." Her voice sounded thick with tears. "If I hadn't missed you so much and gone to work early, I don't know what would have happened."

I had a horrible thought could my murderer possibly know I'd been staying at Sophia's apartment? My bait status had put Sophia in danger! My chest physically hurt. I had to sit down on the bed.

"Jack, I'm sorry," Sophia said. "I have to go. I have to go answer more questions from the police. But thanks for calling."

A JACK BY ANY OTHER NAME

"Of course, Sophia. I miss you, too. Please call me later if you get a chance. We still have a few hours before we take off. Take care. Bye." We hung up.

My mind was reeling. I had to lie back on the bed and try to calm down. I didn't have any evidence it was my fault Sophia's apartment blew up. But my gut was telling me it was. I needed to do something to protect her, but there was nothing I could do from outer space.

Maybe I should stay on Earth and try to protect her from nearby. But there was that damn bait factor again. Me being nearby wasn't safe for her.

First things first. I focused on calming my heart so I didn't die from stress. Somehow, I didn't think Old Jack had had this problem--getting too stressed out.

Calm. I. Am. Calm. I focused on my breathing. In. Out. In. Out.

Eventually, it worked, sort of.

Second things second. I needed more information. I sat up and looked at the photos again.

There was a photo of Noah and old-me, both with stout builds and graying hair, mugging together for the camera in what appeared to be some kind of bar. We looked enough alike to be brothers. We looked happy. Huh. Maybe we were buddies after all.

I decided to call him and ask him to keep an eye out for Sophia. If the explosion was my fault (and I had a strong feeling it was), I must have been under surveillance on Earth. Maybe they could find some evidence of that? He didn't answer, but I left him a detailed message.

I needed to do my own investigation and maybe find some people to help me. The sooner my murderer was caught, the sooner Sophia would be out of danger.

There was a photo of me in a big group of people standing on a planet with blue vegetation. I stared at it intently, but no one sparked the least bit of recognition.

I stood up. Now, if I were old-me, where would I hide my secret stash of data and/or memories?

If I were a secret stash, where would I be? I started searching.

I hunted late into the night but didn't find anything. Finally, I turned in, exhausted.

Sometime during the night, the ship took off from Earth's orbit. Thirty years ago, a launch would have called for parades, confetti, and other assorted fanfare. Now it was business-as-usual. It was jarring. And disappointing. I would have liked a little parade and fanfare. "Yay! Outer space! A big adventure! Yay!" Unfortunately, one person did not fanfare make.

I had a feeling a fanfare-less launch wouldn't be the last odd thing I experienced.

According to the mission schedule, first, we were stopping off at Alpha Catoblepas. In a few days, we'd be giving a performance there, a preview of sorts. It was considered an easy gig. As our closest neighbors, the Catoblepasans were used to us humans. They were our closest galactic friends. Maybe that meant they were our closest enemies, as well. I definitely needed to investigate them regarding my murder.

In the meantime, my first assignment of the day was stage combat. I could live with that. I'd been a little worried I'd spend the whole trip moving boxes around in the cargo bay with Daniel.

As I walked out of my cabin, I had a disconcerting thought: what if that was only Daniel's cover job? Noah said a bunch of the crew were spies. Was Daniel a spy?

When I showed up at the gym and found my trainer was hot, I could really live with it. She was only a little shorter than me, with not an ounce of fat. Yum. And her big brown eyes seemed very happy to see me.

"The rumor's true! Little Jackie!" she yelled and grabbed me in a hug, lifting me off the ground. Why did so many people feel the need to hug Jack?

"Hey! Let me go!" Her arms were like iron bands. I tried to escape, to no avail.

Eventually, she put me down. "Wow. I never was able to do that to your dad. Aren't you a cute little slip of a thing? I was sorry to hear about his murder," she added in a lower tone. Luckily, the two of us had the gym to ourselves.

"Thanks."

She stared at me. "You truly don't know me?" What was she

getting at?

"I take it you knew my dad?" It was disconcerting being manhandled by someone I'd never set eyes on and didn't recognize.

I did recognize her body was just begging for attention, though. And my body was begging to give it to her.

"Yeah, I'm Eva. I definitely knew him." She waggled her eyebrows at me. What did that mean?

"In that case, don't manhandle me, Eva."

She stepped back and arched her eyebrow at me. "This is combat training."

"I thought it was stage combat?" I asked.

"That's a cover. Considering what happened to your dad, you need the real thing." She grinned and took a step closer. "Maybe little Jackie-wackie would like another hug?"

"Don't call me that." I drew up to my full height--which was the same as ever, thank God. "If you don't watch what you say, you'll regret it. Or maybe little Eva would like a spanking?"

She laughed. "In your current state, I don't think you could spank anyone or anything that didn't want to be spanked. What kind of crappy muscle tone did they leave you with? On the other hand..." She looked me up and down. "I could go for some spanking and other activities." She grinned in a way that fired up the imagination. "Your place or mine?"

I felt my cheeks heat up like one of the ship's exhaust ports. I was game, but women hadn't acted like this the last time I was young. "Uh. Did you and my dad..." Since my so-called dad was really me, it wouldn't be a crime if we shared her.

It would be a crime to make love with Eva and not remember it.

And I did need to assemble some kind of team to help me investigate. Eva seemed like she could take care of herself, so to speak.

She laughed at my obvious embarrassment. Finally, when she caught her breath, she said, "Old Jack would never have hooked up with me. When I knew him, he was a one-woman man. But you're not, are you? You're really not him."

My face burned. "What does that mean?" She thought I was Old Jack? Why?

31

"I thought there was a chance you were a clone," she said. "But, no. There's no way you're the Jack I knew."

I finally managed to stammer, "If you think we should hook up, I'm game. But later." I smiled charmingly. I felt a pang for Sophia, but she'd encouraged me to get on with my life. This version of me seemed to be a one-woman-at-a-time man. So far.

"Really?" She grinned. "I didn't think you'd take me up on it. I thought you'd tell me to get thee to a nunnery or something. You're different from your dad."

I was already sick of hearing about Old Jack. But, duh, I needed to investigate. "What can you tell me about Jack's murder?"

She gave me a blank look.

"What's your alibi?"

She shook her head. "I gave a statement back when it happened, but now I don't recall. What day was it?"

"Uh, I'd have to double-check."

"I'd have to double-check my schedule then to answer that question," she said.

"Who do you think did it?"

Blank. Look.

"What do you think did it?" I asked. "Do you think a human did it?"

Blankness.

"Did he have any enemies?"

She shrugged. "I don't know."

I stared at her, but she truly didn't seem to know anything. "Can we just get to work now?" I managed to blurt out. "I think we've established I need some training when it comes to self-defense."

"All right," she said.

Initially, as she put me through my paces, I was very self-conscious, but eventually, all I worried about was breathing and releasing.

Finally, she threw the towel at me. Literally. "I guess you're not hopeless. You improved significantly, dramatically, just in this short session. I'm impressed." She reached for her fon. "Here, I'm sending you your training schedule. It's intense, but an eighteen-year-old can handle it."

A JACK BY ANY OTHER NAME

I glanced at the schedule. It was intense, with at least a couple of hours of workouts a day. "This is a lot. When am I supposed to rehearse? I need to build up the strength in my voice, too. That is my primary assignment, after all." And I needed to put together a team and investigate my murder.

She held up her hands, smiling. "Wait, don't tell me *all the world's a stage.*"

That must be something Old Jack would have said. "Well, yeah."

"You'll have plenty of time to rehearse." She stepped in close. "If you're anything like your dad, you'll want to find out who murdered him. When you confront him or her--or it--you need to be prepared."

"So it's, *screw your courage to the sticking place*?" I said.

"*And we'll not fail.*" She smiled. "I'm all in, Jack. I mean it, whatever you need. Your dad was important to me. I don't like it when people kill my friends. And I have a feeling we're going to be friends as well, good friends. Very good friends."

My throat felt full. I did have some friends on the ship. I nodded, not able to talk for a moment.

We walked toward the locker room. As we got to the hall, I finally said, "Thanks."

She smacked me on the rear with her towel. "And I may not be a flaming youth anymore, but you are. Again." She waggled her eyebrows again. She had very expressive eyebrows. "Join me?" She pointed into the locker room.

Standing so close, feeling her heat, how could I refuse? Plus, we needed to build our rapport if we were going to investigate together--I was guessing. I nodded and took a step her way.

At the same time, she chuckled and stepped into the locker room.

"Dude! Jack!" Someone punched me in the arm. It was Daniel. "Are you gonna hit that?"

Considering I'd tried and tried to hit her and failed to do so for the last few hours... But he was teasing me. He didn't think I stood a chance with Eva. "Sure, yeah," I said. "No doubt."

He laughed. "Yeah, right."

I managed to force a grin. It wasn't his fault he didn't know

Eva and me had a history. I barely knew Eva and me had a history. "Sorry, but I gotta go, Daniel." I pointed into the locker room, where Eva was, no doubt, nude by now. "I've got an appointment."

He shook his head as I rushed inside.

There was no sign of her near the lockers, but I heard water running. I pulled off my sweaty workout clothes and rushed to the showers.

As I approached, she looked over her shoulder. "There you are. I was beginning to wonder. What took you so long?"

At the sight of her perfectly formed naked body, water sluicing off her ass, my eighteen-year-old self jumped to attention.

She laughed in delight. "I guess you're worth the wait."

I crossed the space between us and reached for her. "Sorry, Daniel stopped me in the hall."

"Daniel?" She nodded. "Smart move befriending him." Her hand touched me, and I almost exploded.

My lips caressed her skin as water cascaded over both of us. There wasn't much blood left in my brain at this point. She'd said something. What did she say? "Thanks, yeah. Uh, why is Daniel good to know?"

"He handles all the black market stuff on the ship. Why do you think he works in the cargo bay?"

"Right." I cupped her breasts. "Black market. Yeah." What were we talking about?

Eva giggled.

After that, there was no talking for a while.

"Jack!" A stentorian bellow interrupted our current 'self-defense' lesson.

When I finally focused on the source of the voice, I realized Gina stood there, glaring, hands on her hips.

"Shit," Eva whispered.

"What the hell do you think you're doing?" Gina asked.

As I took in my large, muscular, rather livid ex-wife, I couldn't help wondering why she was so upset.

Was it possible we were still married?

Chapter Four

Somehow Eva faded into the tilework as Gina read me the riot act. "You shit," she said. "We aren't even divorced, and you're screwing the little self-defense trainer?"

"Uh? We, what?" My voice squeaked. Dammit. "What do you mean? You were married to my dad."

"I had your DNA tested, Jack." How? When? "I knew you didn't have a son. I'm not an idiot."

Shit. So much for my cover. Gina knew who I was, and probably Eva knew now, too.

And that answered that pesky marriage question, as well. Still married. Check.

"Keep it down," I said. "And I'm not the Jack you knew. I lost my memories." Standing naked under running water puts a person at a disadvantage in an argument. I turned off the water. "I'm sorry. I don't remember you. And the only reason we're not divorced is you thought I was dead. Considering what you've been doing with Carter, you don't have a leg to stand on, Gina."

"That's Captain Gomez to you!"

I had been starting to get pissed, but she was way ahead of me. My head of steam fizzled out. "I'm sorry you're upset about Eva and me, but you need to get over it. You need to get over me." I pointed down at all my impressive manliness. "Clearly, you still have all kinds of feelings for me, so much so that you have to confront me when I'm naked."

She flushed. "That's not... I'm not..."

"It's understandable." I felt sorry for her. Denied all this, all of me. "But you need to leave me alone in the future, or the TCC will get one hell of a sexual harassment lawsuit, Captain." I was guessing they still had sexual harassment in this day and age.

Gina sputtered. "You little shit. When you were captain, I never--"

Score. "So, we understand each other? You go your way, and I go mine? And you're not going to tell anyone who I really am?"

"Fine." She fumed. She seemed about to say something else but turned and stalked out.

As soon as she left, Eva reappeared. "Nicely handled, Jack. Or should I say, Jack Senior?"

Damn. Cover blown. Check. I was not good at keeping secrets. "Will you keep my cover? I'm supposed to be Jack Junior."

"No problem." The corners of her mouth lifted. "I think I'm going to like this version of you better, anyway."

I gave her a gallant bow. "Where were we?" I grinned.

Eva grinned back. "I think I remember. Here, I'll show you." She reached for the faucet and then me in quick succession.

But something was bothering me. What had Gina come here to say? Did she know Eva and I were having sex? If so, how? I glanced around the showers. Surely, the shower wasn't under surveillance, was it? Exactly how much of this ship was under surveillance?

The surprises just kept on coming. When I got to the music studio after lunch, I discovered Carter was my vocal coach. "You?" I asked in the doorway. The practice room was quite small and rather plain but still nice for this ship; the mural was of a group of medieval musicians. The room only contained an old piano and an old-ish Carter.

He winced. "I'm afraid so." He paused. "But I'm pretty good. You taught me everything I know."

Wait a minute. I taught him? "What do you mean I taught you? You mean, my dad taught you, right?"

"Sorry, Jack." He shook his head. "Gina told me it was you."

Well, shit. It was impossible to keep a secret on this ship. "You can't tell anyone. I'm undercover. And, I'm sorry, I don't remember you."

"Don't worry. I remember you. We were friends, good friends." He held out his arms like he wanted to hug.

I was irresistible. Check.

But I took a step back. "If we were ...friendly, how could you hook up with my wife?"

"We were friends. We are friends, Jack." He stepped towards me. "We thought you were dead."

That was a good point.

"And you know Gina." He read something in my face. "Or maybe you don't. But she's a force of nature. Unstoppable. Whatever she wants, she gets." He paused. "They didn't catch the murderer, did they?"

I shook my head.

"Aren't you worried he'll come after you?"

"Well, that's why I'm supposed to be incognito. Don't tell anyone who I am. Wait. How do you know the killer is a he?" Could Carter be the killer?

"He, she, it." He shrugged. "Who put you back here, anyway? It seems like it might be dangerous."

"Noah Anderson." I didn't say I was supposed to be bait.

"Noah? Shit." Carter's lips pressed into a thin line. "So, what you're bait?"

Now it was my turn to shrug.

"But if you're the bait, who's the fisherman? Who's going to catch the fish?"

"Shit." I hadn't thought that through. The two of us looked at each other like I was screwed. "Maybe Noah's got a guy here?"

"Maybe," Carter said, but he said it in a way that meant 'maybe not.'

"I can catch the fish," I said confidently.

He raised his eyebrows. "So, is our knowledge of your secret going to be a problem? Can you still work with me on voice stuff?"

From Carter's placating demeanor, I was guessing he hadn't heard the full details of Gina's confrontation with me in the shower. He had his own surprise coming. When he figured out she was still hung up on me and I wasn't interested, maybe he wouldn't be so cooperative.

Or maybe he thought I'd get shot again soon. Maybe he'd be glad. Maybe he'd be glad to shoot me.

Ack. He was with my wife. That was a motive if I ever heard

one. "So, uh, where exactly were you at the time of my death?"

He laughed, but there was no humor in it. "You're asking for my alibi?"

I shrugged. "Well, you know, since we're clearing the air..."

"I was questioned extensively by the Terran police and TCC's police as well." He frowned. "I'm sure it's in the reports you must have."

"Oh, sure, I have tons of reports that I've studied and studied." Not. I hadn't had a chance yet. "Remind me."

"I was in Paris," he said. "We aren't on Earth every day. I was taking full advantage of it."

"And this has been verified?"

"Yes." He looked calm, cool, and collected. Not the least bit worried or guilty. Damn. He would have been a great suspect.

"You know, most murders are committed by people close to the victim," he said casually. Too casually? Was he trying to throw suspicion on his wife?

Ack. I swayed, disoriented for a moment. Our wife. I grabbed hold of the door frame. Was bigamy allowed in this day and age?

"What's wrong?" He stepped toward me.

"I don't suppose you know what Gina's alibi was, do you?" I asked.

"Obviously, she was there, on the scene," he said. "You were eating dinner with her, for God's sake. But, supposedly, she'd stepped away from the table. That's what she claims, anyway. She said she missed the whole thing. It happened when she was in the ladies' room."

"And you believe her?" I looked into his eyes.

"Yes." He was still calm and cool. "I wouldn't have married her if I thought she liked to murder her husbands... Yes." But perhaps he wasn't looking quite as collected as he did a moment ago.

"Right." I blew out a breath. I wasn't a very good spy. I couldn't tell when people were lying. I needed a break from all this cloak-and-dagger stuff.

I pointed at the piano. "Let's practice. Start playing."

Once I got into the music, I forgot all about everything else.

My music session made the afternoon and evening fly by.

Carter was a decent vocal coach, but I didn't trust him. Who hooks up with his buddy's wife? What happened to the bro code? Could it have died in the last thirty years?

After dinner, I met up with Eva again for more vigorous so-called training in my quarters.

She rolled off me. "Wow. That was worth the wait."

I levered myself up on an elbow on my now too-small-seeming bunk. "What, wait? It's only been hours since we hit the showers."

"That was just the appetizer." She grinned. "This was the main course." She ran her fingers lightly along my chest. "I meant it was worth waiting for you to--"

I held up my hand. "Don't say the G-word." And technically, I hadn't broken up with Gina.

"Gina?" She smiled. "I was going to say it was worth waiting for you to notice me."

How could someone not notice her? She was hot with a capital H. I reached for one of her perfect breasts. "Oh, I noticed you." I squeezed gently. "I noticed you." Old Jack would have had to be dead not to notice her.

"Mmm."

I felt something stirring in my southern hemisphere. I freaking loved being me. "But speaking of the G-word, where did you go when she showed up?"

Eva arched her back, pushing her delectable chest into me. "Oh, you know. A secret passage."

But I couldn't concentrate on what she was saying anymore.

Much later, we both lay prone, exhausted, on my bunk. "What were you saying about a secret passage?"

She giggled. "Oh, I think we've thoroughly explored my secret passage."

"No."

"We haven't?"

"I mean, sure. We explored your passage." I couldn't help smiling. "But what were you saying about the shower? From this morning?"

"Oh, right." She sobered. "The ship is riddled with secret passages."

Surprise.

"You really don't know anything, do you?"

I couldn't disagree. "Can you help me put a team together to investigate my murder off the record?" Maybe I could catch the fish before he/she/it caught me.

She grinned. "I'll help you if you help me."

I grinned back. "What can I say? I'm all about the helping."

When Eva fell asleep, much, much later, I got up and finally perused the files Noah'd given me. Her easy deep breathing formed the perfect relaxing backdrop for my studies.

The security recordings of the murder itself in the restaurant were holographic, and I watched them from every direction. Unfortunately, the murderer was outside the frames.

There was nothing in Noah's files about secret passages or ship-wide surveillance. It did state that several members of the bridge crew and the featured musicians and performers were spies. I didn't recognize hardly any of the names or faces, however. How could I trust a bunch of people I didn't know? I couldn't, that's how. And were any of them supposed to be my fisherman? I had no idea.

I was going to have to create my own secret band of spies to solve my murder.

I glanced over at Eva, sleeping soundly, chest rising and falling regularly. She looked innocent and naive. I already knew enough about being an investigator to know I shouldn't judge people by their appearances. But she was the only person on board I felt like I could trust.

I'd been backing up my memories religiously when I brushed my teeth. But I didn't want to forget what happened with us tonight, so I did an extra memory backup.

I commandeered the gym first thing the next morning. Supposedly, we were all working out, but in reality, it was a meeting of my newly formed intelligence cabal. Eva had found a couple more people to help us. I wanted men and women working for me *with a lean and hungry look*.

She locked the door behind her and sat down with the rest of us. "Jack, this is Ander Sousa, and this is Sam Jain. Good men. I vouch for them. We can trust them."

They nodded.

I nodded back. "I'm Jack Jones Junior. Thanks for coming."

The two men Eva'd brought looked surprised.

"You're the old captain's son? A scrawny guy like you?" Sam asked. "I'd heard Captain Jones was built." Sam himself was about as wide as a refrigeration unit.

"Afraid so." I shrugged. "I need your help. I need to figure out who murdered my dad. If you're not up for it, if you're too scared or something, you can bow out."

"Scared?" Sam said in a growly voice.

"Why us?" Ander said. "Aren't a bunch of intelligence officers investigating?"

"Yeah," I said. "But I don't know what's going on with the official investigation except they haven't solved anything. And I don't know who I can trust. What if my dad's old colleagues were in on his murder?"

Sam blew out a breath and shook his head.

Ander looked at the floor. "Not. Good."

"Jack Senior didn't know you, and you didn't know him, right?" I asked.

No one disagreed with me.

"You'd have no reason to kill him," I said.

"So, you see, guys, we need you," Eva said. "Are you in?"

"For you, babe, anything." Ander practically simpered at her. What was that about? I was surprised to realize I didn't like it.

"I'm in, too," Sam said. "I don't like people who murder my crewmates." He smiled, but there was no humor in it. "I assume we'll be wreaking some vengeance."

I matched his smile. "Definitely."

"I enjoy vengeance," Sam said.

"Me, too," Ander said.

Eva nodded.

All of our eyes met. We were in agreement. I liked these guys. My murderer would pay dearly. "So, I need you all to sniff around the ship and see if you can find out anything. I'll do the same."

They nodded.

"When we land at Alpha Catoblepas, sniff around there as well," I said.

"I know some enterprising characters there," Sam said. "If

there's something there, I'll find it."

"I know some native females, of shall we say, ill repute," Ander said. "They know everything about everything. I'll consult with them."

"Yeah, I bet you will," Eva said, smiling.

She and Sam snickered a little. There was a story there I didn't know. What else was new?

"What do you want me to do, Jackie?" Eva laughed.

Sam and Ander snickered. I didn't like snickering—at least not at my expense.

I didn't rise to her bait. "Use your considerable feminine wiles. Find out what you can." I grabbed my holo-fon. "I'll shoot you the files, what they've got on the murder so far." I sent them off. "It's pretty skimpy, so anything you can find will be helpful."

"What about you?" Eva asked.

"I will try to investigate on the ship. Unfortunately, I'm supposed to perform in the big show. I'm not sure how much I can accomplish working around that. But I'm going to try to nose around the city."

Eva wrinkled her brow. "Maybe you shouldn't be in the city without a security escort."

She didn't think I could defend myself? That was too much. "*Unkindest cut*!" I jumped up. "I'll have you know I'm still an excellent fighter, with or without weapons."

"Oh, yeah?" She stood up and got her face right in my face. "Show me."

"Whoa, whoa," Ander said, holding up his hands. "I don't want to watch your foreplay, or whatever this is."

I felt the blood rush to my face.

"Yeah, are we done?" Sam asked. "I got stuff to do."

"Yes," I said. "Thanks for your help."

The two men started walking for the door.

"And then *tonight let us assay our plot*," I said.

Ander and Sam turned around.

"Ignore him," Eva said, grinning.

The guys exited.

"You do need to work out, you know," Eva said. "And not the way we worked out last night and today before breakfast."

"Yes, ma'am," I said. "I know. But I also have rehearsal."

"I know," she said right before she lunged at me.

I was slow to react. I had trouble thinking of Eva as a sparring opponent after all our extra 'training.' I barely got out of the way in time. "Shooting for a take-down, huh?"

"Less talking, more fighting, old man."

Chapter Five

Between my murder investigation, voice training, self-defense training and extra-curricular 'training' with Eva, I was pretty worn out when I reported for duty at the cargo bay when we got to Alpha Catoblepas. I moved various boxes where Daniel told me to move them.

"What is all this crap, anyway?" I asked.

"Cultural artifacts, specialized foodstuffs," he said.

"Why?" I asked.

"It's for trade." He shrugged. "I just move what they tell me to move."

Already, I knew Daniel did a lot more than that. Was some of this cargo part of his black market? I needed to stay on his good side. Who knew when I might need black market-somethings?

"So, did I ask you, did you know my dad, Jack Jones Senior?" I asked.

"I knew who he was," he said. "He was the captain."

"Who do you think murdered him?"

He froze for a few moments. "That's a very good question."

"So, no ideas?"

"Nope." Somehow I didn't believe him.

My fon pinged. I was late for disembarkation. "Sorry, boss. Gotta go."

I ran through the halls to join the crowd in the disembarkation lounge. It looked like it was hurry-up-and-wait--what a surprise.

"You look like crap, Ensign Jones," Gina said, filling out her captain's uniform nicely.

"Gee, thanks, Gina," I said.

I couldn't help noticing her lips were full and pouty as she sneered at me. What had she done to Old Jack with those lips? It was probably better I didn't remember.

"I think you mean, 'Yes, ma'am, Captain Gomez,'" she said.

"Okay." I glanced around the lounge. It was only the fifty-odd senior-most officers in here. Some of them seemed confused about why an ensign would even be here with them. But in general, the crew didn't look impressed with Gina throwing her weight around.

And why bother? She must be insecure about something.

"Uh, yes, ma'am, Captain Gomez," I said with minimal enthusiasm.

With my fon, I checked my schedule. It looked like a bunch of rehearsal stuff and some kind of press conference. Crap. How could I investigate my murder if I was booked up? I decided to blow off such petty obligations.

Once Gina turned away, Carter came up behind me and patted me on the back in a fatherly fashion. "Sorry about her, Jack. She didn't mean anything by it. It's just her first mission as captain. She's a little nervous and wants everything to go perfectly."

I didn't know Gina very well, but even I could tell she wouldn't want Carter telling secrets he'd gleaned via pillow talk.

What was his game? Was he trying to lull me into a false sense of security with his purported friendship? Or was he truly trying to be friendly? If so, why? A guilty conscience? Or did he want to be friends, for real? I didn't like being so in the dark.

He smiled at me, waiting for my response. Then he pulled me aside and said, "What's that look?"

"I'm just wondering what your game is." Shoot. A good investigator wouldn't have revealed that.

He chuckled. "I appreciate your honesty, Jack. I'll be honest, too. I don't have a game. You mentored me for years. You were sort of a father figure to me. I thought now, maybe, I could return the favor."

Luckily, no one was near enough to hear us. "I'm Jack Junior, remember."

He nodded. "Right." Was he intentionally trying to blow my

cover?

"The circumstances are weird." I narrowed my eyes. "I guess we'll see if you're being honest or not."

He chuckled again. "I guess we will."

I was glad he was being pleasant because we had to work together. So far, his vocal coaching had been going fine. My voice was stronger than ever.

"I know you're still trying to get your bearings, but, uh, Jack Senior was very popular with the ACs, so keep your eyes and ears open down on the surface. Maybe one of them will let something slip."

"AC?" Air conditioning?

"Alpha Catoblepasans." I must have looked ignorant because he added, "The natives on the planet. You know we get the FTL drives from them. Any clues on how it works or where they got it would be helpful. Any intel at all could be helpful."

I must have still looked ignorant because he said, "You read the briefing materials on the planet, right?"

What briefing materials? Who had time for reading? "Of course. Yeah. You know it." *He doth protest too much.* I smiled to cover.

The outer door finally opened, and the crew surged forward.

We started walking towards the exit.

I didn't like being thought of as an ignoramus. "Did you know the reason there's so much intelligent life in the universe is the Anthropic Principle?" I said. "Only a universe capable of supporting life has living beings in it. Since we exist, the universe must support life, a lot of life."

"Yeah, I knew that," he said. "It's ancient history."

It had been the latest and greatest theory last time I checked--thirty years ago.

He glanced at me, took in my expression, and said, "Sorry."

We stepped through the door.

I was on another planet! Intellectually, I knew Old Jack had been to scads of other planets, but this was my first. As soon as we stepped off the ship, everything smelled alien, and I had to suppress my fight or flight response as my heart hammered in my chest. The scent reminded me of a bakery for some reason.

A JACK BY ANY OTHER NAME

All the people around me (except the *Shakespeare*'s crew) were different. My mind boggled. I mean, there'd been some extraterrestrials at the concert on Earth, but somehow I hadn't paid much attention to them.

The crowd at the spaceport consisted mostly of bipeds, and they streamed around us on their own missions. Apparently, bipedalism was a good design. I wasn't exactly surprised. What could I say? I liked it.

The non-bipeds were bizarre. I couldn't hold them in mind with their strange number of appendages and torso shapes. I twirled around, gaping, checking them all out.

One creature slid by that looked sort of like a six-foot-tall blue octopus, with appendages waving in the air and leaving a faint slimy trail in its wake.

A large group of creatures with exoskeletons, narrow waists, and antennae buzzed past me. They appeared to have small vestigial wings on their backs. I accidentally caught one's eye, and the cold, insectile feeling I got made my blood cool.

I felt something on my back and jerked away.

"Relax, buddy," Carter said. He'd put his hand on my back again. "Are you going to be all right? You look like some kind of a rube seeing extra-terrestrial intelligences for the first time."

I did not point out that I was some kind of rube seeing aliens for the first time. I shrugged. "No worries. I'm fine. Cool."

He grinned like he was humoring me. "Okay. I'll see you later at the show?"

I nodded. That was the official reason the ship was on the planet, showing off Earth's culture. I knew that, at least.

He turned and seemed to search our group for someone. He spotted him or her, smiled, and strode off.

I was tempted to just plant myself on a bench and watch the aliens stream by, but surely spaceports all looked pretty much the same? Plus, it was very doubtful I'd find clues to my murder while sitting at the spaceport.

Once I exited the building, the scenery was even more dramatic. Everything was different, the color of the sky, the color of the sun, the color of the vegetation, and even the smell.

The purple sky reminded me of the grape soda I'd loved as a boy. I felt my mouth stretch into a grin. I didn't know if it was because of the grape sky or not, but the sun here looked green. Very cool.

I stepped towards the planter near the door, staring at its bizarre contents, and reached out to touch one of the blue leaves. Was Alpha Catoblepas where that picture of Old Jack and his friends had been taken?

I took a deep breath of the alien air and held it in. It had a faint tang of spices, maybe cinnamon?

I felt energized and bounced on the balls of my feet. Correction: I felt amazingly energized. Gravity must be lower than Earth's. It felt like I could take off and fly. Maybe the oxygen content was higher too? I loved this planet and couldn't wait to see what an alien city was like.

I followed the crowd to a moving walkway. The right-most strip where you entered moved the slowest. As you stepped left, you embarked on faster and faster-moving strips. On the left-most edge, we fairly flew along. The cinnamon scent pervaded the air. The foliage outside melded together in a blue blur. With the purple sky it all reminded me of Picasso's Blue Period, which I studied in art class--thirty-some-odd years ago, and which seemed like yesterday. I shook my head a little, grinning. Yes, my life was bizarre.

A series of illegible signs started appearing above the walkway, and folks shifted right to exit. I was starting to realize it might have been stupid to blunder into a new city where I didn't speak the language or know the customs, but it was too late now.

Ahead of me, most creatures were exiting, so I deduced we were approaching the city center. I exited.

The city was built of typical-looking stone: gray, white, and red. I guess slate, granite, limestone, and iron ore look the same on any planet. I also studied Earth Science in high school. Who would have guessed all those high school classes would be relevant on Alpha Catoblepas? Maybe I should have paid more attention to the teachers and less to the hotties in class.

I grinned. Nah. I made it into outer space anyway, didn't I? No harm done.

I sat down on a bench made of iron ore and watched the aliens go by on foot and bicycle-like contraptions. I didn't see anything like a car or motorcycle here in the city center.

The most common creatures were bipeds with faces that reminded me of mice with weak chins, prominent noses, and big ears. They must be the natives. Their clothing varied a lot from pants with tunics, to dresses, to large sashes, with colors primarily in the brown to gray to black range. Business attire, I surmised.

They moved quickly along the street, and as I watched them, I was reminded of a quote from one of my favorite books: *These creatures you call mice, you see, they are not quite as they appear. They are merely the protrusion into our dimension of vastly hyperintelligent pandimensional beings.* Heh, heh.

I laughed.

One of the natives stopped, looked at me, and then, presumably, said something. It made noise, at any rate.

I held my hands out. "I'm sorry, I don't speak Alpha Catoblepas."

It fiddled with a piece of tech that looked like a fon. "I said, are you in distress? Do you need assistance?" Surprisingly, the voice that came out of the little fon was very bass and deep.

I couldn't help laughing again.

"Are you having a seizure? Shall I call for medical assistance?" the deep voice asked.

I shook my head, still laughing. When I could talk again, I said, "No. I'm fine. I don't need help."

The creature frowned and muttered as it walked away.

I was lost.

Night was falling, and I was alone and lost in an alien city! I didn't even see any other humans, and the closest ACs were in the distance.

The sky was darkening to a beautiful indigo blue, and another much fainter sun was rising in the sky. It was still light enough outside to read by. Of course, all the street signs and advertisements were in the AC language--which I didn't know--but if I had known it, there was enough light to read the signs.

I couldn't say I'd found any clues about my murder, but somehow I didn't care. I'd had a wonderful day exploring AC.

And I still felt totally energized.

I'd be great if I wasn't worried about finding the concert venue before I had to go on. If I missed the show, would they leave me here? No doubt, Gina would be pissed, at the very least.

I pulled out my fon. Who to call? Whoever I called, I was guessing they'd tease me something fierce about being lost. I was pretty sure I wasn't supposed to get lost. I was pretty sure spies didn't get lost.

I decided on Eva. She was the closest thing I had to a friend.

She picked up right away. "Where are you? I'm at the venue. I thought we could meet up."

"I'm not sure where I am," I said, bracing myself, dreading the worst.

I wasn't disappointed. Peals of laughter assaulted my ears. Finally, she said, "Oh, that's rich." Then she laughed some more. At least her laughter had a lyrical quality.

I found myself smiling, too. "All right, already. Can you help me out? What should I do?"

"I keep forgetting you don't know anything," she said. "Did you even take the meds?"

What meds? "Uh, of course."

She continued. "Turn on the locator app on your fon. Bring up the city map app--"

"Shit," I muttered. It was all so obvious now that I knew. I could see the venue marked on the little map. "Yeah, yeah. I got it. Thanks."

She was still chuckling as she hung up.

I stared at the app. It was almost like my subconscious mind was working against me. Why was the locator app off in the first place?

I got my bearings and started for the theatre. I checked the time, and there wasn't much of it, so I started jogging.

Then, some shards of rock flew off the building I'd just passed. I stopped and stared. Weird. Exactly how alien was this world?

I felt an unsettling prickle of danger, and my subconscious told me to hit the ground.

More shards of rock flew off the building where my head

had been seconds before.

Shit! Someone was shooting at me!

Chapter Six

Time seemed to slow as I lay prone on the sidewalk.

The gunfire was almost silent. All I heard was a kind of *thwack-crumble* as the bullets impacted the building behind me. I could see an AC out of the corner of my eye.

Why was he shooting at me? What'd I ever do to him?

I bet if I was Old Jack, I'd have a gun and could shoot back. Did the asshole shooting at me think I was Old Jack? Had the asshole shooting at me shot old Jack?

Shards of stone flew around me. One grazed my face. Ow! I put my hand up to the pain and came away with blood.

Run away! Run away!

I started standing, getting ready to run, but something whooshed by my head.

Again, I hit the ground, now peppered with pieces of stone.

Crawl away! Crawl away! I got up on all fours and scrambled to a nearby alley as fast as humanly possible. The random grit on the sidewalk bit into my palms. Flying shards of rock continued to follow me. Somehow the lingering smell of cinnamon made it all seem surreal, like I was trapped in some kind of nightmare bakery. Crawl faster, Jack!

Finally, I turned the corner and collapsed on the sidewalk, panting.

The sounds of bullets hitting buildings stopped.

Well, I'd learned one thing from all this: I made awesome bait. And I was pretty darn good at crawling. Yay, me.

As I lay there, one of the natives minced up and stared down at me. "Do you need assistance?" a deep booming voice from a tiny fon asked.

I nodded. "Yes! I need assistance. Please assist me."

"How can I assist you?"

Call the cops? Did this world have cops? Give me a gun? I didn't hear any more shards of stone flying around. Maybe that emergency was over.

Back to my previous emergency. I was late to the show. I levered myself up. "What I really need is a ride."

He--I think, he was wearing pants, anyway--said, "I can procure transportation for you."

Yay.

I hurried through the back of the theatre to the stage area.

Someone grabbed my arm. "Jack! There you are." It was engaging Eva.

"Oh, Eva, I'm so glad to see you." I enveloped her in my arms, pressing my chest into her chest. I could feel her heart beating. Beat, beat. I could feel my heart beating. Beat, beat, beat. Feeling her warmth, I started to calm.

"Where have you been?" She gently pushed me away."They already pushed your first number back."

"I got lost--"

"I know that." She frowned. "What happened to your face? Is that blood?"

"A piece of rock hit me." I felt a giggle bubble up in my chest. "A big man-mouse saved me. He gave me a ride on his big bike." Surreal-city. I started laughing and couldn't stop.

"Are you high?" she asked.

I leaned over, palms on my knees, chuckling and guffawing. My palms were sore, covered with bruises and tiny scratches.

Enveloping Eva grabbed my arm and pulled me up. "You're high, aren't you?"

I straightened, trying to tamp down the bubbling in my chest. "I'm not high. I didn't take anything, I promise."

"Jack!" Enticing Eva did not look happy. "You were supposed to take your meds before you disembarked from the ship. On this planet, the higher oxygen levels and the organic hydrocarbons emitted by the native plants make humans high. I know you're practically a baby, but how do you not know this?"

"No one told me," I said, trying and failing not to giggle.

"Didn't you read the briefings on this planet?"

"I didn't have time."

"Who's your supervisor? This is your first mission, sort of-- they should have briefed you."

"Well, you're my combat supervisor, Daniel's my cargo bay supervisor, and Carter's my singing supervisor. I don't know who my bait supervisor is."

"Your what supervisor?" she asked.

"And for all I know," I said, "I've got even more supervisors. Maybe a funeral supervisor for my upcoming funeral? I don't like supervisors."

"Funeral? Apparently, we dropped the ball." She pursed her lips, which made them very kissable.

I leaned in.

She leaned away. "This isn't the time."

"And I really dislike bullets and bullet supervisors." I touched my injury. It had stopped bleeding, but it still stung.

"Bullets! What the hell happened?"

Carter darted up. "There you are, Jack. We've been holding your numbers. Are you ready to sing?"

"I like singing."

He examined me. "What's wrong with him?"

"He's high. Didn't take any meds."

"I don't like bullets."

"Bullets?" Carter glanced at Eva. "We don't have time for this." He grabbed my arm and pulled me toward the stage. He turned to glance at Eva. "Track down some meds for him ASAP."

Carter dragged me to the stage and pushed me out.

The music swelled.

I closed my eyes, letting the music wash over me, embrace me. Hello, old friend. Now I felt safe.

I sang.

My voice became one instrument among many. I was swept away by the melodies and harmonies, notes converging and diverging. The music swept through me; I was but a conduit of some higher beauty. I kept going, singing all the songs I'd rehearsed.

When I came back to myself, the audience was on its feet, clapping and stomping. Now, that was more like it.

I raised my arms, and the applause thundered. I smiled and

bowed.

I sauntered offstage. That's how you do it.

Eva's eyes were bright with tears.

"You may be a fuck-up--" Carter said.

"Hey!" I said.

"But you're a damn good singer," he said.

Eva stuck me with a needle and depressed the plunger.

"Hey!" I said.

"Hay is for horses," a woman's voice said. Gina's voice. "We need to talk. You three with me back to the ship."

We followed her to what looked like a giant pedicab. Four locals sat at the pedals in front.

As soon as the four of us were inside, Gina slammed the door shut and yelled. "Go!"

It took a few moments, but slowly the vehicle started moving.

Gina wagged her forefinger at the three of us. "What shenanigans have you gotten up to with Jack Junior? He missed the rehearsal and the press conference. He almost ruined the concert. The last thing I need is an interplanetary incident."

I didn't feel like giggling anymore. The planet didn't seem as magical as it had earlier. I was embarrassed about how stupid I'd been acting. I should have read the mission briefing about the planet.

I should have brought a gun with me.

I should have said I wouldn't be bait.

Carter said, "We weren't involved in any shenanigans, at least I wasn't. Jack said there were bullets... Somebody shot at him?"

"Bullets?" Gina peered at the blood on my cheek. "Are you all right, Jack?" She glanced at Eva. "I mean Jack Junior. Your, uh, Dad would be disappointed if something happened to you on my watch."

I couldn't tell if she was being sincere or covering her ass. I was tired; I leaned back into the seat. "I'm okay." We were moving along at a good clip now. The cool breeze felt good on my face.

"But someone was shooting at you?" Eva asked. "Uh, Jack Junior."

Carter looked from Gina to Eva and back. "You know, don't you, Eva?"

"Know what?" Eva asked.

"Know this isn't Jack Junior," Gina said.

"It's not?" Eva raised her eyebrows.

"Oh, good grief," I said. "Yes, you all know. Get over it."

"You told Eva?" Gina asked. "You're undercover."

"Me? It's my secret to tell." I jabbed my finger at her. "You shouldn't have told Carter."

She had the grace to look embarrassed.

Carter snorted. "You may technically be Jack, but you are not good at keeping secrets. The original Jack would have died before he broke cover."

I was sick of this guy pointing out my supposed flaws. My fists clenched. "Or maybe he'd just kill whoever knew his real identity?

The smile on Carter's face died an early death. Maybe Old Jack's reputation preceding me wasn't entirely bad.

Eva grabbed my hand and caressed it gently.

I relaxed a little. "Anyway, that's not the point. We need to focus. Who shot at me and why?"

"Did you get a look at them?" Eva asked. "Take a picture?"

"Picture?" Shit. I should have taken a picture with my fon. I shook my head. "I saw the guy in my peripheral vision. It was a native."

Gina rubbed her forehead. "It's odd for natives to use guns. Are you sure it was a gun?"

"Are you sure it was a native?" Eva asked.

"I didn't get a good look at the actual weapon, if that's what you're asking. I must admit I was too busy ducking and trying to get away to study the weapon or the shooter. It sure acted like a gun. And all I can say is it looked like a native--I didn't test his DNA."

Gina frowned.

"Could you pick the shooter out of a photo array or a line-up?" Carter asked.

"You're kidding, right? These creatures all look the same." I glanced at the drivers of the cab in front of us. They couldn't hear us, could they?

"That's not politically correct," Gina said, but a smile tugged at the corners of her mouth.

"So, to summarize, a mystery native shot at you, and we have nothing to go on," Carter said.

Again, I resisted the urge to punch him.

"Something else was going on," Gina said. "Why did you just give him a shot, Eva?"

Carter's and Eva's eyes met.

"It was just a vitamin cocktail," she said. "Jack asked me to give it to him."

They were covering up the fact that I'd been unprepared for a foreign planet. Why were they helping me? My eyes got heavy. I did have some friends, after all. I wasn't alone in the universe. I blinked.

Gina narrowed her eyes, scrutinizing the three of us.

"Yeah, she was supposed to give it to me before the concert," I said. "Carter pulled me onstage so quickly, we didn't get a chance."

"Yeah, that's what happened," Carter said. For a spy, he was not a great liar.

Eva nodded enthusiastically. "Yep, that's what happened."

Gina pointed her finger at Eva and me. "Or, maybe you two have been having too much sex, and Jack wasn't prepared for the mission."

Was there even such a thing as too much sex? The cab was slowing down as we approached the spaceport.

"Why do you care how much sex they're having?" Carter asked her.

"We're here." She stood as the cab rolled to a stop.

"How do you even know they've been having sex?" Carter asked.

Gina threw open the door and bounded out.

"Gina, don't walk away from me." Carter quickly followed her.

I sighed. I was tired. It must have been an aftereffect of fight or flight. I grabbed Eva's hand. "Speaking of sex..." I wasn't too tired for that.

She pulled her hand back. "We probably have been having too much sex. I'm not doing my job protecting you."

"I didn't know you were supposed to protect me. I'm an adult. I admit I should have done more to prepare for this mission, but I learned my lesson. From here on out, I'm preparation-city. I don't need you to protect me."

"I think the evidence suggests you do need me to protect you. You could have been killed tonight." She shook her head. "I'm not sure this whole thing, us, is a good idea, with Gina and everything else."

"Gina? What does she have to do with it?"

"She was your wife, Jack, for years. From her perspective, it's only been six weeks since you died. Those kinds of feelings don't just turn off. She probably still loves you."

"But I don't even remember her."

"An adult would have compassion."

Damn. Empathetic Eva was right.

Chapter Seven

I lay on my bunk (alone) in my cabin, but my mind wouldn't turn off. The events on the planet just kept going around and around in my brain. Why did that native shoot at me? Did he think I was Old Jack? How would he know that? Why did it happen right after I turned on the locator app? Why wasn't the locator app on in the first place?

Why didn't I take a picture of the shooter? Could I have done something to stop him? Was he hired by someone else? If so, who? And why? I turned and punched my pillow, trying to get comfortable.

My mind spun off onto more personal matters. What was up with Gina? Did she still love me? If so, what should I do about it? What could I do about it? How did Eva feel about me? Was she serious about cooling things off between us?

I couldn't even remember the last time I'd slept alone. Back at the dupe facility? Then, I wondered how Sophia was doing and if she was safe. I wondered if Noah had found anything out about her apartment explosion.

I sat up. Sleeping was hopeless.

I got up and sent Noah a message asking about Sophia and for any updates on my murder case. It'd take a couple of days for my message to get transmitted to Earth and his message to get sent back. Interstellar travel was very inconvenient for communications.

Still jumpy, I accessed the Alpha Catoblepas mission briefings. Sure enough, it said very clearly that we were supposed to get inoculated before going down to the surface. However, it also said the natives were passive and peace-loving, not prone to violence--so apparently, the mission briefings were unreliable.

That was something to keep in mind going forward. I was getting more and more suspicious every day. Was that Old Jack's nature? Or was it because of circumstances? How much of a person's personality was biology, and how much was experiences?

Did I want to get more and more suspicious? Frankly, it didn't sound like much fun.

I returned to the briefing. Guns were prohibited on Alpha Catoblepas, so no *Shakespeare* personnel could procure firearms from the armory for the mission. How inconvenient. Whatever Old Jack had been like, I could see my version of Jack would not be a rule follower. *To thine own self be true.*

I needed to procure a firearm. And I had a pretty good idea of where I could get one: Daniel. Eva had said he was the black market guy on the ship. Now was a perfect time to test that supposition.

The halls of the *Shakespeare* had a kind of cluttered beauty with the lights turned down. It no longer seemed like a spaceship; it seemed like the kind of huge glorious scenery- and prop-filled theatre that The Bard himself would have dreamed of.

I strolled down to the cargo bay and entered. A light shone from the other side of the bay, and I made my way through the literal maze of containers. When I got close, I noticed a wire strung across the path. I carefully stepped over it and crept closer to the light. Daniel, an older man I didn't recognize, and Ander and Sam sat around a cargo container they were using as a table, with playing cards and mugs of something. Ander still looked like a mean son-of-a-bitch. Sam still looked like an appliance.

"Yeah, Jack Junior took fire on the planet," Sam said. "From a native."

They were talking about me. I didn't like being talked about--unless it was how great I was. Still, maybe I could learn something from them. I crept closer.

"A native? That's unusual. Was Jack injured?" Daniel asked.

"Guess not," Sam said.

Ander guffawed. "Those mice don't know murder. I asked 'round the whorehouse--no one knew anything."

Ha. Had he gone undercover, or was that under-the-covers at the whorehouse? Don't laugh, Jack. Was this some lingering aftereffect of the planet's atmosphere? I put my hand over my mouth.

"Someone knew something," Daniel said. "I've never heard of a native committing violence."

"It's a stumper." Ander shook his head.

Well, damn. They didn't know anything, either.

"You could hear better if you got closer," the old man called out.

The four of them looked my way. A little sheepish, I stepped into the light. "How did you know I was here?"

The old man pointed at a small screen. "We got a camera pointed at the wire. Good job avoiding it, by the way. Most people trip the alarm."

I felt my face shape itself into a grin. Maybe I wasn't a lost cause as a spy. Focus, Jack. "Sam, Ander, I'm surprised to see you here. I thought you were working for me."

Ander shrugged.

Sam said, "We're equal-opportunity employees."

Did that mean they'd screw me over if they got the chance? If so, I was sorry to say I didn't see how I could stop them.

Daniel lifted his mug and swallowed. "You can't blame them for that." He put his mug down.

"Relax," Ander said. "We're off the clock."

I peered inside the mug. Was that beer? "What you got there? It looks good."

Daniel elbowed the old man. "Bill, pour my buddy Jack here a pint."

Bill--apparently--fiddled with the keg sitting on the floor and soon passed me a mug of my own.

I took a frothy sip. Stout. Whew. "Strong." I smacked my lips. "Maybe this ship isn't so bad after all." The recreational alcohol and drugs available in the mess hall had been bland.

Daniel pointed at a small cargo container. "Pull up a chair."

"Don't mind if I do." I sat and turned to Bill. "Nice to meet you, Bill. Is this your masterpiece?" I indicated the mug.

He nodded. "Yep."

"Welcome to the *Shakespeare*'s Poker Club," Daniel said.

"Yeah, you want a cigar?" Sam asked. I didn't see any cigars.

I was surprised smoking was allowed on a spaceship. "Cigar? Really?"

The four men laughed.

After a moment, I joined in.

The old man wiped tears from his eyes. "You guys are right; he's hilarious."

Sam said, "I heard he didn't take his meds and was high down on the surface."

"Wish I'd seen that," Ander said.

They chortled.

I was starting to get annoyed. "Laugh it up, Fuzzball."

"Wait, don't tell us." Daniel held up his hand. "You're so inexperienced, you're a virgin, too, right?"

They guffawed.

I resisted the strong urge to brag about Eva and me, or Sophia and me, but even I knew a gentleman doesn't kiss and tell. "*Better a witty fool than a foolish wit.*"

They laughed some more. I wasn't sure if it was because they thought I was a witty fool, a foolish wit, or just thought it was funny someone would quote Shakespeare.

Whatever. I was finally starting to relax. I took a sip of the delicious stout. Mmm. Was that chocolate I tasted? I glanced at the jovial men. Maybe they were just so jolly because they'd had a lot of beer?

"So, anyway," I said. "Did anyone actually learn anything helpful down on the planet?"

Gradually, they quieted.

Ander said, "I'm pretty sure no Alpha Catoblepasans are involved."

"Despite the shooter," Sam said.

"Despite the shooter," Ander said. "Those whores know everything. If there was a plot among the ACs, they'd know it."

"So?" I said. "You're thinking someone from the crew hired the shooter?"

"Yeah," Daniel said. "Or another human. We aren't the only humans on the planet."

"Another alien could have hired the shooter," Sam said.

"So, it sounds like the bottom line is we don't know anything," I said.

Except that someone was after me. That, we knew.

"That about covers it," Daniel said.

"Sounds like it," Bill said.

Everyone nodded.

We paused, and then all took a sip. Beer is good.

Somebody had said something earlier... "What if it wasn't a native that shot at me?" I asked.

"What you talking about, boy?" Bill said.

"You're the one who said it was a native," Daniel said. How'd he even know that?

"It looked like an AC, but why couldn't it be something else disguised as an AC?" I said.

Daniel whistled.

"Shit, man, that ain't good," Sam said.

"You're fucked," Ander said.

We all took another sip.

But neither info (no matter how bad) nor beer (no matter how good) was why I'd come down here to the cargo bay. "In light of recent events, I was thinking I need some way to protect myself, if you know what I mean," I said. "Daniel, you're a resourceful guy. Maybe you could help me out?"

Daniel grinned at me. "I know what you mean. Do you know what you mean?"

They all grinned.

"Yes," I said. "Why wouldn't I know what I mean?"

"I'm shocked," Bill said. "The youngster wants a gun?"

"Do you know how to shoot?" Ander asked, smiling.

Sam snickered, and Bill joined in.

"How hard can it be?" I asked.

"All right," Daniel said. "Give the kid a break. Yeah, I can take care of you. And Ander here will teach you to shoot--"

"I will?" Ander asked.

"Yeah, you will, if you want more beer." Daniel faced me. "But what's in it for me?"

Ah. Payment. "What do you want?" I asked.

Daniel glanced around the circle. Finally, he said, "I want a favor."

"Okay," I said. "What?"

"No," Daniel said. "An unspecified favor. Sometime in the future, I'll ask you to do a favor for me, and you have to do it."

How bad could it be? "Sure, dude." I held my hand out to shake on it.

"Dude!" They all started laughing again.

Daniel shook my hand. "Now, where did those guns get to?" He stood up and walked behind some storage containers. We heard the sound of a large something sliding along the floor. Thump. "Ow." Another slide. A sort of a *snick*. He reappeared.

"Here you go," he said, handing me a gun and a box of bullets. "SIG Pro semi-automatic pistol chambered in nine by nineteen millimeter."

I accepted them and managed not to say 'huh?' "Thanks. So, no rayguns?" They ignored that.

"How old is that thing?" Sam asked.

"It's an oldie but a goodie," Bill said. "Like most things, it improves with age--if it's taken care of."

"I have what I admit is a stupid question," I said, staring at it. "Couldn't this depressurize the ship and kill us all?"

"Yeah," Ander said. They all nodded.

"Don't do that," Sam said.

"Yeah, don't depressurize the ship and kill us all," Daniel said.

I didn't like the sound of that.

"Is it loaded?" Ander asked.

"No," Daniel said. "Jack, give Ander the gun."

I was only too glad to hand the thing off.

Ander did something, and the cartridge popped out. "Good. Not loaded."

"Good." I nodded in what I hoped was a macho and, at the same time, knowing way. "So, maybe you could hold on to it for me?" The more I thought about the gun, the stupider it seemed. "You know, until you get a chance to teach me some stuff."

Ander stared at me as if reading my mind. "Sure," he finally said. "Why don't I hold it for you?"

I nodded macho-ly and knowingly again.

Because, gee, what could possibly go wrong with me and a gun? It's not like anything else had ever gone wrong with me.

A JACK BY ANY OTHER NAME

Yeah, right.

Chapter Eight

The next morning, I was rudely awakened by some loud pounding on my cabin door. Each smack on the door felt like a smack on my head.

"C'mon, kid," a man said. "Get up."

Reluctantly, I sort of fell out of my bunk and stumbled over to the door. I opened it. "What?"

It was Ander. "We're going down to the surface for some s-h-o-o-t-i-n-g practice," he whispered. "Remember?"

I was supposed to rehearse and train this morning on the ship, and after that was another concert on the surface, but Gina was already mad at me, so what did it matter if she got mad again?

I vaguely remembered hatching some plan very late last night, and I appreciated Ander's quiet tone. It made my head throb less. "Oh, right. We wouldn't want to shoot a hole in the ship."

He laughed.

I finally deduced a gun probably would not shoot a hole in the ship. A scowl twisted my face. "Can you at least laugh quieter?"

"Oh, you're killing me, kid." He chuckled some more and straightened up. "If laughter was a weapon, you'd be deadly."

"Great. I'll keep that in mind the next time someone shoots at me."

His expression calmed to a smile. "Let me guess. You have a headache."

I nodded. Too quickly. "Ow."

"You're hungover."

I remembered being hungover when I was a teenager.

"No shit." But what I didn't get was why I was hungover now. I'd hardly drunk anything. Why did it affect me so strongly?

"You're wobbling a little. Are you still drunk?"

"No!" But that was a definite wobble.

"I guess you're not much of a drinker." He clapped me on the back.

From the eighteen years of memories I'd downloaded, I had been a good drinker. But...that'd been another body. "Uh, I guess." Ding, ding, ding. This body had no alcohol tolerance.

"Relax. The medical staff will fix you right up. Hurry up and get dressed, and we'll stop by the med center on our way out."

A cute, young female doc fixed me up with some kind of shot, and I got the required meds for the planet, too. I was momentarily tempted to stay on board and get to know her better, but Ander convinced me otherwise.

Suffice it to say with the proper meds, my second trip to AC was not as magical. The cinnamon scent was slightly nauseating; the blue foliage was boring, and the two suns... Okay, the two suns were still cool. I stared up at them.

"Watch where you're going, Jack." Ander pulled my arm. "We're getting off here."

We exited the walkway in the middle of town, but the area was seedy. The stone buildings were smaller, with an occasional broken window, and there was a lot of trash on the streets and sidewalks. In terms of architecture, it looked surprisingly like a rundown town on Earth.

There were not a lot of people on the street. "Where is everyone?"

Ander shrugged. "This area is livelier at night." He led me to a smallish building with a painting of two giant natives on the front.

"What is this place?" I asked as we walked inside.

A few tired-looking ACs lounged around on couches in the front room. They reminded me of giant mice: pear-shaped bipeds with prominent noses and almost no chins. They were also covered with some kind of hair or fur.

"A whorehouse, of course," he said. "What do you think?" He pointed at the mice, which, I guess, were naked. The body hair threw me off.

"Are those girls? How can you tell?" All I could see was the hair. It had distracted me from their naked status. Come to think of it, yesterday, on the street and at the concert, all the ACs had worn clothes.

Ander laughed.

One of them approached us with mincing steps. She(?) wore a small machine around her neck. "What can we do for you gentlemen?" Her voice via the translator was deep and low. It was disconcerting. "Would you like a girl? A boy? A girl and a boy?"

Ander smiled at her. "Hi, Lisa. This is my friend, Jack. And, sadly, no. I talked to Mary. We're just going to use your courtyard for a secret mission." He winked at her.

Lisa, Mary? Why did the ACs have such boring names?

One of the other ACs stirred from the couch. "Jack?" she said in a deep voice. She stood up and poked her friend. "Look, it's Jack Jones, the singer."

The friend jumped up. "Jack Jones? Ooh. I saw the concert last night. It was great. You're amazing."

They rushed towards me.

"Ack." I took a step back.

Soon, all the ACs were on their feet, crowding around me. I felt uncomfortably like a giant piece of cheese.

"Jack Jones! Wow," one woman said. "I'd be happy to give you a freebie."

"No, me," another said. "Let me do it."

What exactly did that entail? I didn't think I wanted to know.

"But I'll do anything, *anything*. Pick me."

The deep-voiced giant mice were anything but alluring. I glanced at Ander, and he looked like he was trying not to laugh.

"Thank you for your generous offers, ladies." He pushed them away. "But Jack and I are on an important mission."

"Aw." They looked at the floor, frowning. I marveled that I could tell they were frowning. Why weren't these aliens, well, more alien?

"If you change your mind, you know where to find me," one woman said.

"Where to find us." The ladies sashayed back to their sofas, deflated. Aw, poor things. Of course, they were disappointed. But still... I couldn't see myself hooking up with a mouse, no matter how great she thought I was.

I was feeling a little disoriented, and I didn't think it was the cinnamon smell. "Where's the courtyard?"

We went out the back door into a dirt-filled yard enclosed on all sides by a tall wooden fence. It was a depressing space.

I sank to a stool. "I need a minute."

"I've never seen the ACs get so worked up about a human before," Ander said. "Just how good a singer are you?"

"Good." I paused and looked up at him. "Have you, you-know, been with an Alpha Catoblepasan?" Bizarre. How would it even work?

He frowned at me. "Are you a virgin?"

I briefly thought of enticing Eva and her awesome ass. "No. But I haven't been with any aliens, if that's what you mean."

"Don't knock it until you try it. Or are you a speciesist? If you are, you don't have any business being on the *Shakespeare*."

I didn't know what a speciesist was, but I could guess. Was I one? It was yet another thing I didn't know about myself.

I stood up. "I thought we came down here for some target practice. Let's get to it."

Ander'd brought a variety of firearms in his man-purse. He showed me how to load the SIG. "Bullets go here." He popped the cartridge back in and handed it to me. "It doesn't have a manual safety. Hold it in two hands. No." He put my left hand over my right. "Sight along the barrel and squeeze the trigger."

I aimed at a tree and squeezed. Some bark flew off the center of the trunk.

"What were you aiming at?" Ander asked.

"That tree."

"Really? The tree you hit?"

"Yeah. Why do you look so surprised? Isn't that how it's supposed to work?"

"I thought you said you hadn't shot before."

I hadn't. That I remembered. But Old Jack was supposed to be an expert shot. I shrugged. "Beginner's luck?"

Ander put me through my paces with the SIG and some other guns he'd brought along. I was a surprisingly good shot.

I seemed to instinctively know how to operate each gun. I hit everything I aimed at. Did Old Jack, and therefore me, have some type of genetic predisposition for it, or was something else going on?

"You got me, kid," he said. "I bought it when you said you hadn't shot before, but you're an expert. There's more to you than meets the eye."

I decided not to argue with him. I liked the idea of being more than a pretty face. "Thanks for your help. I appreciate it."

He started putting the weapons away.

"Can I take the SIG? I'm going out in the city to investigate yesterday's shooting."

"Not a good idea. Guns are illegal here."

"All the more reason. Clearly, someone has a gun-- someone that doesn't like me. Can I borrow your man-purse?"

"My what?" He looked offended.

"Your, uh, man-purse?" I pointed at it. As far as I remembered, that was what it was called.

"You mean my satchel?" He strongly emphasized the word 'satchel.'

I suppressed a grin. "Yeah, your, ah, satchel. Can I borrow it?"

"If you're going into the city yourself, you need protection. And you know your way around a gun." He paused. "I guess I can get some kind of bag for the rest of the guns from the girls. Okay." He unloaded everything from the man-purse except for the SIG and handed it over. "But it's not a purse."

"Okay. Fine." *He doth protest too much.* "Not a purse." I couldn't help grinning a little when I turned away.

I retraced my path from yesterday, searching for clues. The shooting had to be related to Old Jack's murder, didn't it? The nicer part of the city was much more crowded, with lots of pedestrians and pedicabs.

I didn't see anything out of the ordinary until I got near the site. In the distance, I could swear I saw a large human man checking out the building with the bullet holes. He looked familiar. "Noah?" I called out.

The man jerked but didn't look at me. Instead, he sped

away.

I debated drawing my gun, but it was very crowded, and I didn't want to draw attention to it. Plus, shooting someone for no real reason seemed kind of mean. I ran after the man. "Noah?" What was he doing here?

Again he didn't turn around but sped up. He had bushy gray hair. Was it Noah? I wished he'd turn around.

"Turn around!" I called out.

He didn't.

I ran after him down the sidewalk, the purse thumping against my back.

He went around a corner.

I followed, but he had disappeared. I slowed down, searching every direction. No human males in sight. Well, shit. I stopped. Now what?

I took out my fon and tried calling him. It didn't connect. Did that mean he was back on Earth? Or that he was just pretending to be back on Earth? Crap.

On the corner, a somber gray-stone building with a large sign proclaimed something in many incomprehensible languages. Near the bottom, it said, 'Poleece' in Terran letters. A police station? If so, maybe they could help solve my attempted murder yesterday. Or, at least, help me find a big Terran wandering around the neighborhood. There was one way to find out.

Inside, there were chairs, a counter, and a bunch of desks and chairs behind it. It certainly looked like a police station. The activity behind the counter was bustling, but I was the only customer. "Hello?" There was no kind of bell or anything. "Hello?" I knocked on the blue wooden counter.

A uniformed AC glided up. "Yes, sir?" it said in a deep, translated voice. "Can I help you?" I couldn't tell if it was a male or female. "Nice purse," he or she said.

Uh oh. Maybe I shouldn't have brought an illegal firearm into a police station. "Uh, thanks. I'm not sure if you can help me," I said. "I had an odd experience yesterday."

"Oh?"

"I think a native, an Alpha Catoblepasan, shot at me."

"Oh, dear, sir. That sounds horrible, but very unlikely. You

71

know we abhor violence."

So, why did they have a police station? And why was it so busy? "Okay. Can you check for any reports of gunfire yesterday, just in case?" Surely, they had some kind of paperwork on this planet.

"Yes, sir." He (or she) said something in his native tongue and stared at the computer screen in front of him. "We have an incident report of someone shooting a Jack Jones." He looked up at me. "Is that you? The singer? I heard your concert last night was wonderful."

Who knew the ACs were such music lovers? "Yeah."

"The man in question said he dropped you off at the theatre before he filed the report."

I nodded.

"So, someone did shoot at you? Oh, no. Why didn't you report it? You should have reported it. It sounds very serious."

"Uh, that's what I'm here to do. To file a report." That sounded plausible, didn't it?

"I'd be happy to take your information, sir." She (?) looked at me.

"When?"

"Now. I'm ready. Give me your report."

"Someone shot at me," I said.

She looked at me some more. I got the feeling she was a hetero-female. Or, I guess she could be a homo male. I also got the feeling she was not a speciesist.

"It was around the corner," I said. "You can see some damage on the building there. I don't know the exact address." I stood there, done with my report, such as it was.

She examined me some more. Finally, she said, "Is that it?"

"I guess. Did you catch the perpetrator? Or do you have any information about it?"

She said something in a very high native voice to the computer and nodded at the screen. "Unfortunately, we have not caught the perpetrator."

"Do you have any surveillance or anything of the street?"

She did something with the computer. "The police do not surveil the street. But, I think, yes. There's a bank on that block. Perhaps they have a camera." She accessed some more data

72

and then peered down, squinting at the screen. "Oh, look! There you are! Don't you look handsome for a human? And there's someone following you." She leaned down more. "I can't make out his face, but it does look like one of us. Oh, dear."

"Can I see?"

She glanced back at the desks behind her. No one was paying any attention to us. "That would be totally against the rules. But, maybe... Oh, okay." She lifted the pass-through and gestured me towards her.

Behind the counter, she backed up the recording. We watched a very poor-quality recording of possibly-an-AC raising a possibly-gun and aiming it in my general direction. I wasn't much of an investigator, but even I knew it would not help them or me track down the shooter.

"Thanks for letting me see it," I said. "I appreciate it."

"Do you think I could possibly get an autograph?" she asked with a simper.

"Sure," I said and signed the paper she indicated.

She clutched it to her chest. "Thank you!"

I went back to the public side of the counter.

"I'm sorry I couldn't be more helpful in this matter," she said. "Is there anything else I can do for you?"

"I heard all non-ACs need to register when they arrive." Did the captain register the crew of the *Shakespeare*? "I'm looking for a friend of mine, a human, Noah Anderson. Can you tell me if he's here?"

She accessed her computer and scanned the list of names. Finally, she shook her head. "I don't have a Noah Anderson listed."

"Can you read me the human names from the last three days? Not from the *Shakespeare*."

She read a short list of human names. The last one sounded odd.

"What? Can you say that last one again?"

"Iago Smith."

Chapter Nine

It was unlikely a human on AC was named Iago Smith, wasn't it? It had to be an alias. Who used aliases? People who were trying to remain anonymous. Probably, people who were up to no good, criminal people. I didn't know if 'Iago' was involved with my murder, but it was my only lead for the moment.

Since it was a Shakespearean name, did that mean the criminal was on the *Shakespeare*? But if so, why register again with an alias? Gina must have registered all the crew under their real names.

Unfortunately, as the new kid on the block, I didn't know anything about aliases or the criminal network on AC, or anywhere else for that matter.

I sat down by the front door of the police station, trying to figure out what to do next. I needed criminals for consultation purposes. Did I know any criminals? Ding, ding, ding. If someone had been watching me, they would have seen a light bulb switch on over my head. Daniel was a criminal--or, as he probably would have said, an enterprising businessman--and I would bet large amounts of money (that I didn't have) that he knew about the 'enterprisers' on AC.

I punched his number into my fon.

"Yo," Daniel said.

"Yo?" I said. "What does that mean?"

"Jack?"

"Yeah." He laughed. "It doesn't matter. What can I do you for?"

I wasn't up on the current slang, but that didn't sound right. "Uh, I need to find some criminals."

He laughed again. "Why? Are you going to make a citizen's

arrest? Or, wait, you want to join the gang?"

"Sort of," I said.

"You are hilarious." I heard him chuckling.

"I heard about a human using an alias here, and I figured he might be a criminal. I wanted to talk to him."

"And who better to know about a crook than other crooks?"

"Basically."

"That's actually not a bad idea. Come on over to my office at the whorehouse."

I really didn't want to go back over there. "Uh."

"And, FYI, we crooks prefer the term 'capitalist.'" He hung up.

I guess I had to go. I dragged my feet all the way back over there.

When I got there, the front door swung open before I even had a chance to knock.

"Ooh! It's Jack!" The low voices from the translators didn't sound any more enticing the second time around.

"Jack's back!" They certainly seemed glad to see me. And why not? I was great, after all. Maybe I was being a little speciesist. That was kind of unfair.

I gave them one of my dazzling smiles. "I'm afraid I have a pressing matter to attend to with Daniel."

At the word 'pressing,' the crowd around me giggled.

"I'm good at pressing," one said.

"Yeah, I'll press whatever you like." The crowd pressed closer to me. The feel of fur on my bare arms was disconcerting.

I had to struggle to keep my expression pleasant. "Gosh, ladies, give a man some room. Close quarters are bad for my voice."

"Oh, no," one of them said.

They backed away.

Once I could see more of my surroundings, I became aware of Daniel standing in front of an open doorway. He chuckled, gestured to the room, and walked inside.

I quickly followed before the uh, ladies, could pin me down again. "Gee, thanks for the assist, Dan." Except for the large bed, the office's decor was totally nondescript: desk, assorted chairs, lamps, and window.

He chortled. This was one happy guy. "I wanted to see what you'd do."

"If you don't mind me saying, did you skip the required meds, Daniel? You seem unusually happy."

He just smiled at me in return. "What do you want?"

"I'm looking for Iago Smith."

He erupted with laughs like he was some kind of laughter volcano. Possibly he was too annoying to ask for help. I waited impatiently for the laughs to subside.

When he finally quieted, I said, "I know it's a fake name. I'm trying to find the guy. Is there any way to find him or figure out what he's up to?"

"Why do you want him? You got a plot you need carrying out?" He snickered. "Maybe you want to make somebody believe their wife's cheating?"

I almost said, 'I think he's involved in my murder,' but I remembered in time that info was need-to-know. Instead, I said, "I think he's the one who shot at me yesterday."

"Oh, right, that." The smile leaked down his face. He pointed at the chair in front of the desk.

"So what kind of illegal activities do humans participate in here on AC?" I asked.

Daniel leaned back in his chair, steepling his fingers. "Mostly smuggling, prohibited drugs, food and drink with the occasional guns or other weapons. And whoring." He paused.

"Can you tell me anything else? A place they hang out?"

My fon pinged, and then I heard Eva's voice: "You're supposed to be at the theatre now, Jack." I'd forgotten. "Where are you? Don't tell me you're lost again." How did she talk to me without me answering it? I could see I needed to study my fon more.

When I glanced Daniel's way, he was smirking.

I picked up my fon. "Of course, I'm not lost. I'm just running a bit late. I'll be there soon."

"Okay," she said. "See you soon." She hung up.

"Is that your momma, Jack?" Daniel asked. "Does little Jackie have a babysitter?"

I scowled. "No. It's Eva. She's just--"

"Hot Eva from the gym? Are you hitting that? She's smokin'.

You dog."

I felt a grin slip onto my face. I knew it wasn't polite to kiss and tell. *"When love speaks, the voice of all the Gods makes heaven drowsy with the harmony."*

He nodded. "Oh, yeah. I'd be drowsy, so drowsy, after harmonizing with her all night."

Honestly, he could make anything sound cheap. "Anyway, places I might find this Iago character? Any ideas?"

He grabbed a piece of paper and wrote down an address. "Here. This is the address of a club we capitalists like to frequent. They have some excellent refreshments." He handed it over.

"Thanks."

My fon pinged again.

I quickly grabbed the piece of paper and bolted out.

The show went off without a hitch. I did an excellent job. Afterward, I was inundated with fans onstage--as was my due.

I invited Eva and a quartet of human (I think) lovelies with a beautiful rainbow of skin tones to check out the gangster-- sorry, capitalist--club with me.

"Go, have fun," Eva said. "I don't have any claim on you. I said we should cool it, and I meant it." Aw. I'd hoped she'd changed her mind.

"I want to go to a club!" one of the lovelies exclaimed.

"Me, too. I want to go," another lovely said.

"Me, too."

"Count me in."

"Suit yourself, Eva," I said. I put my arms around all four of them, to the best of my abilities, as we walked to the theatre exit.

At the club, we had no trouble getting in. It was dank and dark inside and seemed to be mostly filled with humans and other non-AC aliens. One popular libation was some kind of injection mask you put over your mouth and nose.

"Let's try that!" one of my companions said.

"Yes." I held my arm up and snapped my fingers. "Garçon!"

A male human in a soiled apron sidled up to our table. "Yeah." He sighed as if he was sick of human tourists. "What do you want?"

"What are those masks?" one of my women asked.

LESLEY L. SMITH

"It's a concentrated dose of the local atmosphere. It overcomes any meds you've taken to render the atmosphere harmless."

"Let's do that!"

"I want that."

I glanced around the table at four beautiful young women who all clearly wanted to have sex with me. My life was good. I felt a little sad for Old Jack in that he was missing all this.

"So?" our waiter asked.

Based on my memories from yesterday (before the shooting), the mask did sound good. Very good. "Masks all around!" But thoughts of Old Jack reminded me that I was here on a mission. "Before you go, garçon..."

He'd started walking away.

"I'm looking for an old friend of mine, a human. A big, burly sort of fellow. He said he'd meet me here, but I'm a bit confused about when. Has anyone like that come in here?"

The waiter sighed again. "I don't know. You can ask the manager if you want. His office is in the back." He pointed to the hallway with a sign above it, *Restrooms*.

"Thanks. I appreciate it."

He walked off.

I stood. "Ladies, please excuse me." I leaned my head towards the back. "I have to go see a man about a fish." Huh. That didn't sound right, somehow.

The women looked confused but smiled back at me.

I walked through the dimly lit main room to the dimly lit back hallway. Before the restrooms, there was a closed door with a sign containing several letters I didn't recognize and the word *Office*.

I raised my hand to knock on the door but paused. Did they knock here on AC? There was only one way to find out. I knocked.

An incomprehensible sound came from within.

I gingerly turned the doorknob. Nothing happened. I continued messing around with it. By accident, I pressed it in, and the door opened. I stuck my head inside. "Does that mean *come in*?"

The AC sitting at the desk pressed a button on his/her

78

translator and grunted.

I entered.

The AC said through the translator, "What do you want?" The office looked more like a storeroom, filled with shelves and boxes of stuff on said shelves. The 'dimly-lit' decorating theme continued in here.

"I'm looking for a human, a big human," I said.

"What's his name?" he asked in a very deep voice.

"Uh, I'm not quite sure." Damn, I probably shouldn't have admitted that. "I mean, he told me his name was Iago Smith."

The AC rubbed his face. "I might have some information, but it'll cost you."

I hardly had any credits. "No problem. Let me know what you got, and I'll be happy to reimburse you."

He made a strange noise, and his body shook. Laughter? Why were people always laughing at me? "Ha. That's a good one, human. No. Pay and then get the information."

"So there definitely is information to be had?" That, at least, was something.

He didn't respond.

"Okay. How much?"

"A thousand credits."

Damn. I didn't have a thousand credits. I barely had a hundred credits. "That's too rich for my blood."

"What does blood have to do with it?"

"Nothing. Never mind. It's a human expression. I don't suppose you'd accept a hundred credits?"

He made that odd noise again, and his body shook some more.

"Uh. All right." I headed for the door. "Thanks, anyway."

Damn. I really needed to get some credits. How was I ever going to solve the mysteries of my murder and the recent attempted murder with no capital for information?

Chapter Ten

When I awoke the next morning, two shapely arms were draped across my bare chest. Surprisingly, they were attached to two different shapely women. Who knew three people could fit in these little bunks?

I smiled, recalling just how well we'd all fit. I'd performed admirably. Apparently, I was gifted in this area.

As I gazed upon their aesthetically pleasing forms, something nagged in the back of my mind. Something wasn't right here, something I needed to remember...

A klaxon sounded, and a loud mechanical voice announced, "Warning. Unauthorized personnel aboard. Warning. Unable to launch ship."

Oh, right. That's what I was supposed to remember: get the girls off the ship before takeoff. How did the ship know there were unauthorized personnel on board?

The women stirred. "What is that racket?" the brunette said, scrunching up her adorable nose.

"What time is it?" the blonde said. They looked at each other over my chest.

I gave them my most charming smile. "Morning, Beautiful."

"Which one of us is beautiful?" the brunette said, smiling engagingly.

"Both of you, of course. *Who ever loved that loved not at first sight?*" As they leaned in to kiss me, I felt every part of me wake up to greet the dawn.

The blonde giggled.

"Jack?" Gina's stentorian voice interrupted, coming from my fon on the desk and deflating the mood. Apparently, the ship had some kind of intercom system. My guests leaned away from me.

I grabbed my fon and pressed the 'chat' button. "Uh, yes, ma'am." My voice may have squeaked a bit. "Can I help you?"

"That's, 'Yes, Captain Gomez.'"

"Yes, ma'am, Captain Gomez."

"Do you have one or more stowaways in your cabin?"

Did she have cameras in here? I practically got whiplash looking around the cabin for cameras. "No, Captain Gomez. Absolutely not. That's a negative. No stowaways here."

One of my lovelies grabbed an extremely sensitive part of my anatomy and giggled.

I reluctantly removed her hand. It was the brunette; she pouted.

"Was that a giggle?" Gina asked. "You do have someone in your cabin!"

"Nope." Technically, I did not have someone; I had some two. "That was me. I giggled."

"Seriously?"

"Yes, Captain Gomez. You know my situation has made me more, uh, youthful, of late. I giggle now."

"Yeah, right," she said. "I'm sending a security detail to your cabin immediately. Gomez out." I put my fon back on the desk.

At the sudden quiet, both my lovelies reached for me.

"Alas, ladies, you must go forthwith." Ideally, without getting me into more trouble. But how?

"Aw," the brunette said, still pouting prettily.

"I like the way you talk," the blonde said.

"Thank you." My mind was racing and not over the topics you'd suspect. What we needed was a secret tunnel. I tried not to dwell on the word tunnel. One part of my body wanted to dwell on tunnels. A lot. "Please get dressed. Posthaste." I extricated myself from the bed and threw on some pants and a shirt. "Posthaste!"

They shimmied into their slinky dresses from last night, each wriggle a symphony. Did they truly have to go? How much trouble could I get in by delaying the ship's takeoff?

Focus, Jack! I turned back to the cabin. Now, if I was a secret passageway, where would I be?

"Ensign Jones!" Someone pounded on my cabin door. "Open up!"

The two women looked at me questioningly. I held my finger in front of my mouth and said, "Shh."

"We're coming in!"

Shit. I examined my cabin again.

There were some fumbling sounds from the direction of the door.

The only open space, the only open wall, was next to the desk. That had to be it. I really hoped that was it.

"Dammit!" one of the guys in the hall said. "Do you have illegal modifications of this lock, Jones?"

I didn't, but hurray for Old Jack. I rushed to the wall and started pressing and pulling.

"Jones, open the door!"

One of the wall panels swung open as if by magic. I wasted no time in pointing into the opening. Hello, secret tunnel.

The women nodded, grabbed their purses and got in.

I quickly followed, pulling the panel closed behind us. The passage was lined with metal and seemed like a giant vent.

Very faintly, I could still hear the security guys yelling, "Jones, open the fucking door!"

I whispered, "Thank you for last night, ladies. I had a lovely time."

"Oh, we did, too," the blonde said.

The brunette bobbed her head in agreement.

Of course, they did. "I'm sorry to make you rush off like this. I guess we overslept." I gave them one of my rogue-ish looks. (I'd been working on it.)

They nodded. "It's understandable. We were up very late."

"Yes, we were." It was funny how adrenaline could wake a person right up, no matter how little sleep he'd gotten. "Let me show you to the exit." I hoped I could find the exit.

We found the exit, no problem because someone had helpfully put exit signs with arrows in the secret passageway. Nice. I'd buy him or her a beer if I knew who they were.

I popped open the panel in the disembarkation lounge (it was much easier from this side because you didn't have to search for it) and checked for crewmembers without sticking my head out. I didn't see anyone in the lounge but didn't want to risk any security cameras seeing me.

I pointed. "There's the exit right there. *Love is a smoke raised with the fume of sighs.*"

"What?" the blonde said.

"Goodbye," I said. "*Being purged, a fire sparkles in lovers' eyes.*"

"Huh?" the brunette said.

"Goodbye." I pointed some more.

They disembarked.

I rushed back in the direction of my cabin. When I approached said cabin, totally out of breath, I noticed there was some kind of something attached above the exit to my cabin. Upon closer inspection, it was an old-school paper envelope containing a large number of data cubes. Could this be Old Jack's secret stash of info? "Awesome!"

"I heard something," one of the guards said in the hall. "Jones! Open the door!"

Wow. They still hadn't broken through the door? That was some impressive extra security Old Jack had installed.

I quickly slipped into my cabin, closing the panel behind me and stashing the envelope in the desk drawer.

I stepped toward the door to the hallway but paused. I shucked my pants and shirt and threw them on the floor. I had to go for verisimilitude, didn't I?

I finally palmed the lock. "What is going on out here? You guys woke me."

The security guys' eyes bugged out--no doubt at my manliness. They were probably jealous, or maybe a little turned on--or both.

One of them muttered something that sounded like, 'Asshole,' but that couldn't be right.

"What took you so long, Jones!" the pointy-headed head guy said. "We've been out here forever."

"I just woke up." I grinned. "I'm a deep sleeper."

"Yeah, fuck you," he said and pushed himself into the cabin. But of course, there was no one else there (now) and no place to hide.

"What's this about?" And, okay, I couldn't help grinning some more--which may have been construed as a little asshole-ish.

The security guy was already pushing his way out again and thumbing his comm. "I'm sorry, Captain Gomez. There's no sign of any unauthorized personnel in Ensign Jones' cabin."

One of the other guys was also on his comm. He looked up at his colleagues. "Security says we're clear. No stowaways."

In the hall, they all scowled and/or frowned at me.

I tried not to grin too much.

Eventually, they stalked off.

I went back inside, closing the door behind me.

I recorded my recent memories, not wanting to forget what had happened with the two(!) beauties last night.

Once that was squared away, I grabbed my fon and the envelope, emptying it on my bed. I sat on the bed, leaning against the wall and grabbed the first data cube.

It seemed to be blueprints of the *Shakespeare*. Okay: slightly helpful. At least I wouldn't get lost on the ship itself. Then I noticed the images labeled 'Secret Camera Locations' and 'Secret Passageways.' Okay: quite helpful.

The second cube contained personnel records. The name 'Noah Anderson' caught my eye, and there were a lot of Gigabytes associated with it. I scrolled through headings like *Education, Employment, Missions, Family, Personal* and stopped at *Top Secret*.

I held the drive up to my fon and opened that file. *Noah has been my best friend for decades, but I've deduced over the years that what originally drew him to me was a homosexual attraction. I believe he's in love with me and has been for years. At the same time, he's very jealous of my success as a singer and within the TCC. Do not trust him.*

I knew it!

Under The *Shakespeare,* there was a cryptic entry saying only *The FTL drive utilizes quantum entanglement and improbabilities. If it's out of alignment, probabilities can become misaligned. Improbability can become probable, and vice versa.*

What did that mean? I didn't recall anything about the FTL drive in any of the official information about the ship. Had Old Jack uncovered some kind of secret? Hadn't Noah said something about investigating that?

I'd have to think about that later.

A JACK BY ANY OTHER NAME

I returned to the main menu with categories including, *The Shakespeare crew* and *Terran Cultural Committee* and scanned the list of names, including *Gina Gomez* and *Carter Nillion*. I had a lot of reading ahead of me.

I grabbed another cube: *Top Secret TCC Missions*. Under *Alpha Catoblepas,* there was a long list, including *Gun sales* and *Smuggling*.

This had to be it, Old Jack's info stash. I threw my fist into the air. "Yes!"

Now I had a real chance to figure out what the hell Old Jack had been up to and, by extension, who was trying to murder us, me.

I reached for another cube. But when I tried to read this one, there wasn't anything intelligible on it. I could tell it contained many Terabytes of data. Huh. My brain whirred. This cube must be encrypted. What if it was Old Jack's memories?

I glanced at the array of cubes spread out on my bed. Old Jack was supposed to be a spy, a good spy.

Why could I read any of this? Why weren't they all encrypted? Were they really what they seemed? Innocent, straightforward data cubes? Or were they something else?

"*Something is rotten in the state of Denmark*."

Chapter Eleven

"What do you mean I can't play Frederic?" Carter asked. "I always play Frederic."

I was a little confused. Was Carter acting like a friend? Or an envious competitor?

We were starting rehearsal for a new show, *The Pirates of Penzance*, in preparation for our next planet, Tau Ceto. The entire cast was standing around waiting to get started.

"I think Jack, uh, Junior, should play Frederic," Gina, I mean Captain Gomez, said. I was standing right next to the two of them. Apparently, the *Shakespeare*'s captain was also the artistic director. That was the first thing I'd heard that made me regret I wasn't captain.

"He always plays Major-General Stanley," Carter said.

"Careful, Carter," Captain Gomez said softly. "Jack Junior's never played anything with us. And he's not old enough to play Stanley."

Carter frowned at me. Finally, he said, "Okay. I'm Major-General Stanley."

Captain Gomez peered into his eyes. "Can I trust you to direct? Can you be objective?"

"Yes, fine!" Carter said in a tone that sounded nothing like fine. I guess artists were melodramatic all over the universe.

Captain Gomez pivoted and walked out of the rehearsal space.

Carter sighed and turned around to face the cast. "Welcome to *Pirates*."

Quite a few people groaned.

Why? *Pirates* was a classic. Even I remembered it with my messed up memory, and I remembered it as being a lot of fun.

A JACK BY ANY OTHER NAME

"I know we've done it before, but the Tau Cetoans love it, so we're doing it again. At least we're mixing it up. Since Jack's gone, I'll be directing," Carter said.

Of course, technically, Jack was only partly gone.

I looked around at the cast. Did they look sad at the mention of Old Jack's death? Mostly they looked bored.

"And I'll be playing Major-General Stanley," Carter said. "Jack Jones Junior will be playing Frederic. Olivia Lee is Mabel."

A feminine-sounding someone squealed. If that was Olivia, I was eager to meet her. She sounded cute.

"Ander Sousa is the Pirate King, etc." Ander? I didn't even know he was a performer. Carter continued, "Check your fons for roles, music, and scripts."

Everyone looked at his or her fon.

My first musical number was "Oh! False One! You Have Deceived Me!" I scrolled through the music. It wasn't complicated. Hopefully, my pirate costume would be sexy and swashbuckling. I scanned the music and lyrics for "Stop, Ladies, Pray." Piece of cake.

Now "Oh, Is There Not One Maiden Breast" looked a lot more challenging, with a larger range of notes, and many of them held for a long time. I was gonna be great in this role. All the women would swoon for real, the human women, anyway. I wondered what Tau Cetoan women looked like. Hopefully, not like any kind of rodent.

"Jack, pay attention," Carter said. Oops. Apparently, I'd missed something. "We're going to run through the musical numbers first and see who's ready to go and who needs more time to practice." He narrowed his eyes at me. "Those of you new to the show, study, study, study."

He walked across the stage to the piano. "The Major-General Song," he said to the accompanist. "Ready?"

She nodded. I hadn't noticed her before. She had gray hair, so she was clearly older, but somehow she managed to pull it off and look attractive.

"*I am the very model of a modern Major-General,*" Carter sang after she played the intro. I had to admit, he had a nice voice, not as good as mine, but still nice.

"*I've information vegetable, animal, and mineral, I know*

the kings of England, and I quote the fights historical. From Marathon to Waterloo, in order categorical I'm very well acquainted, too, with matters mathematical, I understand equations, both the simple and quadratical, About binomial theorem I'm teeming with a lot o' news, With many cheerful facts about the square of the hypotenuse."

I couldn't help humming along. Good song.

"Jack." Someone poked my arm. It was Ander.

"Ander! Dude! I didn't even know you were a performer."

He shrugged. "Yeah." He paused. "Do you want help?"

"Huh? Help with what?" Humming?

He smirked at me. The effect was quite a bit reminiscent of a pirate. How had I never noticed it before? His criminal, er, capitalist, aura was very pirate-y. He was a space pirate!

I snickered.

"What are you giggling about?"

"I'm not giggling. I don't giggle." I hoped he didn't compare notes with Gina, but why would he? "Um, help with what?"

"Help with your part. Duh. You're the least experienced cast member, and you've got the biggest role."

I knew better than to assume he was offering to help me out of the goodness of his heart. "What'll it cost me?" I was a quick learner, or at least quick enough.

"I'll add it to your tab." He started to pull me off to a rehearsal room.

"Wait," I said. "I want to meet that Olivia Lee who's playing Mabel." I had a feeling we were really going to hit it off. She was playing my love interest, after all.

"Yeah, okay. I know Liv." Ander strode in the direction of the piano.

I quickly followed him.

He stopped in front of a beautiful woman with some beautiful Asians in her gene pool. "Jack, this is Olivia Lee, Mabel."

I played it cool; not so easy to do when you're a little out of breath. "Hey." I nodded, trying not to stare at her golden-hued skin and wide-set almond eyes.

"Liv, this is Jack Jones Junior, playing Frederic." He pointed at me.

Her eyes passed over me from the top of my head to the tips of my toes. I waited for her girlish screams of delight at getting to play my leading lady. "Hey." Then, she turned to face Ander and smiled beguilingly.

What? Where were her shrieks of excitement?

She said, "How's your buddy Sam? Is he still h-o-t?"

What was happening here? My mind couldn't process it. I put my hand on her shoulder. "Maybe you didn't understand. You're playing Mabel to my Frederic."

She turned her head and gave me a deadeye stare. "I understand." She faced Ander again. "Is Sam seeing anyone?"

For his part, Ander seemed amused as he glanced from Olivia to me and back again. "You know Sam's just waiting for you to say yes, Liv. You should call him."

This woman actually liked Sam Jain more than me? Sam looked like a refrigerator. Could he even sing?

They continued to chat about Sam.

Ah. That must be it: Olivia hadn't heard me sing. "Do you want to come to rehearse with us, Liv?"

"It's Olivia," she said, stressing each syllable. "And, we're talking here. Quit interrupting."

Huh. This Olivia chick was a mystery wrapped up in a hottie. I guessed there was no accounting for taste. I turned back to Carter, who was still singing.

"*For my military knowledge, though I'm plucky and adventury, Has only been brought down to the beginning of the century; But still, in matters vegetable, animal, and mineral, I am the very model of a modern Major-General.*"

Fun song. I was plucky and adventury. Give me a nice gray beard and sideburns, and I could totally play the Major General.

Everyone clapped.

"Who's next?" Carter asked.

I raised my hand. "I can go. I'll go."

"Have you ever sung any of these songs?" he asked me.

"Well, no, not professionally. But we did *Pirates* in high school, and I'm a good sight-reader."

I may have heard some groans from the assembled company. How could that be?

Carter grimaced and pointed at Ander. "Ander, help Jack.

Run through his songs."

As Ander and I walked to one of the rehearsal rooms, he said, "So, what'd you think of Liv?"

I thought there was a good possibility she had some kind of mental issues or at least very bad taste in men, but I knew that wouldn't be a tactful thing to say, and I was nothing if not tactful. So, what to say?

"Jack?"

"Pretty. She's pretty."

He chuckled like he knew what I'd been thinking.

I'd made plans to eat dinner with Eva because I needed to pick her brain about my data-cube mystery. And she was the only person I trusted that knew Old Jack. Were the cubes encrypted? If so, how could I decrypt them? Reading Old Jack's secret files could only help solve his murder. His comments on the FTL drive were also very intriguing, and I wanted more info. Did everyone know the drive was tied to improbabilities?

Luckily, while on AC, I'd picked up a variety of foodstuffs, including wine and some supposedly delicious cake. I knocked on Eva's door.

She answered right away. "Hi, Jack." I offered my gifts. "Oh, yum!" She grabbed the wine and glanced at the label. "I love AC wine, and this cake looks scrumptious. Thanks, Jack. Come on in."

"Wait." She narrowed her eyes at me. "What do you want? When I said we shouldn't have a romantic relationship, I meant it."

"I know." I smiled in a friendly but not too sexy way. "I just want some info."

She stared at me for a few seconds more, and I got the distinct impression that she'd wanted me to protest our lack of romance. Women were complicated.

"Of course," I said, "I would be honored if you deigned to bestow your affections--"

"No." She shook her head. "No. We shouldn't." Who was she trying to convince?

On a table folded down from the wall, she'd laid out dinner. "We should eat."

I poured the wine, and we dug in. I didn't know if it was the company, the food or the wine, but dinner was tasty.

I pushed my chair away from the table. "Mmm. That was good."

Eva finished off her glass of wine. "Yes, it was."

I poured her another.

"So, what are you doing here, Jack? Plying me with wine and cake?" She eyed the untouched cake on the table. We hadn't gotten into it yet.

"Well, I have a little mystery."

She laughed uproariously. Finally, she caught her breath and said, "Yeah, Ander said Liv didn't take to you, and you didn't know what to make of it. He said you acted like you'd never had a woman not be thrilled to meet you."

Geez. News traveled fast on a spaceship. How annoying. "No. That's not it. That's not what I'm talking about."

"No?" She arched an eyebrow.

"I mean, that is a mystery. I have never met a woman who wasn't happy to meet me." And, frankly, happy to have sex with me, but I didn't add that. Wow, I was getting mature.

Eva leaned back. "Seriously?"

"Yes." I paused. "Except maybe for Gina--and I'm not a hundred percent sure about that; she does seem very passionate. Perhaps you're forgetting I'm only a month old."

"Whoa. Yeah. I do keep forgetting that. Sorry." She reached for my hand. "All this must be very confusing for you."

I nodded. Her skin on my skin felt very good, like home. I relaxed a little more. "Thanks for saying that, Eva." I told her about Old Jack's encrypted data stash. "I need some help decoding it."

"Well, don't look at me. If you want to learn epee, I'm your woman, but I'm not a tech person."

"I know that. But you know the crew. You know who knows what. I just need a name and maybe an introduction."

She dropped my hand. "You were with Ander all afternoon at rehearsal. Why didn't you just ask him? Or Daniel?"

"I seem to be accumulating a deficit of favors with them. I'd rather not incur any more." I needed to figure out how to start paying off what I owed.

"So you're not worried about incurring a debt with me? You didn't think I'd charge you?"

Now it was my turn to reach for her. Her warm hand fit in mine perfectly. "On the contrary, I'm happy to owe you a debt. I'll pay whatever you think is fair."

She squeezed my hand and grinned. "Somehow, I think we can work something out." She was definitely one of my favorite people. Who could resist her? Not me.

She stood. "Strip, boy!"

"Well, as long as it's not a relationship." I grinned. I loved the barter system.

Chapter Twelve

The day was about to begin, and I was still in enchanting Eva's bed. I gazed at her as she opened her eyes.

She smiled. "Morning."

I smiled back because, truly, who wouldn't? "Morning. *This bud of love, by summer's ripening breath, may prove a beauteous flower when next we meet.*" That would make her swoon.

"Maybe you shouldn't quote Shakespeare so much. It's pretentious. And a little annoying."

"What?" No swoon?

She leaned in. "Quit talking." She pressed her luscious lips against mine. Every part of me tingled and rose to meet the new day.

And then... I felt odd. I sort of deflated.

Eva reached for my most sensitive part, looked down and frowned. "Huh."

I panicked as she moved away from me and sat up. "I don't understand what's happening," I said. "What's happening?" Very unfortunately, what was happening was: nothing. Nothing at all. How was that possible? I was healthy, and Eva was very hot.

She shrugged. "It happens."

"Not to me! It's never happened to me. It's impossible." I sat up next to her, leaning against the headboard.

"I think we've already established your experience is limited."

"I'm telling you, something is seriously wrong." What could it be? It couldn't be me. I was great. It couldn't be Eva. She was great.

It had to be something else. Impossible was just another

word for very, very improbable. "The ship," I said. "It must be the ship. The FTL drive must be malfunctioning!" Thanks to Old Jack, I knew the FTL drive utilized improbabilities. So it stood to reason that it must be related if something very improbable happened--like my manliness or lack thereof. Could the drive be leaking improbabilities or something?

The corners of Eva's mouth turned up. "Yeah, honey, I bet that's it. The ship's FTL drive's malfunctioning." She patted my shoulder.

I shrugged off her hand. "I'm telling you, I can tell." My manhood twitched. "The FTL drive's not working right!" Twitch.

I stared at my manhood. "FTL." Twitch. "Whoa."

Eva couldn't help staring at it either. "Do that again."

"FTL." Twitch.

"Huh," she said.

If something this impossible could happen, what about other impossible, or at least very improbable, things?

Despite the obvious tragedy with Eva, this could be an opportunity if probability was out of whack. Old Jack's notes didn't mention taking advantage of improbabilities, but it stood to reason, didn't it?

If I could harness some improbability, I might be able to solve some of my problems and at least accrue some credits. I jumped out of bed and reached for my fon.

My intuition was telling me more improbable things might be easier to instantiate than less probable things. "I have a secret credit account with one billion credits, and the access code is..." I typed in *awesome jack*.

"Gee, greedy much?" Eva said.

The little screen on my fon said, *Accessing*.

I stared at it.

Accessing was replaced by *Balance: 1,000,000,000*.

"Yes!" I pumped my fist into the air. "Yes! Hoo-rah!"

"That worked?" Eva frowned.

"Yes, it did." I showed her the message on my fon.

"Holy shit!" She straightened up. "I got a promotion to Officer Second Class with a raise." She reached for her fon. "Nothing happened." She got up and looked in her closet. "Same dress uniform. I don't get it."

A JACK BY ANY OTHER NAME

I stared at the *1,000,000,000*. "You're not thinking grandiose enough. It has to be very improbable." I had a thought: what would be the most grandiose thing? "I am emperor--," twitch, "of the universe."

But I didn't suddenly feel imperial. Instead, my body started acting as it normally would when a beautiful naked woman stood before it.

Eva looked at me, all of me, smiling. "It is over?"

"Oh, this is just the beginning, babe." I stepped forward and enfolded her in my arms.

I'd have to record these memories as soon as I could.

I was cognizant of the old Earth idiom *Easy come, easy go*, and while antique Terrans didn't have to deal with probability engines, I figured it still applied. My newfound riches might disappear at any time. I planned to disperse the windfall as far as possible and as fast as possible before that happened. I gave Eva 100,000 credits before I left her quarters.

After that, I rushed to the cargo bay to find Daniel. I already owed him for the gun and deduced I'd probably end up owing him more in the future. I made my way through the now-familiar maze of containers and found Daniel, Ander, Sam, and Bill sitting in their spots. Did they sleep here?

"Greetings, young Jack," Bill called out. "What brings you out so early?"

I decided not to ask them why they were here. I was probably better off not knowing their nefarious schemes. "Greetings, all," I said. "I'm here to settle my debts."

Daniel raised an eyebrow. "Oh?"

I held up my fon. "Yeah, I just came into my, uh, inheritance and wanted to pay you what I owed you." Inheritance, brilliant! Sometimes I amazed even myself.

Daniel smirked. "I told you he was good for it."

The other men scowled as they typed into their fons.

Ander said, "You're killing me, kid."

Daniel glanced at his fon. "We had a bet. They thought you'd welch."

"So, we didn't settle on a number," I said, trying to hurry things along. "How do 100,000 credits each sound?"

"It sounds like too much," Daniel said, eyes narrowing.

"For services rendered and for future services," I said, thinking fast.

"What kind of future services?" Bill asked. "You're not going to ask us to kill anyone, are you?"

"No!" I said too quickly. "If, uh, there's any killing to be done, I'll, uh, do it." Bad-ass spies killed people, didn't they? Or at least people thought they did. I wanted people to at least think I was a badass.

Sam snorted, but Ander gave me an appraising look. He may have been remembering my facility with a gun.

"Okay, kid," Bill said. "If you want to give me 100,000 credits, go for it."

I started typing on my fon, and soon my windfall was down 500,000 credits.

They all looked at their fons with surprise.

Finally, Daniel said, "Thanks. Is there anything I can help you with at the moment?"

"Yes, as a matter of fact," I said. "I came into some encrypted data and need to decrypt it."

"You mean you stole some encrypted data?" Bill asked. "Not that we care."

"No, I, uh, inherited it, too," I said.

"But you didn't inherit the decryption key?" Sam asked.

"No," I said. "At least, I don't think so."

They all gave me looks that said, 'Gee, that's not suspicious.'

"Sam, here's your man," Daniel said. "The best data jockey on the ship. If anyone can decrypt your mystery data, it's him."

"What do I owe you for that tip?" I asked.

Daniel smiled. "Considering your generosity this morning, it's a freebie."

The last time I'd been offered a freebie, it'd been an AC whore. I shuddered.

I manned up and barreled on. "Sam, what do you think?" I asked. "Can you help me out?"

"Sure," he said. "Hand over your data."

I didn't like the glint in his eye. I didn't want him reading Old Jack's secret data stash. "Maybe you just have some decryption code you could give me?"

"Maybe I do." He nodded. "But, it'd be quicker for you to just hand it over."

"Not yet," I said. "I'd rather try the decryption code myself first."

Sam raised and lowered his shoulders. "Suit yourself. I'll send it to you now."

My fon said, *New code received.*

"You can have the code for free," he said. "When you can't figure it out and come back to me, I'll charge you plenty." He grinned.

"Thanks, I think," I said. What did all those credits get me?

Ander nodded. "It's much easier to decrypt something when you have the decryption key. Isn't there any chance you can get it?"

"Did you inherit the data from your dad, the old captain?" Daniel asked. "Maybe his wife, Captain Gomez, would know the decryption key."

That was a good idea. Gina might know something. "I'll investigate." I turned to go. "Thanks. See you later." Were these guys my friends? I was gonna be an optimist and say: yes.

"Later," Sam said.

"Yeah," Daniel said.

"See you at rehearsal," Ander called after me.

I really didn't want to talk to Gina. Truth be told, she scared me a little. But even I realized I could probably build up some goodwill with an 'inheritance.'

I located her in the mess hall. "Hi, Gin--, er, Hi, Captain Gomez." I sat down next to her.

She put down her fork. "What do you want?"

I decided to try some small talk and slowly build up to important matters. "So, how's breakfast today? Is that scrambled eggs? Mmm. Looks good."

"Yeah." She didn't elaborate.

"So, how's the ship doing? Everything all right? I could have sworn the probability drive was acting up earlier this morning."

She leaned toward me. "How did you know that?"

Shoot. I shouldn't have revealed that. She made me

nervous. "I, uh, just knew."

"Jack always knew, too." She talked quietly so we wouldn't be overheard. "He would never admit how he knew."

"Oh?" Could it be that Old Jack had the same special skill as me? If so, how had he discovered it? What had he done with it? The more I learned about Old Jack, the more interesting he got.

"How did he know?" she whispered forcefully. "How did you know? Does he have some kind of computer surveillance installed? Or maybe secret cameras on the bridge or in engineering?"

I leaned away from her. Her intensity was intimidating. And she wouldn't believe me anyway if I told her how I knew. I'd experienced it and still found it pretty hard to believe.

When I didn't answer, she straightened up. "What do you want?"

"Jack's attorney contacted me, and apparently, he left me some money."

"We both know that's not true."

"No, it's true." Not. "TCC's still claiming Jack's dead back on Earth. I guess that set some things in motion."

"Anyway." I brainstormed that Gina might soften if she thought Old Jack had been thinking of her. "The attorney said Jack left you some money as well." I held up my fon. "I can transfer it to you."

"I don't believe you," she said. "If 'Jack' did have any money, and you had it now, there's no reason why you would give it to me."

Good grief, she was a tough asteroid to crack. I sighed. "Would you believe I'm just trying to make nice? I don't want to be your enemy." Darn it, more honesty. I was going to have to stop that.

She blinked, almost as if she was holding back tears. "How much money are we talking about?"

"100,000 credits. Not a fortune, but nothing to sneeze at."

"Okay." She held out her fon, and I transferred the money.

"I am sorry things are so difficult between us," I said.

She looked at the balance on her fon. "It's a difficult situation. It's not your fault."

"It's not your fault, either." I placed my hand over her hand on the table.

After a moment, she pulled her hand away. "Thanks, Jack." Her voice sounded heavy with emotion. "If there's anything I can do for you..."

"Thanks for saying that." Or at least starting to say it. "I also inherited some data, but it's encrypted. You wouldn't happen to know what the decryption key is, would you?"

"So that's what this is about," she said.

"No," I said.

"You're trying to buy Jack's decryption key!"

Did that mean there was a decryption key?

And she knew what it was?

Chapter Thirteen

I tried sweet-talking Gina some more, but she wasn't buying it. I guessed she knew Old Jack too well. But, geez, you'd think a hundred grand would buy a fella a little cooperation. Times must have changed over the last thirty years.

As I was walking away from the mess hall, my fon pinged and said, "You're overdue at rehearsal, Jack." It was Ander. My fon ordering me around was an annoying feature; I'd have to figure out how to turn it off.

I didn't bother answering him. I just started jogging to the rehearsal space.

The first person I ran into there was Olivia, still as beautiful as ever. "Hi, Olivia." I smiled sexily. "Did you miss me?" The rehearsal room was jammed full of people and scenery, as usual.

"Yeah." She frowned.

She did miss me. I knew it! I knew we were going to hit it off.

"We've been waiting for you to rehearse 'Oh, Is There Not One Maiden Breast,' and 'Poor Wand'ring One,'" she said.

"I'm your man," I said with a charming smile.

She didn't look convinced. "Come on." She walked to the piano without checking if I was following. The women of the chorus were already crowded around the piano.

The pianist started playing before we even got there. Shit. I needed lyrics. Quickly, I got out my fon and searched.

The pianist stopped.

When I glanced up, both the pianist and Olivia were glaring at me. "You missed your cue," Olivia said.

I smiled widely. "I was just testing you." I finally found the music and started singing.

"*Oh, is there not one maiden breast--*" I loved this song. I loved my job!

"*Which does not feel the moral beauty of making worldly interest subordinate to sense of duty?*"

The accompanist hurried to catch up to me.

"*Who would not give up willingly all matrimonial ambition, To rescue such a one as I from his unfortunate position?*"

Not surprisingly, a bunch of delectable young women crowded around me. Yes, I did sound good. I didn't think I'd met any of these women before, but I was going to remedy that very soon. That one with almond eyes and glossy black hair looked enough like Olivia to be her sister. Maybe I could win Olivia over via her sister?

They all started singing, "*Alas! There's not one maiden breast which seems to feel the moral beauty of making worldly interest subordinate to sense of duty!*"

They paused, looking at me expectantly.

Ooh, my part again. Maybe I should pay attention to the song. Sadly, I withdrew my focus from the nubile women clamoring around me, making beautiful music.

We were just finishing up rehearsal when my fon pinged again. "Jack, report to the bridge immediately," Gina said.

I picked up my fon. "Can it wait? I'm busy." I was about to get busy meeting my female co-stars, and maybe after that, I'd be a whole other kind of getting busy.

"No!" she said. "Now!"

I frowned. Shit. She sounded upset. What did I do now?

I made my way to the bridge posthaste. When I entered, Gina stood up. She was surrounded by a bunch of security officers who did not seem happy to see me. Sadly, they were also not nubile.

"Uh, what's up, G--, er, Captain Gomez?"

She put her fisted hands on her hips. "Did you kill Sam Jain?"

"*Whaa?*" My mind struggled to catch up. Dead? "Sam's dead? What happened?" How could he be dead?

Gina sat down, deflated. "Yeah, he's dead. We found him in your cabin."

The high spirits I'd gotten from singing surrounded by

beautiful women deflated. Ugh. "That's horrible. How'd he die?" Sam was the biggest, strongest man I'd ever met. I knew it sounded clichéd, but he seemed full of life. I wondered if he had a family. And poor Olivia, she'd be crushed.

One of the security team stepped forward. "How'd you do it, Jones?"

"Do what?" I said. I couldn't wrap my mind around the idea Sam was gone.

"We found his body in your cabin."

"I didn't do anything. Wait. In my cabin? What was he doing in my cabin?" How did Sam get into my cabin? How did security get into my cabin? Why were they in my cabin? "Who's 'we'? Who found the body?"

"We're asking the questions here, asshole," the security officer said. Come to think of it, his pointy head looked familiar. The way he said 'asshole' was definitely familiar.

I needed to mend some fences here. "Hi, Officer...?" My voice went up at the end, politely asking his name.

He didn't respond.

I forged ahead. "I don't think we got off on the right foot. I'm Jack Jones, uh, Junior. Pleased to make your acquaintance." I took in the entire security detail. I don't know about nubile, but a few of them were kind of handsome. "I'm pleased to make all of your acquaintances. Maybe we could go for a beer sometime. My treat." That reminded me: I was rich. And use it or lose it. "Or maybe you'd like some cash?" I held up my fon. "I'd be happy to tip you guys since you're doing such a good job."

"Jack!" Gina was standing again.

"Brig, ma'am?" the pointy-headed security guy, who, besides not liking me, apparently didn't like beer or cash either, said. Go figure.

I was starting to get good at interpreting Gina's moods, and right now, I'd say she was livid. "Yeah." She gestured at me. "Take him away."

I must have heard her wrong. She knew me. She knew I wasn't a murderer.

The officers grabbed my arms and started leading me away. They must have heard her wrong, too.

"But I didn't do anything!"

Outside the security area was a rather hedonistic painting of a Midsummer Night's Dream. Was it supposed to be irony? I waved to Puck as I was hauled past him.

The brig was delightfully old-fashioned with lots of strong vertical metal bars. It looked like a jail set, but somehow I knew it wouldn't be as easy to get out of.

They threw me into the cell without taking my fon. I decided to take advantage of the brief lull in my activities and practice for the show. I ran through 'Oh! False One, You Have Deceiv'd Me,' 'Oh, Is There Not One Maiden Breast?,' 'How Beautifully Blue The Sky,' 'Stay, We Must Not Lose Our Senses...,' and 'Finale Act 1' before anyone came to see me. I was very good if I did say so myself.

Honestly, I didn't think they'd leave me alone for so long. I figured they'd let me out as soon as Gina cooled off. Or as soon as they heard me sing.

I had been at rehearsal all day, so I must have an alibi.

My first visitors were a very young-looking security officer and Daniel.

The security officer said, "Wow, you're a good singer." Of course. He had a nice smile.

Daniel scrutinized me. Finally, he said, "I don't think you did it."

"Good," I said. "I didn't do it. He was found in my cabin?"

"I don't think you could do it," Daniel said.

"I..." I realized that arguing I could have done it was not in my best interest. "I'm very sorry for your loss."

He nodded.

"Can you tell me what happened?" I asked. "They haven't told me anything. How did he die? How does my cabin figure into it?"

Daniel shrugged. "The body's in the medical bay right now. They're doing an autopsy." He shook his head. "I heard through the grapevine he didn't have any apparent injuries."

"Are they sure he's dead?"

"Yeah," Daniel said. "They're sure. Doctors are good like that."

My brow furrowed. "How'd he die then?"

103

"Good question," Daniel said.

"Do you know when he died, at least?" I asked.

"I saw him yesterday," he said. "So, after that."

My mind whirred. What had I been doing for the last twenty-four hours? Yesterday I rehearsed and ate dinner with Eva. I spent last night in her cabin. I was at rehearsal all day today. I did have an alibi.

When I started to say that, I realized Daniel'd already left.

The young security guard was still standing in front of me.

"I have an alibi," I said.

He stepped closer. "Of course you do. Someone who can sing like you wouldn't go around murdering people."

He had the longest eyelashes I'd ever seen.

Before I could react, he leaned over and kissed me through the cell bars.

His lips felt warm with just the right amount of strength. His kiss felt good. Who knew men kissed as good as women? Did Old Jack know?

When he finally withdrew, his face was flushed. "I hope that was okay."

"More than okay. You're a good kisser." Suddenly, I was wondering what else he was good at. I admit I was intrigued. We stood there staring at each other for I don't know how long.

Someone cleared his throat.

Another security guard followed still-Angry Gina into the brig area.

"Jesus Christ, Jack!" she said. "Is there anyone you won't screw?"

I glanced back at the young officer, who seemed embarrassed now. "I have an alibi," I said, very reasonably, I thought.

"Dammit, Jack," she said. "I know you have a fucking alibi."

I raised my eyebrows. "So, why am I here, then?"

"Because you're infuriating!" She was very worked up. Could it be she was jealous? Could it be she wanted some Jack? Could it be she missed our lovemaking?

"What's that goofy look?" she said.

"I'd be honored, Captain Gomez, if you wanted to do dinner sometime and..."

She clenched her fists and breathed heavily through her nose. Finally, she said, "You're here partly because you just tried to bribe my security officers." Her breathing calmed a bit. "Come on, Jack." She sighed. "I know you're a smart man. You need to get your big head in the game. Quit thinking with your little head."

Yeah. She thought I was smart. And she was thinking about my little head. I smiled. "Your wish is my command, dear lady. Can I get out of here, then?"

"No," she said.

"Why not?" I asked. "You know I didn't kill Sam. You know I didn't mean anything by offering to tip security."

"Think." She stared at me.

It seemed important that I think. She thought I was missing something. I tried to clear my mind of how hot she was, how hot the young security guy was, of hot-ness in general.

Sam died. Yeah, that did it. All thoughts of hotness were gone.

It happened in my cabin. He didn't have any visible injuries... How was he killed? Could it have been some kind of poison? Why was my cabin relevant?

"Was there some kind of trap in my cabin?" I said.

"And he gets it in one try," Gina said.

"So, someone on the ship right now is trying to kill me."

She grimaced. "I'm afraid so."

Shit.

Chapter Fourteen

I should have been worried about the fact that a murderer was on board the ship, but instead, I was just pissed. How dare he come after me? How dare he kill my friend Sam?

"Can I see Sam?" I asked Gina from the brig.

She shook her head. "I don't think it's a good idea. You're safer in there."

"I'm not staying in the brig because it's safer. You don't have to protect me. I'm not a kid." Despite appearances to the contrary. And my month or two of life experience.

She sighed. "It's better if you stay there."

I grabbed the bars and shook them. "Let me out of here!"

Gina favored me with a baleful stare.

Yelling wasn't getting me anywhere. "*Our remedies oft in ourselves do lie*," I said. "After all, *men at some time are masters of their fates.*"

She frowned. "Yes, but *When clouds appear, wise men put on their cloaks; when great leaves fall, the winter is at hand; when the sun sets, who doth not look for night*?" I should have known Gina would know her Shakespeare quotes--she lived with Old Jack, after all.

"Come on, Gina." I smiled charmingly.

"All right!" She threw up her hands. "You are exasperating. Let him out. But if you get murdered, I'll kill you."

I didn't tell her how stupid that sounded. I didn't want her to change her mind. "Yes, Captain. I'll be careful."

The good kisser let me out of the brig. He looked at me hopefully from beneath those amazing eyelashes.

"*This bud of love, by summer's ripening breath, May prove a beauteous flower when next we meet,*" I said to him.

"Oh, good grief." Gina stormed out.

"*Never doubt I love*," I called after her.

I had to see Sam and pay my respects. I jogged to the medical bay. It was a fairly large room, about twenty feet by thirty feet, filled with medical beds and instruments. The equipment all had small LED lights, illuminating the room very faintly. It was one of the few spaces on the ship without any props, scenery, or decoration; it was all business. I didn't like it.

When I stepped inside, it seemed dark and deserted. I turned on the overhead light. "Hello? Anyone here?" The evenly spaced medical beds filled the large room. Only one was occupied.

A woman said, "Yeah." She sat next to a covered body. I could barely see the top of her bowed head. Then she glanced up and said more sharply, "What do you want?" It was my co-star, Olivia, whose sorrow-filled eyes were still as bewitching as ever. But even I knew this was not the time to make a play for her.

I stepped around the table. "I just wanted to pay my respects to Sam." I indicated the body on the table.

Tears rolled down her cheeks. "I can't believe he's gone."

"Me neither," I said. "It's a real shame. I'm very sorry for your loss." Clearly, she needed help and comfort. I held out my arms for a hug as I approached her.

She collapsed against my chest, sobbing.

"There, there." I rubbed her back as her tears soaked through my shirt. Poor thing. She must have truly cared about him. "There, there." My words were insufficient, but I couldn't decipher what else to say. *For in that sleep of death what dreams may come*? Or *O proud death*? The quotes didn't seem appropriate. For the first time, the Bard was failing me.

I stood there quietly, and Olivia cried into my chest for a long time.

Finally, she pulled away. "I'm sorry. I guess I got carried away. It's just that... I thought we'd have more time." Her eyes overflowed again.

I pulled over a chair. "Do you want to tell me about it?"

"He-- We--" She paused. "We had a thing." She paused.

"Or, not really. I mean, he kept asking me out, and I wanted to go out with him, but we just never--" She paused yet again. "I guess I don't want to talk about it. Too many regrets."

We sat silently together for a few minutes.

Goodbye, Sam. You were a good man. I'm glad I knew you.

He didn't deserve this. The fact that he was lying there dead was not right. My blood began to simmer again. I turned to Olivia. "He didn't suffer, did he?"

"The medical officer said he went very quickly, seconds, so if he did suffer, it wasn't for very long."

"That's good, at least." Seconds? What poison worked in seconds?

"I guess," she said slowly. "If anything about this is good."

I must have looked confused because she said, "It wasn't poison, if you're wondering. It was nanobots."

"Huh? Nano-what?"

"Nanobots. Tiny sub-microscopic robots attacked his cells. As I said, it was quick. The med officer said they would work on any species."

Well, crap. Here was an invention of the last thirty years I could have done without. I shivered, imagining tiny robots crawling on my skin, into my skin. Ugh. I shivered. "That sounds bad. Are they sure the, uh, robots are dead, or deactivated, or whatever?"

"Yeah." She nodded.

"So, when will they bring him back?" If they could bring me back, they could bring him back, right?

"I don't know," she said. "We don't have the facilities or the resources on the ship to clone somebody. So, at the earliest, they could do it when we return to Earth, but that's not for months. And the company doesn't pay to clone everyone. It's expensive. I'm not sure..." She sniffled.

Her breaking heart was about breaking mine. "Oh, right. That makes sense." They cloned me back on Earth. How many times would they do that? I was guessing not a lot. I gulped. I better not die again out here.

"Jack, will you stay here with me the rest of the night, just sit with me?" she asked in a little voice. "I don't want him to be alone."

"Yes, Olivia, I can do that. I don't want him to be alone, either," I said. "Or you."

"Rise and shine!" someone annoyingly chipper said. It was an older, fit-looking, dark-skinned man.

I had a terrible crick in my neck--which was a surprise because if asked, I would have said I hadn't slept. My mind had kept turning over the events since I'd woken up in my new body. Sophia had been bombed, and now Sam was dead, presumably all because someone was after me. Again. Why? What had Old Jack done or known that would make someone want to kill him so badly?

How many other people would get caught in the crossfire before the murderer accomplished his goal?

And what had I been doing to stop him? Not much. Having entirely too much fun, too much sex. But, my body had a mind of its own when it encountered a delectable woman (or man?) who wanted to have sex with me.

These were not happy thoughts. I needed to change.

From Olivia's expression, she'd had a bad night, too.

"What are you folks doing here?" the chipper man asked.

"We wanted to keep Sam company, Dr. Sharma," Olivia said.

"That's kind of you, but I'm here now," he said gently. "Olivia, honey, you need to go to your cabin and get some rest. I insist. Don't make me call in Captain Gomez."

Olivia nodded and stood up. "Yes, sir." She walked to the door, then turned. "Thanks, Jack. You're not nearly as big a jerk as I thought."

I was rubbing my neck. "Uh, thanks. I guess."

She left.

The Doc stared at me. "You look familiar. Who are you? Jack? Jack, who?"

"Jack Jones," I said.

He narrowed his eyes. "Isn't Jack's cabin where the body was found? And I knew a Jack Jones, and he wasn't you."

"Junior!" I said.

"Huh." He leaned back a bit. "I guess I see the family resemblance, especially around the eyes. And you seem to have an old soul, like your dad."

If I was a good investigator, I'd ask him about his alibi. "Did you know him well?" I asked, apparently not much of an investigator.

"Yes. He was one of my closest friends. I thought. But I can't say I knew he had a son, so maybe we weren't as close as I thought." That was a little sad, or maybe everything just seemed a little sad to me right now.

"I was a surprise," I said. "He only found out about me recently. Right before he, uh, died."

"Did you ever get to meet him?" he asked.

With the stabbing pain in my neck, I couldn't remember all the details of my fake backstory. "No. Can I get some pain meds? My neck is killing me."

"Yeah." Dr. Sharma went over to some machine, pressed some buttons, and returned with a couple of capsules in a tiny paper cup. "Here."

"Thanks." I quickly swallowed them down and handed him back the tiny cup.

"So," I said as he was throwing the cup away. "Can you tell me anything about Sam's murder?" I needed to step up my game when it came to investigating murders.

"I can tell you his body was found in your cabin," he said. "Do you have anything to say about that?"

I felt the corners of my mouth turn down. "Nothing good."

He nodded. "Your dad was a good man, a good friend. For his sake, if I can help you with anything, just ask."

Before all this trouble, I had been looking for Old Jack's decryption key. "When things settle down, I would like a chance to talk to you about my dad, maybe get to know him a little."

"Sure. I'd be happy to. That's easy. Anything else?"

Sam's murder must be related to my murder. "Can I get the autopsy results?" I held up my fon.

He paused. "I guess. There are so many spies on board you'd probably get the info almost immediately from them, anyway. I'll send you the report, right after I send it to Captain Gomez, okay? Anything else?"

I was reminded of Gina's *thinking with your little head* comment. "Ah, actually, Doc. I've been having some trouble, uh, focusing. So many beautiful people are on board; they're hard to resist. And I'm so hard for them to resist." What would it be like to be with that beautiful security officer? For that matter, the Doc here wasn't bad-looking for an old guy. I shook my head. Focus, Jack!

Dr. Sharma laughed. "Believe it or not, I remember what it was like to be a young man."

Oh, I believed him. "Do you maybe have some medication that could maybe help me focus on work, not be distracted..."

"That sounds pretty extreme, Jack. Maybe you should just lay off the ladies and concentrate."

If I laid off the ladies, who knew what I'd lay on? "I'm just asking," I said. "There seems to be a murderer gunning for me; I need to figure out who it is. Or at least keep my wits about me in case they try it again."

He sobered and pursed his lips, staring at me. Finally, he said, "All right, I've got something that should work." He walked to the med dispenser and returned with another capsule in another tiny paper cup. "Are you sure?"

"Yeah." I took the cup and downed the pill. "Thanks."

"Well, if there's nothing else, I should finish up the autopsy results and send them off to Captain Gomez."

It was as if a cloud had lifted from my mind. The capsule must have taken effect. "Did you run all the trace evidence from Sam's body through the mass spectrometer?"

"Not yet," Dr. Sharma said. "I'm guessing you want the data when I do?"

"Yes. If I find evidence in my cabin that security missed, can I bring it to you as well?"

"Yeah. But isn't that unlikely? Security knows what they're doing."

"Yes. But they aren't as motivated as me." No one was as motivated as me.

I got up and strode for the door.

"Jack."

I turned around. "What, Dr. Sharma? Hey, this medication is great."

He pursed his lips again. "Never mind. Good luck with your investigation."

What was that about?

Chapter Fifteen

After spending the night with Sam's body and seeing how broken up Olivia was, I was more determined than ever to figure something out. I rushed back to my cabin to collect evidence to bring back to Sharma, but when I got there, security was inside gathering trace evidence.

I hung back in the hall and let them work. While cooling my heels and enjoying *The Tempest* mural outside my quarters, I couldn't help noticing the very unobtrusive cameras placed at even intervals down the corridor. Surely, security had a record of who approached my cabin?

I knew from the night featuring my two female guests there weren't any cameras inside my cabin, however, or at least if there were, the run-of-the-mill security guys didn't have access to the footage. Too bad for them. I grinned. Too bad for me; I wouldn't mind having an external record of our activities that night.

Following the memory, I realized the killer could have entered my cabin through the secret passageway--or maybe just sent the nano-whatevers in that way.

Speaking of entry, how did Sam get in? Who found the body and how? And how did the security team get in today?

As I pondered all this, someone tackled me from behind. Was it the killer? It took me a few seconds to catch my breath and sort out the tangle of limbs on the floor.

"Jack!" Eva cried. "You're all right! The last I saw of you, you were going to talk to Gina. What happened? I heard there was a body in your cabin--some people said it was you, some said it was Sam. I also heard you were in the brig." She wrapped her arms around me.

So, the tackler was not the killer. I attempted to extricate myself. "Yes, I'm okay, Eva. I'm sorry I didn't contact you."

"I was worried. But, sorry, I didn't know you'd fall on the floor just now. I wasn't trying to get you on the floor. We have some more training to do, obviously."

One of the security guys in my cabin saw us lying on the floor and snickered.

"Please get off me." I tried to push her off, but sadly, she was still in better shape than me. "No need to worry. I'm fine."

She got off. "*I have no other but a woman's reason.*"

"Huh?" Oh, she was giving me some of my own medicine: Shakespeare quotes. "I said I was sorry."

"Someone's after you," she said more quietly when we were both vertical.

"If you two are done rolling around on the floor, the Chief has some questions for you, Jones," the snickery security guy said. "Here? Or do you want to come down to the security center?"

I flashed back to my boring stint in the brig; I didn't want to go anywhere near that again. "Here."

The security officer said, "Come on in, then," and waved me into my own cabin. Gee, thanks.

As Eva and I entered, the long-lashed security officer exited, holding an evidence container. "Jack! It's so good to see you." I'd swear he batted his eyelashes. "Are you all right?"

Eva looked from him to me and back again with raised brows.

"It's nice to see you again..." If I'd ever known the guy's name, I didn't recall it now.

"Ted," he quickly said.

"It's nice to see you again, Ted. This is my lovely friend Eva." I waved at her. "And Eva, this is my lovely friend Ted." I waved at him.

She nodded to him.

"Say, Ted." I stepped closer and gazed into his eyes. "Can you keep me in the loop on what you guys discover?"

"Sure thing, Jack." He nodded. "You can count on me."

"If you're quite finished flirting, Jones, get over here," the head security officer bellowed. I didn't know this guy's name either, but I didn't care.

Most of the other security left.

"I guess you have an alibi, Jones," the head guy said.

Duh. Hadn't I said that? But I said, "Yes, sir."

"But that doesn't mean you didn't booby-trap your room," he said.

Huh. I hadn't even considered that. I knew I didn't do any booby-trapping, but maybe Old Jack did, causing the release of the nano-things when his extra security measures were breached. It was a sign of the severity of events that the term *booby-trap* didn't make me even think of sex--until just now, dammit.

"Young Jack here is only eighteen-years-old," Eva said, grabbing my hand. "He doesn't have the expertise, connections or resources to obtain these proscribed nanobots."

The security guy stared at me for a good while, and I tried to look young and ignorant (it wasn't difficult). I hoped Eva didn't think I was as ignorant as I looked.

"I hope not," he finally said. "Because the nanobots are not a good way to go. It's quick, but all your organs and cells are attacked at once, essentially eaten alive."

I grimaced. That wasn't what Sharma had told Olivia.

"I don't hold with that, kid," he said. "I don't care who you know or who you were related to."

Shit. I didn't hold with that, either. Who was the jerk who killed him in such a horrific way? If it was Old Jack via some kind of timer, he was a brigand, an evildoer, a huge asshole...

"You're not much like your old man, are you?" the Chief said, shaking his head.

Was that true? "What do you mean?" I asked.

"Jack had plenty of resources and connections, as well as expertise in all kinds of ways to kill a man. And he wouldn't look like he was about to puke when discussing a murder." He turned to the sole remaining security officer in the room, and they both took a step toward the door.

So, not like Old Jack: check. If he was an evil nanobot-killing jerk, that was a good thing, a very good thing.

But they couldn't leave yet. I wasn't through with them. "Wait. I have some questions for you."

The Chief smiled like *what could he have to fear from a kid like me*? "Sure. What?"

"How did you guys get in here today?"

"The door was unlocked. We assumed Sam left it open."

Eva hissed like she didn't believe it.

"But I didn't leave it unlocked. Is that unusual--to leave a cabin door open?"

"Not at all," he said. "The ship is secure."

Eva's expression said she didn't believe him. I didn't, either.

That was one question answered. I hadn't left it unlocked and never would. Maybe I was a bit like Old Jack in terms of paranoia. "How did Sam get in? What was he doing here?"

He shrugged. "No idea. We checked the security feeds for the hallway outside here, and Sam doesn't appear on them, at least not for the last couple of days." He looked at me. "What do you think he was doing here?"

He had some decryption info for me? Or maybe he had some kind of information about my shooting on AC? Had someone shut him up before he could give me answers? I wasn't ready to tell the Chief this hypothesis. "No idea. But, wait, how could you not have footage of him?"

The Chief grimaced. "I'm guessing the security feed was hacked. And I'm not happy about it. We're investigating that, don't worry."

So, the Chief didn't know about the secret passageway to my cabin? Interesting. "Could I see the security footage you've got?"

"I guess. I'll get your little buddy Ted to send it to you."

Eva sighed.

Little buddy? What was that supposed to mean? I'd had it with this jerk.

"*Come not between the dragon and his wrath,*" I said. "*Nothing can allay, nothing but blood.*"

Eva squeezed my hand.

"What?" the security guy said. "Whatever, kid. But," he held up his forefinger. "No vigilante shit on my ship. Got it?"

No.

He and his minion turned and left.

Still holding hands, Eva and I sank onto the bed.

"What do you think happened to Sam?" I asked.

"I don't know, but it's not good," she said. "I'm just glad it wasn't you who died. Those nanobots sound like a bad way to go."

What if it was old-me that killed him? I couldn't get that thought out of my mind. Was I responsible for the sins of my predecessor? Was he me? Was he a murderer? Was I?

Even though she'd shared my bed, I couldn't bring myself to share these thoughts with Eva.

"Jack?" She rubbed my shoulder. "We've been sitting alone on your bed for several seconds, and you haven't made a move. Are you all right?"

Hurray for the meds; they must be working. "I'm not okay." I looked at her. She was a sweetheart, and I should cut her loose for her own safety. The next murder attempt could kill her.

"What's that look?" she said. "If you're thinking of letting me go for my own protection, think again."

How did she know what I'd been thinking?

"Like many teenagers, you show everything you're thinking on your face. It's sweet," she said. "And, frankly, you need my protection at this point."

"I don't want to be sweet," I said. "I want to be badass. I mean, I am badass." Yeah, I was trying to convince myself as well as her.

"Let's do some training and make you even bad-assier."

I patted her hand. "It's a nice thought."

I had a not-nice thought. The last thing I'd talked to Sam about was inheriting data and looking for an encryption key. Maybe he was looking for Old Jack's data cubes? Had he had some kind of nefarious aims?

"I need to go talk to Daniel," I said. "He may have known what Sam was up to."

"Have you considered that Sam might have been leaving some kind of trap for you?" she asked.

Crap. "No. But that's just another reason to talk to Daniel. Plus, he may know where the nanobots came from."

"You're learning, kid," she said. "But I'll see you in the gym later?"

I needed all the help and training I could get. "Yeah."

Daniel was in his usual place in the cargo hold. He stood up as soon as he saw me. "So, they let you out of the brig, huh? Is that wise?"

"What do you mean?" I thought I knew what he meant, and I didn't like it. "You think I need to stay in the brig to stay safe? You think I can't take care of myself?"

He shrugged as if to say, *Yeah*. He sat. "What do you want?"

"What can you tell me about nanobots?" I'd looked them up on my fon and hadn't found out much more than Olivia had told me.

"Nothing."

"What do you mean, nothing? I just gave you a big consulting fee. You don't know anything about them?"

"Oh, I know plenty," he said. "But not only are you somehow mixed up in the murder of my buddy Sam, you blew off work here the other day."

Shit. How was I supposed to fulfill all my duties on the ship? There were just too many of them. Or, maybe I'd been goofing off too much. "If I do some work for you now, will you tell me what you know about nanobots afterward?"

"I guess." He shot some instructions from his fon to mine.

I got to work shifting cargo from AC away from the airlock.

I'd moved about a dozen various crates, and I was on the last one, about four-feet-cubed in size, which was being uncooperative. For some reason, the anti-grav dolly wasn't working on it. I grunted and repositioned it underneath.

The dolly clanged, and suddenly it and the crate zoomed up and came right back down, crashing on the floor. I fell backward and the crate cracked in front of me.

Was that another murder attempt? My pulse flew faster than the speed of light.

"Jack!" Daniel ran over to me. "Are you all right?"

I nodded, trying to calm my pulse.

"Damn dolly. Oh, no," he said. "It's one of the high-security crates from AC."

"Sorry, but it wasn't my fault. The dolly's acting up. Has that ever happened before?"

118

But Daniel wasn't paying any attention to me. He was trying to get a peek at what was inside the crate. "I've never seen one not installed in a ship, but I think that's an FTL drive."

I examined the item inside. It was a featureless sphere. Boring. "How can you tell? It doesn't look like anything."

"Yeah, mysterious, isn't it?" He stood up, smiling.

"It's surprising we get our FTL drives from AC," I said. "They don't seem smart enough to produce them."

"They aren't," he said.

"So?"

Still grinning, he said, "I don't know what's going on. But it's very, very interesting."

"What does the paperwork say about the box?" I asked.

He pointed his fon at the crate's label. "It's in AC, but the translation is something like Ephesus Holding Company." He looked up. "Does that mean anything to you?"

It did sound vaguely familiar, but I couldn't put my finger on it. "No, sorry. Is there any other info on the crate? Trace evidence? Fingerprints? Do the AC have fingerprints?" I paused. "Paw prints?" Was that a thing?

Daniel waved his fon over the surfaces of the crate. "No, nothing, at least according to my fon. I might have some more precise scanners somewhere. But it's too clean. Why would a crate be this clean? Weird."

Why did it seem like the mysteries were mounting? "I'm glad I could pique your interest," I said. "Now, about those nanobots-- what do you know?"

"I guess you've earned it. Rumor has it they were developed on Geryon 180b. They're proscribed tech."

"What does that mean?"

"Forbidden tech. It's banned."

"How the hell did it end up in my cabin, then?"

"That's a very good question."

Chapter Sixteen

I stood in the cargo bay, intuition tingling. There were just too many mysteries, including Old Jack's murder, Sam's murder, Sophia's apartment bombing, my shooting and the secret FTL drive in the cargo bay. All this mayhem at once was too much of a coincidence. It all had to be related.

When it came to physical evidence, however, I didn't have much. Old Jack's autopsy hadn't held any surprises; the cause of death was a bullet wound to the back, nothing unusual about the bullet and no trace evidence. There hadn't been anything physical in my quarters or on the crate. But I didn't know about Sam's body or Sophia's apartment bombing.

Hadn't I called Noah to ask him about Sophia a while back? I double-checked my fon, and there weren't any messages from him. Maybe he could help me decrypt Old Jack's data. I left him another message.

Lacking any other leads, I decided to go down to engineering and see what they could tell me about FTL drives. Was I the only person on the ship who knew it utilized unusual probabilities? Eva had certainly seemed clueless when I'd mentioned it.

In engineering, I found Olivia. Surprise.

"Hi, Jack," she said, as lovely as ever. "Did you come to check on me?"

No. I had no idea my beautiful, but sad Pirates co-star was an engineer. "Yes. Of course. *Love comforteth like sunshine after rain.*"

Her nose scrunched up. It was good I was on Sharma's meds, or I would have thought she was adorable. "I may not think you're a jerk anymore, but I'm still not interested in you."

I resisted the urge to say something dramatic about how she'd wounded me and broken my heart. I cleared my throat. "So, how are you doing?"

"I'm hanging in there." Her eyes filled, and she looked at the floor, trying to regain her composure.

"Good." I glanced around engineering. This-Jack, me, had never been in here. It was full of banks of machines with lots of little glowing lights and faint humming sounds. The aisles between the machines were narrow. "You know I'm new. What do you guys do around here?"

"Make sure the engines work." Her current expression said she thought I was an idiot.

"Well, sure. Right. Of course. I figured." I looked around but couldn't make heads or tails of anything I saw. "There are two kinds of engines, right?"

"Yes. We have the sub-light engines and the FTL drive."

"How do they work?"

"The sub-lights work just like any other engines. And the FTL drive is a proprietary secret, a black box. We don't know how it works."

"Surely you have some guess as to how it works?" I said.

Her fon pinged, and she glanced at it. "Rehearsal. Do you want to walk over there together?"

I was glad I'd managed to turn off the feature where my fon ordered me around. "Sure."

She said goodbye to someone, grabbed a bag, and we headed off down the hall.

"Is it really true the FTL drive's mechanism is secret?" We walked past a mural of three witches. They were a little scary. I wasn't sure I approved of the dark, overly dramatic decor down in the bowels of the ship.

Checking me out, Olivia looked like she was about to smile. "Yeah. It's top secret."

I waited for more. More was not forthcoming. "What do you think?" I asked. "How does it work?"

She shrugged. "I don't know. I'm just a regular engineer."

"So, what do you do when it malfunctions?"

"Why do you ask that?" she said. "Have you heard something? What have you heard?"

I tried to look innocent. "Me? I haven't heard anything. What have you heard? Is there something to hear?" Clearly, there was something to hear.

She didn't answer. "Lift or ladder?" she said at the end of the hall. The rehearsal space was near the top of the ship, and we were presently near the bottom of the ship.

I wanted to take the lift, but I knew the ladder was manlier. "Ladder, of course."

She did smile then. "Because you're a manly man?"

I was glad I could cheer her up a little and smiled back. "Ay, and *a bold one, that dare look on that which might appall the devil*."

She laughed. "That's what I thought."

What did that mean?

At rehearsal, Olivia and I practiced 'All Is Prepar'd; your Gallant Crew Await You' and 'Stay, Fred'ric, Stay.'

Carter seemed pleased, and I was strangely pleased by his pleasure.

Then, we tried to block out the entire show, and he was much less pleased. The whole company in the stage area was in disarray from where I'd disarrayed them. They'd had to keep avoiding me as I flailed around because of Carter's hand-waving instructions.

"Christ, Jack! It's like you have no idea what you're doing!" Carter said.

I didn't know what I was doing, and his instructions were vague. No one else seemed to be struggling, but they'd all done the show together before.

I just looked at him. Had he mixed me up with Old Jack? Finally, I said, "I'm sorry, Sir, but I've never done this show before with this group. I don't know what you want. Explain it better."

"Oh, right," he said.

"I'll tell you what," he said. "I'll play your part, and you can see what I mean." He walked to the center of the group. "From the top."

I got out my fon and started recording. That way, I'd have a specific record of what he wanted, and I could practice at my leisure. Huh. Like I had any leisure.

A JACK BY ANY OTHER NAME

I texted Eva to tell her I'd be late to the gym.

After rehearsal, I ran to the mess hall, grabbed a quick protein bar, aka dinner, and ran to the gym.

"There you are," Eva said. "I was beginning to wonder if you were going to make it. What--did you hook up with someone on the way here?" She grinned.

"Hook up? No, of course not. I wouldn't do that." We both knew that I would do that. But she didn't know I'd gotten meds from Sharma that helped me focus.

Before I knew what was happening, I was on the ground. "What happened?"

Eva was sitting on top of me. I was too tired to appreciate it. "You need to work on your defensive skills," she said. "That's the second time I took you down today. Have you learned nothing?"

I didn't like being chastised. "I've learned something. I'm just tired. It's been a long day." Had I even gotten any sleep last night in the med center? "Following a long night."

"So you did hook up with someone!" she said. "I knew it."

I came to a realization she was jealous. "Why are you so interested in who I hook up with?"

"I, uh, I'm not that interested." She struggled to get off of me without poking any sensitive parts.

I pulled her back down. "I can tell you're interested. You're jealous. You care about me."

She quit struggling. "Fine. You caught me. I care about you."

I leaned toward her. "I care about you, too," I whispered.

We kissed gently; it was much different than our other kisses had been--lacking the lust component. Wow, Sharma's drugs were powerful.

"What's up with you?" she asked. "You seem different."

I leaned back on the floor and grinned. "If I told you, I'd have to kill you."

She got off me and lay next to me. "What's that mean?"

"Nothing. I'm just joking around. Spy humor."

"Oh, so you're a spy now?"

"No. But aren't most people on the ship?" We lay there next to each other for a few moments. "How do I know you're not a spy?"

"You don't." She grinned. "I can't believe you haven't made a move yet."

"I'm tired." My stomach growled. "And hungry."

"Did you eat?"

"Sort of."

"Only sort of? I tell you what. Let's go over to the mess hall, and you can tell me why you're different and what you got up to last night. I'm buying." That was a joke; mess hall food was free.

I sat up. "It's a date."

The mess hall was deserted; I guessed it was late in the day for dinner. We each got some food.

As we sat, Eva said, "Okay, spill. What's up with you?"

"I got some meds from Dr. Sharma that suppress my libido."

"Seriously?" Her eyebrows had migrated well up into her forehead.

I nodded and took a bite.

"That doesn't sound plausible," she said. "I know Sharma. I'm calling him." She did so. "Dr. Sharma, could you stop by the mess hall for a few minutes?" She hung up. "He's coming."

We consumed our comestibles for a few minutes.

Sharma strode in. "What's this about?" He slowed at our table. "Ah. Mr. Jones."

"I'm glad you're here," I said. "Did you have another dose of that anti-libido stuff?" I'd become increasingly aware of enticing Eva sitting beside me on the bench, her thigh pressing against my thigh.

"About that." He sighed and sat down.

"I was wondering," Eva said. "I didn't think you gave out anti-libido drugs."

"I'm not at liberty to discuss my patients," Sharma finally said.

"Jack doesn't care, do you, Jack?" Eva poked me with her elbow.

"Eva and I have no secrets," I said.

"I think you do," he said.

Eva was looking from one to the other of us with increasing confusion. "What's going on?"

I wished I knew what was going on.

Sharma stared at me.

"Just tell us," I said.

He sighed again and leaned toward us. "Fine. I did give Jack some meds that suppress libido."

"What?" Eva asked.

"I don't give those meds to people," he said.

"What?" I said. Was he saying I wasn't a person?

Eva looked even more confused. "What are you saying? He's not human?"

"Hey! I'm human!"

"They're clone-specific meds," Sharma said.

"Oh." Shit. How many people were going to figure out my secret?

I glanced at Eva. She didn't say anything.

"You knew?" he asked her.

She nodded.

"But..." I didn't know what to say. "I don't understand. Are you saying my feelings and desires have been some kind of side-effect of the cloning process?"

Sharma steepled his fingers. "Some clones are starved for affection when they're first duped." He stared at me. "It's a chemical imbalance in the brain. Your dupe engineer should have corrected it."

I felt like someone had punched me in the gut. Oh, Sophia. Had she made some kind of mistake? Or... I couldn't finish that thought.

"If you're Jack's clone, why did you act like you didn't know me?" Sharma asked. "I thought we were friends, Jack. Don't you trust me?"

"I'm sorry," I said. "I don't know you. They lost thirty years of Jack's memories."

Sharma blew out a short breath and then looked down at the table. "Then, I'm sorry, too. My old friend is really and truly dead. I'd hoped..." He looked up at me.

I shook my head. "Sorry," I whispered. I was so confused. How could Old Jack have so many good people he counted as friends and yet possibly leave lethal traps in his cabin?

Finally, Sharma put his hands on the table. "Well, is that it? I need to get back to the med center."

"Can I get some more meds?" I asked quietly.

"The ones I gave you should solve the problem, but yeah, come see me if not."

"Will you keep his secret?" Eva asked.

"Yes." He stood. "I take doctor-patient confidentiality very seriously."

I was still reeling from what he'd said. Was I just some kind of affection-starved clone? It made sense in a way: babies needed physical contact and affection to develop properly.

"Any news on Sam's death?" Eva asked Sharma.

"I sent him the autopsy report." He pointed at me as he turned. "Ask Jack." He walked out.

"You got the autopsy report and didn't tell me?" she asked.

"When would I tell you?" I said. "I haven't even had a chance to·read it yet."

"Show me."

I pulled up the report on my fon, and we read it together. "Nothing new," I said when we were done. Nanobots ate him from the inside out. What a horrible way to go.

"Eva..."

"What?"

"You knew him. Do you think Jack was capable of murder?"

She froze for a moment. "I assume you want me to be honest."

I nodded.

"Yes. I know for a fact he was capable of murder." She looked away from me. "It was part of his job."

Ugh. "So...could he have left a nanobot trap in his cabin?"

"Could have, but why wait so long to deploy it? No, I think whoever killed him is after you."

So, I was officially good bait. Check.

Eva leaned back. "What's that recording?" She pointed at the rehearsal file.

I thumbed it open. "It's Carter's blocking for the show *Pirates of Penzance*. He couldn't explain what he wanted; he had to act it out."

"Let's see it." She leaned forward.

We watched the recording of people dancing around, walking to and fro and getting on and off stage. It helped me relax a little.

"Wait. Who's that guy?" She leaned over my fon.

"Who?"

"That big guy in the back. He sort of reminds me of Sam."

It was a big guy. "That's not Sam." I peered into the fon. "That's Noah, Noah Anderson." What the hell was he doing here?

"Who? I don't think I know him."

"That's because he's not in the crew." I paused. This was more than a little suspicious. "He's supposed to be back on Earth."

She exhaled. "So, he's like a stowaway? Captain Gomez will not like that. You need to tell her."

She was right, but Gina still intimidated me a little. What if I told her something she didn't want to hear, and she put me back in the brig? "I'll just text her the recording." I sent it off.

Chapter Seventeen

That night Eva was kind enough to invite me to stay in her cabin. I was creeped out about what happened to Sam in mine. We didn't have sex. And it wasn't because of my anti-libido drugs or a malfunctioning FTL drive; I think I was worn out. And creeped out, really creeped out.

After breakfast, we went to the gym to work out. There were about a dozen other crew members already there. I tried to watch them all--which was impossible. But how did I know who I could trust?

"You need to learn to protect yourself," she said. "People are after you."

"I know," I said.

We began sparring, and distracted, I mostly unsuccessfully blocked her various jabs and whatnots.

At one point, I fell on the floor.

"Come on, Jack. Are you even trying?"

I lay back. "I don't know. I have a lot on my mind. Where is Noah? What's he doing here? Should we have reported him to security?" I'd tried calling him again last night, and he didn't answer. Again.

"Maybe I should forget this self-defense training," I said. "I feel like there's too much going on. I have to do the show. I have to learn self-defense. I have to solve Jack's murder. I have to work in the cargo bay. I mean, give me a break."

"I don't know what giving you a break would entail, but I'm in," a male voice said from near the doorway.

I couldn't help it; I laughed. It was Ted.

I got up off the floor. "Hi, Ted. You remember Eva?"

He nodded.

"Hi, Ted," she said. "What are you doing here?"

"I thought I'd bring the footage from outside Jack's cabin in person."

"Of course you did," she said, smirking. "How'd you know he was here?"

I hadn't thought to ask him that. Eva was a better investigator than me. Darn it.

"We security officers have our ways." He grinned.

"Spying on us?" Eva asked.

Ted shrugged. "So, do you want to see what we've got or not?"

"Yes," I said. "Thank you for bringing it by. It was very kind of you." He seemed like a good guy.

"You got an office or anything with a bigger monitor?" he asked.

"Yeah." Eva walked to a closed door in the gym. "Come on." The three of us went into what was apparently her office.

Ted did something with his fon, holding it up to the monitor, and then typed some stuff on the keyboard.

The view of the hallway outside my cabin appeared on the monitor. Somebody I didn't know walked by, followed by a bunch of nothing.

"This is thrilling," Eva said.

I was starting to realize investigating stuff was boring--at least when people weren't shooting at you or leaving tiny deadly robots in your cabin.

"Yeah, I can speed it up." Ted typed something else.

The recording fast-forwarded, showing mostly empty corridor with occasional people speed-walking by. Then the recording seemed to jump.

"Was that hacked?" I asked.

"Yeah," he said. "And that's not the only place. Keep watching."

We did and saw two more jumps.

"That's pretty much it," Ted said.

"Three jumps is odd," Eva said. "Does it means three people went into your cabin?"

"Sam, and..." I paused. "No. They'd have to exit, too. One guy entered and left."

Eva and I looked at each other, and both said, "Noah."

"Who's Noah?" Ted asked.

"He's a stowaway, we think," Eva said.

"But he works for TCC," I said. Noah was supposed to be a super-spy. Of course, he was the one that told me that...

"TCC?" Ted asked. "Don't we all work for TCC?"

"He's a secret agent or something, right Jack?" Eva said.

"Yeah, I guess," I said.

"Do you think Captain Gomez knows he's here?" Ted asked.

I felt my eyebrows rise. "I sort of told her last night."

"How do you sort of tell someone something?" Ted asked very reasonably.

"I sent her a file," I said.

"But we don't know if she watched it," Eva said.

"She probably already knew," I said. "She should know who's on her ship. And she seems very capable--but who knows?"

"Well, I don't want to tell her," Eva said.

"Me neither," Ted said. "She's scary."

"You should talk to her in person, Jack," Eva said.

"Yeah." But I didn't want to talk to her. "I hate to say it, but I'm out of my depth."

Eva snorted. "You hate to say it? You've been whining about it all day."

I mentally reviewed my morning. Instead of focusing on working out, I had been whining and randomly watching other people working out. "Sorry."

"Don't apologize," she said. "Just quit acting like a pussy." She was right.

"*Once more into the breach, dear friends, once more*," I said. "*When the blast of war blows in our ears, then imitate the action of the tiger!*"

"I can be a tiger," Ted said. "*Roaaar!*"

Eva and I started laughing. Ted joined in.

Once we all caught our breath, Ted said, "What do you want me to do?"

I considered. "Can you give me any pointers on how to investigate crimes?" I wished I'd thought of asking for tips on how to investigate earlier. I needed all the help I could get.

"I just graduated from the academy back on Earth," he said. "The main thing they taught us was to interview everyone associated with the crime. And whoever lies is probably involved. And killers usually love the victim--or used to." That was a chilling thought. Who loved Jack? Gina loved Jack.

"Noah lied to you, right?" Eva said. "He said he was on Earth."

Noah may have loved Jack. "Yeah," I said. "He's got to be involved somehow. Can you try to find him, Ted?" I smiled. "Using your special security ways?"

"Sure."

I swear, then, he batted his lashes at me. He was amusing.

What else could I do? "I could interview that young female doc that helped me before and see if she knows anything about Sharma or what he might be hiding."

"Sure you could," Eva said with a wry smile.

"What are you going to do?" I asked her.

"I'm going to go do my regular job." Her fon pinged. "Speaking of which, I have a training session." She stood. "Come on. You guys get out of here." She hustled us out. Back in the main gym, a group of crew members I didn't know stood waiting for her.

Ted and I exited, stopping outside the gym in the hall.

"So, can I see you later?" he asked.

"Sounds good. We need to compare notes." He looked a little disappointed, so I added, "And I know where there's bootleg liquor on board."

"Liquor!" His eyebrows rose. "Wow, I thought that was prohibited."

Finally, someone greener than me! I liked this guy. "I'll text you the secret location. Stick with me, kid, and I'll show you the ropes."

He nodded.

I walked toward the med center.

"Jack!" a man called out from behind me. "There you are." It was Carter. "I'm glad I found you. You're late for rehearsal. We're doing a run-through of the entire show. Come on."

Did I mention I had too much shit to do?

Rehearsal went fine; Carter even said I was much improved. I guess scrutinizing that video paid off.

By the time I got to the med center, the cute young doc wasn't working. Darn.

Sharma was working. "What can I do for you, young man?"

It was time to nut up, or as Eva would say, quit acting like a pussy. "Why didn't you come out and tell me the anti-libido drugs were for clones? Isn't that against the doctor's code or something?"

"Yeah, but Captain Gomez told me to do it."

"She told you to suppress my libido?"

"No. It's complicated. Let's just say you've got an issue with Captain Gomez."

That was not good. She could definitely be involved in Old Jack's murder. She had a motive: she got Old Jack's job, for one. She inherited his money if he had any. She loved him, at least at one point. And she may have been having an affair with Carter when Old Jack was still alive; the two of them got together pretty quick after he died.

I got a text from Ted: Bootleg time?

I texted him back to meet me outside the cargo bay. If I was going to confront Captain Gomez, I needed some fortification-- and that didn't make me a pussy.

Daniel wasn't happy to see Ted and me when we'd picked our way through the maze of containers in the cargo bay to the bar. "What the hell, Jones? You think this is your own personal speakeasy?"

"No," I said. Somehow I didn't think reminding him that I'd paid him enough money that it should be my own personal speakeasy would turn out well.

Ted smiled. "I'm security."

"Shit!" Daniel said. "This operation, booze, is illegal. Did you turn me in?"

I said, "I didn't turn anyone in."

"I just meant I'm not a threat," Ted said. "It's not like I'd steal your booze, and I'm not arresting you."

"What does it hurt to give him a drink?" I asked.

"So, what, are you two on a date or something?" Daniel

asked.

Ted looked hopeful. I shrugged. "Sort of."

"I should have known befriending a teenager would be trouble," Daniel said.

"Relax," I said. "It's not like I'm hosting a rave here."

Ted giggled. "What's a rave? It sounds kinky."

Raves, wild unsupervised parties, were popular the first time I was eighteen. If Ted didn't know what they were, they must have fallen out of favor. I tried to cover. "I don't know."

"Why'd you say it then?" Daniel asked, peering at me. "How old are you?"

I peered back at him. When did people stop having raves? Did he know about them? "How old are you?" He looked like he was in his twenties but didn't act like it. Shit. Was Daniel a clone?

We stared at each other for a few more moments, but neither of us said anything.

"I'm nineteen, and I'm thirsty," Ted said. "Bring on the hooch."

Daniel snickered. "You guys remind me of each other. He talks funny, too." He turned around. "Bill."

Bill appeared, carrying the hooch. He poured us all a mug.

We sat in a circle on cargo containers.

"Did you come to tell me you discovered something about you-know?" Daniel asked.

"What's you-know?" Ted asked.

I wanted to know what you-know was, too. "What do you mean?"

"You know, the thing we discovered the other night," Daniel said. "In the container that was mislabeled."

"Oh, the FTL drive!" I said.

"Is it safe to talk in front of this guy?" Bill asked.

"Sorry." I introduced everyone to everyone and then said, "Sure, talk in front of him."

"I don't have anything to say," Daniel said. "I thought you did."

"What were we talking about?" I asked.

"About the FTL drive!" Daniel said.

"Wait, you discovered an FTL drive?" Ted asked. "Besides the one in engineering?"

"Yeah," I said. "I don't know anything new."

"Why did you come here, then?" Bill asked.

"For a drink." I raised my mug.

"What's the story with the FTL drive?" Ted asked.

"We don't know," Daniel said. "The documentation for it was fake. I'm trying to figure out where it came from. It was loaded on AC."

"I might be able to help with that," Ted said. "We probably have outside security feeds of when it was dropped off at the ship. They might tell us something."

"That would be great," Daniel said. "When can you show us?"

"Now." Ted punched some buttons on his fon and stared at the little screen. "I'm pulling up the footage outside the cargo bay before we left AC." He stared at the screen some more. "Well, I don't see anything weird. Do you guys want to take a look?"

"Yeah," Daniel said.

"Sure," I said.

Ted passed me the fon. I stared at the images. "Is it just me, or does that AC there look weird?"

"Let me see," Daniel said.

I passed him the fon.

"I don't think that's an AC," he said. "I think that's something else disguised as an AC."

"Why do that?" Bill asked.

I had a few ideas... To sneak onboard the *Shakespeare*. To shoot at a handsome singer on the surface of AC. To plant nanobots in said singer's cabin. To lurk about the ship...

Chapter Eighteen

Bright and early the next morning, I was berating myself. I was not a good investigator. The more I investigated, the more questions I seemed to have.

I also didn't want to talk to Old Jack's wife, Captain Gina Gomez, and I needed to. She was my best lead to decrypt Old Jack's data. I was afraid of her--not that I would ever admit that to anyone.

I was guessing she also really needed to know about Noah--stowaways didn't seem like a good idea. So, with reluctance, I forced myself to go to the bridge to talk to her.

The bridge was approximately twenty-feet by twenty-feet, with display screens on all the walls. Against the walls, there were desks with computer workstations. Every chair was filled. Gina'd called me up here before, but I'd been so busy with her yelling at me I hadn't had a chance to notice any details.

I saw Gina sitting in her captain's chair and stepped toward her.

A man I didn't recognize said, "What's your business here, Ensign?" as I entered.

Everyone swiveled to look at me.

"I, uh, wanted to talk to Gina, er, I mean Captain Gomez, if possible," I said.

The man said, "That's not protocol, Ensign. You need to talk to your CO and use your chain of command. Only if it's deemed necessary do you talk to the captain."

Gina stood up. "It's fine, Harris." She walked toward me. "Let's go talk in my cabin, Jack. Get back to work, everyone."

The bridge officers looked surprised but turned back to their display screens.

She ushered me to a nearby cabin the same size and layout as my cabin. Had Old Jack spent a lot of time here? If he'd been the captain, why wasn't this his—and now, my--cabin? She sat down on the bed and patted the mattress beside her.

I hesitated. She looked like she could break me in half, almost as tall as me and more muscular under all those delectable curves. She wasn't going to like me telling her about a stowaway.

"I don't bite, Jack." She gave me a lascivious-looking grin. "Well, I mean, I do as you know, but not if you don't want me to."

"Uh." I stayed put near the door. I didn't know.

She chuckled. "At least close the door."

I did so.

"What's on your mind?"

I debated asking her about what kind of deal she and Sharma had about me but decided against it.

"I think I discovered something you need to know," I finally said.

"Intriguing. I'm not sure an ensign has ever discovered something I didn't already know." She patted the bed next to her. "Come sit next to me. It's not like you haven't done it before."

I slowly walked across the small cabin and sat down on the bed. It squished down, the softness bringing my thigh into contact with Gina's. She was very sexy, in an intimidating way.

"So, what have you discovered?"

"I'll, uh, tell you in a minute," I said. "First, I'd like to ask you something. What can you tell me about Jack's decryption key?"

"His decryption key?" she asked. "Is that what this is about? I thought we talked about this already."

And then I felt weird. I looked down at my lap. Surprise. Part of me was suddenly standing at attention. It was bizarre because I didn't think I was excited. The timing was horrible. Could Sharma's meds be wearing off?

Gina noticed me noticing and looked down at my lap. When she realized what was there, she laughed. "Same old Jack."

But I wasn't the same old Jack. I wasn't even the same new Jack. Those meds were working, and Sharma said they wouldn't wear off. And I wasn't feeling excited. I was feeling nervous and, yes, maybe a little scared.

Something felt off here. And this wasn't the first time I'd felt this way... The FTL drive! It must be malfunctioning!

She put her hand on my thigh. My pulse raced. "I don't have the decryption key, but why don't you just let me have the data? You help me, and I'll help you." Exactly what kind of help was she talking about?

Twitch. It had to be the drive. I needed to take advantage of the improbabilities. It had to be something big. My heart started jackhammering as I realized anything could happen--if I could imagine it.

Distracted, I pushed her hand off. "What are you doing? I thought you were with Carter now." Twitch.

She smiled. "I'm the captain. I can do what, who, I want." She caressed my leg, her hand quickly approaching my super-fun zone. Despite my best efforts, I was starting to get interested in what that hand might do next. "You want to. I want to."

Somehow, that didn't ring true. Was she lying? I wish I could tell.

Twitch. There was no telling how long the malfunction would last. I needed a very improbable idea that the FTL drive might instantiate, and I needed it now. "I can tell when people are lying!"

"What?" she asked.

My manhood deflated. I brushed her hand away and stood up. "I don't think this is a good idea. I just came to ask you some questions and tell you something."

Her expression seemed to say she didn't believe me.

"What?" I said. "You know I'm not Old Jack. You know I don't remember you. I'm sorry if that hurts your feelings..."

She laughed. "My feelings aren't hurt."

It felt like she was lying.

So, her feelings were hurt? Why was she acting this way? Did she want to get back together? Or was it something else? "Are you trying to manipulate me?"

"No."

Lie.

She smiled and leaned back against the wall. "Maybe you're not a complete idiot, after all. Maybe there is some of Old Jack in there."

That was kind of bitchy, but it didn't seem like a lie. "Can you help me with the decryption or not?"

"No," she said.

Lie. Talking to her was a waste of time.

"I sent you a recording, and I'm guessing you didn't look at it."

"That rehearsal thing?" she asked. "No. Why would I need to watch that? Carter told me about rehearsal." She laughed a little. "He told me you were hopeless..." At my expression, she shut up.

"I need to tell you there's a stowaway on board," I said. "I think it's Noah Anderson."

She paused for a second and then said, "I knew that. It's for a TCC mission."

Lie. Wow, she lied a lot. Why did she lie so much?

"Captain Gomez, report to the bridge," a man's voice coming from somewhere said. "There's an, uh, issue..." Yeah, I knew what kind of issue--an FTL issue.

She pressed a button on her fon. "Message received, Harris." She jumped up. "I'll be right there."

Not a lie.

And then I went cold. Maybe she lied about Old Jack's murder. Ted had said loved ones were usually the killers.

"Did you murder Jack?" I asked. "Did you shoot at me on AC? Did you leave a nanobot trap in my cabin?"

"I don't have time for this."

Truth. But she didn't answer my questions. "Did you murder Jack?"

"Get out."

Truth.

She opened the door.

I jogged to my cabin and quickly entered, closing the door behind me. My heart was pounding. I sat down on my bed. How long would my lie-detector skill last?

I checked my fon. The money was still in my account. Wow. What if my lie-detector ability didn't go away either?

Gradually, I calmed down. I needed to make use of my special skill while I could. Questioning Gina had led nowhere. If Noah was here, I needed to question him.

A JACK BY ANY OTHER NAME

If I were a stowaway, where would I be?

My eyes strayed to the hatch to the secret tunnel. A secret tunnel would be a good place for a stowaway to hide. It was as good a plan as any: search the tunnels.

My fon rang as I entered the tunnel and was about to put the hatch back. It was Daniel.

"Jack, you're on the schedule to work in the cargo bay today," he said. "We're approaching Tau Ceto, and we have to get ready to offload cargo." Truth. Huh. It worked over the fon. "Where are you?"

"Hi, Daniel. Yeah, I'm sorry. I had an important meeting with Captain Gomez."

He snorted. "Ugh. Better you than me. Are you coming now, then?"

I had a great idea. "Sorry, Daniel, I have to rehearse extra for the show on Tau Ceto."

"Yeah, I heard you were pretty bad." He chuckled. Truth. "Okay. Later." He hung up.

I called Carter. "Hi Carter, I'm sorry I can't come to rehearsal. I have to work in the cargo bay."

"Who's this?" he asked. "Jack?"

"Yep. Sorry."

"You need to practice--" Truth.

"Bye." I hung up. Free at last. It turned out that having a bunch of bosses wasn't so bad. Who knew?

I stepped back into my cabin, got my gun and went back into the tunnel, closing the hatch behind me.

Using my fon as a light, I scrutinized the area. This was where I'd found Old Jack's data. Was there anything else? Had the nanobots been released from here? I suddenly felt sick.

If there were nanobots here, I was already dead. I froze, but it didn't feel like anything was eating me from the inside out.

I turned around and followed the tunnel, sneezing. Damn. So much for sneaking around quietly. Other than a lot of dust, nothing seemed to be in here. I froze for a moment, trying to figure out if anyone had heard me. No reactions that I could tell.

I came to the first junction. Which way?

As I pondered it, I realized the tunnels weren't exactly hospitable. No stowaway would lie on this dusty, exposed metal for long. Where would be hospitable? An empty cabin? Unfortunately, I had no way of knowing if or where they would be.

On the other hand, the cargo bay was huge, with lots of nooks and crannies. A stowaway might even use an empty crate as a bedroom. And we did see that probably-fake AC near the cargo bay. I decided to head that way.

Near the cargo bay, I heard raised voices.

"What do you mean he's not here?" It sounded like Carter.

"What do you mean he's not here?" It sounded like Daniel. "He said he was with you." Truth.

"He told me he was with you," Carter said. Truth.

Well, shit. I peered through a grating in the tunnel. Sure enough, two of my bosses stood in the cargo bay, glaring at each other. Not good. Carter must have come looking for me.

"What an asshole," Carter said, lifting his fon. Truth. Yikes. He thought I was an asshole. I'd thought we might be friends.

I silenced my fon just in time as a 'Call from Carter' came through. To be safe, I turned it off.

"No answer," Carter said. Truth.

"I don't know what to tell you," Daniel said. "He's a kid; this is his first tour. He's not reliable." Truth. Hey, I hadn't missed that much cargo duty.

"Knowing him, he's off screwing someone," Carter said. Truth. Ouch. I wasn't sure I actually liked this skill.

Daniel chuckled. "He did say something about a meeting with Captain Gomez." Truth.

Carter looked alarmed.

What Daniel said was almost a lie. I'd told him I'd had a meeting with Gina earlier; he knew I wasn't with her now. This skill was trickier than I first assumed.

"I have to go." Truth. Carter practically ran out of the cargo bay.

Daniel returned to work, and I directed my attention back to myself. Phew. I stood there for a moment, feeling my pulse slow.

Approaching the outer hull but still adjacent to the cargo bay, I discovered a bunch of large boxes in the tunnel near another hatch.

And no dust. "Interesting," I said quietly.

A JACK BY ANY OTHER NAME

"Is someone there?" someone answered.

Chapter Nineteen

Exactly how many people knew about these so-called secret tunnels, anyway?

I reached for my gun and snuck around one of the big boxes.

Noah sat on the other side. "Whoa." He put up his hands. "Don't hurt yourself, kid. Do you even know how to use that thing?"

I remembered exactly why I didn't like this guy. "Yes." I gestured with the firearm. "What are you doing here? You're supposed to be on Earth." I pointed the gun right at his head. "Did you try to kill me?"

"Take it easy there, young Jack," he said. "No, I didn't try to kill you." I couldn't tell if he was lying or not. "Why would I do that? I'm on your side," he said.

Shit. I wasn't getting anything from him. My truth detecting didn't seem to work anymore. They must have fixed the FTL drive or at least turned it off. "Damn."

"What?" he asked.

"Are you on my side?" I said. "I don't think you are."

From inside the cargo bay, Daniel faintly said, "Did you hear something?"

"Yes," Noah whispered. "I'm on your side. Can we go to your cabin?"

"Talking? I might have heard something," a voice I didn't recognize said from the cargo bay.

I nodded. "You first." I pointed the gun.

Noah went, and I followed him to the hatch and inside my cabin.

He lay down on my bunk. "Ahh." He made a sound like a

tire losing its air.

"Did I say you could lie on my bed?"

"Put the gun away, kid. Ahh. It's been too long since I was in a real bed."

I did put the gun down and sat on my chair. So, what had I learned? He liked beds. He might or might not have tried to kill me. He might or might not be on my side. If only I'd been able to detect the truth for a few more seconds... "Argh." I put my head in my hands.

"What's wrong with you?" Noah asked.

"Nothing. Why are you here? When did you get on the ship? Does Gina know you're here?"

"Relax, kid. It's all part of the plan."

"What plan?" I didn't shriek and was very proud of myself for it.

"The plan where you're bait. You're supposed to draw out your killer so that I can catch him. Remember?" That answered the question of who the fisherman was.

"Why didn't you just tell me you were coming along on the ship?"

He ignored my question. "What I don't get is why he came after you so soon? Two attempts already. I thought you were posing as Jack's son?"

I shrugged. "Someone, or maybe a couple of someones, figured out I was a clone of old Jack."

Noah stared at me from his supine position. "How many people?"

"Oh, just Eva." I paused. "And Gina." I paused again. "Carter."

"Well, damn," he said. "Is that it?"

"Dr. Sharma." I finished.

"Shit. That's a lot of people. You are definitely not a spy." I didn't need a truth-detector to know that one was right. Ouch. "And there's no telling who they told."

"They didn't tell anyone," I said.

"Are you sure?" he asked.

"Yes." But was I sure? Not totally sure. But I was totally loyal. "I'm totally sure."

"Someone tried to kill you, probably because of the old

Jack," he said. "If your friends didn't tell anyone, that means one of them is the killer."

Good point. "I'm not sure."

"So, give me the rundown of what's been going on," he said.

I gave him the unfortunate highlights, including getting shot at on the planet and the nanobot attack in my cabin. I didn't tell him about all the fortunate highlights, aka all the sex I'd been having.

He jerked at the mention of nanobots but quickly settled down again. "Is that it? Is that everything that's been going on? Bullets and nanobots?"

"Yep."

He stared at me. "I think you're lying." Did he have the power?

"Uh, that's it." Except for sex, loads and loads of sex. And singing, there was some singing, too.

"Tell me the whole story."

Someone knocked on my cabin door. "Jack? Jack? Are you in there?"

Noah held a finger up in front of his mouth, indicating, 'Be quiet.'

"It's Ted," the guy in the hall said. "I have a, uh, feeling you're in there." I knew what prompted his feeling: the surveillance cameras. "Your fon's off. I just wanted to see if you wanted to hook up, I mean meet up, and go down to Tau Ceto together."

I realized I'd grinned at his Freudian slip. "Sure, Ted," I called out. "I'll hook up with you later, okay? I'm busy now. I'll call you."

"Okay," Ted said.

Noah raised his eyebrows at me. "Hook up? What, you're gay now?"

I smiled. "*My bounty is as boundless as the sea.*" Except for mice; I drew the line at giant mice. I held up my hands. "But don't be getting any ideas, Noah. I know you have feelings for me, but I'm not feeling them for you. You're just too old." That wasn't diplomatic. "Sorry."

He sputtered for a minute. Finally, he said, "Feelings? Sex-type feelings? What? And what do you mean I'm too old!"

144

I was very confused. "Old Jack said you were in love with him. And you are lying in my bed."

He sat up abruptly. "I'm not in love with him or you or any version of him!" Truth. I was guessing (rather than using a special power), but he seemed pretty convincing.

My feelings were hurt a little. "Why not?"

"Shut the hell up," he said. "Did you say Old Jack told you that? How did Old Jack tell you anything?"

Why didn't he love me? I was lovable.

"Jack!" Gee, grumpy much?

"I found Old Jack's data stash." Oops. Maybe I shouldn't have told him that? On the other hand, maybe he could help decipher them. I turned and opened the desk drawer and took out the data cubes. "They were outside my cabin in the secret tunnel."

Noah sat up and reached for the cubes.

"Jack?" Ted said from the hall. "Who's in there with you?"

I took a step toward the door. "Nobody."

"I hear talking," Ted said.

"I'm acting," I said. "Rehearsing. I'll meet up with you later, okay?"

"All right." And then he must have walked away because he didn't say anything further.

Noah was reading the cubes. He turned very red when he read one of them--I assumed it was the one that said he loved Jack.

"I have some questions for you, too, you know," I said. "Are you Iago Smith?"

"What?" he said. "Shut up." He held one up. "What's up with this cube?" That must be the encrypted one.

"Encryption?"

He curled his lip. "Yeah."

I shrugged. "Don't look at me. I can't decode it. I don't know anything about Old Jack." I knew even less than I thought I did--and I hadn't thought I knew much. "You were, uh..."

He glared at me. I got the impression he was about to growl. But people don't growl. Right?

"You were, uh, buddies with Jack. Didn't you know him well? Maybe you should try it."

LESLEY L. SMITH

"Huh." He examined it. "I might have something..." He did something with his fon and held the cube up near it.

I leaned back in my chair. Something about all this stuff wasn't adding up.

Why had Old Jack said Noah was in love with him? Maybe he thought he was. That did add up. I was pretty awesome.

I wondered what Ted really thought about me. I turned my fon back on. There were a whole bunch of missed messages.

"Dammit!" Noah jumped up.

"What?"

"The cube did something to my fon!" he said. "It's all screwed up."

I stood and leaned over to look. Sure enough, the screen showed a bunch of nonsensical characters. Then it made a weird grinding sound.

"I never heard a fon make a noise like that before," I said.

Then, Noah made a growling noise I hadn't heard a person make before.

Then, his fon made a popping sound, and a wisp of smoke drifted from the back.

"Ow!" He dropped it on the floor, where it continued to smoke. "What the hell?"

"I never saw a fon do that," I said.

He glared at me and sort of trembled as he stood there like he was struggling to keep control of himself. Finally, he said, "Give me your fon." He held out his hand.

I pulled my fon in close to my body. "No. I need it."

He leaned toward me and growled. "Give. Me. Your. Fon."

"No."

Noah trembled some more.

My fon rang. It was Daniel. "Hi, Daniel."

Noah growled.

Daniel said, "Oh, so, now you answer your fon?"

"Fine," Noah said.

"Just a sec," I said to Daniel.

"We don't have a clue what's going on here." Noah pointed at his fon. It was still emitting an occasional wisp of smoke on the floor. "But, you're on your own." He reached for the access hatch to the tunnel. "And FYI--those two M.O.s were very different. It's

146

probably two different assassins."

"Wait, what?" I said. Two assassins!

Noah left via the tunnel, closing the panel behind him.

"What what?" Daniel said.

"What?" I said.

Daniel sighed. "I talked to Carter. Get off whoever you're on, and come do your work in the cargo bay!"

What was he so worked up about? He didn't have two assassins after him.

"Jack!"

"Fine. I'll be right there."

As I moved large boxes from one location to another, my mind was spinning. Who was trying to kill me, and why? It didn't really make any sense. I clearly wasn't the same guy as Old Jack. I guess the assassins thought I had all of Old Jack's memories? And decrypted data? What did Old Jack know that was so important?

Could one of my friends--or sort-of friends, anyway--Eva, Gina, Carter, Dr. Sharma, really be involved in my murder?

What exactly had Noah been up to these last few days? Was he really on my side?

Who was Iago Smith? Had he been shooting at me? My truth-detector might be gone, but Noah hadn't seemed to know what I was talking about when I asked him about Iago.

"*If this were played upon a stage now, I could condemn it as an improbable fiction,*" Ted said behind me. Where'd he come from?

"Hey, Ted," I said. I knew there was no point in asking how he tracked me down. "You know Shakespeare? What's improbable?"

"This is the *Shakespeare*. Everyone on board knows Shakespeare. The improbable thing is that you should be depressed." He smiled.

"I'm not depressed," I said. I couldn't help smiling back. "I've just got a lot on my mind."

"Sam?"

Ugh. Was Sam's murder my fault? "Yeah." Among other things.

"Well, don't worry. We'll catch the bastard that killed him." He glanced around the cargo bay. "Can you get out of here? It's Tau Ceto! I want to go down ... with you."

I laughed. His double-entendres were so obvious they were charming.

In the disembarkation lounge, we ran into Carter. "Not so fast," he said. "I'm not letting you out of my sight, Jack. We're going straight to the venue."

"Can Ted come?" I asked.

"Yeah, fine," Carter said.

"There's no shots or anything we were supposed to take, are there?" I asked. See, I was learning.

Carter gave me a beady-eyed stare that he must have learned from Gina. Finally, he said. "No."

"What's that about?" Ted whispered.

"Long story," I said. "Tell you later."

It was immediately clear Tau Ceto e was completely different than the last planet we were on. And completely different from Earth, too, for that matter.

For one thing, it was very hot, and the gravity was much stronger. "How are we supposed to dance in this?" I asked Carter as we exited the ship.

"We need to rehearse," was his clipped response.

I was already sweating. The spaceport did resemble the Alpha Catoblepas spaceport. Look at me, getting to be an experienced space traveler.

"Whoo," Ted said. "I feel twice as heavy as usual." I kept forgetting Ted was actually around my apparent age. I liked Ted.

"You are twice as heavy," Carter said.

In the spaceport, Carter made us get goggles immediately. He put his right on. "Ted?"

Ted stared at him for a moment but then put on his goggles.

"Jack?" Carter said. "Goggles."

Looking around, I noticed almost everyone was wearing them. I did see some humans without them, but all the aliens seemed to have them.

"What's with the goggles?" I whispered to Ted.

"Didn't you read the orientation on the planet?" he

whispered back.

I said, "Uh..."

"The sun here is twice as bright as Earth's sun," he said quietly. "You can seriously hurt your eyes if you don't wear the goggles." The spaceport itself was very brightly lit.

"Oh." I shrugged. "Sure. Knew that." I quickly put on the goggles. I felt like some kind of googly-eyed bug, but they did shade my eyes.

"Come on," Carter said.

I couldn't tell when we exited the spaceport because we stayed inside on enclosed moving walkways. "When do we go outside? I want to smell the planet. I want to experience the flora and fauna."

Ted and Carter looked at each other.

"It's, like, a hundred and fifty degrees out there," Carter said. "The surface is mostly desert. We won't be going outside."

"Humans have to wear an environmental suit," Ted said.

That was disappointing. "Hey, wait a minute. If we have to stay inside, why do we need these goggles?"

Carter laughed. "Yeah, you don't have to wear them inside." He took his off. "I wondered how long it'd take you to figure it out. I knew you didn't read the orientation."

"Ted, how could you?"

"You should have read the orientation." He shrugged as he took off his goggles, wearing them around his neck like a necklace. "Oh, come on. It was funny."

We stayed on the moving walkway until we passed into a huge cavern. It was so big you couldn't see the other side of it. The whole thing was made of tan-colored sandstone. Tan, tan, everywhere you looked was tan. The walls, the floor, the ceiling, the rows of seats: tan.

"Our venue," Carter said.

"Wow," Ted said.

"Wow," I said.

Chapter Twenty

In a giant cavern on Tau Ceto e, I kissed a boy, and I liked it. Ted and I were getting to know each other better behind part of the *Pirates of Penzance* set.

"Jack! Where the hell are you?" Carter shouted from center stage.

Ted pushed me away. "You should probably go, get to work."

"Aw." I didn't want to get to work. "I don't need to get to work."

"Jack!" Gina's stentorian voice called out.

I felt my body tense. No doubt about it, I was afraid of her. "I need to get to work."

Ted smiled. "I'll be in the front row, watching rehearsal."

We walked towards the front of the stage. "This set is amazing." It resembled an authentic rocky seashore. Upstage center looked like the sea with a giant ship anchored in the distance. "How'd they make the sea look so realistic? How long did it take to make all this?"

A dry, gritty voice said, "Twenty-four hours." When I realized the dry voice was attached to a lizard-looking creature, I jerked back. "We used nanobots," it said.

"Ack!" Since nanobots killed Sam, I did not like nanobots.

"What is this 'ack'?" the reptilian man asked. He had gray scaly skin and powerful-looking thick arms and legs. His back was rounded, almost like he had a shell. I glanced around him, but his back was covered by a tunic in shades of gray and brown. I didn't think I'd ever seen an alien quite like him. It was as if an Earth turtle had grown to human size and stood up on two legs.

"It's a human expression of delight, Sir," Ted said loudly. Softly, he said, "Wow, you didn't read the dossier on the planet, did you? Whatever you do, don't say the t-word."

What t-word?

"I thought nanobots were dangerous, Sir." Suddenly, it felt like they were creeping and crawling all over me. I resisted the urge to brush them off. Mostly.

"Dangerous? How so?" Turtle-Man asked. As some kind of membrane flicked over his eyeballs for a moment, I realized he spoke English perfectly.

"Jack!" Gina yelled from the front of the stage. "Quit your jibber-jabbering and get in your place." She turned to Carter. "I thought you were the director. Direct!"

We all pivoted to stare at her, even Turtle-Man. Oh, wait, the t-word was turtle.

Carter gulped and said, "Yes, ma'am." It looked like I wasn't the only one who was afraid of her. He turned and stared at me.

I didn't need to be told twice, or at least a bunch of times. I hurried to the back of center stage and sat on a rock. Ack. Was it a nanobot rock? I lifted my body away from the rock and attempted to sit without actually sitting. It was quite uncomfortable, especially in this heavy gravity. Luckily, I didn't have any trouble looking despondent.

"*Pour, oh, pour the pirate sherry,*" everyone sang. "*Fill, O fill the pirate glass; and to make us more than merry, let the pirate bumper pass.*"

Truth be told, my singing was not up to its usual amazing standards. I got tired of fake-sitting and truly sat on the rock but kept squirming. Were nanobots about to dissolve my body from the inside out?

It didn't help that the character in the scene was named Sam. The actor playing him sang, "*For today our pirate 'prentice rises from indenture freed; strong his arm, and keen his scent is. He's a pirate now indeed!*"

The real Sam was dead. Poor Sam.

In the short lull between verses, I heard someone whisper, "That Jack kid can act. He looks sad."

Everyone sang, "*Here's good luck to Frederic's ventures! Frederic's out of his indentures.*"

I heard a loud creaking noise. And then...

My head hurt. My eyes were closed.

"I want to be here when he wakes up," Ted whispered fiercely.

"No, I want to be here when he wakes up," Eva whispered equally fiercely.

"For Pete's sake, take it out in the hall," Dr. Sharma said.

I opened my eyes and discovered I was in the med bay. "I'm awake." I tried to sit up. "Ow." It didn't work. "Ow. What happened?"

"There was a little accident," Dr. Sharma said, leaning over me.

Oh, my God. Not nanobots! Did they eat me? I restrained myself from babbling.

"A big piece of setting fell on your head," Sharma said.

"Accident, my ass," Eva said.

"Yeah, I don't think it was an accident," Ted said.

"Am I okay?" I didn't feel eaten from the inside. "Did the nanobots get me?"

Dr. Sharma said, "What nanobots? No, there were no nanobots. You'll be okay." He twisted around to address Ted and Eva. "Will you two shut up and at least step back a bit?"

Eva's eyes flashed, and she crossed her arms in front of her.

Ted bit his lip.

They both looked pretty adorable. Uh oh.

I gestured for Dr. Sharma to lean in closer.

"What is it?" He put his ear near my mouth. "Are you in pain?"

"Yes, but is there any chance my anti-libido meds wore off?" I whispered.

"No." Dr. Sharma stood up and glanced behind him. "You two, leave. Now. And close the door behind you." He glared while he waited for them to exit.

Eva opened her mouth to protest.

"Now," Dr. Sharma said.

"I'll be right outside," Eva said quickly.

Ted nodded. "I'll be right outside, too."

They left.

Dr. Sharma must have seen something in my face because he said, "Are you worried about those two?" He pointed at the hall. "Don't be. It's human nature to care about people. But let's focus on the matter at hand. Part of the set collapsed on you down on the planet. You're lucky you weren't more seriously injured. It could have been much worse."

I took a mental inventory. My head hurt. I tried to get up again. "Ow." Correction: nothing else hurt unless I tried to move.

"What hurts?"

"My head is killing me. But nothing else hurts unless I move."

"Well, then, don't move. I'm going to give you something." He leaned in and gave me a shot.

The next time I woke up, the med bay was quiet and dark. No one was there waiting for me or with me. Aw. No Eva, no Ted. *"A hit, a very palpable hit."*

I checked my fon messages, and they both sent me *'get well soon'* messages. Aw. (In a good way.)

I also had a message from Sophia, which had taken a few days to get to me from Earth. The gist of it was she missed me (Aw.), and regarding the explosion at her apartment, the police wanted to question someone named Noah Anderson. She'd attached a grainy surveillance photo of a large, older white man. I squinted. It might be the Noah I knew. Or it might not. The quality was too poor to know for sure.

I don't know if I dozed off or what but the next thing I knew, Gina was sitting next to my bed in the dark. "Well, thank you for screwing up the rehearsal," she said.

At least she wasn't yelling. "You're welcome?" I tried a charming grin.

"Carter insisted on playing Frederic, so we didn't have anyone to play the Major General. I ended up doing it." She seemed...pleased.

Was this a bad thing or a good thing? "Okay?"

"You don't think I could do it?" she asked.

I knew I was drugged up, but I didn't think I'd said that.

"I'm very well acquainted, too, with matters mathematical,"

she sang softly. "*I understand equations, both the simple and quadratical.*" She smiled. She had a really nice smile. I'd forgotten.

"I'm, uh, sure you are acquainted with all kinds of matters." That sounded dirty--which hadn't been what I intended. Oh well, I went with it and grinned.

She grinned back. "I'm sorry we haven't been getting along very well lately. This situation has been unusual."

"Oh, yeah," I said, nodding. Hey, my head didn't hurt anymore.

"I guess I'm worried about you. I don't know how to protect you." She sort of laughed. "The old Jack never needed any kind of protection."

"Isn't Noah here to protect me?"

"Noah?" A storm passed over her face. "I can't abide stowaways."

"I thought you knew he was here?" Hadn't that been what she'd said when I'd mentioned him?

"You caught me off guard. Being unprepared was always a bad thing with Old Jack. I reacted instinctively and lied to cover my ass."

She couldn't be off guard with her husband? That didn't sound good.

"I've had the security detail scouring the ship," she said. "We can't find him."

"I, uh, probably know where he is."

Thus, in the middle of the night, I led Gina and some security officers I didn't know through the secret tunnels to the area near the cargo bay. We entered through the hatch in the disembarkation lounge. Even I wasn't idiot enough to show them the hatch in my cabin.

Finally, we got to where I thought Noah would be. I struggled not to sneeze in the dust as we snuck up on him.

A light glowed ahead of us in the tunnel.

Gina made some mysterious gestures, and somehow the security officers knew to rush Noah's location quietly. There was a commotion at said location.

When we caught up, the officers had surrounded Noah and were pointing their guns at him.

He stood with his hands up. "What's this about? Oh, Gina, Jack. Hi. Nice to see you. This is all some kind of misunderstanding." He seemed nervous. I'd never seen him nervous before.

"What are you doing here? Did you do something to Jack on the planet?" Gina asked hands on her hips.

"Me? The planet? Not me. I haven't been to Tau Ceto e." Lie.

I knew that was a lie because around his neck hung a rather large obvious pair of Tau Ceto goggles.

Chapter Twenty-One

The next day I was trying to get out of the medical bay, but Dr. Sharma wasn't cooperating.

"I don't think it's a good idea for you to perform," he said. "I'm pretty sure you have a concussion. You could easily become dizzy or disoriented with the pain meds and the heavier gravity."

"Nonsense!" If I'd learned anything from all those school shows when I was a kid, it was "The show must go on!" Besides, I'd been practicing and rehearsing since we left the last planet, and I was determined to do my first real show in this body.

On Tau Ceto e, before we got into places, I peeked through the curtain at the crowd. Every seat was filled, most with turtle-people. I hoped they would enjoy the show. I didn't understand how they could identify with it, being from another planet and all.

In the right orchestra aisle towards the back of the auditorium, I saw a big burly human man--it looked like Noah! But Noah was in the brig; how could it be Noah?

The bell rang for places.

I felt a hand on my back and jumped orbiting-spaceship-high.

"Relax, Jack," Carter said, dressed as the Major General, complete with a giant gray mustache and a funny hat. I resisted my sudden urge to giggle. "Get to your mark," he said.

I closed the curtain. "I think I saw Noah out there."

"Noah Anderson?" Carter said, shaking his head. "Impossible. He's back on the ship, in the brig."

"But--" I said.

"Get to your mark. We're about to start." Jeez, this guy was bossy. What a director!

He clearly didn't believe me. But I knew what I saw. What did it mean?

I sighed. "Break a leg, Carter."

He nodded as he walked away.

In my place onstage, before the curtain went up, I had pterodactyls flying around my stomach. My first show! My first starring role! I had memories of teenaged-me starring in some shows back on Earth, but this was the debut of this version of me. What if the copy wasn't as good as the original?

Then I had another clone thought: what if the Noah I saw in the audience was a clone? If so, was he evil? Or what if the one in the brig was the clone?

But then the curtain went up, and the lights went up.

I was Frederic!

"Then, again, you make a point of never molesting an orphan!" I said with pirately gusto. I held all the humpbacked turtle-men and turtle-women in the palm of my hand; they were riveted. And why wouldn't they be? I was the sexy Pirate Apprentice!

Someone else said their dialogue.

"Yes." I grinned out into the packed auditorium. "But it has got about, and what is the consequence?" I held up my hands in a charming fashion. "Everyone we capture says he's an orphan. The last three ships we took proved to be manned entirely by orphans, and so we had to let them go. One would think that Great Britain's mercantile navy was recruited solely from her orphan asylums--which we know is not the case."

The Sam character, the King character, the Ruth character and I said some more dialogue.

The music started.

The King sang, *"Oh, better far to live and die under the brave black flag I fly, than play a sanctimonious part, with a pirate head and a pirate heart..."*

I thought I might enjoy being a pirate. I wondered if there were any pirates in outer space. Could the Noah in the audience be a pirate?

One of the chorus members poked me. "Pay attention!" she whispered. She was pretty in her wench costume. She poked me again and glared.

"Yes, ma'am," I whispered and got down to business: performing admirably.

A little later, I said, "Thank you, Ruth. I believe you, for I am sure you would not practice on my inexperience. I wish to do the right thing, and if--I say if--you are really a fine woman, your age shall be no obstacle to our union!" I could really identify with this Fred guy.

The Ruth character glared at me.

I focused on the task at hand: being an amazing Frederic.

"*Did ever pirate roll his soul in guilty dreaming*," I sang, "*and wake to find that soul with peace and virtue beaming*?"

Mabel--played by that cute Olivia--sang, "*Did ever maiden wake, from dream of homely duty to find her daylight break with such exceeding beauty!*"

I sang, "*Did ever pirate loathed, forsake his hideous mission to find himself betrothed to a lady of position!*" Was I 'betrothed' to a lady of position, namely, captain? What were the rules of marriage for clones, anyway? Was Gina watching me? Was Noah--or who- or whatever it was--still watching?

Could I be in danger?

The Pirate King said, "I shouldn't be surprised if it were owing to the agency of an ill-natured fairy--you are the victim of this clumsy arrangement, having been born in leap-year, on the twenty-ninth of February; And so, by a simple arithmetical process, you'll easily discover, that though you've lived twenty-one years, yet, if we go by birthdays, you're only five and a little bit over!"

Ruth and the King said, "Ha ha ha ha! Ho ho ho ho!"

I said, "Dear me! Let's see!" I held up my fingers and counted. "Yes, yes; with yours my figures do agree!" I felt kind of dizzy.

Everyone but me said, "Ha ha ha! Ho ho ho ho!"

"How quaint the ways of Paradox!" I said, swaying under the hot lights and heavy gravity. "At common sense she gaily mocks! Though counting in the usual way, years twenty-one I've been alive, yet reckoning by my natal day, I am a little boy of five!" I felt odd; I wished I'd been around five whole years.

Ruth and the King said, "He is a little boy of five! Ha ha ha!"

A JACK BY ANY OTHER NAME

Everyone except me said, "A paradox, a paradox, a most ingenious paradox! Ha ha ha..."

Frederic and I were just alike. We were both younger than everyone else. We were both paradoxes.

"Upon my word," I said, "this is most curious--most absurdly whimsical. Five-and-a-quarter! No one would think it to look at me!" Was the stage spinning? No one would think I was actually a few months old to look at me. I reached out to a piece of the set to keep myself from falling.

Huh. Dr. Sharma'd been right. I probably shouldn't have performed. The way I was feeling right now, I wouldn't need some evil clone Noah to do me in. But the show must go on...

I said, "General Stanley, the father of my Mabel--He escaped from you on the plea that he was an orphan?" I was an orphan.

The King said, "He did."

"It breaks my heart," I said, "to betray the honored father of the girl I adore, but as your apprentice I have no alternative. It is my duty to tell you that General Stanley is no orphan!" My heart felt a little broken.

Ruth and the King said, "What!"

I said, "More than that, he never was one!" I was still an orphan.

A little later, I sang, "*Away, away! Ere I expire--I find my duty hard to do today! My heart is filled with anguish dire, it strikes me to the core. Away, away!*" I felt tears run down my cheeks. I didn't have any parents, and they'd been dead thirty years longer than I remembered.

The cast went on about how the General was doomed, a traitor, going to die. "Tonight, he dies!" I cried and cried. I couldn't help myself.

A little later, I sang, "*Ah, must I leave thee here in endless night to dream, where joy is dark and drear, and sorry all supreme -- where nature, day by day, will sing, in altered tone, this weary roundelay, 'He loves thee--he is gone. Fa-la, la-la, Fa-la, la-la.'*" I couldn't stop crying. I didn't have any relatives. I was totally alone.

Mabel, aka cute Olivia, rubbed my arm. '*What's wrong?*' she mouthed.

I shook my head. The show must go on. I tried to pull myself together.

Eventually, at long last, Mabel and I were reunited, and we all sang together. *"Poor wandering ones!"* and so forth.

With a final musical flourish, we were done.

The audience jumped to its feet, clapping wildly. Of course. They also made a hissing sound, but no one in the cast seemed to think that was a bad thing.

Looking closely, the hisses came when they jerked their heads. Whatever. I shrugged.

I took my bow. The rest of the named cast took their bows and took their places at the back of the stage. The applause and hissing continued heartily.

Once the individual bows were done, I grabbed the pretty chorus wench's hand, and we all marched to the front of the stage, held hands, and bowed in symphony. It felt magical as if the waves of applause were lifting us, the entire cast, out of the gravity well, up to heaven together.

When the turtle-people finally started winding down, I began to sing. *"Poor wandering ones!"* The cast joined in immediately. I waved my arms and said to the audience. "Join us!"

Soon, we all were singing as one, *"Though ye have surely strayed, take heart of grace, your steps retrace. Poor wandering ones! Poor wandering ones! If such poor love as ours can help you find true peace of mind, why, take it, it is yours!"*

Even though I kept smiling, I felt exhausted. This high gravity was a bitch.

Everyone cheered and clapped. I felt connected to every sentient creature in the auditorium.

Who knew the turtle-people of Tau Ceto e were so sympatico with a wandering troupe of Terran space pirates?

My legs were shaking like they couldn't hold me up anymore.

Music could unite the galaxy in love and peace.

I forced myself to remain standing until the curtain finally came down.

I collapsed on the stage.

Chapter Twenty-Two

I'd been spending entirely too much time lately in sickbay. I was tired of the small room filled with medical equipment, small beds, and medical personnel. I groaned and heaved myself out of bed.

"Where do you think you're going?" Dr. Sharma asked, turning around from his workstation.

"Out of here." I had to figure out if I'd truly seen Noah in the auditorium or not.

"Where exactly?"

I stood. "Relax. I feel much better." I'd felt immediately better after I got off the planet and away from that strong gravity. "I'm just going to the brig."

He stood up. "What?"

"I'm going to see if that Noah guy escaped or if I saw his clone down on the surface." I paused. "Or, could it have been a drug-induced delusion?"

Sharma shook his head. "I didn't give you drugs that were that powerful. And you would know if you saw his clone. He'd look younger. It's very difficult to have a clone the same age as a person unless they were cloned right after the person was born."

"Really?"

"You're seriously asking me?" Dr. Sharma's eyebrows were raised way up on his forehead. When I didn't answer, he added, "You're a clone."

Ugh. Sometimes it was hard to remember I was a clone. I felt regular. "Right. But they accelerated me. Couldn't they just accelerate a clone's growth even more?"

"It's dangerous to accelerate a clone's growth, especially if you do it out past ten years," he said. "Too many things could go wrong."

Well, crap. He and I both knew my body had been accelerated to grow more than ten years. I felt my face stretch into an unaccustomed frown. "Can I go?"

"Are you sure you feel okay?"

I nodded.

"No more dizziness?"

"Nope."

"All right." He held up a forefinger. "But you have to promise to come right back here if you start feeling poorly again."

"Yes, sir!" I bounded for the door and smacked right into Eva. How fortunate.

"Whoa," she said. "I was just coming to visit you. Where are you going so fast, tiger?"

"I think I saw Noah down on the planet during the show," I said. "You didn't see him did you?"

"No." She shrugged. "I didn't see anything out of the ordinary--until you collapsed. But I'm not sure I'd recognize that Noah guy if I saw him."

"I'm going to the brig to see if he escaped."

"Why not just call over there?"

"I have to see for myself."

"Ohhh-kay. But I think I would have heard about it if he escaped." She glanced at Dr. Sharma through the doorway as if checking with him. "Maybe I should come with you."

Sharma didn't say anything, so I assumed we were good to go.

"Beauty itself doth of itself persuade," I said, "the eyes of men without an orator." I reached for her, and we walked over to the brig hand-in-hand.

At the brig, my new friend Ted was on duty. Nice. He jumped up from his chair when he saw us. "Jack!"

"Hi, Ted. Nice to see you." I craned my head, trying to see if anyone was in the holding cell, but he kept moving in front of me. "Did Noah escape?"

Ted started. "What?" His head whipped around to look behind him. "No. Phew. You had me worried there for a second."

Sure enough, grizzled old Noah was sitting in the holding cell on his cot. "What was that?" he asked. "Did I escape? Why would you say that?"

I approached the cell. "I thought I saw you down on the planet."

"When?" he asked.

"Just now." I had no idea what time it was. "During the show."

"Today?" Noah asked. When I nodded, he added, "I've been here all damn day, as you should know. You put me here!"

I took a step back. "Whoa. Relax, dude."

Next to me, Ted snickered.

"Are you sure you feel all right, Jack?" Eva asked. "You seemed pretty out of it down on the planet."

"You were down on the planet?" I did not recall her down on the planet. I had been out of it. But not anymore. "How'd you like the show?" I grinned. "It was good, right?"

She laughed.

Ted said, "I thought you were amazing."

"Thank you." I dazzled him with my smile, then turned to Eva and waited for another compliment.

"Okay," she said, smiling. "You were pretty amazing."

In the cell, Noah cleared his throat. "Gee, don't let me interrupt you. Maybe you guys just want to have a threesome here on the floor in front of me."

The three of us turned and stared at him.

I glanced at Ted and Eva. Surely, they wouldn't want to? The floor looked very uncomfortable, for one thing... "No, that wouldn't be right. Right?" I asked the duo.

"I'm in the damn brig!" Noah interrupted. "I couldn't have been down on the planet. And, more importantly, I didn't do anything! Get me the hell out of here!"

"Captain Gomez said you were a stowaway," Ted said, crossing his arms. "That's not nothing. That's something."

Noah stood on the balls of his feet, his hands clenching and unclenching at his sides. He breathed in and out loudly and rapidly. "That is a minor offense," he said like he was just barely stopping himself from yelling. "If you just let me talk to Gina, I'm sure we can straighten this out. We're old friends."

"You can't be that good of friends if she put you in here," Eva said.

163

I agreed.

"I'm not going to disobey orders and bother the captain," Ted said.

"The only reason I'm here at all is to help you, Jack," Noah said.

He didn't seem like he'd been that much help.

"Help with what?" Ted asked.

"Find his murderer!" Noah said.

"What?" Ted asked. He was pretty cute when he was confused.

Eva glared at him. She was pretty cute when she was annoyed.

I was pretty much in trouble, possibly falling for both of them...

"I mean, find his father's murderer," Noah said. "Kid, you are infuriating."

"Your dad was murdered?" Ted asked. "Sorry. That's intense."

He didn't even know how intense it was. "Yeah." I nodded.

"What's going on?" Another voice came from behind us.

The three of us turned around.

Another security officer had arrived on the scene. "It's the asshole!" he said to me. His pointy head did look familiar. I'd had run-ins with this guy before, and surprisingly, it hadn't gone well.

"Hello?" I said. "Hi, I'm Jack. It's nice to see you again. I'm not sure I caught your name in our other interactions." Was he one of the officers I'd offered money to? If so, he must not like money?

"Get him out of here," he said. "I don't want to see his face. I'm here to relieve you anyway, Ted. Go."

Whatever. If he didn't want to get to know me better to correct his incorrect impression, it was his loss. The three of us walked away from the brig.

"Hey! Come back!" Noah called after us. "Get me out of here!"

A little way down the hall, I stopped. "So, now, what?" I didn't know about Eva and Ted, but I couldn't stop thinking about Noah's threesome comment.

Eva stood next to me, grabbing my arm. "I was hoping we

could have a date."

"Aw," Ted said. "I was hoping we could have a date."

"Both of those ideas sound very nice. This is a mysterious conundrum," I said. "Whatever shall we do? Let's go back to my cabin and try to sort it out."

Much, much later, I was exhausted. I'd had no idea threesomes were quite so tiring. Frankly, I could barely move. "That was lovely," I said. "*Eternity was in our lips and eyes, bliss in our brows' bent.*"

"It was surprisingly good," Ted said. "Women aren't nearly as bad as I'd assumed."

"Gee, thanks." Near the wall, Eva shifted in the bed. "And you're not nearly as bad as I'd assumed. But somebody's got my hair pinned to the bed."

Yeah, these bunks weren't built for threesomes. Bad planning!

Eva tried to move again. "Ow. Get off my hair."

"Ow," Ted said, shifting and poking his elbow in my stomach.

"Ow," I said.

Ted grimaced and got out of bed. "Ow! I stepped on something." We all glanced down at the floor. He'd stepped on Noah's ruined fon, still lying lonely and discarded on the ground. At least it'd stopped smoking.

"Sorry," I said. "It's Noah's fon. I should have picked that up."

Ted gingerly sat down on my desk chair, and I moved away from the wall to make more room in the bed for Eva. It took every last bit of energy to move.

"Why do you have Noah's fon?" Eva asked.

"You knew the stowaway Noah was on board?" Ted asked.

"Yeah," I said. "I was hoping he could help me decrypt something, but no go."

Eva poked me on purpose and said softly, "Does Ted know about you-know?"

I yawned. Did Ted know I was a clone? I didn't think so. I shook my head.

"Decrypt what?" Ted asked. "You know I'm pretty good with

that stuff. Maybe I could help."

"Go for it," I said, practically talking in my sleep. "That would be great. I really want that data." It seemed like it might be key to what was going on.

Ted leaned over and picked up Noah's broken fon. "Well, this thing isn't doing anything." He examined it. "It's fried. How did..."

I may have drifted off.

"Jack?" Eva asked.

"Sorry." I yawned. "What'd I miss?"

And then, very suddenly, part of me was totally wide-awake and ready for action.

"Whoa," Ted said. "You're an animal. You're already ready for round two?"

"More like round seven," Eva said. "But I'm impressed."

My brain was still very tired. Somehow this didn't make sense. Oh. We must be FTL-ing away from Tau Ceto.

"I'm pretty tired," Ted said.

"Me too," Eva said.

I needed to wake up. Focus, Jack! I shook my head and sat up in the bed. What did I want most? I glanced at Ted and Eva. Maybe I already had my heart's desire. I smiled.

Besides that, what did I want? And what was very improbable?

Ted still held Noah's ruined fon in his hands.

"I know Old Jack's decryption key!" I said forcefully.

And it came to me like magic; the key was The Moor. "Quick! Hand me my fon and the data cubes in my desk drawer." Hindsight was twenty-twenty. I couldn't believe I hadn't tried the names of Shakespearian characters before.

Ted scrabbled in the drawer and handed the stuff over.

I held the mystery data cube up to my fon. I looked at Ted. I looked at Eva. I smiled.

"Othello," I said.

"I remember the story of Othello." Eva frowned. "Is Captain Gomez in danger?"

Decrypted data started scrolling across my fon.

As I watched it, I belatedly realized I should have tried out my truth-telling ability again. Darn.

Chapter Twenty-Three

I almost couldn't believe I'd decrypted Old Jack's mysterious data. The gibberish was gone. I was pretty impressive. Anyone else would have been stymied.

Eva asked, "Well, what does it say?"

"Yeah, what does it say?" Ted asked. The three of us were still ensconced cozy-style in my cabin.

"I'm not sure." I yawned. I was tired again. I glanced down. All of me was exhausted. So, either the FTL drive was off, or it had quit acting ...up. Heh, heh.

"Is it decrypted or not?" Eva asked.

"Yeah, is it decrypted or not?" Ted asked.

Eva scowled at him. "Quit repeating what I say."

Ted scowled back.

"It's words and numbers and stuff," I said. "So, it's not encrypted. But I couldn't tell you what it says." I held the fon out.

"Yeah, I got nothing," Ted said. "I don't know what that is."

Eva frowned. "Ditto. Maybe equations? Algorithms?"

"It looks technical," I said. "Maybe Olivia in engineering can figure it out?"

Someone knocked on my cabin door.

"Come in," I said.

The door slid open.

"Jeez, Jack! I don't want to see this." Gina's mouth hung open in the doorway.

"Uh, Captain." Ted froze for a second but then ended up saluting. "Ma'am." Somehow without his uniform, the formality was lost.

"Ma'am." A red flush crept from Eva's face down her neck

and to her very pretty chest.

In hindsight, I probably shouldn't have said 'come in' when I was standing around naked in my cabin with two other naked people. "Sorry, Gina."

In the hall, a man said, "What's going on in there?"

Eva sank back down on the bunk and pulled the covers over her head.

"Nothing!" Gina blurted out before taking a step backward. The door slid closed.

"I didn't know you were friends with Captain Gomez," Ted said.

"I'm not sure what Gina and I are." I took a step towards the door.

Eva peeked out from under the covers. "Pants, Jack."

"Oh, right." I snagged some pants off the floor and slid them on.

Out in the hall, Gina was still standing there, eyes wide, shaking her head.

"Sorry, Gina," I said again. "I should have thought before I said 'come in.'"

"No." She stared at me, face slack. "I should have called first." Did that mean she wasn't upset? She seemed kind of upset.

We stood there for several seconds. I yawned again.

Finally, I said, "Was there something you wanted?"

"I, uh, yes, I was just stopping by to warn you that I asked Carter to play Benedick in *Much Ado About Nothing*."

Why did she think this was worth a personal visit? "Okay."

"We start rehearsals tomorrow morning," she said.

I figured we'd start rehearsals for a new show. "Okay." We stood there for several seconds.

She expelled a burst of air. "What am I doing here? You don't even remember."

She was right in that I had no idea what she thought I should remember. I raised my eyebrows and tried to look understanding. Whatever she was doing here, it was apparently important to her. "I apologize if I hurt your feelings? I remember you're Captain Gina Gomez, and you are a very attractive woman even if you're not quite as young as..." I petered off.

She frowned. Didn't she like being called attractive? Who didn't like that?

"You're attractive in a totally-appropriate boss-subordinate way."

She was shaking her head again.

In a low voice, I added, "Do you want a divorce?"

She was still shaking her head.

"Do you want to get back together?"

"No. Forget about that stuff. Jack and I always played Beatrice and Benedick. It was our most famous role. Everyone loved it. You don't remember!" She looked like she would start crying--if she hadn't been the tough, capable captain.

Aw. I held out my arms and took a step toward her. "Let me comfort you." I wasn't entirely sure what I'd done, but I was sorry she was upset.

She glanced at the now-closed door to my cabin. "No." She took a step away. "Never mind." She started walking down the hall, shaking her head. She was quite good at it. "See you at rehearsal."

"Wait, who am I?" I called after her. The star, no doubt.

"Balthasar." The name was not familiar.

Back in my cabin, Eva was dressed. Aw.

Ted was wearing everything except his pants. That was a little odd.

"Those are my pants," Ted said, pointing at my trouser-clad legs.

Ah. I took off his pants and handed them to him.

"Is Captain Gomez okay?" Eva asked.

"I'm not sure," I said.

"What was that about?" Ted said, putting on his pants. Aw.

I shrugged. "She told me Carter's going to play Benedick."

Eva sucked in a breath.

"I don't get it," Ted said. "Who cares?" He wasn't the only one.

"Jack--" Eva glanced at me. "I mean, Jack's Dad always was the one to play Benedick to Gina's Beatrice."

"I didn't know your Dad was in the crew," Ted said.

"He's not," I said. "He died."

"Wow. I didn't know that," he said. "Sorry. So... Captain

Gomez's your mom?" he asked.

"No," I said.

"Oh, I see. Awkward," he said. "Are you a bastard?"

Was I? Who would even care? I couldn't keep my cover story straight anymore. I decided to ignore that. "She said I was Balthasar. Who's that? I don't remember."

Eva smiled. "He's one of the attendants to Don Pedro."

That didn't sound right. "So, I'm basically in the chorus?" I asked. How could that be?

"No," she said. "You are the chorus. He's a singer, the only singer. I don't think you have any lines."

Singing sounded good, but no lines did not.

"How do you know so much?" Ted asked her.

"I'm Hero." She sighed. "Plus, I'm old and wise compared to you two teenagers." Did I know how old she was? She looked to be in her twenties. Even I knew it was impolite to ask.

Ted nodded. "Nice. The hero of the show." That was not what I recalled.

Neither I nor Eva had the heart to correct him.

"So, what's next?" I pointed at the bunk. "Slumber party?"

Eva shook her head. "No offense, Jack, but your bunk isn't very comfortable for three."

"Yeah," Ted said. "And I have an early shift at the brig."

They both stepped towards the door and looked at me. They didn't leave.

"Thanks?" I yawned. They still didn't leave. "Good night?"

They left.

Why were they so slow to leave after they said they would leave? Normally I'd ask Eva for advice about people, but I couldn't ask her for advice about herself. Maybe when I was asking Olivia about the decrypted data, she could explain it.

As I trudged through the ship, I was too tired to even enjoy the murals. That was a first. I didn't even wave at Puck like I usually did.

A little later in engineering, I'd tracked down Olivia. For the night shift, the joint was jumping. The whole engineering crew must be here studying all the blinking lights, or at least the equipment they were attached to. "You're pretty hard core, working tonight after the show," I said. "Very nice job as Mabel, by the way. *Thy eternal summer shall not fade*."

"Thanks. It's all hands on deck here." She sighed. Where was my compliment? "I probably shouldn't tell you this, but the FTL drive has been acting up."

I tried to act super-shocked and surprised. "No!" I knew, however, that the malfunction had been short-lived because my twitchiness had been short-lived.

Her eyebrows rose. Maybe I'd gone overboard. "You can't tell anyone," she said. "I'm swearing you to secrecy."

"Okay." I shrugged.

She continued, "I don't have to tell you, a malfunctioning FTL drive is potentially very bad."

She did have to tell me because I wasn't sure what she was getting at. "Oh?"

"We could end up somewhere we don't want to be, like across the galaxy or inside a star. Or we could get trapped in FTL space and never return to regular space."

That did sound bad. "What's wrong with it?" I asked.

"We don't know." She shrugged. "So, what do you want?"

I blurted out, "How did I do in the show?"

"Seriously?" she asked. "That's what you're doing here? I do have work to do." I waited. She still didn't compliment me.

"So, uh, anyway," I said, "I wondered if you could give me some advice."

"I guess." She didn't look too enthusiastic.

"Say, uh, hypothetically, a person had hooked up with someone and invited them to stay over afterward, and they hung around a little but didn't end up staying. What does that mean?"

She smiled slightly. "They're just not that into you."

Aw. That didn't sound right. Who wouldn't be that into me?

"Wait. Spill. Who was it? I won't tell. A girl?"

"Yes."

She had kept talking. "Or a boy?"

"Yes."

She paused. "Which?"

"Hypothetically, both?"

"What? A hermaphrodite? Human? I didn't know we had any on the ship. Who?" She suddenly looked lost in thought.

"No," I said. "A girl and a boy. Two people." I paused. "*The sight of lovers feedeth those in love*?"

She winced. "Well, that's another kettle of starfish entirely. Did you invite them both to stay?"

I nodded. "Hypothetically."

"At the same time?"

I nodded. "Hypothetically."

"Maybe they were each waiting for a private invitation."

"Aw." Maybe I needed to give that word a rest.

"Was that it?" she asked, frowning. "Love advice?"

"Uh, no. I came across some technical data that I can't interpret. Can I show it to you?" I held up my fon.

"Whatever." She stared at my fon.

And then she grabbed my fon. "Oh. My. God. It's the holy grail of engineering. One of TSS's major objectives."

"What is it?" I asked. "Do you understand it?"

Her eyes were wide open when she looked up at me. "I've never seen them before, but I think these are specs for the FTL drive. They're supposed to be top secret, more than top secret, tip-top super-secret! I'm not sure any human has ever seen them. The authorities on most worlds, like Alpha Catoblepas, would hurl you in jail and throw away the key if they knew you had this. It could destabilize the whole galaxy. It might start a war."

She shook my fon at me. "Where did you get it?"

"Uh." Somehow I didn't think I should tell her I basically got it from myself.

What had Old Jack been up to?

Chapter Twenty-Four

Olivia and I stood in engineering amidst all the blinking lights and folks rushing to and fro and back and forth.

"You have to let me give these specs to my boss, Jack," Olivia said. "They could help us fix the FTL drive once and for all."

I started to panic. It all sounded too dangerous. This data could cause a war? Plus, if the FTL drive was fixed, my superpower would go away. I didn't want that. But it might be the right thing to do. I was torn.

"Jack!" Olivia held my fon right in front of my eyes.

I grabbed it. "It's, uh, not what you think. And, uh, it's not mine to give away." Why did I say that?

"So you stole it?" She put her hands on her hips. "That makes more sense than you having the most desirable information in the galaxy. Did you steal it from Daniel?"

"Yes." But wouldn't that get him in trouble or put him in danger--at least from Olivia? "I mean, no."

"I bet it was Daniel. I've heard of him. He's bad news. He's the black marketeer on the ship. Are you afraid he'll do something to you?"

I wasn't sure what to say. I wasn't afraid of him. Until now. Should I be afraid of him?

"Oh, my God!" she said. "I bet he's the one who killed Sam! They knew each other. Did you get this data from Sam? Did he steal it from Daniel?" She was spinning out, but it made sense since she and Sam had a thing.

I hugged her. "Please calm down, Olivia," I said to the top of her head. "I know you're stressed out about the FTL drive, and I know you miss Sam, but getting all worked up isn't going to help anything."

After a moment, she clutched me. We stood there for a few minutes.

I yawned.

She pushed me away. "You're not going to give me the data, are you?"

"Not right now," I said.

"Please think about it," she said solemnly.

"I will." I was dead on my feet. "Please don't tell anyone about it. You might put them in danger."

"Danger?" she asked.

"I'm worried that Sam's murder might be related to all this." I stared into her eyes.

They filled with tears. "What do you mean?"

I shook my head. "I'm not sure. I'm still investigating. Rest assured, I'm trying to keep you safe."

"I'll hold off telling my boss for now," she said. "But you have to let me know when you figure something out."

"Okay." I dipped my head. "Thank you. I appreciate it."

Threesomes and big discoveries both took it out of you. I had to get to bed.

The next morning Gina said, "I wonder that you will still be talking, Signior Benedick: nobody marks you." Her voice was rather gentle.

Carter said monotonously, "What, my dear Lady Disdain. Are you yet living?"

We were all in the ship's rehearsal space. I yawned, which made no sense because I'd gotten a good night's sleep after talking to Olivia.

"Is it possible disdain should die while she hath such meet good to feed it as Signior Benedick?" Gina said. "Courtesy itself must convert to disdain if you come in her presence."

I was bored. When did my part start?

"Then is courtesy a turncoat," Carter said.

"Is it just me," Eva whispered in my ear, "or are they really bad?"

"They're definitely boring," I whispered in her ear. I caught her delicious scent and breathed in.

"You look cozy. What are you two doing?" Ted whispered. Where'd he come from?

"None of your business!" Eva whisper-shouted at him.

"It is too my business!" he whisper-shouted back.

"Calm down," I said.

The dialogue stopped in the play. The three of us looked up.

"You three shut up," Gina said.

"Yes, ma'am," I said, giving both Eva and Ted dirty looks in turn.

We shut up.

Gina said, "Scratching could not make it worse, an 'twere such a face as yours were." She was so bland it was hard to believe she had a good reputation for this part.

Carter said, "Well, you are a rare parrot-teacher."

Their body language was too mild. It was like they were afraid to be mean to each other.

Eva put her hand on my leg.

Ted glared at her and put his hand on my other leg.

"Stop it," Eva whispered to him.

"You stop it," Ted whispered to her.

"Good grief," I said. "Both of you, stop it." Threesomes could apparently cause trouble.

The dialogue stopped again. The cast stared at the three of us.

"Don't make me put you in the brig again, Jack," Gina said with heat in her voice.

I stood. "That's more like it." I pointed at her and Carter. "Do your dialogue more like that."

"Are you the director now?" Carter said.

"Well, someone needs to be," I said. "This isn't working."

"It's not final yet," Carter said. We're rehearsing."

Behind me, Ted and Eva were still fussing.

I glanced back. "These two would do a better job."

Gina crossed her arms. "I highly doubt that."

I turned to Ted and Eva. "Go ahead."

Eva said, "A bird of my tongue is better than a beast of yours!" She had a great sneer on her face.

Ted said, "I would my horse had the speed of your tongue and so good a continuer!" He sneered back. "But keep your way, i' God's name; I have done!" They looked like they were on the verge of tearing each other apart.

I chuckled. I wasn't bored, that was for sure.

The rest of the cast--minus Gina and Carter--clapped.

"The casting assignments have been made," Gina said.

"Give them a chance," Olivia said. Where did she come from?

"I think they'd be good," I said.

Gina practically looked like steam was coming from her ears. "Fine. We'll let them try it if you leave the room, Jack."

"Leave?" Surely she didn't mean that? "What about my part? I need to rehearse, too."

"You can rehearse in your cabin," Carter said.

Everyone was staring at me like they wanted me to leave. But that couldn't be right, could it? "Fine." No worries; they'd ask me back soon. I started walking towards the door.

"Take your instrument," Carter said. "It's the mandolin."

"Fine," I said.

They started the scene from the top as I rooted through the bin of instruments, picking out the mandolin. Did I even know how to play the mandolin? I strummed it. It sounded nice.

Everyone was staring at me again.

I hurried out into the hall.

Once outside, I strummed the strings again. The clear, mellow tones were very pleasing to the ear. I put the fingers of my right hand on the frets. The strings under my fingertips felt great. I strummed away. It reminded me of playing the guitar. I strummed and hummed as I walked down the corridor.

"*O, good my lord, tax not so bad a voice*," I sang, "*To slander music any more than once.*"

Somebody I didn't know walked past. "Sounds good," he said.

I nodded because, of course, he was right.

Wait a minute. I stopped. Since when did I know how to play the guitar, much less the mandolin? I had no explicit memories of playing either.

I knew I was awesome, but why did I seem to be so good at everything, from singing, to playing instruments, to shooting a gun? It was a bit mysterious.

Could it have something to do with Old Jack? Must be.

Practically the only person on the ship who knew Old Jack was Gina. I glanced back the way I'd come. Somehow I didn't think she'd be inclined to answer random questions about Old Jack at the moment.

There was someone else who knew Old Jack well: Noah.

I changed directions and hummed and strummed my way to the brig.

The pointy-headed security officer that didn't like me was on duty. "Oh, no, it's Jones. No mandolins in the brig area, Jones."

Surely, that wasn't a real rule.

His attitude was quite suspicious. "Are you nefarious, Mr. Security Officer?"

In the brig, Noah guffawed. "You may be annoying, Jack, but you can be funny."

"What do you mean by nefarious?" the officer asked. "Like a pirate?"

I was going to make this guy smile if it killed me. "Yes!" I smiled. "Are you a space pirate?"

Noah laughed.

I got right up next to the officer and gave him my most charming smile.

"You just have pirates on the brain after that *Pirates of Penzance* show," he said.

"So you saw the show? I was good, right?" I smiled some more. "Did you like it? Tell me you liked it."

"It was pretty good," he said grudgingly. "I guess."

"I knew it!" I said. "I'm glad you liked it."

He smiled.

Ha!

"Why do you insist that everyone like you, Jack?" Noah asked. I glanced over at him. Right. The business at hand.

I sidled right up to him. "So, in the past, Jack--if you know who I mean--didn't want people to like him?" I said quietly through the bars.

"No," Noah said quietly. "He didn't care about stuff like that. What's up with you?"

The security officer acted like he was busy with something on his computer.

What was up with me? Dr. Sharma said something about clones being emotionally needy. It might be related to that. I didn't like the thought of being so controlled by my clone biology.

"*Anyway...*" I strummed. "*Because you talk of wooing, I will sing...*" I sang.

Noah interrupted me. "There was no talk of wooing. Why are you wandering around singing and playing music?"

"I'm rehearsing."

"Well, go rehearse somewhere else. Gee, here's an idea: rehearse in the rehearsal space. I mean, I know I'm a captive audience, but this is just cruel." But he grinned.

"I did come for a reason," I said. "What can you tell me about my, uh, dad? He was a good singer, right?"

"Yeah," Noah said. "But you knew that."

"Was he a good musician?"

"Yes." He gestured at the mandolin. "I never saw an instrument he couldn't play. Mandolin. Guitar. Whatever. But it took him years to learn all that."

"Interesting," I said. "And was he a good shot?"

"With a gun?" he asked.

"Yeah." I nodded.

"Sure. He was an excellent shot. I've never seen anyone better. Why? What's this about?"

"Is there any chance I 'inherited' his skills?"

He just stared at me for a few minutes. Finally, he said, "I've never heard of that in your, ah, situation." He meant a clone who didn't have the original's memories. "Of course, I'm not sure I've heard of your situation before. But I can see how that would be very useful."

"What other skills did he have?"

"Why should I help you? You aren't helping me." He gestured at the bars. "The only reason I'm here is to solve your, er, your dad's murder."

If that was true, I was letting him down by leaving him in the brig. The problem was I didn't know if that was true.

I thought of something else. "I decrypted that data I showed you. And it looks very, very interesting. Why would Dad have something like that?"

His eyes narrowed. "Interesting how?"

"Valuable interesting," I said. "What was he into before he died?"

"I don't know what he was into," he said. "If I knew that, it might help me solve his murder. Show me the data." He seemed very eager.

"I don't think that's such a good idea." I wasn't sure I trusted him.

"Show me the data. Is it on your fon?" Why was he so worked up?

"No." Not everything he said added up.

Noah tried to shake the bars of the brig, but they didn't budge. "Show me!" He had quite a temper on him.

"Quit riling up the prisoner," the security officer said, approaching us.

"You need to get me out of here, Jack!" Noah said. "Talk to Gina! You owe me!" If he had been in love with Old Jack, could he have killed him in some kind of crime of passion? He sure seemed to have a lot of passion. He'd make a good Benedick.

I studied him, but I didn't get a murderer vibe.

"Jack!" Noah said.

It seemed more likely that Old Jack's murder was tied to the FTL drive data. Could Noah have killed him for that? But then why act so ignorant about it?

"Maybe you should leave now, Jones," the security officer said.

I was finding it hard to believe this middle-aged man standing in the brig in front of me murdered me. "I'll do it," I said to him. "I'll talk to Gina."

"Thank God." Noah seemed to relax a little.

Of course, the way she felt about me right now, it might hurt more than help...

Chapter Twenty-Five

After rehearsal, I tracked down Gina in the mess hall. She was eating dinner and practically the only one in there. The large table-filled room was mostly empty.

"What do you want?" she asked, lifting one corner of her lip.

"From your attitude, I'm guessing rehearsal didn't get any better," I said, sitting beside her.

She sighed. "No, it was fine. Your little friends ended up being good." She looked sad. "But I enjoyed that role. It's the end of an era."

"I'm sorry it didn't work out with Carter," I said.

"He's no Jack, that's for sure."

I raised my eyebrows to say, 'That's obvious.'

"You're no Jack either, Jack," she said, glancing at me.

That was becoming more and more obvious. "I'm sorry, Gina." I put my hands over her hand. "You miss him, huh?"

She nodded. "I was so angry when he died. How could he do that? To himself? To us? To me?"

"Well, I'm pretty sure he didn't get shot on purpose," I said.

"I know," she said. "I guess I also feel guilty. We weren't getting along very well at the time of his murder. He was acting secretive, lying all the time. I thought he might be having an affair. The last thing I said to him..." She trailed off.

"I know he loved you very much." I would in his position, and he was me, right? "Try not to feel bad about things. Try to focus on the good times. You guys had some good times, right?"

She perked up. "So many good times." She smiled. "There was this one time on Geryon 876 d in the mud springs..."

I raised my eyebrows to say, 'Please continue.'

She stopped. "It doesn't seem appropriate to tell you about

it."

"Aw," I said. "You can tell me. I'm a big boy." No doubt she knew exactly how big.

She flashed a wicked smile that I'd never seen before, darn it. "Suffice it to say, we had f-u-n."

"No. It's not sufficient to say," I said. "Tell me the story."

She laughed. After she quieted, she said, "Thanks, Jack. I feel better."

I tipped an imaginary hat. "*Your Highness' part is to receive our duties, and our duties are to your throne and state.*"

She smiled. "Now, what do you want?"

I tried to look young and innocent. "To clear the air between us." What a good idea. How come I hadn't done this before? I guess Gina scared me a little.

"Okay," she said. "Consider it cleared. What else?"

"Maybe you could reconsider if Noah needs to be in the brig," I said hopefully. "He didn't really do anything."

"Stowing away on the ship is something," she said, pointing her fork at me. "And what if he killed Sam?"

That would be bad. I wished I had my lie-detector skill back. I scrunched up my nose. "Haven't you known Noah for years? Decades? He says he's here investigating Jack's murder."

"He does? I have known him for years, decades. I thought he was trustworthy."

"Yes." I nodded solemnly.

"It's about time!" she said. "I've been trying to light a fire under TCC's ass since it happened. You know, at Tau Ceto I heard someone suspicious was spotted in the audience during the show."

"It couldn't have been Noah," I said helpfully. "He was in the brig at the time."

"I know that," she said. "But I want him off my ship."

"Good idea!" My mind whirred. I wanted to investigate Tau Ceto. I wanted to solve my murder so it didn't happen again. "Can we borrow a shuttle?"

"No," she said. "We need the shuttles. Besides, the shuttles don't have FTL drives. We're too far away already."

"Then, how's he supposed to investigate Tau Ceto e if he can't get there?" I asked reasonably. "Could the *Shakespeare* make a little jump back there?"

"And then what?" she asked. "Leave him stranded on Tau Ceto e?" She paused. "Not that that's an entirely bad idea."

"Maybe we could pop back and pick him up?"

She turned to glare at me. "Do you have any idea how much that would screw up the schedule?"

"A lot?" I smiled engagingly. "But *whoever does not have enough will is not smart enough*, and I know you're smart enough."

"*Asses are made to bear, and so are you*." She held up her finger. "And don't you dare finish that quote."

'*Women are made to bear*,' was on the tip of my tongue. Instead, I said, "Yes, ma'am. Does that mean we're a go?"

"Does he have any other leads?" she asked.

The FTL drive data.

Then I had a genius idea. If I went with Noah, we could install the secret FTL drive on the shuttle. Whoa. Then I would know in advance when it would be turned on. And then, with advanced planning, I could use my special skill to do something amazing.

"Jack?" she asked. "Leads?"

"Gosh, no." I frowned. "No other leads."

"Hmm." She stared at me. "You make some good points, but, no, sorry, he can't borrow a shuttle."

"That's not fair." Me and Noah needed to go back to Tau Ceto e! We were going to investigate! Maybe we'd finally solve the murder. I felt my lips move into an unaccustomed frown.

"And, Jack." She narrowed her eyes. "Don't get any ideas. You're not going either. The shuttles are off limits."

Damn.

Noah was glad when I let him out of the brig. Gina hadn't said expressly that I couldn't release him. The security officer believed me when I said she'd authorized it. He could use a little lie-detector skill.

"Finally!" Noah said. "What took you so long, you little twit?" Maybe he was not as glad as he should have been.

The security officer snickered. He was the one I'd won over earlier. I gave him a big smile.

I turned back to Noah. "Would you rather go back inside?" I pointed to the cell.

"No," he said. "I want a drink. Hook me up."

"Drink?" I asked. "They don't serve hard alcohol in the mess hall."

"I know that--" He seemed about to say something else, but he restrained himself. He glanced at the security officer. "Let's go."

Once we were in the hall, he said, "Yes, booze. Where? Jack would know. Don't tell me you don't know."

How could he even consider I didn't know? "I know."

I stared at the *A Midsummer Night's* mural on the wall, all cool and calm. He couldn't rile me up. It was pretty. "Hi, Puck." I wondered who had painted it.

"Come on," I said.

We walked and talked. "Not only did I get you out of jail, Noah--"

"Didn't you get me in jail?" he asked.

Ugh. Maybe. Move on. "Not only did I get you out of jail, but you're going back to Tau Ceto e."

His eyebrows flew up his forehead. "How?"

"Uh." Darn. He would ask me that. I hadn't quite worked it out yet. "Uh, Gina's loaning you, us, a shuttle." How tight could security be?

"Loan me a shuttle? I've never heard of TCC just giving out shuttles." He glanced at me sideways. "Are you screwing her, Jack?" He chuckled. "I do not understand how you always seem to win over the ladies."

"No, I'm not screwing her. Don't be crude." Why had Old Jack been friends with this joker?

"Well, if you're not screwing her, she wants you to be screwing her."

"I don't think that's true." I thought me and Gina had shared a moment, a genuine friendship moment, a connection. "No. You're wrong."

Noah chuckled. "*He doth protest too much.*"

Jerk.

A little later, in the cargo bay, Daniel made a big show of being surprised to see me. "Who is this young fellow? He looks slightly familiar, but I can't quite place him." The cargo bay hadn't changed a bit; it looked as crowded and disorganized as ever. Clearly, I hadn't missed anything here.

Noah turned to me. "I thought you said you knew this guy?"

"He's pulling my chain," I said. "Hi, Daniel. What, are you annoyed I haven't helped you move big boxes from one spot to another recently?"

He opened his mouth. He closed his mouth. Then, he said, "Basically."

"Sorry about that. I've been busy." Busy being a pirate. Busy lying in sickbay. Busy charming the captain. I had been busy!

"Anyway, this is Noah." I pointed. "He wants a drink."

"What's in it for me?" Daniel asked, crossing his arms.

"I seem to recall I paid you a bunch of money for just such occasions," I said, irritated. Geez, thousands of credits just didn't go as far as they used to--I was guessing not having all that much personal experience.

He shrugged and stared at me. Somehow I got the message that he wanted me to do some work for him, even though he didn't explicitly say it.

"All right." I sighed. "I'll move some boxes around."

"Now you're talking, kid," he said. "Right this way, old-timer." Daniel walked away.

"Is he talking to me?" Noah asked.

Now it was my turn to shrug. "Do you want a drink or not?"

"You stay there, Jack," Daniel called back to me.

The two of them disappeared into the maze of boxes and crates.

A few minutes later, Daniel reappeared, rubbing his hands together. "Have I got a bunch of boxes for you."

I sighed again. "Did you fix that anti-gravity dolly?"

"Yes."

As I moved one of the many, many boxes Daniel asked me to move, I noticed the mysterious crate that had broken open the last time I worked here. That would be the mysterious crate that appeared to contain an FTL drive. Probably, a secret, very valuable FTL drive. Possibly my ticket to Tau Ceto.

Possibly a war-starting FTL drive--if Olivia was to be believed.

I was staring into the crate when Daniel came to check on me. "It's a thing of beauty, isn't it?" he asked.

"More like a thing of mystery," I said.

"Yeah." He grinned. "No one knows how they work."

I fingered my fon. Almost no one.

What if the data on my fon was related to this drive? What if this drive was a clue to my murder? What if it was *why* I was murdered? A shiver shimmered up my spine.

"Did you run any tests or anything on the drive or the crate?" I asked.

"What?" He grinned. "Like hook it up to a ship and see if it works?"

Uh Oh. If anyone was going to hook up this drive and use it, it would be me.

"Jack?" Daniel asked. "You still with me?"

"Yeah, I'm with you," I said. "I meant, what about more mundane tests on the drive? Forensics. Like, did you check it for biometric data?"

He snorted. "Anybody who can get their hands on a contraband FTL drive knows better than to leave their DNA on it."

"Just humor me," I said.

"All right. I've got a biometric scan somewhere..." What didn't he have in here? He walked away.

A few minutes later, he pointed what looked like a souped-up fon at the mystery crate. He waved it along all the crate surfaces and even pointed it inside.

He pulled the machine close to his face and stared at the screen. "Huh." He glanced up at me. "See? I was right. There's no DNA on this but yours. Why did you have to go and touch it all over?" He turned and walked away. "Stupid kid."

But I didn't touch it. I'd never touched it.

The drive itself was a clue, a huge clue.

What had Old Jack been up to?

Chapter Twenty-Six

I couldn't believe how smart I was: I'd figured out a solution to all my problems. All I had to do was hook up the renegade FTL drive to a shuttle and fly it back to Tau Ceto e. And as a huge plus: I'd be able to use my special power when I engaged the drive.

Of course, I personally didn't know how to hook up an FTL drive. Or drive a shuttle. Or navigate to Tau Ceto e. Or get a shuttle out of Gina's clutches. Or how to investigate murder when I got back to the planet of the turtle people.

Huh.

"You all right, little buddy?" Noah asked, putting his arm around me. He was considerably mellower since he'd drunk a bunch of Daniel's moonshine. We were sitting around in the cargo bay with Daniel and Bill.

"There you are!" Ted appeared amongst the crates. "I've been looking all over for you, Jack." He sat down right next to me, thigh to thigh. "When I couldn't find you on the security feeds, I finally figured out you had to be somewhere we didn't have security feeds. By the process of elimination, I deduced you must be in the cargo bay and, look, here you are in the cargo bay."

I thought I heard Noah mutter, "No, shit." I frowned at him.

Daniel and Bill chuckled.

"What?" Ted asked, raising his eyebrows.

I smiled. I'd finally met someone more naive than me, and I liked it.

"Don't mind these old-timers," I said. "They're just jealous of your cuteness." I leaned over and kissed his cheek.

Ted actually blushed. "He doesn't look that old." He pointed at Daniel. That was true, but who the heck knew how old anyone was these days, anyway?

Noah cleared his throat. "So, what are the sleeping arrangements tonight, Jack? Am I in your cabin?"

I stared at him. He didn't want to sleep with me, did he? He'd sworn he didn't have a thing for me. It'd been hard to believe, but I'd taken him at his word. Was that the wrong thing to do? "You know I respect you, Noah," I said. "But, we've been over this..."

"Oh, Christ!" he said. "I don't want you. I just want your damn bed. What is wrong with you?"

Was there something wrong with me?

Ted pressed against me. "You could stay with me if you needed a place. You know I'd do anything for you, Jack."

Ha. Of course, people wanted to be with me. There wasn't anything wrong with me. It was only curmudgeons like Noah that were too old or whatever to have good taste.

I turned and considered Ted. He'd do anything? Like, help me steal a shuttle, anything? There was only one way to find out.

"Sure, Noah," I said. "Take my cabin. I can stay with Ted here." I reached for Ted's hand and squeezed it tenderly.

In Ted's cabin, a long, long time later, Ted sighed in satisfaction. "Wow. You're great, Jack."

Yeah, I was. "You're great, too, Ted."

"Thanks," he said. "*Hear my soul speak. Of the very instant that I saw you, did my heart fly at your service.*"

"Nice." I nodded. "*Love sought is good, but given unsought is better.*"

"Yeah," he said.

We shared a tender kiss.

"I didn't know you were a Shakespeare expert," I said after we separated.

"*All the world's a stage, and all the men and women merely players,*" he said, grinning. "I've been studying. I know how much you like the bard."

Wow. That was dedication. My shuttle caper was starting to look more likely. "So, I know you're good at monitoring the security feeds. Do you have any experience with, I don't know, maybe turning them, or shuttle security, off?"

"No." He looked at me guilelessly. "Why would someone do that?"

"I don't know, maybe, if they wanted to do some kind of nefarious deeds undetected."

"Nefarious deeds?" Ted chuckled. "Jack, you're awful. But, no, turning off security is a bad idea. It would just draw attention to your nefarious deeds. You'd want to replace the live feeds with fake ones or spoof the shuttle security to show everything's normal."

"That's brilliant!" Ted was even better than I'd thought he was, and I'd thought he was pretty great. "Do you know how to do that?"

He blushed. "I think I could figure it out. Are you thinking of taking a shuttle?"

"Uh, Gina might be sending me on a super-secret mission." It was so secret she didn't even know about it.

He nodded like that made sense. "When might such an event occur?"

"Maybe tomorrow night?" I grabbed his hand and kissed his palm. "I'll keep you posted."

"Heh, heh, posted. Sounds fun." Ted reached out and turned off the light.

As we settled in for the night, I did feel a little guilty about corrupting today's youth. Of course, technically, compared to me, Ted was a wise old man.

I had to stop by my cabin in the morning to change clothes and pick up my mandolin.

Noah had been snoring loudly, but as soon as I entered, he sat up, instantly alert. "Oh, it's only you."

That wasn't a very nice greeting. "Yes, only the man who generously loaned you the use of his cabin." What had Old Jack seen in this guy?

"Whatever. Oh, by the way, a real cutie stopped by last night looking for you."

"Who?"

"I don't remember," he said. "How many cute young women would stop by for a late-night visit?"

I grinned. "You'd be surprised." But I know who I hoped it was. "Was it Eva?" I hadn't seen her in hours. I missed her.

"Eva?" He nodded. "Yeah, I think she said her name was Eva."

"Excellent!" If memory served, among Eva's many skills, she had experience as a shuttle pilot.

"What's that look?" Noah asked. "If I didn't know better, I'd say that's Jack's 'I'm planning something' look. Are you up to something?"

I was so surprised Old Jack and I had a look in common I didn't immediately answer.

"Kid?"

I smiled mysteriously. "I may or may not be working on something to get us back to Tau Ceto e."

He laughed. "Yeah, right, kid."

"Just be ready to go tonight."

Phase one of my plan was to be asked to leave rehearsal so I'd be free to scheme. Since they asked me to leave yesterday, I was guessing this phase of the plan would be pretty easy.

First, I had to greet enchanting Eva. I sidled up behind her. "*Psst.* Eva. Hi."

She turned and smiled. "Hi, Jack."

She had a beautiful smile. "Hi, Eva."

"You already said that." She paused. "I must admit I've never heard anyone actually say *psst* before."

"Did it work for you?"

"It was fairly effective."

"I heard you stopped by my cabin last night," I said. "I'm sorry I missed you."

Her smile slipped, and I surmised she was wondering where I was, or rather, who I was with.

I took her hand. "You know you're my favorite girl." True.

"Really?" She made a sound suspiciously resembling a giggle.

"Of course," I said. "*She's beautiful, and therefore to be wooed. She is woman, and therefore to be won.*" Ah, there was that gorgeous smile again.

"So, didn't you say you were a stupendous shuttle pilot?" I asked.

"Yes, well, I'm a regular shuttle pilot," she said. "I don't know about stupendous. Why?"

I leaned in and whispered. "Gina's sending me on a secret mission, and I need a shuttle pilot. Are you available?"

"Well, no." She glanced over at Gina. "You got Ted and me the leads in the play."

"Gina understands," I said. "The mission is more important. And you know about our special relationship." Eva was one of the few people who knew I was technically married to Gina. "So what do you say?" Of course, the real specialness of my Gina relationship was it was pretty non-existent.

"If it's okay with Gina, I guess it's okay," she said.

"Great!" I pecked her on the cheek. "I'll keep you posted."

I walked away in awe of how good I was getting at lying. Was that one of Old Jack's skills I'd inherited?

Rehearsal started. I strummed and strolled around the rehearsal space, singing, "*Sigh no more, ladies, sigh no more. Men were deceivers ever, one foot in sea and one on shore, to one thing constant never.*" I wasn't sure I liked this song.

"Take it outside, Jack," Gina said.

I said, "Gosh, are you sure?" Then I sang, "*Then sigh not so, but let them go, and be you blithe and bonny...*" Maybe it was a good song.

"Outside!" she said.

Geez, I wish Gina was at least a bit blithe and bonny.

I strolled out the door. "*Converting all your sounds of woe into hey nonny, nonny.*" The door closed behind me.

All right, phase one accomplished.

A key element of my nefarious scheme was the renegade FTL drive, so I went to the cargo bay to check it out. Unfortunately, the drive was not where I'd seen it last. "Damn."

"What are you up to, Jack?" Daniel asked behind me.

I jumped sky-high. Where had he come from? "I'm, uh, looking for you."

He crossed his arms in front of him. "Why? It's a bit early for a drink."

"Right," I said. "I'm here to work. Can I help you move something?"

"What's going on here?" He pointed at me. "You're acting suspicious. Jumpy."

"Nothing," I said. "Nothing's going on here. I'm not acting suspicious."

He narrowed his eyes. "I don't believe you, Jack. Maybe you should leave."

So, my lying skills only worked on people I'd slept with? That was probably not a good thing.

I glanced at Daniel. He was not unattractive with his smooth, clear skin and thick brown hair. "Do you have a girlfriend?" I asked. "A boyfriend?"

"Out!" He pointed at the door. "Get out!"

He followed me until I was all the way out in the hall, then slammed the door closed.

Well, crap. Now what?

Chapter Twenty-Seven

If I couldn't get Daniel on board or at least sufficiently distracted, this mission to Tau Ceto would be over before it even started.

Lacking any better ideas, I strolled and played my mandolin to my quarters.

I opened the door to Noah snoring loudly. He sat up, instantly alert. "Oh, it's only you." Again.

I clenched my fist but resisted the urge to pop him in the nose. "Still asleep, huh? Must be nice to be retired."

He frowned. "I'm not retired."

"Could have fooled me," I said. "Or do your snores somehow fight crime?"

"My snores fight crime better than you do, kid," he said.

I didn't dignify that with an answer. Mostly because I was worried he was right. I sat down in my desk chair and strummed the mandolin.

"Did you want something, kid?" he asked.

"I ran into a snag with my nefarious scheme."

"Your what?" He looked puzzled.

I debated how much to tell him about my scheme. I landed on nothing. I didn't trust him at all. "I need Daniel out of the cargo bay for a while." I wasn't about to tell him why. "If you're such a super-spy, you can take care of that, right?"

"Why do you need access to the cargo bay?"

"I can't tell you. It's part of my secret mission from, er, for Gina."

"Daniel, the purveyor of liquor? Daniel, the black marketeer?" He reached for a fon. Where'd he get that? "No problem. I have a huge dossier on him."

"Great." I put down the mandolin. "Give me an hour at least

in the cargo bay." I didn't know where the renegade FTL drive was, but the crate had been pretty big. I should be able to find it. I thought I'd easily recognize the crate. It did have some pretty distinctive cracks in it. Now.

He scratched something under the covers. Ick. "Give me an hour to get dressed and get some chow."

An hour? Good grief, old people were slow.

While I was killing an hour, I decided it was the perfect time to recruit Olivia. She was crucial to the scheme since she was the only person I knew who knew anything about FTL drives.

I found her in engineering. It seemed like she was always there. "Wow, Olivia. You work hard." Even in the middle of the morning, the lighting was still subdued, and all the blinking lights stood out--I guessed that was on purpose.

"You would think so," she said. "Since you never seem to work at all."

"Aw. That's not nice. And here I came to offer you an exciting opportunity." I paused. "Besides, I don't know what you're talking about. I did musical interludes on Earth, was a pirate, and now I'm Balthasar. And I worked--I work--in the cargo bay. And I train with the combat expert."

She harrumphed. "Yeah, I know what kind of training you do with Eva."

Even I knew arguing with her would not get her to help me. "I concede the point that you work harder than me."

"You got that right," she said.

"That's what I said," I said.

"That's what I'm saying," she said.

This was getting us nowhere. "So, anyway, I've been considering your wise words about the--" I stepped closer to her and whispered "--FTL drive. It should be shared with someone like you who can understand it."

"FTL drive!" she said.

"Shh!" I glanced around engineering, but no one was paying us any attention.

"FTL drive!" she whisper-shouted. "We didn't talk about a drive. You just showed me some data on your fon. Do you have a drive?"

I stared into her beautiful almond-shaped eyes. "I do have a drive." Soon. "I need your help to install and operate it. You would get to make use of all that lovely data." I shook my fon.

"What!" she shrieked.

The other folks in engineering turned to stare at us.

I smiled and waved. I tried to say, 'Nothing going on over here,' with my expression. They looked away.

"You already know I have data about the drive," I said. "Well, now Gina--"

She gave me an odd look.

"Er, Captain Gomez is sending me, us, on a secret mission to test it out."

"Why didn't she ask me herself?"

"Did I mention the secret part?"

"Well, yeah..." She wrinkled her brow, and I was guessing she was considering my offer. Why was it taking her so long, though? Who wouldn't want to help me?

"No."

"Great." I started to hug her but paused. "Wait. Your 'yes' sounded a lot like a 'no.'"

"It was a 'no.'" She crossed her arms in front of her. "No."

"How can you say no?"

"Like this: nooooooo."

She was crucial to my nefarious scheme. I found a chair and sank into it. "I don't get it. Why don't you want to help?"

She pulled up a chair next to me. "This mission sounds too important for me. You need Dr. Wilson, the head of the FTL team. Or Commander Bello, the chief of engineering."

"Gina, er, Captain Gomez needs them to stay here and deal with the *Shakespeare*'s FTL drive. You said it was acting funky, right?"

"True." She nodded. "I guess that makes a certain amount of sense."

It did? Of course, it did. "Come on." I smiled charmingly. "You know you want to help me."

She gave me a sharp look.

"You know you want to become an expert on FTL drives."

She appeared to be wavering.

"If you play your cards right, you could become one of the

top FTL experts in the universe."

"Really?"

Yes. I would make it happen for exquisite engineer Olivia. "Yes."

She narrowed her eyes. "I'm not sure I believe you."

"It's a very important secret mission for Captain Gomez. She asked for you specifically. She's depending on you. I'm depending on you." I brushed her arm with my fingertips.

She frowned. "If you stop coming on to me, I'm in."

"Yes!" I thrust my fist into the air.

She started to grin but squashed it when she noticed me noticing. "So, what's the plan?"

I stood. "The plan is you come with me right now to find, er, get the drive and we install it in the shuttle and take off tonight."

She stood slowly. "Tonight? Why so soon? Why not more testing?"

"Did you miss the 'secret' part?"

"All right," she said. "Just let me tell my boss where I'm going."

I put my hand on her arm to stop her.

She stared pointedly at it and then at me.

"Sorry." I withdrew my hand. "Captain Gomez already took care of all that." Blatant lies seemed to be easier to carry off than subtle lies.

"All right," she said. Huh. I could effectively lie to some people I wasn't sleeping with.

As we left engineering, I quashed my feelings of guilt about lying. It was all for a good cause, right? Solving an evil murder, murders. Sam's murder must be related to all this. And Olivia would get to learn about the FTL drive. And Gina did know about the mission. Sort of. So, it was all good.

I had a niggling suspicion that I was also getting good at lying to myself.

In the cargo bay, there was no sign of Daniel. Yay. Noah was good for something, after all.

"There's an FTL drive in here?" Olivia asked, glancing around. "Where?"

That was an excellent question. I nimbly climbed up onto

the biggest crate. "*Romeo, Romeo, wherefore art thou, Romeo?*"

Down on the ground, Olivia said, "You named the drive Romeo?"

I shrugged. "Why not?" I scanned the large room. Over against the far wall, I spied a likely candidate. I jumped down. "This way."

We ambulated over there and, sure enough, found our heart's desire. I recognized the markings, or more accurately, the cracks I'd put in the crate.

"Is this the Alpha Catoblepas's language?" Olivia asked.

"Yes, it is." I nodded wisely. "It says Eph-something." I didn't want to tell her too much.

"What does that mean?" she asked.

"It's an AC thing." I had a sudden vision of being mobbed by AC ladies of the evening, wanting to give me a freebie. That was very kind and generous of the ladies, but ick.

I'd snagged the anti-grav dolly on the way across the bay. I started maneuvering it underneath the crate.

"It is just me, or is this crate cracked?" Olivia asked.

"Hmph," I said noncommittally.

"Jack, did you do this? Drop it or something?" she asked. "You didn't break it, did you?"

I flashed her a charming smile. "You sure look pretty in your engineering uniform."

She couldn't help herself, she smiled back.

"Come on, Romeo," I said as I positioned the dolly underneath it.

"What's the end of that quote?" she asked. "*Deny thy father, and refuse thy name?*"

Gee, that wasn't ominous at all. I started wondering what my father, er, Old Jack's father, would have thought of me. And his Mom. I had Old Jack's memories of them, but somehow, it wasn't the same. I knew they'd loved him, but they never met me. Would they have loved me? Ugh. Being an orphan was hard work.

"You all right, Jack?"

I shook it off and turned to Olivia. "*Be but sworn my love?*"

"Give it a rest, Jack," she said, trying to sound gruff. But I saw a split-second smile. That's what I'm talking about.

A JACK BY ANY OTHER NAME

We loaded up the secret FTL drive on the dolly and walked it right out of the cargo bay. I planned to walk it over to the shuttle bay like we had every right to do so.

What could possibly go wrong?

Chapter Twenty-Eight

It turns out that traipsing down the corridor with a secret stolen FTL drive like you have every right to totally works. No one stopped us. No one questioned us.

A few people even said, 'Hey, how's it going?' Of course, I said, 'It's going great. How's it going with you?' and smiled in return.

At the shuttle bay, we ran into our first hurdle. We couldn't get into the shuttle. It was kind of a big hurdle.

Olivia frowned. "Jack, did you lose the security code?"

I was a little insulted that she thought I would lose something so important. Obviously, I wasn't about to tell her I'd never been authorized any security codes. "Uh..."

"That's a yes," she said. "Honestly. Well, I'm going to get lunch. Sort this out." She turned and walked away.

For such a small woman, she sure contained a lot of bossy. "*For I am he am born to tame you...*" It would be fun to try to tame Olivia.

But right now, I needed to tame this lock. I got out my fon and contacted my main man in security, Ted. He said he'd be right over.

He was as good as his word. "Hi, Jack." He smiled widely as he sauntered up. "Is this where we do it? Dirty deeds?"

That smile looked pretty lascivious. Did he think we were going to have sex here in the hall outside the shuttle, in front of the secret stolen FTL drive? Even I wasn't up for that.

He gave me a peck on the cheek when he got close.

"What dirty deeds are you talking about?" I asked.

Ted inclined his head towards the shuttle. "Breaking into the shuttle."

Geez. Could he say that any louder? "Shh!"

He giggled. He was pretty cute when he giggled.

I whispered, "Yes, Ted, those dirty deeds. I'm counting on you."

Ted took something out of his pocket and waved it in front of the security pad. The shuttle door slid open. "Ta-da!"

"Nice job--" I started to reach for him to give him a congratulations kiss.

"What the hell is going on here?" a man behind us said.

Ted and I both whipped around. It was that pointy-headed security guy I'd been trying to win over for days. Had I truly won him over? I was about to find out.

I really didn't want him to investigate the mysterious crate that was right in front of him. My heart started staccato-ing in my throat. Nothing to see here; just move along.

"Uh, hi, uh, boss," Ted stammered. "Nothing going on here. I just thought I'd, uh, stretch my legs. And I saw my buddy Jack here and thought I'd say hi. And--"

Ted's boss wasn't buying it. He crossed his arms and scowled at us.

Please, don't ask about the crate. "That's enough, Ted," I said. "We're doing something for Captain Gomez."

Ted's boss took out his fon and scanned it. "Nope. Whatever you're doing here, it's not on the schedule."

So far, bald-faced lying had been working great. "Yes, we are," I said. "It's a special secret project for Captain Gomez. I guess she didn't let you in on it." My expression implied he wasn't special or secret enough to be in on the project.

His expression implied, 'Yeah, right, kid.' "Nope. But I can call Captain Gomez and check with her if you want." Crap. That was the last thing we needed.

I took a step toward him. "No. We don't need to bother her. She's a busy woman." Was I being foiled? That was disappointing. My spirits sank. "*I have a soul of lead*," I muttered.

"Of course, I don't bother the captain when she doesn't need to be bothered," Ted's boss said. "I'm very good at my job."

Brag much? "Okay."

"I'm super-good at my job," he said. "Really, very super-good."

Was I about to enjoy the amenities of the brig again?

"I'm so good, I deserve a bonus."

Ted and I just stared at him.

"A bonus from Captain Gomez, or maybe another crewmember..."

Arrest us already, if you're going to arrest us.

"Shit, kid," Ted's boss said. "Get a clue."

Ted poked me and whispered, "Credits."

Ah ha. He was one of the guys I'd offered a tip to earlier. Then Gina had been standing right there with us, however. Now, she wasn't. "I'd be happy to offer you a remuneration since you're doing such a good job." My heart started settling down.

"I might be amenable to some nice remuneration."

"What about fifty thousand remunerations?" I asked.

"That would be effectively remunerative," he said.

"What?" I was losing track of this conversation.

Ted's boss walked to us, holding up his fon. Bribe: okay. I transferred fifty thousand credits to him.

He checked it, nodded, turned around and started leaving. "You're on your own, boys. I don't know what you're up to, and I don't want to know." He paused, turned, and gave us the evil eye. It was pretty scary. "And I better not find out." He left.

Phew. I collapsed against the shuttle.

"So that just happened," Ted said. "We bribed my boss."

"Please don't talk so loud," I said.

And then, Olivia appeared from around the corner. "Oh, good, you got the shuttle open." She checked us out. "What's wrong?"

I straightened up. "Absolutely nothing. We're just waiting for you."

"We are?" Ted asked.

"Yes, we are," I said. "Come on. Let's get this, uh, piece of equipment into the shuttle."

We dollied the drive to the shuttle's bridge. The earlier damage to the crate made it easy to open. We carefully carried the drive to the main control panel and set it down on the floor. It was surprisingly light.

"Are we sure this is a real drive?" Olivia asked.

I shrugged. "I don't know."

Ted said, "Does anyone know how much FTL drives are supposed to weigh?"

"I don't know," Olivia said.

"Don't look at me," I said. As far as I'd been able to tell, no one--no humans anyway--knew anything about FTL drives.

This was getting us nowhere. "So, anyway." I called up Old Jack's FTL data and specifications on my fon. "Here." I handed it to Olivia.

She took it and started scanning through the data. "I'm not sure I can do this; install it, you know."

"*To climb steep hills requires a slow pace at first*," Ted and I both said at the same time. We looked at each other and smiled.

"Ack," Olivia said. "It's spreading. Don't tell me quoting Shakespeare is contagious. Sharma should put you two in quarantine."

I snickered. I assumed she was joking. She was joking, wasn't she?

"Ha, ha," Ted said. "We are here to assist you, Miss Olivia."

"Yeah, anything you need," I said. "We can hold a wrench or whatever."

"Yes," Ted said. "I'm good at holding ...screwdrivers."

Was he joking?

Olivia lifted her head from the fon and scanned him. "You two are annoying me. Go away. Come back later."

"Yes, ma'am," Ted said.

The two of us started walking away.

"So, what now?" Ted asked. "We have some time to kill. Whatever could the two of us, two strapping, handsome young men, do?" It may have been Olivia's influence, but Ted was starting to get on my nerves a little.

It had been a long time since breakfast. I was hungry. "I'm going to the mess hall. Would you like to join me for lunch?"

He agreed. Of course.

The mess hall was one of the biggest rooms on the ship, filled with tables and chairs, with murals of forest scenes on all the walls. It was currently crowded; there were hardly any seats available. We got some food, elbowed our way through the crowd and found two spaces at a table.

"Ted." Gina appeared next to us from out of nowhere.

I guessed the crowd masked her approach. "I wish you'd reconsider quitting the show." I didn't know he'd quit.

"Sorry, Captain," he said.

"I suppose you had something to do with this," Gina said to me. "Why did you suggest Ted and Eva for Benedick and Beatrice if you were just going to make them quit?" Eva quit, too? Oh, right, she had to because she was going to Tau Ceti with us.

"Jack?" Gina asked.

"Uh, after you and I talked," I said to her, "I thought you and Carter should give it another chance. I think the two of you could be good." I smiled. Old Jack was gone. Gina needed to truly move on.

"Really?" she asked.

I nodded solemnly. "Yes. Go for it."

"Hmm." She didn't seem completely convinced, but she departed. Phew.

"What was that?" Ted asked. "It almost seemed like you were giving the captain romantic advice."

I kept forgetting he wasn't in on my secret. And that was probably safer for him. "No." I shook my head. "We were just talking about the show, only the show. I'm a talented performer, you know."

He nodded agreeably.

The rest of lunch passed uneventfully.

Back in the shuttle, Olivia was lying on the floor with her head inside the front console, surrounded by instruments, cables and meters. The FTL drive looked exactly the same as when we'd left.

"Everything all right in here?" Ted asked. "It looks like some kind of machine exploded."

"Where'd you get all this equipment?" I asked.

"Engineering, of course," Olivia said. "What'd you think? The equipment fairy?" Her bad attitude was getting on my nerves, too.

I tried to calm myself. "So, how's it going?"

"It's going," she said. "I think I might be able to do it."

"Might?" Ted asked.

She ignored him and went back to work.

"So, what now?" Ted asked me.

I needed a break. What had I gotten myself into with all of this? "I need to think. I'm going to my cabin."

"I can..." he said.

"Alone," I said. "I need to finalize the mission plan."

Or make a mission plan.

But when I got to my cabin, Noah was there. I deflated.

I should ask for his input on the mission plan, but I didn't want to deal with his condescension. Because he was older, he acted like he knew way more than me.

"Out," I said. "Get out." I sighed. "Please." I'd had it. Everyone was getting on my nerves.

He took one look at my face and got out.

I was starting to think I was in over my head.

Chapter Twenty-Nine

Alone at last in my cabin, I lay on my bunk thinking deep, important thoughts pertaining to our secret mission to Tau Ceto e. What should we do when we got there? How could we obtain info? Basically, I was pondering how to solve my murder and how to find out more about the mysterious FTL drive.

Sadly, so far, I hadn't come up with much.

Someone knocked on my cabin door.

"Enter," I said. I wasn't procrastinating. This person might have important info for me. In fact, they probably were crucial to the mission. Yeah, that was it.

It was Eva, and she flashed me her beautiful smile. "Hey, Jack. How's it going?"

I couldn't help smiling back at her. "Much better now that you're here."

"So, what'cha up to?" she asked. "Napping?"

"No," I said. "I'm planning our important mission."

"It looks like you're napping."

I tried not to lose my temper. "Then, looks are deceiving." I patted the bunk next to me. "Come here."

She examined me for a moment with a hint of a smile on her face but then lay down next to me. "So now we're both planning?"

"Yes. Look at us plan." It wasn't too convincing.

She grinned. "You wanna fool around?"

"You know me so well." I turned to face her. We pressed our lips together. It felt lovely as if we were one.

"*Doubt thou the stars are fire*," I said. "*Doubt that the sun doth move; doubt truth to be a liar; but never doubt I love*."

Eva pressed her whole self against me. "Less talking, more

kissing, kid."

I wholeheartedly agreed. But...

Eva glanced below my waist. "You all right down there? I would have thought something would be going on by now."

I would have thought the same.

The FTL drive must be malfunctioning. I sat up. "The FTL drive must be malfunctioning!" If the FTL drive wasn't malfunctioning, foreplay with a beautiful, desirable woman would excite me, all of me.

She sat up, too. "What?"

What was my most pressing current need? Finishing what I started with Eva. My eyes caressed her smooth skin and beautiful form. But she was not my most pressing need overall. Focus, Jack!

I needed a mission plan. "I have a kick-ass mission plan!" I said.

"Okay?" she said. "Brag much?"

I smiled broadly as a whole big plan blossomed in my mind. It started with getting the FTL drive to take us to Tau Ceto e. I kissed her forehead.

I jumped out of bed. "Come on!"

"Wait," she said. "What's happening?"

"We're going to the shuttle bay."

"Right now?" But she followed me as we rushed out of my cabin and down the hall.

At the shuttle bay, Olivia stood talking to an older man I didn't recognize. He was handsome with his strong physique, full head of gray hair and beard, sort of a silver fox. She looked nervous.

Just inside the shuttle, Ted looked super-mega-nervous. "There you are, Jack!" he said loudly as Eva and I approached.

"Who is this guy?" the older man asked.

"This is Jack Jones Junior, sir." Olivia pointed at me with the screwdriver in her hand. "Captain Gomez authorized him to lead this mission."

The man stared at Olivia for a few moments. "This kid is an ensign," he finally said. "He's not leading any missions. For the last time, we need you in engineering, young lady. The FTL drive crapped out again."

"Ah ha!" I knew it.

He turned to look at me and flashed me a big frown. "Ensign Jones, mind your business."

In my peripheral vision, I could barely make out Ted trying to communicate via a series of hand motions. I faced him. "What?"

Ted said, "We dropped out of FTL space. We're in regular space."

Comprehension dawned. Thanks to my big new plan, I knew we needed to launch the shuttle when we were in regular space. "Ah, Olivia, I have the authorization forms inside the shuttle. Come with me. Let's get them to show to your ...boss." I was guessing he was her boss anyway. He was bossy enough (even bossier than her) to be her boss. "Come on, Eva. We need your help as well."

Eva looked startled. "To get the forms?"

"Yes," I said. "Excuse us." I pushed past the older man and grabbed Olivia's arm as I entered the shuttle.

"Just a moment, sir," Olivia said.

Once all four of us were well inside, I said, "Shuttle, close exterior doors." The doors started closing.

"Wait. What are you doing?" Olivia's boss said, but he was cut off when the airtight doors latched.

"Eva, get in the pilot's chair," I said. "We're taking off."

We heard someone pounding on the exterior doors.

"But..." Eva said.

"I haven't finished installing the FTL drive," Olivia said.

"Everyone strap in," I said. "We're leaving."

They didn't look happy about it, but they all sat and strapped.

I sat in the back.

Eva started flipping switches on the front console. "Are you sure about this?"

"Yes. It's all according to my excellent plan." I tapped my forehead with my finger.

"*Hhmpf.*" Olivia scowled. "If this wasn't a super-secret mission for Captain Gomez, there'd be no way I'd be here."

Eva glanced at me with a wry expression. How much did she know?

"Here we go," she said. The shuttle glided forward through

the launch bay doors. When it was sufficiently far from the ship, the propulsion system ignited. We were all pressed back in our seats as we flew into space.

Soon we were surprisingly far from the *Shakespeare*.

"Shuttle One, what do you think you're doing?" a communications officer on the *Shakespeare* said over the comm. "Your launch was not authorized."

"Not authorized!" Olivia said. "What's he talking about?"

Everyone turned around to stare at me.

"Jack!" Olivia said.

I noticed Eva and Ted didn't say anything. I was having trouble keeping my lies straight. What had I told who?

"Shuttle One, come in," the comm officer said.

Eva punched the comm button. "This is Shuttle One. Our launch was authorized. Everything is normal here. Routine, perfectly routine."

Ted muttered under his breath, "These are not the droids you're looking for."

"What?" I said.

"Who am I talking to?" the comm officer asked. "Pilot, identify yourself."

Olivia had unstrapped and stalked back to me. She punched me on the shoulder. Hard.

"Ow," I said.

"What's going on, Jack? If your shenanigans hurt my career, I'll kill you." She shoved her face in my face.

"Shuttle One?" the comm officer said.

"What do you want me to say, Jack?" Eva asked.

"Jack!" Olivia said. Loudly.

"Use your best judgment, Eva," I said.

Eva activated comm. "This is Jack Jones. I'm on a secret mission for Captain Gomez." That was her best judgment?

Everyone froze.

"Come again, Shuttle One," the comm officer said.

"This is pilot Jack Jones," Eva said. "I'm on a secret mission for Captain Gina Gomez."

The officer didn't answer immediately. Finally, he said, "You don't sound like a Jack."

"What can I say? I'm a girly man," Eva said.

Ted laughed nervously and then put his hands over his mouth.

Olivia punched my shoulder again.

It really hurt. "Ow."

The comm officer said, "Captain Gomez says to return to the ship immediately, uh, Jack, or we're leaving you behind."

Everyone looked back at me. I shook my head *no*.

"Sorry, *Shakespeare*," Eva said. "I'm not coming back." She flipped off the comm.

Wow, that took balls. So, not such a girly man after all. I didn't think the *Shakespeare* would risk destroying its shuttle, but I wasn't sure.

Almost immediately, the *Shakespeare* accelerated away. I'll admit it: it was a little nerve-wracking watching it get smaller and smaller.

Olivia punched me again.

"Ow! Stop that!" I said.

Olivia drew her fist back to punch me again, but I dodged her.

"Is security officer Ted going to have to restrain you, Olivia?" I said.

Ted stood up and tried to look menacing.

"Is this an authorized mission?" Olivia asked.

Ted and Eva exchanged a look that said, 'Probably not.'

"Yes," I said. "Of course." I pointed at the FTL drive. "Please finish the installation."

She scowled and muttered, but she did go up to the FTL drive.

Ted followed.

Olivia started bossing Eva and Ted around.

I rubbed my sore shoulder and relaxed back in my chair. Being captain wasn't so tough.

My fon rang. It was Gina. No way was I answering that.

Another call came in: Noah.

I picked up. "Hey, Noah."

"What are you playing at, Jack?" he growled. "I thought I was coming with you to Tau Ceto, and I thought we weren't leaving until tonight."

"I saw an opportunity, and I took it." The opportunity to run away from Olivia's boss.

"What opportunity?" he asked.

"We entered regular space," I said. "The shuttle needs to launch when the *Shakespeare*'s in regular space."

"We're going to be in regular space for several days now, traveling to Geryon and for our away mission there," he said. "What's really going on?"

I made the sounds of static. "Gosh, Noah," I said. "You guys must be getting out of range for real-time conversion." Static, static. I hung up.

Ted came back to me. "Who was that?"

"Gina, er, Captain Gomez," I said. "Wishing us good luck on our important super-secret mission."

Eva shot me a look that seemed to say, 'Yeah, right.'

On the bright side, I was getting good at reading facial expressions.

Olivia stood. "I think that does it. I think the FTL drive is ready to go."

"Everyone strap in again," Eva said.

Once we were all strapped in, Eva said, "Here goes nothing." She engaged the FTL drive.

Nothing happened.

Chapter Thirty

Being stranded in outer space in the middle of nowhere was not part of my excellent mystery-solving plan.

"Try it again," I said.

Eva shrugged. "Okay." She did not say, 'Here goes nothing' again. She did engage the FTL drive again.

Nothing, indeed.

Ugh.

Everyone twisted around in their seat and looked back at me.

"Can you take another look, Olivia?" I asked.

She unstrapped and stood but looked scared. "I've never installed an FTL drive before. I never said I had." She approached the front of the shuttle.

I had a moment of panic. If the shuttle wasn't stocked with air, fuel, water and food, we might all be dead. My excellent plan was starting to look much less excellent.

I looked over the three wonderful humans essentially in my care. I couldn't screw this up.

"Ted," I whispered and crooked my finger at him.

He unstrapped and leaned down to me.

"Can you double-check the stores of food and water?"

He nodded and stepped towards the cargo area.

I unstrapped and approached Eva. I leaned down. "How are we set on fuel?" I whispered.

"Uh oh," she said at a normal volume.

"Shh!" I said.

She glanced at the rest of the crew. "It doesn't look good," she whispered. "Fuel tanks are less than twenty percent. I'm not sure we can reach any stations or planets with that."

Shit. I felt sick. But we weren't dead yet. I needed to focus on the positive, but I felt a little like a limp noodle and leaned against the shuttle wall.

I definitely wasn't ready to explore the undiscover'd country.

"What about air?" I whispered.

She glanced around the small shuttle. "For four people, maybe a day of air, maybe."

The fault, dear Brutus, is not in our stars, but in ourselves, that we are underlings. But that wasn't positive.

"Can you chart a course towards the nearest station?" I whispered. "We only have to get within comms range."

She nodded and turned back to her console.

Ted approached me and put his mouth right near my ear. "Bad news," he whispered. "No food and not much water."

It felt like a gut punch. Had I killed all my new friends? I sort of collapsed against the wall. My so-called excellent plan was the opposite of excellent.

"What is with all the whispering?" Olivia said. "Aren't we all in this together at this point?"

She was right. I straightened. "Sorry, Olivia. You're right." I turned to Ted. "Please tell the group what you found out."

Ted cleared his throat. "There's no food on board. And I'd guess there's about one day of water for four people--if we ration it."

"Shit," Eva said almost under her breath.

"What?" I asked.

"At the shuttle's max speed, it will take five days to get to the nearest space station."

Gut punch. I leaned against the wall again.

No one said anything for a few moments.

"So, we need to get the FTL drive working," I said.

"I say we need to space Jack," Olivia said.

"No!" Ted said. Ted was my new favorite person.

But I'd rather space myself than kill these good people.

"No, Olivia's right," I said. "The cold equations don't lie. If it comes to it, I will space myself."

"No!" Ted said. "You can't."

I put my arm around him, drawing comfort from him. "Eva lay in a course for the closest space station."

"Aye, aye, Captain," Eva said.

I wracked my brain, trying to come up with a solution. Unfortunately, my guilt about endangering the others was getting in the way.

"What can I do?" Ted asked.

"Please be quiet and let me think," I said. There was something on the tip of my brain. It was something associated with Eva.

I walked to the front of the shuttle and sat in the co-pilot's seat.

Olivia looked up at me from the floor, where she was entangled in the FTL drive. Her eyes were full of tears. "I can't do it, Jack," she whispered. "I'm sorry." She handed me my fon.

"Now, who's whispering?" Ted asked from the back of the shuttle.

"Please be quiet, everyone, and let me think," I said.

I faced Eva in the pilot's seat. "What did you say to me after our first training session?"

"So, I don't have to be quiet?" But, she smiled gently. "When are you talking about?" She glanced back at Ted. "In the shower?"

"Kill me now," Olivia muttered on the floor.

"No, earlier. Right after the workout--the official workout." But I remembered. "You said I'd improved dramatically."

"How is this helping?" Olivia said. We ignored her.

"Yes," Eva said. "It was dramatic, surprising, how quickly you improved."

And I'd been a crack shot almost immediately. And I could play the mandolin.

And I'd gotten very, very good at lying. My eyes scanned the group. That wasn't necessarily a good thing.

I'd almost figured it out earlier. I didn't totally understand it, but apparently, I'd inherited a lot of Old Jack's skills, even without his memories. When they brought me back, somehow, I knew what he knew. I just didn't know that I knew it.

Old Jack must know about the FTL drive; he had all kinds of info and data about it. "I might be able to figure out the FTL drive," I said.

"You?" Olivia asked. "I thought you didn't know anything

technical."

"Maybe I do." I pointed at her. "Switch places with me."

I studied the data on my fon, focusing especially on the circuit diagrams. Time passed.

I turned my attention to tracing the circuits on the floor in front of me. More time passed.

Eva asked, "What are the sleeping arrangements going to be?"

"You guys go ahead," I said. "I'm gonna keep working. And I'll keep an eye on the autopilot."

They turned out the lights in the back of the shuttle. More time passed.

I realized Olivia had mixed up two connections and corrected it. I powered on the FTL drive, which emitted a very faint hum and floated up off the floor a bit.

Promising.

But we still had to lay in a course through FTL space. I studied the navigation data on my fon. Suddenly it clicked. FTL space was not like regular space. It was fuzzier and more subjective. I programmed a course to Tau Ceto.

I stood up.

Should I execute? From the back of the shuttle, a mixed trio of sleeping sounds washed over me. Ted and Eva snored softly. Olivia turned over in her cot. "*O sleep. O gentle sleep. Nature's soft nurse,*" I whispered.

I couldn't just execute without their permission. Something could go wrong. I couldn't just kill them in their sleep. I felt kind of nauseated. And thirsty.

I tried to find my voice. "Hey, guys, wake up. Hello?"

They stirred.

Eva jumped up first, landing in a fighting stance. "What?"

Olivia just turned over again and looked at me.

Ted swung his legs over the side of his cot. "Did you get it to work?"

"I think so," I said. "But I don't want to execute the FTL drive command without your permission. Something could go wrong." The way things had been going, something would go wrong. "Should we vote?"

Eva sat back down on her bunk. "Usually, that's not how

things work on a spaceship, Captain."

"I don't care," I said. "Let's vote. All in favor of trying out the FTL drive, say 'aye.'"

"Aye," Ted said immediately, holding up his hand.

"Aye," Eva said.

Olivia sat up. "What the hell. Aye."

"Really?" I asked. I was surprised.

"Well, if we don't do this, we have to kill you, right?" Olivia said.

"Yeah," I said.

"Do it," Eva said.

I turned up the shuttle lights. They all got up and joined me in the front of the shuttle.

"*Once more unto the breach, dear friends, once more*!" Ted said.

"*There are few die well that die in a battle*!" Eva said, getting into the spirit of it.

We all looked at Olivia.

She shrugged, "Sorry, I don't know any quotes."

I said, "*He which hath no stomach to this fight, let him depart; his passport shall be made*." I examined the rest of them.

They all nodded.

I pressed the button.

We entered FTL space. The view out the windows changed. Instead of the star-sprinkled void of space, we now saw a fuzzy blue-white glow.

"Yay!" We all cheered. "Yay!" We cheered some more.

Then we didn't know quite what to do.

We all looked at each other.

"I can double-check the course," Eva said, sitting in the pilot's chair.

"I'm going back to bed," Olivia said.

"Do you think I could have some water?" I asked.

"Yes!" Ted said. "I'll get it."

He rushed off to the cargo area.

I asked Eva, "How are we on air?"

She nodded. "I think we might be okay."

Phew. "*For this relief much thanks*."

Once Ted and Olivia were distracted, Eva said, "Any sign of

you know?"

"You know?" I asked.

"You know!" she said. "Your special skill."

"Oh! My special skill." My manhood acted opposite the way I expected when weird possibilities were in flux. I focused on my nether regions. Nothing seemed to be happening. But why would it, right now? Nothing provocative was happening.

"Do you want to make out?" I asked Eva, grinning. Of course, she would.

"No," she said. Aw. "I'm flying the shuttle. Do the others know you can basically control reality sometimes?"

The sometimes were few and far between, namely, when I was in FTL space, and something weird was going on with the FTL drive.

Was my special skill working right now? I couldn't tell. "I wish I had a bacon cheeseburger."

Nothing happened. Did that mean my special skill wasn't working? I didn't know.

"No," I said. "They don't know about my skill."

Ted came back with a thimbleful of water.

"Thank you," I said. I gulped it down.

"Do you want to make out?" I asked him. In the past, reactions to lovemaking had been how I knew my special skill was working.

"Okay," he said. Of course! He led me back to his bunk. We gingerly sat on the edge. They folded down from the wall; how much weight could they handle?

I guess we were about to find out. Ted and I kissed.

"Kill me now," came faintly from Olivia's bunk.

"Should we stop?" Ted asked.

"Yes!" Olivia said.

"No," I said. "It's important."

Ted giggled. "Okay."

We made out some more, and my special skill did not make an appearance. My regular awesome bedroom skill was raring to make an appearance, but it didn't seem to be the time or place.

I had to stop, or I wouldn't be able to stop. "Whoa." I stood up. "That's it for me."

"Aw," Ted said.

LESLEY L. SMITH

"Sleep tight," I said.

He turned over.

I went up to Eva in the front. "How's it going?"

She jerked. She must have been dozing. She glanced at the console. "Everything's ship-shape, Captain." She grinned. She seemed to enjoy calling me captain. Or, maybe she was mocking me?

"How's everything going back there?" she asked.

"No special skill."

"Too bad," she said.

"I don't get it," I said. "Why does it work on the *Shakespeare* and not here?"

She tilted her head slightly. "Different FTL drive? The *Shakespeare*'s drive is broken or something, right?"

"I guess so," I said. None of this stuff really added up.

Why had this FTL drive been on the *Shakespeare*? Where did it come from? Was it stolen? Could it lead to war?

What had Old Jack been up to?

Had it gotten him killed?

Chapter Thirty-One

Eva landed the shuttle on Tau Ceto e like a champ. Luckily, the *Shakespeare*'s landing credentials were still good. Even in orbit, the higher gravity had been noticeable.

I was proud of Eva. "Yay!"

Everyone joined me in shouting and clapping. "Yay!" "You go, girl." "Huzzah!"

We'd arrived at the planet in the nick of time, almost out of air and very thirsty. I was guessing the group was not proud of me for getting us in this fix.

"Let's get some water and something to eat," Olivia said.

"Huzzah," Ted said again. "That's what I'd call a plan."

"I agree," Eva said.

"Me, too. Great idea, Olivia," I said. "And, my treat. Whatever you guys want." Thank God I still had plenty of credits.

We locked up the shuttle and sauntered into the station. Again, it was very hot. Again, the gravity was very strong. It smelled dusty, like the desert and maybe sage. I wondered what kind of plants grew here.

"I forgot how heavy I feel here," Olivia said.

Ted said, "Jack, you better get some of those goggles." He snickered. Last time he and Carter had convinced me I needed to wear goggles here on the planet. But that reminded me Noah had had some goggles. That might be a place to start, barring any other ideas.

In the meantime, I decided I'd be better off not complaining. About anything. "Heh, heh."

"There's a pretty good cafe over here that caters to off-worlders," Eva said and started walking.

My companions were surprisingly good sports, considering

I'd practically kidnapped them. They must be true friends. I felt a smile break out on my face. "We're like the Four Musketeers," I said as we walked to the cafe.

Olivia grunted.

The cafe, with one wall open to the station, seemed to have been carved out of the red-orange sandstone, with stone walls, floor, ceiling, tables, and benches. Between the cafe and the station was a row of knee-high planters filled with Terran (at least they were familiar-looking) desert plants. Nice. The lighting was bright, like the sun, but not too bright. It felt cheery.

The sage odor of the station blended nicely with the aromas of human food. My stomach rumbled. "Mmm."

The hostess, a giant turtle (don't say the t-word) person, seemed kind of agitated as we walked up. "Oh, praise the gods, you're Jack Jones, the famous singer, aren't you?" she said in perfect English.

"Yes, miss," I said. "I'm afraid you're right. I am he." I smiled, tipped an imaginary hat, and bowed--not so easy in the high gravity.

Eva poked me in the ribs with her elbow when I came back up. Hard.

Olivia and Ted looked confused.

"Er, I mean, I am the famous singer Jack Jones Junior. I also sing magnificently."

"Were you the one who starred in that concert a few days ago? I heard it was amazing."

I liked this turtle lady. "Yes. I am he." I smiled.

Olivia sighed very loudly.

"Oh, I've got our best table for Jack Jones, the famous singer and his friends." She led us to a large table in the front, open to the station.

As we settled in, she said, "Is there any chance you could grace us with a song?"

She was so cute; turtle women were growing on me. "I think that could be arranged. What did you have in mind?"

"My favorite is that one from *Man of La Mancha*," she said. "The one about the beautiful maiden."

"Dulcinea?" I starred in *Man of La Mancha* just a couple of years ago (to me) in school. "Yes." I stood up again.

"Ooh, I'll go get the music." Sure enough, in a couple of minutes, the opening strains of Dulcinea swelled through the restaurant.

Olivia said, "I'm going to the head." She darted off.

I cleared my throat and then sang, "*I have dreamed thee too long,*
Never seen thee or touched thee.
But known thee with all of my heart.
Half a prayer, half a song,
Thou hast always been with me,
Though we have been always apart." The music carried me away.

"*Dulcinea... Dulcinea...,*" I sang. "*I see heaven when I see thee, Dulcinea. And thy name is like a prayer. An angel whispers... Dulcinea... Dulcinea!*"

I went on for a while. Sentients inside and outside the restaurant crowded around--as they should. When I finished, many made hissing sounds. Interesting. You gotta love other planets. *Vive la difference*!

I tried out my doffing-the-invisible-hat-and-bowing move again. It was well received. Of course. The crowd started dispersing.

Finally, after all the excitement, the hostess said, "Oh, that was wonderful. You are all welcome to whatever you like on the menu, no charge."

Eva nodded her head. "Thanks."

"Yeah, thanks," Ted said.

"This has been the greatest moment of my life," the hostess said.

"Talk about singing for your supper," Ted said.

The three of us got comfortable at the table and studied the menu.

"What happened to Olivia?" Eva asked.

"You don't think she missed my performance, do you? That would be a pity," I said, still examining the menu. Some of the items on it were difficult to decipher.

"I think we may have another problem," Ted said, pointing towards the cafe entrance. Olivia strode towards us, arms crossed, accompanied by several large turtles in some kind of uniform.

"Station security!" Eva said, jumping up and landing in a fighting stance. "Ted, you're a security officer. You've got to be a good fighter, right? Jack, get behind us."

"Does anyone else have the urge to yell 'Turtle Power'?" I said.

"What?" Ted pointed at the open space behind us. "Why don't we just run?"

"I like the way you think, Ted!" We all managed to climb over the stone planters and into the station proper.

It took a while for station security to catch up to us, but when they did, it was almost like a chase in slow-mo. None of us were moving super fast in the high gravity.

"I hate to say it," Ted said. "I think they're gaining on us." He was hardly puffing at all; he was in better shape than me. We were all sweating.

We were running through the entertainment portion of the station. I saw a sign showing a nude turtle. Puff. Puff. "Eva, do you think that's a brothel?" I knew all about off-world brothels from my time on Alpha Catoblepas. They were often a hotbed (heh heh) of criminal activities.

"Yes," she said, giving me a weird look. "Why?"

I pointed. "We're going in here." I jogged into the brothel. "Close the door behind us."

Ted and Eva followed me, closing the door.

I jogged up to the proprietress. "We need a room." Puff. Puff.

"For all three of you?" I couldn't read turtle expressions, but her tone of voice was surprised.

"What are you doing?" Eva asked softly. She wasn't out of breath either.

"Yes," I said. Puff.

"Pay in advance," she said.

I handed over my fon. "Quick, make it quick." Puff.

"It's an emergency? Quick billing costs extra."

"Fine," I said, starting to catch my breath.

"Okay." She handed back my fon. "Gigi will take care of you." She gestured, and a turtle in a filmy dress approached us.

"Right this way, ah, lady and gentlemen." I couldn't get used to proper English coming out of a giant turtle. She led us up the stairs to a large bedroom, closing the door behind us. It had red-orange sandstone walls, floor, and ceiling. I was sensing a design trend. I concentrated on catching my breath. The stairs had been a challenge.

"There's a bed," Ted said. "I wasn't sure what to expect."

"Who's first?" Gigi asked. "Or were you thinking all at once? I'm not sure I can handle that."

"Jack, you're much more adventurous than I expected," Ted said.

"No, he isn't," Eva said. "Gigi, we don't want your services."

"Yeah," I said. "We just needed a place to lay low for a little while."

"What do you mean you don't want my services?" Gigi said. "You better not be saying there's something wrong with me." She put her hands on her middle. She didn't have a waist.

"No, of course not," Eva said. "You're beautiful."

"Very beautiful." I had no idea how to elaborate. Pretty shell?

"I should hope so," Gigi said.

"I'm confused," Ted said.

"Actually," I said. "We'd love it if you could get us some food, Earth food, and water."

"So, I'm to be your waitress?"

I smiled. "Yes, please."

"Oh, all right." She stomped over to the door and exited.

The three of us collapsed on the bed.

"I must admit, I don't even know how..." Ted said.

"Me neither," I said and started giggling.

It was contagious. We all leaned back on the bed, giggling.

After the giggle fit passed, Eva said, "What do you think happened with Olivia?"

"She must have decided we were too nefarious for her," Ted said.

"What he said." I pointed.

"You didn't tell her what was really going on?" Eva asked.

"My bad," I said. "I thought we needed her to get the FTL drive working."

"How did you get the FTL drive to work?" Ted asked.

Eva and I exchanged a look.

I said, "I'm a fast learner."

"Why are we here, in the brothel?" Eva asked.

"It's a good place to hide out for a little while. And on Alpha Catoblepas, I found out brothels are a locus for, shall we say, shady activities."

Ted snickered. "More like undercover activities."

That started another giggle fit.

Finally, Eva said, "So, you don't have a plan, do you? Be honest."

"Of course, I have a plan." I tapped my forehead with my forefinger.

"Are you going to tell us the plan?" Ted asked.

"Of course," I said.

"Now?" Eva said.

"Yes, jeez," I said. "During my last incident of special skills..."

"Huh?" Ted said.

"Long story," I said. "I wished for a plan to solve my mystery, and I thought of one."

Eva cleared her throat. "Jack."

"Your what?" Ted said. "And don't say long story again!"

"You have to tell him," Eva said, looking serious.

"Tell me!" Ted said.

"Okay, Ted," I said. "I should apologize. I haven't been entirely honest with you. I'm not Jack Jones Senior's son. I'm Jack Jones, Senior."

He stared at me for a moment before saying, "Huh?"

"I'm a clone," I said.

"Huh." He shook his head. "I didn't see that coming. So, what, you're like a super-rich hundred-year-old guy who grew himself a new body? I have to say, you don't seem a hundred years old."

"Uh, thanks, I guess," I said. "Biologically and memory-wise, I'm only eighteen-ish."

"Why's that?" Ted asked.

I shrugged. "I was murdered, and the murderer somehow managed to irretrievably purge thirty years of my memories."

"Wow," Ted said. "That murderer sounds bad. Memories are

precious. You aren't supposed to ever delete them. You're not supposed to be able to delete them. Aren't there safeguards or something?"

"Supposed to be," Eva said.

"Yes," I said. "So, anyway, I'm trying to find the murderer." And what? Bring him to justice? Get my memories back? Huh.

"So, back to the plan?" Eva said.

"Uh, yeah. The plan is to go back to the last known location of the mystery human and where the FTL drive was loaded, namely here, and poke around and ask questions."

"The big plan is to come to Tau Ceto and act like a detective?" Eva asked.

"That's not much of a plan," Ted said.

"It is much of a plan. I ingratiate myself with the natives to get their cooperation. We check out dens of iniquity like brothels." I pointed around the room. "We ask questions and shake things up. Something will shake loose. And then we'll go where the clues lead us."

"Why didn't you just wish you knew who the murderer was?" Eva asked.

Shit. "Uh..." I said.

"I don't understand what wishing does," Ted said.

"I'm guessing Jack Jones Senior wasn't much of a detective," Eva said.

"He was a worlds-renowned detective!" I said.

"I'm getting confused again," Ted said. "Aren't you supposed to be Jack Jones Senior?"

"Yes," I said. "I'm Jack Jones, Senior. They took the tissue sample from the up-to-the-minute Jack, and I seem to have his skills--just not his memories."

"I'm still confused," Ted said.

Eva nodded. "It's confusing."

"Okay," I said. "We're all somewhat confused."

"It's all well and good to find Jack's murderer," Eva said. "But I also want to solve the mystery of the FTL drive. That would be good for Earth. Where did it come from? How does it work?"

She didn't just want to help me? Aw. "I know the FTL drive is important."

Gigi burst in with a large tray laden with food.

223

We all got off the bed.

"Yeah!" Finally, some food.

"Lucky for you, our kitchen is getting pretty good at Terran food," Gigi said, setting down the tray. "We got another Terran staying here."

I stopped reaching for food and reached for my fon. "Oh? We're looking for a Terran. Can you look at a picture?" The mystery man from the concert.

But I was interrupted as a big burly man stepped into the still-open doorway and said, "Eva?" in a surprised voice.

Despite his gray hair and beard, wrinkles, and muscular build, I would recognize the man anywhere. *I follow him to serve my turn upon him.*

"Jack?" she squeaked.

It was me.

Chapter Thirty-Two

"Gigi, please give us some privacy," Old Jack said.

Gigi left.

My mind was spinning. The room was spinning. I couldn't breathe again. Puff. Puff.

"Is that you? Eva?" Old Jack said. How could Old Jack say anything? Old Jack was supposed to be dead. Spin. Puff. Spin. Puff.

She nodded.

He grinned a wolfish grin. "Wow. You look much younger than you did the last time I saw you."

Huh? What was he talking about? What was happening? I sort of fell, sort of sat, onto the bed. Spin. Spin. I tried to calm my breathing. Breathe in. Out. In. Out.

Ted said, "Huh? What's going on here?"

Eva glanced at me.

I stared at her and, apparently, old me. "I agree. What. The. Hell. Is. Going. On?" My mind wasn't working right.

Old Jack looked me up and down. He frowned. "Rush job, huh? He's pretty scrawny."

"Hey," I said. "I'm right here!"

"I demand to know what's going on," Ted said.

"Who's this kid?" Old Jack said.

"Jack, this is Ted," Eva said. "Ted, this is, ah, Jack."

Ted pointed at Old Jack. "Jack, who?" He turned to me. "I thought you were Jack." He turned back to Old Jack. "Is this your father? I thought you said your father was dead."

"I thought he was!" I said. I did not feel well. I lay back on the bed. My mind was reeling. If Old Jack was still alive, what was I?

Old Jack chuckled. "Oops."

"It's not funny, Jack," Eva said. "If you're alive..."

"What?" Ted asked.

I sat up. "I'm his clone," I said. "If he's still alive, I guess I'm an illegal clone." I felt like I might vomit. "They'll put me down like a dog."

"No!" Ted rushed to my side and embraced me. "Never. I'd never let them hurt you, Jack."

I felt my eyes fill as I rested my cheek on his warm chest.

Eva walked over and patted me on the back. "He faked his death. He's the criminal, not you, Jack. I'll protect you."

Old Jack had helped himself to our room service. He bit off a chunk of bread and chewed and watched us.

Finally, he said," I guess you have a way with the ladies and the, ah, gentlemen, Jack. Like father, like son. Sort of." He grinned his wolfish grin again.

"I'm nothing like you!" I shifted away from Ted. "Explain yourself, Jack."

"Explain yourself, Jack," Old Jack said. "What are you doing here?"

"We were looking for your murderer," I said.

"Well, mystery solved." He grinned. What an asshole. "Eva, why do you look so hot?"

"What do you mean?" I asked. "Why wouldn't she look hot?"

"Well, she is about seventy years old," Old Jack said.

"What!" I said. I would have guessed she was twenty-five years old, max. And I'd seen all of her, so I would know.

Eva smiled and shrugged. "TCC assigned me to protect you, Jack, er, Young Jack. They thought you'd respond better to someone your age."

I felt a little good that TCC thought I was worth protecting.

"Am I the only one here who isn't a clone?" Ted asked.

"I'm not," Old Jack said.

"No, but you faked your death," I said. "And someone died in my, er, your cabin. Was that your fault?"

He didn't answer, and I had a brainstorm. "You're not using me as bait, are you?"

He grinned. He was using me as bait!

"Aw," Eva said. "That's not nice, Jack, er, Old Jack. You've

226

made my job more difficult, and I don't appreciate it."

"And we know you've been doing something nefarious with an FTL drive," I said.

Old Jack narrowed his eyes. "FTL drive? What do you know about an FTL drive?"

I said, "I know it has something to do with my, er, your, er, the alleged, er, attempted murder." I wasn't sure what else to say. Should I be afraid of him?

"Did you install it?" Old Jack asked. "Is that how you got here?"

"He has a lot of your skills," Eva said, brow wrinkled. "I don't totally understand it."

"That is weird," Old Jack said. "Especially since you only have my most basic memories."

"Yeah!" I said. "Why is that?"

He didn't answer.

"The cell samples they used to, ah," I glanced at Ted, "grow me was from your mature body."

"Yeah," Eva said. "How'd you pull that off? How did you trick TCC into thinking you were dead?"

"None of your business," Old Jack growled. He was intimidating when he wanted to be.

Eva took a step back. "You know I have to report this."

"No, you don't." Old Jack took something out of his pocket. It was a stun gun. He shot Eva without hesitation. She crumpled to the floor.

I jumped up and rushed to her. "Eva!"

Old Jack shot Ted. Ted crumpled.

"Oh, no, Ted!" I stood up. "You fucking asshole!" I yelled at Old Jack. He would be dead by the time I finished with him. I clenched my fists and rushed him, preparing to attack.

He pointed the gun at me and shot.

Sometime later, I woke with a giant headache.

Ted and Eva were also awake, lounging on the bed, wincing.

"What happened?" I asked.

"He stunned us," Eva said.

"Where'd he go?" I asked.

"He ditched us, I guess," Eva said.

"Thank God it was only a stun," Ted said.

Considering as an illegal clone, I had zero rights; he could have shot me dead with no consequences. "Thank God," I agreed. There was supposed to be only one version of a person at any given time. 'Copies' were executed with extreme prejudice. There had been a couple of instances when cloning was first perfected... I shuddered.

I was very, very glad it was only a stun. I rubbed my head. "Where do you think Old Jack went?"

"Good question," Eva said. "I don't know, but we need to find him. There's no telling what he might do."

"Does anyone have an idea?" Ted said.

I shrugged. "I'm not sure." Finding Old Jack should be our number one priority, but I was selfish. I wanted to save my own life. I didn't say that. "What's our next move?"

"Technically, my next move should be reporting Old Jack is alive. But. . ." Eva frowned. "I should report his life to TCC, but it's unclear what that would mean for you, Jack."

"Don't kill him!" Ted said.

Wow. We were all on the same page.

"I'm not going to kill him," Eva said. "But, as an illegal clone..."

I didn't want to be an illegal clone. I didn't feel like a clone. I felt like me. I frowned. What a screwed-up situation. Unfair. I was starting to hate Old Jack.

"This shouldn't be our first priority, but could we get me some kind of fake identity?" I asked. We were in a whorehouse at a spaceport. There had to be all kinds of criminal activity around here. "We can go after Old Jack right after."

"With what money?" Eva said.

I grabbed my fon and shook it. "I have money!"

"Technically," Eva said, "Jack has money. You have nothing."

"So, don't report Jack alive," Ted said.

"I second that idea," I said. "Come on, Eva. Please. I thought we cared about each other." I gazed into her eyes, and I thought I saw something there, a connection between us.

She exhaled. "All right. I won't report him alive until we get you fixed up." She pointed at me. "But TCC already knows you're a clone, obviously. I'm taking a big chance here."

"I know, Eva, and I really appreciate it," I said. "Thank you."

"Yeah, thanks, Eva," Ted said.

"And all this must be related to the FTL drive," Eva said. "We have to figure out what's going on there."

"Yeah," Ted said. "I'm not a diplomat or anything, but if TCC figures out FTL drives, couldn't it destabilize this whole region of the galaxy?"

"Yes," Eva said grim-faced. "On the other hand, TCC wants the tech. It's one of their primary goals."

"I wish we'd had time to ask him if he killed Sam and shot at me on Alpha Catoblepas." I sighed. "It's all a big mess."

My stomach growled. I looked around for our comestibles. When I found them, they were the worse for wear. Old Jack must have eaten most of them. Jerk. "I'm still really hungry. Let's get something to eat."

"There's also the problem of Olivia," Eva said. "Presumably, she reported us for stealing the *Shakespeare*'s shuttle."

"That is a problem," Ted said.

"Yeah." I agreed. "What if the authorities confiscate the shuttle and figure out it has an unauthorized FTL drive?"

"That would be bad," Eva said. "Very bad."

I was too hungry to think straight. "Let's try to get some more food from Gigi."

Eva touched her stomach. "Yeah, I'm still really hungry, too." She nodded. "Go ahead. Try it." She held up her fon. "I need to check some local contacts."

Ted and I gathered up the dishes and went downstairs to the main floor of the brothel.

Gigi bustled up to us. "I don't know what you did to that other guy, but he ran off after meeting you."

Ted and I exchanged a look.

"Can we get some more Terran food?" I asked.

"Show me the money," she said.

I showed her.

"I'll bring it to your room when it's ready."

Later, after we'd finally eaten, Eva said she'd made an

appointment for me to get a new ID. So, the three of us crept through the seedy area of the spaceport to her contact.

We entered a very run-down bar.

"Are you sure this is the place?" I asked.

Eva nodded. "What, it's not fancy enough for you?"

The guy behind the counter said, "You Eva?" I wasn't familiar with his species. He was very short and squat, but besides that and his bright green color, he looked human. I debated asking him what species he was but decided it might label me species-ist.

She nodded and pointed. "Pay the man."

I paid him out of my rapidly dwindling funds.

Once he was satisfied the funds had been transferred, he gestured to the back. We followed him into the back room and then through a hidden door.

He pointed to a chair. "I need your fingerprints and retina print."

I glanced up at Eva. "Is that safe?"

She shrugged. "You must have accurate fingerprints and a retina print associated with your ID."

I turned back to the ID guy, who scanned my fingerprints and retina. Then, he got to work doing something on the computer.

It seemed like we had to wait a while. I got up and paced around.

The ID guy said, "Go to the bar and get a drink; you're making me nervous."

I felt all cooped up, so I agreed. "Come on, guys."

The three of us left, sat at a table and ordered drinks.

We'd just been served our beverages when a bunch of human men and women in uniforms burst into the bar. They had determined looks on their faces and weapons, which they pointed at us quite rudely.

"What now?" Ted muttered.

"Olivia strikes again?" I asked. Had we evaded station security only to get caught by some other security?

One of the uniformed men, a particularly fierce-looking one, said, "Put up your hands. You're under arrest!"

Chapter Thirty-Three

I was confused. Why were we under arrest?

The people in uniform had us surrounded in the bar--and they were people, homo sapiens, which was odd for Tau Ceto e. The few native turtle people in the bar didn't seem bothered by the influx of homo saps. They continued drinking, glancing over at all the hubbub occasionally.

I'd wasted no time in putting up my hands. I tend to do what people say when they point guns at me, especially after already getting shot once today.

I studied the insignia on said uniforms as the officers approached us. The uniforms did seem familiar, especially the insignia. It said, 'TCC.'

"Uh, guys," I said. "You know I am a TCC agent, right?" It probably wouldn't go well for me if they scanned me, whatever the reason for them being here.

Eva piped up. "Yes. All three of us are from the *Shakespeare*. I'm the special agent in charge. Can I get my ID out of my pocket?" I always knew Eva was special. I would have given her a big smile if things hadn't been so dire.

The TCC agents' stun guns wavered. They looked confused.

The fierce head guy said, "IDs can be faked." That was ironic, considering what was happening right now in the back room. I really hoped they weren't going to go into the back room. "I'm going to come closer and do a retina scan." Yikes. I was done for if they knew I was an illegal clone and scanned me. I tried to look unobtrusive and not handsome at all.

He stepped towards Eva. "Don't try anything funny."

She smiled. "Wouldn't dream of it. We're on a sanctioned

mission. Above your clearance, I'm guessing."

Wow. Eva was even better at lying than I was.

He scanned her eye and then scrutinized his fon. And then he looked super nervous. He wasn't as good-looking when he was nervous. "Ah. Sorry, ma'am. I'm very sorry." He put down his stun gun and twisted around to face the other agents. "Stand down, men. Olivia, a crewmember from the Shakespeare, reported that you'd stolen a shuttle craft and were on some kind of crime spree." They lowered their weapons.

He turned back to Eva. "We're very, very sorry, ma'am." Exactly how special was Eva?

"You can put your hands down," he added for the benefit of Ted and me.

Eva had already taken hers down.

Ted and I glanced at each other. Hopefully, this wasn't a trick, and they wouldn't shoot us if we put our hands down. Slowly, we both took our hands down.

I waited for the pain of an electromagnetic stun gun, but it didn't come.

"Yes, ah, Captain," Eva said, staring at something on his uniform. "I'm on a very special mission, and I need all of you to stand down." Yeah, a fake-ID special mission. "In fact, you need to leave here now."

"But..." The captain stepped next to Eva and said something in a very low voice. I couldn't hear, dammit.

Eva nodded and said something back to him in a low voice. Had she betrayed us?

The captain stepped away. "Come on, men." He ran back out of the bar, and his soldiers followed.

"Did you betray us?" I stepped to Eva. "*Et tu, Brute*?"

Ted joined me. "Yeah. *Et tu, Brute*?"

"Relax," she said. "I didn't betray you. If I wanted to betray you, why would we even be here?"

"Good point," I said.

"Where do you think Old Jack went?" Eva asked me.

"There is a good chance he'd be interested in our ship, the shuttle, considering it's got his FTL drive on it," I said. "He might not know that now, but if he gets on board..."

"What if TCC finds him?" Ted said.

I gulped. "They'd know he's not dead." That didn't bode well for me.

"Yes," she said. "We're in new territory. Usually, a clone of a person who's still alive would be totally illegal. The clone would be put to death immediately."

I sagged, and Ted caught me. Yay, Ted.

He was a good guy. He smiled at me.

She continued. "But, Old Jack deceived TCC and cost them a lot of money. They were very suspicious about what he'd been up to. We, the three of us," she pointed, "know he faked his death and stole an FTL drive and as soon as TCC figures that out..."

"We don't know for sure that he stole it," Ted said.

She gave him a dirty look. "He had an FTL drive. FTL drives are strictly regulated. He shouldn't have one. What are you saying? Someone gave one to him?"

"That does sound implausible," Ted said. Even I had to admit, I was charming but I wasn't charming enough for people to just give me FTL drives.

She continued. "Old Jack could cause an intragalactic incident. To say stealing an FTL drive is a felony would be putting it mildly."

I held up a finger. "Uh, didn't we steal an FTL drive?"

"It's not stealing if you take it from a criminal," Eva said. That didn't sound quite right.

Then, I thought about how he'd ambushed us at the brothel. And shot us. Old Jack was a villain. "*O villain, villain, smiling, damned villain!*"

"What do you think this Jack senior will do next?" Ted asked

I said, "He's looking for his FTL drive." It was weird totally understanding someone I'd only interacted with for a couple minutes. But, I felt like I did know him.

"Yes," Eva said. "I agree."

He wanted the drive and there was nothing stopping him from taking the drive. "Uh oh," I said. The DNA locks would let him right into the shuttle. "If he finds the shuttle, what's to stop him from taking the shuttle?"

Eva looked surprised for a second, and then she said,

"Crap."

Her fon pinged and she answered. "Eva here. Yes." She paused. "Okay, let me know." She hung up and stared at the two of us. "That was the guy that tried to arrest us; the shuttle's gone."

"Shit!" Ted said. "We're stuck here."

"*How now?*" I said. "*A rat!*"

The three of us stared at each other with glum expressions.

"Why didn't you finish your drinks?" the fake-ID guy, Mr. Green, had come out from the back. "Did I miss something?" Gee, a phalanx of TCC officers?

"You could say that," Ted said.

"No," Eva said. "You didn't miss anything important."

"Then, why so gloomy?" he asked.

"We're not here to chitchat. Are you done?" Eva asked.

"Yes." The guy held out an ID. "John Smith, welcome to your new ID."

"John?" I said. "I want to be Jack!"

"You do usually have to change your name when you get a fake-ID," Ted said.

"Relax, John." Eva quirked a smile. "Jack is a nickname for John."

"True." Ted nodded.

"I could always keep the ID," the ID-guy said. "And your money, of course. No refunds."

"No. I want it." I grabbed the ID, but I wasn't happy about it. Could he come up with a more boring name?

We grabbed our drinks and sat down at a table. "What now?" Ted asked.

Eva's fon rang again. "Eva here. Yes." She paused. "The TCC captain says they just got a positive ID on a fugitive. Jack Jones. He stole the ship in slip thirteen." She paused again.

That was our ship. "Damn," Ted said.

I took a sip of my drink. Tequila sunrise. It was pretty good, especially considering they didn't have our kind of tequila or our kind of sunrises here on Tau Ceto e.

"Yes, the galaxy is a big place," Eva said loudly into her fon. "Maybe." She stared at me and said softly, "Do we know where Old Jack, er, I mean Jack Jones might have gone in a stolen ship?"

I felt my mouth stretch into a smile. "Oh, we know. We know, all right." I knew where I'd go if I was him--and I was. Sort of. He'd be frustrated and disappointed with the shuttle's FTL drive as soon as he discovered it didn't work as he expected, i.e. no special skills.

"Where?" she asked softly.

"He's going to the *Shakespeare*," I said.

"The *Shakespeare*," she said into the fon. "I'm sure?" She raised an eyebrow at me.

I nodded adamantly. "One hundred percent."

She said into her fon, "I'm sure." She paused yet again. "Why's he going there?" she asked softly.

"Special skills," I said.

"Ah, long story," she said into the fon.

"Can we get a ride?" I asked.

"Actually, can we hitch a ride?" she asked into the fon. Then, she stared at me. "Why would you take us?"

"Because we know Jack," I said. "I can predict what he'll do."

She said into the fon, "Of course we'll be helpful. We've, ah, been studying Jones. We know every move he'll make almost before he does." She smiled. "Yes. I guarantee it." She hung up.

"Well, drink up, gents," she said. "We're headed back to the *Shakespeare*."

After we slammed our drinks and as we walked to the port, she said, "You better be right about all this, Jack."

"I am." If there was anything I knew in this whole big galaxy, it was myself.

The TCC ship, the *Assyrian*, made the *Shakespeare* look like a decrepit barge. It was small, sexy and very sleek; if it had been any smaller, I might have tried making love to it. It looked like it could zoom through intergalactic space and do Mach 20 in atmosphere.

As we approached the *Assyrian*, Ted whispered, "What am I missing? Isn't it bad if they find out who Jack, here, really is?"

"Yes," I said. "Instantaneous death seems like it would be bad." My voice squeaked a bit.

LESLEY L. SMITH

"Relax," Eva said. "You're John Smith." She stepped onto the gangway. "Permission to come aboard, ensign."

"Permission granted," the ensign at the door said.

"As long as they don't look closely at your ID, everything'll be fine," she said quietly.

We reached the door.

"IDs please," the ensign said.

Chapter Thirty-Four

Me and my two comrades-in-arms stood outside the main door of the *Assyrian*, our ticket out of here. I wished they were in my arms instead, and we were in bed.

"IDs?" the ensign asked again.

There was no help for it; the best offense was sexiness. "Have we met?" I smiled charmingly. "You look familiar."

He studied my face. "I must admit you look familiar as well." Hopefully, not from a *Most Wanted* bulletin.

I stepped closer and stared into his eyes as if I wanted to have sex with him.

"You don't need to see our IDs," Eva said.

He didn't break eye contact with me. "I don't need to see your IDs," the ensign said in a dreamy voice, still looking at me.

I leaned down and planted a juicy kiss right on his lips. Mmm.

When we separated, he was flushed. "Wow."

I smiled engagingly as we walked past him onto the ship.

Everything was small and sleek inside, too. The lack of murals made it all seem very businesslike, or maybe military. I bet the *Assyrian* could blow stuff up good.

"What was that with the ensign?" Ted asked with wonder in his voice.

I said, "*Love all, trust a few, do wrong to none.*"

"I don't think I fully appreciated your mojo until now," Eva said. Her fon chirped. "I'm borrowing some quarters. Here's the info. Meet me there." She pushed some buttons on her fon. "I want to go check out whoever's in charge." She turned to walk away but called back, "Try to keep a low profile."

Ted and I scrutinized our fons trying to figure out the way to our quarters.

"I think it's this way." He pointed left.

"I think it's this way." I pointed right. We both squinted and held up our fons. I shrugged. "Okay. Let's try left." We started walking. After a bit we both realized we were on the wrong level. The ship seemed bigger than it initially appeared. Or with its drab, dark-gray carpeting and slightly lighter gray walls it was just monotonous. We went down a level and tried again.

Somewhere in there while we were wandering around, the ship took off. I knew because there was an announcement, "Prepare for takeoff. Three. Two. One. Takeoff."

As we approached a junction in the hallways we heard a strident female voice. "I demand you let me out of here!" It sounded a lot like Olivia...

"She sounds familiar," Ted said.

She did sound familiar, Olivia-familiar. I held out my arm to stop him. I peeked my head around the corner. Sure enough, Olivia stood in the small brig, face red, fists clenched. "I didn't do anything!"

"Quiet down, Miss." It was the cute ensign from the exterior door.

I started backing away. "What are the odds?" I shook my head.

"Knowing us," Ted said, "I'd say pretty high."

I crept back down the hall and Ted followed. "We'll have to find another way to our quarters."

"What about *do wrong to none*?" he asked. "You just said it."

"What about it?" I knew exactly what he meant.

"We can't just leave her there," he said. "She didn't do anything except try to help us and we tricked her."

Dammit. He was right. Truth be told, I was peeved because I didn't understand why Olivia didn't like me. "Well, she did turn us in to station security and/or TCC." I didn't see how else they could've found us so quickly.

Ted frowned at me. His expression seemed to say, 'Do the right thing.'

"I know, I know! We should get her out." Although it was a little amusing that she ended up in the brig when she was trying to put us there. "We'll get her out. Give me a minute. We need some kind of plan."

"Oh, yeah," he said. "A plan would be good."

We leaned back against the wall, thinking.

"That ensign seemed to really like you," Ted said.

"Yeah?"

"Maybe you could use your charm to get Olivia out of the brig?"

I was pretty charming. "Not bad, Ted." I bumped my shoulder gently against his shoulder.

I stood up straight, squared my shoulders and marched into the security area.

When the ensign saw me, he seemed surprised.

When Olivia saw me, she seemed really surprised--if her screaming at the top of her lungs was any indication. "Oh, my God! It's the devil! Devil Jack!"

Ted was loitering near the door and I gestured with my head towards Olivia. He rushed over to her. "Shut up!" Their voices dropped so I couldn't hear what else they said.

"Hi, there, ensign," I said. "I didn't catch your name earlier."

"Hi. I'm, uh, Demetrius."

"Hi, Demetrius," I said. "I'm Jack, er, John, er, Jack." I was confused.

"Hey, what's your friend doing with the prisoner?" He pointed.

I stepped between him and the brig. "Nothing."

"I found out you guys are big spies, huh?" he said. "You're posted on the *Shakespeare*?"

"Yes." I stared into his eyes.

"What do you do?" he asked. "What's your cover? Are you, like, a dancer or actor or what?"

"I do it all." I paused to give him my bedroom eyes again. "But, probably my best skill is singing."

"Really?" Demetrius smiled. "I like singing. Sing me something. Oh, I know. Sing that three-little-maids-from-school song."

I felt my brow start to furrow, but smoothed it quickly. "From *The Mikado*?"

"Yeah." He nodded. "It's my favorite."

I glanced at Ted and Olivia. It could work. "I generally sing more manly roles, but I'd be happy to sing it for you, if you like. Especially if my colleagues Ted and Olivia helped out."

"I don't know," Demetrius said.

"Don't you want the full effect?" I said. "Plus, we're in outer space, what's gonna happen?" I gazed into his eyes some more. Without losing eye contact with Demetrius, I called over to Olivia and Ted, "You guys know *Three Little Maids from School* don't you?"

"Yes!" they said in unison.

Demetrius almost giggled. "I guess it would be okay." He grabbed something from the counter and walked over to the cell. He waved it in front of the door and it sprang open.

Olivia smiled and walked out of there. "Ah, did you say something about singing?" she asked.

"Yeah." Demetrius nodded. "Ooh, I should call the rest of the guys." He started punching buttons on his fon. "This mission has been b-o-r-i-n-g."

"Is that a good idea?" Ted asked.

Demetrius nodded. "Sure."

In what seemed like seconds, the room was full of people.

"Are you ready?" Demetrius asked.

"Ah ..." Ted said.

"Whatever," Olivia said.

What could I say? I liked to sing. "One, and a two, and a go."

I channeled my inner geisha. "*Three little maids from school are we...*"

All three of our voices rang out in perfect harmony.

"*Pert as a school-girl well can be. Filled to the brim with girlish glee.*"

Ted camped it up with an imaginary fan and I was having trouble not laughing.

I had to join him in his antics.

"*Three little maids from school. Everything is a source of fun...*"

We really got into it, dancing, and generally acting like Japanese schoolgirls. Everyone was laughing by the time we finished.

"*Three little maids from school!*"

240

There were even more people in the room at the end than when we began.

As we bowed demurely, we were met with thunderous applause. Ah. Earth really did have great culture. I was proud to be a Terran.

"Woo hoo!"

"All right!"

"Bravo!"

"That was great!"

Eventually, most of the crowd cleared out, until Ted, Olivia, Demetrius and I were almost the only ones left standing.

Almost.

Eva and that good-looking fierce TCC Captain we'd met in the bar were also left standing.

"I should have known you wouldn't be able to keep a low profile," Eva said.

Oops.

Eva and the captain brought Ted, Olivia and me to some meeting room.

"This is Captain Wu," Eva pointed at him. Uh oh. Was this safe? What was stopping Wu from throwing us all in the brig? "He's an old friend," she said.

"Wow," Captain Wu said. "That performance was really something." He chuckled. "I see why the *Shakespeare* has a galactic reputation as entertainers."

"I'm sorry," I said to Eva. "We got a little carried away." Our cover--such as it was--was blown.

"You know," Eva said, "Jack Senior would have never done that Mikado song. He would say it was beneath him. He's too macho."

I frowned. "Please don't compare me to him. He's an asshole." I glanced at the captain. Did he know who I was?

He was grinning. "I know who you are, Jack. But I can keep a secret."

My heart started pounding like someone who was about to be executed. "Are you going to throw me out the airlock?"

"No," Ted whispered and put his hand over my hand on the table.

Even Olivia looked a little disconcerted. Good.

"What?" Captain Wu said. "No. We need you to catch -- " he glanced at Eva" -- Jack Senior? Is that what we're calling him?"

She nodded.

"I'm confused," Olivia said.

She wasn't the only one. "You're not going to execute me?" I asked.

"I'm sorry I turned them in," Olivia said, hands up. "Stealing a ship isn't a capital offense, is it?"

"For the last time, I didn't steal the ship," I said. "I borrowed it. Gina knew I took it." Sort of. She could figure it out anyway. She didn't try very hard to get it back, and she could have.

"And Captain Gomez wouldn't order the execution of her own, ah," Ted glanced at me, "husband, would she?"

"Husband!" Olivia shrieked.

Good. I was glad to see I wasn't the only person whose voice gave out on them in times of stress.

"Jack, are you telling me Olivia still doesn't know?" Eva said.

I wracked my brain. I couldn't remember who knew what at this point. I sighed. "I don't know."

"Somebody tell me what's going on!" Olivia said, still shrieking a bit.

Eva said, "You have to swear to keep it quiet unless or until it becomes declassified." She had some steel in her.

"Okay." Olivia's expression said, 'What's the big deal?'

Captain Wu pointed at me. "This Jack Jones is a clone of the real Jack Jones, galaxy-famous singer and TCC officer."

Real? I wasn't real? That did not sound good.

"I still don't get it," Olivia said. "You don't, he doesn't, seem like an officer, or an old guy, for that matter."

"I lost my memories," I said. "Or, his memories. The memories. Most of the memories were deleted."

"Oh," Olivia said with a small voice. "Sorry."

Eva looked sad. She must be imagining what it would have been like if her clone had lost her memories.

"What happened?" Olivia asked.

"I'm not sure we have time to get into all that now," Eva said.

"No. We don't," Captain Wu said. "We've got to come up with a plan to catch this Jack Jones Senior, ASAP."

"Before he causes an intragalactic war," Eva added.

Gee, no pressure.

And once we caught Old Jack, what then?

They'd execute me?

Pressure!

Chapter Thirty-Five

In Captain Wu's small ready room off the bridge, he seemed to really want to capture Old Jack and bring him to justice. I could see that stopping an intragalactic war would be a big motivator. The agreements among the various species were balanced on a knife-edge, with each having its acknowledged areas of expertise. If homo sapiens figured out FTL drives they'd disrupt all of it. For one thing, FTL drives were the major export of Alpha Catoblepas; they were the only official distributors of the drives. And only the ACs knew who manufactured them.

But I was pretty sure Old Jack hadn't stolen the FTL drive to incite a war, or even to give it to the TCC—which he should have done, so they could reverse-engineer it.

I was pretty sure Old Jack had stolen the FTL drive for person gain of the special skills variety.

Whatever his motivation, Old Jack was an asshole who should be stopped... But what would happen to me once he was captured?

I sighed. I couldn't worry about that now. Lives were at stake.

I absolutely did know what he was up to. He was going back to the *Shakespeare* to steal their FTL drive. He wanted it because of his special skill. Our special skill. He could do anything with that defective FTL drive. So far, it had granted me any wish, it had instantiated the most improbable possibilities. "*A man can no more separate age and covetousness than he can part young limbs...*"

"What?" Ted asked. We were all still sitting around the captain's table.

I wasn't sure if Old Jack was planning on stranding the

Shakespeare in space when he took the drive. Was he that evil? (I could never do that.) If he did that, he'd be condemning the whole crew to die--unless we could get to them.

Eva nodded. She understood me.

"Yeah, what?" Captain Wu asked.

Olivia just looked worried.

"I know what Jack's up to," I said. "He's going to the *Shakespeare*."

"You already told us that," Captain Wu said. "Or you did through Eva. Why is he going there?"

"He's going to steal their FTL drive."

Olivia gasped. "That's dangerous! He could strand the ship in the middle of nowhere and kill everyone."

I nodded sadly.

"Doesn't he already have an FTL drive? Why would he need two?" Captain Wu looked upset. "Are you sure?"

I nodded. Eva nodded. Ted looked at me and then nodded. There was a lot of nodding going on.

"That's also top-secret, by the way." Wu stood up. "Just a minute." He talked into the comm system. "This is Captain Wu. We must determine the *Shakespeare*'s position, immediately." He listened for a few minutes. "All right. Keep a close eye on them. Set an intercept course."

"It's too bad we don't have instantaneous communication," Eva said.

I had to agree. Where was a nice ansible when you needed one?

He came back to the table and sat down. "They're approaching Geryon 180b."

"Good," I said. "They're still on mission."

"And they're close enough to the planet that they won't die if someone steals their FTL drive," Eva added.

That was a huge relief.

"Why is Jack, er, original Jack, doing all this?" Captain Wu asked.

I wasn't sure how much to tell them. "Can we keep this between the five of us? The FTL drive on the *Shakespeare* is malfunctioning somehow."

Olivia interrupted. "Yes. That's true. It's not acting right. And

245

it's not a secret." At my annoyed look she quieted.

"As I was saying, as a consequence of this malfunction," I said, "probabilities are malleable. Old Jack and I can take advantage of this malleability to manipulate reality."

"Say what now?" Wu's eyebrows had risen up his forehead.

"We can control reality," I said.

"Wow," Ted said. "That explains a lot."

"Seriously?" Wu said.

"Huh," Olivia said. "The FTL drives are rumored to work via quantum entanglement." She nodded. "It could make sense. Quantum field theory is based on wavefunctions of probability."

Eva interrupted. "It doesn't matter if you believe him, Wu. Old Jack believes it. He's going for the *Shakespeare*'s FTL drive."

"Well, I guess we'll find out when we get there," Wu said. "Jack got a head start, but our ship is much faster in normal space. Hopefully we can overtake him."

Hopefully.

Seven hours later found the *Assyrian* pulling up on the *Shakespeare* in orbit around Geryon 667 Cc. Surprisingly, I'd managed to sleep during the down time. It had been a long time, too long, since I slept. I felt much better, much more like myself. We were going to catch nefarious Old Jack.

Captain Wu had let me and my merry band onto the bridge and told us to stay out of the way. The bridge was exactly as sexy as you would expect, sleek, with all the latest tech and gadgets.

Eva, Ted, Olivia and I crowded around one of the exterior viewscreens.

Thus, we had a perfect unobstructed view of Jack's shuttle docking with the *Shakespeare*.

"Damn." I groaned.

"*Shakespeare*?" Wu said over the comms. "I thought I told you to halt that shuttle docking."

"We tried to stop him," the comm officer said. She sounded familiar; she must have been the one on duty when we, ah, borrowed the shuttle in the first place. "But he had all of Captain Jack Jones' security codes."

"They didn't change the codes?" I said.

"You didn't change the codes?" Wu asked over the comms.

"We thought he was dead!" the officer said. "TCC told us he was dead."

Ouch. I should have told them he was alive. What must Gina be thinking about all this?

"Where is he now?" Wu asked.

"Ah..." She paused.

"Where?" Wu asked again.

"We don't, ah, know," she said. "He disabled all the interior sensors." Ouch.

Gina, er, I mean Captain Gomez, and her whole security team met us at the airlock.

Captain Wu said, "What are you doing here?"

"Waiting for you," she said. "And Jack." She pointed at me.

All thirty armed security officers and superspies turned to stare at me.

A lesser man might have been nervous. A lesser man might have been intimidated. A lesser man might have been shaking in his boots.

Thankfully, I wasn't wearing boots. I smiled. "To the secret tunnels!" I threw my fist into the air and ran towards my cabin. "*Cry havoc and let slip the dogs of war!*"

The group followed. We sounded like thunder roaring as we ran down the corridor.

At my cabin door, I hesitated. The corridor looked like it always did. *The Tempest* mural was as beautiful as ever. Ariel was beautiful and powerful. She looked a little like Gina. It was disconcerting how everything looked the same on the ship when everything had changed. The last time I'd hung out here, they'd been investigating Sam's murder.

Eva stood at my elbow. "What's wrong?"

"We need to be careful. We never did resolve Sam's murder with the nanobots." I sought out Olivia's face in the crowd.

She blanched. She must have heard me. Darn.

"What, you're worried now? You think Old Jack might have left a nanobot trap in your cabin now?" Eva asked.

"Someone did before," I said.

Ted was right there next to me, too. "We can send an electromagnetic pulse in first," he said. "It'll disable any nanobots inside." He waved over one of the security guys.

Ted conferred with the guy. I was impressed. He was apparently a pretty good security officer. I had no idea. I'd just thought of him as a pretty face. And a good snuggler. And good at other, pre-snuggling activities. Shame on me.

The mystery security officer ran off.

Gina had elbowed her way through the crowd. "What's the hold-up?"

"We're gonna sweep the cabin with an EM pulse," I said. "In case of nanobots."

She jerked back. "Oh. Good idea." She must have forgotten about the nanobots.

Suddenly, her comms squawked. "..aptain Gomez! Help! Intruder...engineering!"

She turned to her security team. "To engineering! Double-time!"

They all thundered away.

As she ran off at the back of the crowd, I heard a scream through her comms.

Eva turned to me. "Do you still want to go into the tunnels?"

"Yeah," I said. "Even if he steals the FTL drive he has to get back to his ship. Crap." I turned to Wu. "We didn't leave his ship unguarded, did we?"

Wu said, "Of course not. I left some officers at his ship and our ship."

I had a brainstorm. "We should uninstall the FTL drive on the shuttle. It'll slow him down if he has to reinstall an FTL drive. And the *Shakespeare* needs it if Old Jack takes their drive."

"Good idea, kid," Wu said. He spoke into his comms. "Uninstall the FTL drive on the shuttle." I wondered if everyone knew how to uninstall an FTL drive.

But somebody on the other end of the comms quickly said, "Yes, sir." So, at least some people knew how to uninstall FTL drives.

"Don't worry," Captain Wu said, "there's no way he's getting off the *Shakespeare*."

And then the gravity turned off, and we all started floating.

"Dammit!" Wu said, trying to grab something on the wall.

Old Jack must still be in engineering. Did that mean he hadn't procured the FTL drive yet?

Duh. If he got away with the *Shakespeare*'s FTL drive, I was about to miss out on a huge opportunity to stop him. We needed to turn on the FTL drive. I needed to use my special skill.

At the end of the corridor, Ted's security officer friend was carrying something that looked a lot like a ray gun, but he, and it, floated up like the rest of us. The gangly stranger had a horsey face and buck teeth.

"Go help him," I said to Ted, pointing at the guy. He looked like he could use all the help he could get.

Ted sort of ran, sort of swam off towards his colleague.

"Olivia," I said. "Does the *Shakespeare*'s FTL drive always malfunction?"

She slowly nodded. "Yeah. Lately."

Into my comms, I said, "Gina, we need to turn on the FTL drive."

She answered. "Just a sec." Then, I heard, "Security, take engineering! Go! Go! Go!" Then, more quietly, she said, "What now?"

"We need to turn on the FTL drive," I said. The floating was starting to make me feel woozy or dizzy or something.

"There's a firefight right now in engineering," she said. In the background, I heard what sounded like pulse rifles. Old Jack was only one guy. How could he hold off so much firepower?

No gravity was kind of fun. Why didn't we do it more often? Focus, Jack.

"And, ah, anyway, we're too close to something. We're too close to Geryon 667 Cc," she said. "We can't enter FTL space so close to a planet, right?" She paused. "Right."

The pulse rifle blasts quieted. Over the comms, I heard someone yell, "He's gone!"

I giggled. Why? Old Jack escaping wasn't giggle-worthy.

Over comms, Gina giggled.

Eva giggled but then said, "Something's wrong."

"Old Jack must have messed with life support," I said, suppressing a giggle. "CO_2 must be building up." Then, I did snicker. "Gina, fix life support! Gina?"

LESLEY L. SMITH

She didn't answer me.

Chapter Thirty-Six

Me and my merry band floated outside my quarters on the *Shakespeare*. We couldn't seem to stop laughing.

Ted floated over and showed me a big ray gun. Hilarious.

Oh, wait. We were supposed to do something with the ray gun. I took it, cracked my door, and sprayed my cabin with EM radiation.

"Ha!" I said. "*Art thou Beldam*, er, *Bedlam*?"

Everyone thought that was hilarious.

I was very, very funny, but something was off...

I went into my cabin and didn't feel quite so hilarious. There must not be so much CO2. "Get in here!" I gestured to everyone in the hall. There was something helpful here... What was it?

Ted, his security friend Eva, and Olivia floated into my cabin. They sobered.

"I think something's wrong," Eva said. "Did you say something about CO2?"

Oxygen. I had a bottle of O2 in here. That's what I was looking for. "The CO2 scrubbers must be offline. Does anyone have the codes to restart them from here?" I found the O2. I grabbed it from my closet and cracked the valve. It hissed and the room filled with oxygen.

Olivia giggled as she floated up to me. "As part of the engineering team, my codes should work."

I pointed at the computer console on my desk.

She floated over to it. "Oh. I'm starting to feel more normal. There are emergency protocols." She typed. "Yeah. I got the CO2 scrubbers back online."

"Try the artificial gravity," Eva said.

Olivia typed some more.

In the meantime, I tried my fon. "Gina? Are you there? Are you all right?"

She didn't answer. I was getting a very bad feeling. Was she hurt? Dead?

"What should we do?" Ted asked.

"Can you get internal sensors back online?" I asked. We needed to see what was up with Gina. And we really needed to find Old Jack.

"Oh, yeah, maybe," Ted said. He and his security buddy put their heads together over their fons.

"I can't seem to get the gravity back on," Olivia said, still typing.

"It's not important," Eva said, elbowing her way past me. She pressed a spot on the wall, and a compartment popped open. A compartment full of weapons.

"What the hell?" I said. "How did that get there? And how did you know?"

Eva reached in and pulled out pulse guns. "I told you me and Jack went way back." She tried placing them down on the floor, but they floated away.

Apparently, there was a lot I didn't know about Eva--but I wanted to. "You'll have to tell me about it sometime."

She grinned. "If we live through this, I promise I will." She closed the panel and grabbed one of the guns from the air.

If we live?

"We got good news and bad news," Ted said.

"Uh, okay," I said. "Hit me."

Ted said, "We got the internal sensors back on."

"That sounds good," I said carefully.

"The bad news is there's no sign of this Jack guy," Ted's friend said. "Except, maybe..." He trailed off.

Old Jack must be in the tunnels.

I realized I hadn't officially met Ted's friend. Awkward. Especially since he was in my bed--or at least hovering over it. "Hi," I said, holding out my hand. "We haven't officially met. I'm Jack."

"Jack must be in the tunnels," Eva said.

The stranger said, "Wait. You're Jack? I thought we were looking for Jack. Ah. Yes, I'm getting your bio-sign here. No wonder. Why are we looking for you?"

"We're not actually looking for me," I said. "You're supposed to be looking for another me."

"What?" Ted's friend said.

"I'm on it. Later. It's a long story." Ted sighed. "Jack, this is Bertram." He pointed in Bertram's general direction.

"Hi." Bertram shook my hand. Not the most attractive man I'd ever met, he looked like he had an old soul to match his name.

"It's nice to meet you," I said, smiling handsomely.

"Uh, hi," he said, still holding my hand, trapped in my gaze.

"You're not a clone, are you?" I asked. See, I had learned something through all this; you never knew who might be a clone.

"A what now?" Bertram said.

"Never mind." Ted moved Bertram's hand out of mine.

"I still can't get the gravity," Olivia said.

Duh. We were still floating.

"Forget that for the moment," I said. "Can you tell if the FTL drive is still online?"

"I'll check," she said.

"Are we going after Jack or not?" Eva asked impatiently.

"Yes," I said.

Eva turned to the panel in front of the secret tunnels. Gosh, she knew about all my secret panels. I felt like giggling again but refrained.

"Olivia?" I asked. "The FTL drive?"

"Not sure yet," she said.

"What about the bio-scan for the other Jack?" Bertram asked.

"We'll scan as we move," Ted said, scooping two guns out of the air.

"Stay here, Olivia," I said, scooping my gun out of the air. "If the FTL drive isn't online, try to put it back."

"Okay," she said.

Eva dove into the tunnels. "Let's head for engineering."

"I'm right behind you." I followed right behind her. "*Cry havoc and let slip the dogs of war*!"

"You already said that," she said.

"Okay," I said. "*The fire-eyed maid of smoky war all hot and bleeding will we offer them!*"

She sighed.

Following closely behind her, I had a great view of her ass. It was a very nice ass. I resisted an impulse to reach out and caress it.

When I turned around, Ted was glaring at me as he and Bertram followed us. Yikes.

Swimming through the featureless tunnels, I flicked my fon. "How's it going, Olivia?"

"It's going," she said.

"Keep up the good work," I said. We zoomed along.

I flicked over to Gina. "Gina? Are you there? Gina?"

She didn't answer. We had issues, but I didn't want her to die or get hurt.

"Can you guys try to raise the other security forces?" I asked Ted and Bertram, twisting around to look behind me.

"I'll do it," Ted said.

"I'm still scanning for this Jack guy," Bertram said.

I sneezed. Our passage must be disturbing the dust in the rarely used tunnels. I sneezed again.

Ted pressed some keys and mumbled some stuff. I was impressed with his multitasking abilities. And his lack of sneezing.

I looked at Eva's fine ass as we kept moving.

Ted said, "Security has Old Jack cornered in engineering. Captain Wu and his people are there, too."

"What about Gina?" I asked. "Is she all right?"

Ted consulted his colleague and made a loud gulping noise. "She's down."

I twisted around again. "What does that mean? Is she dead?"

"They don't think so, but they can't get to her," Ted said. "They can't move. They're in Jack's line of fire."

"It sounds like Jack has them cornered," Eva said.

My blood was starting to boil. Old Jack was a real asshole. "Let's hurry." We picked up the pace.

A few minutes later, the four of us gathered outside the

secret hatch to engineering.

Eva whispered, "I'm going to take this panel off. Everyone draw your weapons. We're going to try to sneak up on Old Jack."

"I got it!" Olivia said loudly over the fon.

We all jumped. "Shh," I said. "What do you have?" I asked more quietly.

"The FTL drive is still online," she said.

My mind was racing. If I could manipulate reality before Old Jack knew what was happening, we could get him.

"Turn it on," I said.

"Wait a minute," Eva whispered. "We're very close to the planet."

"Do it," I said. "We don't have to go anywhere. Just get ready to go somewhere."

"Okay," Olivia said over the fon. "Here goes."

What should I wish for Old Jack? Drop his gun? Confess? No. To be on the safe side, it needed to be something improbable...

Eva turned back to the panel. "Now, be quiet," she whispered. "We're sneaking."

"What are you doing?" a voice boomed out, Noah's voice.

We all jumped.

"Shit!" I said.

Eva turned and shot him in one fluid motion. Wow.

Noah sort of crumpled and floated away.

"That was harsh," Ted said.

"Who was that guy?" Bertram asked.

"Noah," I said.

"I just stunned him," Eva said. "What the hell was he doing here? I don't trust him."

I shrugged. You couldn't argue with success.

Eva reached for the panel yet again. "Now, all of you, shut the hell up," she whispered.

Olivia whispered, "The drive is on."

"Hurray," I whispered. "Good job."

Eva took off the panel, and we floated into engineering. The main lights were off, but all the equipment still showed off its blinking green lights. We passed one panel of red lights. Artificial gravity?

We slowly and stealthily snuck up behind Old Jack; he didn't see us coming. Instead, he peered out the doorway, holding his gun up. He still looked like he could be Noah's brother; he was a big bear of a man with too-long gray hair and a barrel chest.

Eva charged ahead to him.

Was the FTL drive running? I needed to know if my special skill was working. I grabbed Ted and kissed him.

He obliged. I didn't feel anything. We separated.

I whispered, "Old Jack is paralyzed. He can't move his arms or legs until I say so."

At my whispering, his head turned, and he gave us a weird expression and then looked down at his hand, which didn't move. "What did you do to me?" he asked.

My merry band all swiveled and looked at me.

I grinned. "*The arms are fair, when the intent of bearing them is just.*"

Eva sighed and then turned to Ted. "You might as well call in security."

"And get a doctor for Gina and any other injured," I said.

Ted talked into his fon.

"You're such an asshole," Old Jack said as we all floated right by, ignoring him.

Into my fon, I said, "Turn off the FTL drive, Olivia. Try again to fix gravity."

"Yes, sir," she said.

Wow. Had I ever been sirred before? It felt good.

Ted patted me on the back. "Nice job, Jack."

Eva peeked out the door. "Yeah, not bad, kid," she said.

"Wow," Bertram said. "You're kind of awesome, Jack."

Had I ever been awesomed before? It felt really good. "Yeah, I am," I said. "Thanks."

"What the fuck did you do to me?" Old Jack said. "Release me!" He tried to shake loose but didn't move much.

Security forces started streaming into engineering. They surrounded Old Jack.

Ted's boss, the head security guy, approached us. "What's wrong with him?"

I grinned. "I guess he's paralyzed with guilt." I wanted to keep my special skill secret, if possible.

A JACK BY ANY OTHER NAME

Old Jack tried moving some more. Unsuccessfully. "Fuck you, Jack! Fuck all of you!" His attempts to break free were making him float up and down like a yo-yo. Up. Down. Up. Down.

The security guys surrounding him pointed and laughed.

Eva scooped up his gun and fon.

My work here was done. "*Our revels now are ended.*" I bowed elegantly.

Gina's number two, Carter, approached us, frowning. I guess he was number one with Gina out of commission. "We need to have a conversation," he said. "Now." No doubt it would be a conversation about my illegal clone status and impending execution.

I gulped.

Chapter Thirty-Seven

We were all in the hall outside engineering. Everyone watched soberly as Dr. Sharma came to help Gina. She floated near the corridor floor like a rag doll or a sad old piece of trash; it broke my heart. He leaned over her, taking her pulse. "She's alive, barely." She looked so vulnerable lying there near the ground.

There were other injured folks. A few dark-red globules of blood floated in the air. Ick.

A big crowd of security forces milled in the hallway or kneeled over the injured. It was a little jarring to see all the uniformed, armed men and women in front of the mural of the ghost spirit of the late King Hamlet. I really hoped the ghost wasn't an omen. (And why was a mural of a ghost outside engineering?)

Captain Wu approached. "Nice job securing the suspect, Jack, Eva, ah, other people." He clearly didn't remember or know Ted's and Bertram's names.

"Thanks," I said. But looking at the injured, it didn't seem like a nice job.

"I'm going to go check on my crew," Wu said and departed.

A bunch of medical personnel appeared and started ministering to the other wounded. Old Jack had managed to shoot a lot of people in a short amount of time.

I stepped toward Gina.

"Gina?" Dr. Sharma said and shook her gently.

She didn't answer.

Dr. Sharma frowned. "Non-responsive."

He turned to look at me. "What happened to her?"

"Are you looking at me?" I said. "Why are you looking at me?"

One of the security guys stepped up. "She was first on the scene. She went in to talk to the suspect. For some reason, she thought she could calm or deal with him."

I knew the reason. The suspect was her husband. The suspect might well be the love of her life. I exhaled. That was harsh, being attacked by the love of your life.

"So, what happened?" Dr. Sharma asked him.

"We didn't, ah, see the actual assault," the security guy said.

Ugh. Assault? Poor Gina. If--or I mean, when--she made it through this, I would give her a huge hug. Not all Jacks were evil.

Dr. Sharma pointed at the gurney he'd brought with him. "Help me get her back to med bay."

Everyone jumped up to help.

Almost under his breath, he said to me, "It's unlikely she's going to make it. Prepare yourself." His group took Gina to the med bay.

I watched them walk away. Oh no. Poor Gina.

"I'm still working on gravity," Olivia said over my fon. I had a thought.

"Actually, Olivia, turn the FTL drive back on," I said.

"What?"

"Just do it." If it was unlikely Gina would survive, I could change the probabilities and make it likely.

"Okay," Olivia said. "I got it. It's on."

"Gina fully recovers," I whispered. "Immediately."

"What?" Olivia said.

I ignored her for a moment, concentrating and focusing. "Gina's better. It's a miracle." After I'd concentrated for several moments, I said more loudly, "Okay, turn it off again, Olivia."

"Okay," she said.

Suddenly, Eva was standing next to me. "What are you up to, Jack?"

Carter was there, too. He dragged me and my merry band (currently Eva and Ted) to the Captain's ready room. The ready room was a small meeting room near the bridge, containing a table and a bunch of chairs. It had rose-pink walls and several vases of fresh-looking flowers. Were they real? They must have been bolted down somehow to avoid floating away. I floated towards them to investigate. Somehow, I doubted the room looked this nice when I was captain. The flowers smelled real. I reached out to touch them. They felt real.

Carter cleared his throat. When I looked at him, he pointed toward the table.

I floated in that direction. It was kind of ballsy of Carter to bring us here since he wasn't technically the captain, but maybe sleeping with the captain lets you do stuff like that?

If I was captain and we were sleeping together, I'd probably let him use my ready room.

"What is that look you're giving me?" he asked me.

We were all sort of floating around the table.

I shrugged. "You're welcome?"

"Huh?" he said.

"We did save the day." I glanced around at my cohorts. Let the accolades begin. We deserved them. I smiled. Ted smiled back at me.

"Huh?" Carter said.

Eva sighed.

"What the hell is going on around here?" Carter demanded, glaring.

We all fell on the floor. Ow.

On my fon, Olivia said, "Jack, I got the artificial gravity!"

I flicked my fon. "Nice job, O." Carter was still glaring at me. "Uh, maybe you should report to your boss in engineering."

"Roger that," she said.

"Since when do you order my crew around?" Carter said as we all picked ourselves up off the floor.

Eva and I exchanged glances as we sat in the chairs around the table. "Well, technically, they used to be Jack's crew, and he did hire a bunch of them," she said.

I pointed at him. "You know I'm a clone, right?" I was having trouble remembering who knew my secret. Of course, maybe at this point, it wasn't a secret anymore.

Carter's face was turning red. He was breathing hard. Finally, he said, "Good." He reached for me. "So no one will care when I kill you." He held his hands out and reached for my throat.

I scooted my chair back. "Whoa, there. You don't seem very grateful that we saved the day."

A JACK BY ANY OTHER NAME

My merry band and I were all still armed, and Ted had unholstered his gun. "Maybe we should all calm down. I'd hate to have to shoot the acting captain," he said.

I smiled at Ted. He was such a good guy. I loved that he always had my back.

Carter turned and reached for Ted's throat.

Ted scooted back.

"Everyone calm down," Eva said. "Carter just wants to know what's going on. You can't blame him, can you?"

She was very reasonable. And beautiful. *"Beauty itself doth of itself persuade, the eyes of men without an orator."*

Eva flashed me a smile and then turned to Carter. "Thanks," she said. "But I can orate for myself. As you know, Jack here was murdered. So TCC cloned and put him on the ship undercover to find his murderer. This is top secret, by the way."

"Captain Nillion?" Carter's fon said.

He jerked back in his chair and flicked his fon. "Captain? Oh no. Is Gina dead?"

"No. Sorry sir," the voice on the fon said. "She's been successfully transferred to sick bay. Dr. Sharma says she's made a full recovery. He says it's a miracle."

Phew. My special skill worked.

"Thank God." Carter relaxed. "So, she'll be okay?"

Eva stared at me, considering.

I smiled at her.

"Yes, sir," the voice said. "I should have said Acting Captain Nillion."

"Yes, you should have," Carter said. "What did you want?"

"Just to tell you, Captain Gomez is going to be okay."

"All right," Carter said. He visibly relaxed. "Thanks. I'll stop by to see her in a little while." Aw. He loved Gina. That was nice.

He turned his attention from his fon and back to the folks seated around the table. "You were saying?"

Eva nodded at me.

"Yes," I said. "I was investigating my murder. And--"

"So, who murdered you?" Carter asked.

"I didn't actually figure that out," I said. Come to think of it, that was a little embarrassing.

"But..." Ted said. "If that other you took the ship hostage,

261

he's not really dead, is he?"

I pointed at him. "Right. The original me isn't dead. We did figure that out. So, there was no murderer!" A little less embarrassing.

Ted's fon said, "We've secured the prisoner. He's in the brig. This is Bertram."

Ted said, "The prisoner's in the brig. Who's the prisoner again?"

Carter frowned.

"The prisoner is the original me," I said.

"What about Noah?" Eva asked.

I pointed at her. "Oh, yeah." I turned to Carter. "You need to secure Noah. We left him unconscious in the tunnel outside engineering."

"What! Noah Anderson?" Carter said, jerking back.

We nodded.

Carter already was flicking his fon. "Security, come in."

"Yes, sir," someone in security said.

"There's another suspect in the access tunnel right outside engineering." He glanced at me, and I nodded. "Unconscious. He needs to be taken into custody immediately."

"Yes, sir," the guy on the fon said.

"Where were we?" Carter asked us. "Oh, right, you're telling me what the hell's going on around here."

"Uh," I said. I had lost track of what we'd said so far.

"We were investigating the original Jack's murder," Eva said. "And we found out he wasn't dead."

"Right!" I said. "*He wasn't dead but he was up to no good. And therefore think him as a serpent's egg, which, hatch'd, would as his kind grow mischievous, and kill him in the shell.*"

Eva sighed.

"So, wait," Ted said. "Doesn't that quote say you're the serpent's egg?"

"Uh," I said.

My fon dinged. Yay. Saved by the fon. "Jack?" It was my old friend-slash-boss Daniel from the cargo bay.

"Daniel, old buddy," I said. "Long time no see."

He grunted. "Since I'm your boss, Jack, that is not a good thing. But that's not why I'm calling." He paused. "You need to get down here to the cargo bay ASAP," he whispered.

"Everyone, turn off your damn fons!" Carter said. He made a big show of turning his off. Everyone else followed suit.

"Gotta go," I said to Daniel and turned off my fon.

"As acting captain, I demand to know what has been happening on my ship!" Carter said. "Why did the original Jack fake his death? Why did he come back here? Why did he hurt Gina?"

I couldn't remember who knew what at this point.

Ted said, "I'm not totally sure." So, Ted didn't know everything. Check.

Eva and I frowned at each other. She nodded at me. Did Eva know everything?

"So," I said. "I was working in the cargo bay and found a secret FTL drive."

"What!" Carter said.

"And it had my fingerprints all over it," I said.

"But let me guess," Carter said. "You didn't touch it."

I nodded. "So, it turns out the *Shakespeare*'s FTL drive has been malfunctioning."

Now it was Carter's turn to nod. "I know that."

Eva and I frowned at each other again. She nodded at me again.

I took a deep breath. "This is super top-secret, need-to-know. Me and Old Jack seem to have a special ability to control reality utilizing the improbabilities leaking out of the *Shakespeare*'s FTL drive."

"Huh?" Carter said.

"We'll try to explain later," Eva said.

"Old Jack wanted to have this ability at his disposal, so somehow, he obtained his own FTL drive," I said.

"It makes him very powerful," Eva said.

Ted just stared at me.

"He may have thought his special skill would work with any FTL drive, but I don't think it does," I continued. "It turns out he has to have the *Shakespeare*'s FTL drive." I resisted mentioning the serpent's egg again--even though it was totally relevant. Old Jack was a serpent if I'd ever met one.

Carter was shaking his head like he couldn't believe it.

Someone pounded on the closed ready room door. We all jumped.

Carter got up and opened the door.

A security guy stood there, panting. "Captain Nillion, we can't find that Noah guy. He wasn't in the tunnels where you said."

"Why didn't you call?" Carter said.

"We did call," the security guy said. "A bunch of times."

Carter pulled out his fon and grimaced at what he found there.

"We do think Noah was working with Old Jack," Eva said.

"We have to find him!" I said.

Chapter Thirty-Eight

Still, in the ready room, Carter pointed at Ted. "You're security?"

He nodded.

"Report to your supervisor immediately. And don't repeat anything you've heard here today to anyone or anything else about all this."

Ted left. I trusted him to keep my secrets.

"What do you want me to do?" I asked.

Carter frowned.

Eva piped up. "I can keep an eye on Jack."

"Okay." Carter rushed out, leaving Eva and me alone.

"And by keep an eye on me, you mean let me help you search the tunnels so we can find him and save the day?" I asked.

She smiled. "Okay."

"Do you not think I can save the day?"

She opened her eyes wide. "Did I say that?"

"No." I was sensing her negative vibe and didn't like it. "I think we should start in my cabin. Noah was staying there for a while. Even if he's not there, he might have left a clue."

She smiled again. "Okay. *Lead on, Macduff.*"

"I think you mean, *Lay on, Macduff, and damned be him who first cries 'Hold! Enough!'*" I said.

"Do I?"

Now it was my turn to smile. "Yes."

We were on the hunt for my former best friend, Noah. Er, that wasn't quite right. The former me's best friend, Noah.

We made it back to my cabin without incident. We made it inside my cabin without incident. We searched my cabin without incident.

I sank into the bunk. "Damn. I thought there might be something here."

Eva sat down next to me. "Me, too."

My fon pinged.

"Who keeps calling you?" she asked.

I checked the messages, and Daniel had called several times. "What is up with him?"

"There's one way to find out," she said.

I called Daniel.

"Jack! Finally! I've been calling and calling. Why haven't you picked up?"

"I've been busy," I said. "What's up?"

"That guy Noah was here."

I jumped off my bunk. "What!"

"Noah was here, hiding in the cargo bay."

"Why didn't you tell me before?" I asked.

"What?" Eva asked.

"Noah was in the cargo bay," I said quietly to her.

"What!" she said.

"Is he still there?" I asked Daniel. "Keep him there."

"He left," Daniel said.

"He left," I said quietly to Eva.

"Well, where did he go? Did he say?" Eva said.

"He said something about saving his best friend if that means anything to you," Daniel said.

"It does. Thanks, Daniel." I hung up. "Noah's going after Old Jack."

"How do you know?" she asked.

"Daniel said so."

"Well, come on!" I ran for the door and headed to the brig. Eva ran after me.

I flicked my fon on and called Ted. "Where are you?" It was a little tricky running and manipulating my fon simultaneously.

"I'm working at the brig," he said and sighed.

"Noah's coming for Old Jack. Keep your eyes open. Get reinforcements."

"Roger that. I better go!" He got off his fon.

We ran and ran. The ship seemed surprisingly large when you wanted to get somewhere fast. I paused.

Eva said, "Come on, we're almost there."

I made myself start running again, and we soon reached the brig. It was full of security personnel.

Old Jack was in a cell.

Eva and I elbowed our way through the crowd to Ted.

He waved his hands around. "I got reinforcements, as you said. But nothing's happening. It's a little embarrassing."

"Huh." The three of us turned and stared through the crowd at Old Jack.

"Maybe Noah's just not here yet?" Eva said. "We did run over here pretty fast."

"Maybe. What's he been up to?" I asked.

"It's a little embarrassing." Ted scowled. "He keeps playing with himself. It's like he's obsessed or something. Did you say he was you?" He frowned. "Oh, jeez. There he goes again." He pointed at the cell.

The security guys mostly flinched and turned away, giving us a clear view of Old Jack. Sure enough, his hands were in his pants, and he was doing something. Honestly, I did not want to know what that something was.

"It's weird, though," Ted continued. "When he gets himself, ah, excited, he stops."

"That is weird," Eva said, looking at me like she didn't think it was weird at all. Obviously, she'd put it together as I had. Old Jack was trying to see if his special skill was active, i.e., if the FTL drive was on, i.e., if he could master improbabilities.

"You don't masturbate this much, do you?" Ted asked me.

Eva snorted. "When would he have time?"

I thought about saying something like masturbation was normal and perfectly healthy. "I think we're getting off track," I said instead.

And then the lights went off.

In the dark, I heard a lot of 'Hey!' and 'Watch it!' and 'What was that?'

"The power's out," Ted said.

"Really?" I said drily.

"I mean, the power's out is a bad thing. The cell locks are electromagnetic," he said. "He may be able to escape."

"Check the cell!" I said, turning my fon light in that direction.

Following my lead, a bunch of fons lit up the room.

"It's empty!" someone yelled.

Sure enough, the brig held a big bunch of nothing. "Damn."

"He can't have gotten far. We might be able to catch him," I said to Eva and ran for the hall.

"I'm right after you," she said, running right after me.

In the hall, the lights flickered back on.

"At least someone's on the ball--getting the lights back on," Eva said, stopping next to me.

The long corridor stretched out in front of us; it was the only way he could have gone. There was no sign of Old Jack.

"Where'd he go?" she asked. "He didn't have that big of a head start on us."

The rehearsal space door near us was open. "Look." I pointed at it. "I don't think that door was open before. He must have gone in here."

She nodded, and we both ran through the door. "Why come in here?"

My brain raced. "I think there's a tunnel opening backstage."

We both ran that way. The stage still contained the *Much Ado About Nothing* set. The fake Italian villa and grounds were pretty.

At the back of the stage, a big bear of a man was pressing on a section of the wall.

"Stop, knave!" I yelled.

I happened to be standing right near a cache of swords. I grabbed a pointy one and approached Old Jack. "I said, stop!"

He turned around and stared at me.

I pointed the sword at him. "*En garde*, knave!" I lunged.

His mouth fell open.

I waved the tip of the sword around dramatically as I appeled. "*Thou shouldst not have been old till thou hadst been wise.*"

He grimaced. "*How sharper than a serpent's tooth it is to have a thankless child.*"

Was I his child? My sword tip dipped. How odd. I sort of was his child. I hadn't thought of it that way before.

Then Old Jack frowned. "Isn't that a prop sword, kid?" He shook his head, turning back to the wall. "Idiot."

A JACK BY ANY OTHER NAME

"Your gun, Jack!" Eva ran up next to me. Her gun was drawn. Oh, right, we had guns. I dropped the sword and unholstered my weapon.

"Stop," I said. We had him now. I was a little disappointed we weren't going to have a sword fight.

But a section of the wall popped open, seemingly by itself. Then Noah stuck his head out. "What's taking you so long?" He saw Eva and me pointing guns his way and ducked back into the tunnel. "Come on, Jack!"

Old Jack started climbing into the tunnel. "Why didn't you turn on the FTL drive?"

I stared at him, feeling the heavy weight of the gun in my hand. I should shoot him. Somehow, shooting a running-away unarmed man seemed different than shooting at inanimate targets.

Inside the tunnel, Noah said, "I couldn't get to the FTL drive. I turned off the power. And it worked, didn't it? You escaped."

Eva gave me a dirty look for a split second and pointed her gun more pointedly at Old Jack. "Stop, Jack, or I will shoot."

He froze for a second, looking out at her.

She said, "Confess. You stole the FTL drive and data, didn't you? Did you shoot at poor Jack on Alpha Catoblepas? You were skulking on Tau Ceto e?"

"It sounds like I don't need to confess." His hands were up, but he didn't look scared. "You already know everything."

"Knave! You risked a war! And you killed Sam!" I said. "And you blew up Sophia's apartment!"

"No, wait," Old Jack said. "I didn't do all that." He turned to look at Noah. "Did you do that?"

I couldn't hear what Noah said.

Eva turned and looked at me. She looked very sad for some reason. And then she abruptly shot Old Jack.

He made a sound like 'Oof' and crumpled onto the floor, gushing blood.

She darted into the tunnel and shot her gun again. I heard a thump as a large something fell onto the metal floor.

She poked her head out. "I got Noah, too." She didn't use her stun gun. Why not?

Frankly, Eva was a little scary. "Ah, good?" I said. Frankly,

Eva was a lot scary. "Remind me not to get on your bad side," I said.

She grinned a little. Yikes.

Blood was geysering out of Old Jack like Old Faithful back on Earth. I whispered, "*And either victory, or else a grave,*" as I knelt and put pressure on the wound. "Don't just stand there," I said, "call for medical help."

She shrugged and pulled out her fon.

Old Jack didn't die. Quite. He came really, really close, but what can I say? Modern medicine is really good. It also helps when you have a blood donor with an exact blood match. Suffice it to say, I spent a lot of time over the next few days in the med bay.

Everybody said I was crazy and should have just let him die. It would have simplified my legal status, for sure. But letting someone die when I could help them didn't seem right.

Eva only winged Noah, so he wasn't in mortal danger.

On the plus side, Gina was very nice to me.

When she saw Old Jack in the bed next to me, she said, "Will he make it?"

"Yeah." I smiled at her. I was so relieved she'd recovered.

"Too bad," she said, grimacing.

"I'm sorry he hurt you," I said. "That must have hurt."

She just looked at me.

"I mean, it must have hurt emotionally," I said. I remembered that I owed her a hug. I leaned over her and wrapped her in my arms. "I'm glad you're okay. We, the whole crew, need you. I need you." I felt my eyes fill. How could her husband hurt her like that? Eventually, I let her go.

She seemed to be blinking back tears as she tried to get up.

Dr. Sharma swooped over. "Not so fast, Captain. It wasn't so long ago you were lying in one of my beds. Please sit down and let me check you out."

Later, me and Gina and Carter, Ted and Eva were sitting around that table in the captain's ready room.

Gina cleared her throat decisively. "So, there's the little matter of your legal status."

"It wouldn't even be an issue if the original had died." But Eva shut up as we all turned to stare at her. "I was trying to help you, Jack. Trying to save you." She seemed sincere. Of course, she was still armed, so I had to believe her. Had she always been such a badass, and I just didn't notice?

"What are my options?" I asked, my voice squeaking a little bit. Surely, they wouldn't execute me after I helped save the day. Multiple times.

Surely.

"You know we averted a galactic war," I said.

"Speaking of averting war," Eva said, "what's going to happen to the extra FTL drive? If it's discovered we have it, there could still be trouble."

Carter frowned and rubbed his chin. "Well, it should go back to Earth so the tech guys can reverse-engineer it."

"It should," Gina said. She paused. Everyone followed her lead and was silent for a moment. Both Gina and Eva were tougher than all of us men put together.

"What?" I asked. "What are you thinking?"

"I'm thinking we should keep it," Gina said, "just in case." She had a sly smile.

Carter was nodding, hair flopping about.

Eva said, "I like that idea. But it only works if we keep it quiet."

"Yes." Gina looked at each of us in turn, steel in her eyes. "Can we keep it quiet?"

"Yes." We were all in agreement.

"So back to execution, you can't execute Jack," Ted said earnestly. Yay, Ted.

"Well, Noah and Jack are going to prison back on Earth," Gina said. "Captain Wu's taking them on the *Assyrian*. Wu's pretty confident he can get to the bottom of Sam's murder, too. He'll take Sam's body back to Earth. And he can hush up whatever happened at the spaceport on Tau Ceto e."

"Good," I said. "And Sophia's apartment bombing?"

"Yes, yes," Gina said. "All of that. He can get all the details. He's TCC's best interrogator."

I didn't even want to know what that might entail.

Eva said, "Of course, they're going to clone Sam, so if worst comes to worst, they can just ask him when he wakes up."

That did make things simpler. "If he knows."

"He might not know," Gina said. "Anyway..."

"TCC is embarrassed that they cloned someone who wasn't dead," Carter said. "They're trying to keep the whole thing quiet."

"Yeah," Eva said. "That's not allowed. At all."

"I can keep quiet," Ted said. "Especially since talking might get Jack executed. And I think everyone else here can, too, right?"

Everyone nodded. I carefully scrutinized their faces. I thought I could trust them.

I said, "In that case, is there any chance I could just be the official Jack Jones?"

Gina smiled. "We were hoping you'd say that." She had a beautiful, powerful smile.

"Yes," Carter said. "I think TCC would go for that."

Did that mean I was off the hook? I wouldn't be executed? "Yay?"

"Yay!" Ted said.

Everyone smiled.

"So, what happens to the original Jack?" Eva asked.

"He becomes someone else," Gina said. "We can't have two versions of the same person."

"What? He gets a different identity and name?" I asked.

"Yes." Gina nodded. "What do you think it should be?"

"Jackass," Eva blurted out.

"Jack-off," Carter said and snickered.

"John Smith," Ted said.

I looked around the table. "Taking away his name just seems cruel. I thought most of you guys were close friends with him."

Gina frowned. "That's probably why we feel so betrayed."

"He can be Jack Jones," I said. "Just not the TCC officer and excellent singer Jack Jones. That's me."

Gina nodded. "That can be arranged."

Ted clapped a little. When we all turned to look at him, he quit.

"So, Jack, you should download your missing memories before Old Jack leaves for Earth," Eva said.

"No!" I said. "God, no. The last thing I want is that guy's memories." Memories make us who we are.

My memories made me me. And I liked being me.

Gina smiled. "That can be arranged, too."

"In that case, maybe you should stay undercover as Jack Jones Junior," Carter said. "I'm not sure people would believe you were the original if you don't have his memories." He held up his hands. "But still perfectly legal."

"If you think that's best," I said. "I'm Jack Jones undercover as Jack Jones Junior." Could be fun. Strike that. I'd make sure it was fun.

I looked around the table at my friends: Eva, Ted, Gina and Carter. We'd already made some fun memories.

And I had a feeling we'd make even more good memories together.

"So..." Carter said.

"So, what?" I asked. "I can stay on the *Shakespeare*? And I'm all legal and everything?"

"Yes," Carter said. "We'd like you to stay on."

I practically melted with relief. "Yes! *The noblest Roman of them all*!"

"We'd also like to promote you to Lieutenant Junior Grade," Gina said. "We need someone with your, ah, special skills." She grinned.

They wanted me to fly around the universe, sing, and use my special skills? Yay!

But I just smiled and said, "I think that can be arranged."

Science Fact: The Speed of Light

There are a surprising number of terms to describe light. Light, also known as visible light, is made up of a whole spectrum of other colors of light: red, orange, yellow, green, blue, indigo, and violet. Rainbows and splitting a beam of light with a prism illustrate this. The different colors of light correspond to different wavelengths: red light has the longest wavelengths (and least energy) while violet has the shorted wavelengths (and highest energy).

Let's take a step back and talk about charged particles. A charged particle is a particle with a positive or negative electric charge. If you've ever seen a bolt of lightning or gotten shocked as your feet shuffled across carpet, you're familiar with charged particles. The flow of electrical charge (called current) creates electricity. If you're reading this right now on a screen, you're using electricity.

An electric current produces a magnetic field, and conversely, a changing magnetic field produces an electric current. It turns out that electricity and magnetism are two sides of the same coin. This relationship or 'coin' is called electromagnetism.

Thus whenever charged particles are accelerated, electromagnetic waves are produced. Another term for electromagnetic waves is electromagnetic radiation. Visible light is actually a subset of electromagnetic radiation or energy. Other subsets of electromagnetic radiation include radio waves (less energetic), microwaves, infrared light, ultraviolet light, and X-rays (more energetic). So, light is electromagnetic radiation. Light is also, thus, energy.

A JACK BY ANY OTHER NAME

In the early twentieth century, famous physicist Albert Einstein realized that these electromagnetic waves could be subdivided into small pieces or particles he called quanta. This is an important point: light itself is quantized. Quanta of electromagnetic waves are called photons, and they are massless. So, light is also photons.

The speed of one of these massless photons through the vacuum of outer space is officially called 'the speed of light' and is very accurately measured to be 671 million miles per hour. (Now, that's fast!) In Einstein's theory of special relativity, the speed of light is the maximum speed possible in the universe. This is worth repeating: the speed of light is the maximum speed at which all matter and information can travel. It is impossible to travel at a speed greater than this. I'm not saying we don't have the technology to exceed the speed of light; I'm saying no one will ever have the technology to exceed the speed of light.

Since the observable universe is 91 billion light-years in diameter, the speed of light is bad news for explorers. For example, it would take 91 billion years for a photon to travel from one end of the observable universe to the other. Another example, the closest star to earth (besides the sun) is Alpha Centauri at 4.367 light years, so it would take 4.367 years for a photon to get there. Due to nonzero mass, it would take a person in a spaceship considerably longer.

Since the universe is so big, this speed of light limitation is pretty bad news for science fiction. To avoid this problem, science fiction authors employ their imaginations. A common faster-than-light (FTL) scheme is to leave regular space-time and enter some special FTL space, called jump space, hyperspace, warp space or similar. This idea is loosely based on the idea of wormholes which could theoretically create a shortcut between distant points in spacetime. While general relativity does allow the existence of wormholes, accepted physics does not allow matter or information to traverse such wormholes. Furthermore, the idea of a space outside, or different from, space-time is problematic. Space-time encompasses all space and time that exists, so how could space exist outside this?

The second main way authors try to avoid the speed of light limitation is with quantum mechanics, or more precisely, quantum entanglement. Quantum entanglement is a physical phenomenon in which pairs or groups of particles are created in a dependent way. Let's look at an example: if a pair of entangled particles are created so the total spin of the pair is zero, and I measure the spin of one of them as plus one, then the spin of the other one must be minus one--no matter how far away it is. In other words, the particle with minus one spin somehow knows that a measurement has been performed on its entangled partner particle--even if it's across the galaxy. Albert Einstein never did like this "spooky action at a distance" idea. But quantum entanglement is an active area of current research, including its possible utilization in communication. Who knows what we'll discover?

For more information and details about these and other topics, check out the Physics Is Fun website: www.physicsisfun.net

Thank you for reading *A Jack by Any Other Name*. I hope you enjoyed it!

- For more info about me or my work, please visit my author's website, http://www.lesleylsmith.com/. Sometimes, I post links for free fiction downloads!
- Please check out the Physics Is Fun website www.physicsisfun.net for lots of information about fun physics topics.
- Reviews help other readers find books. I appreciate any and all reviews.
- A sneak peek at my new novel *Conservation of Luck,* follows.

−Lesley L. Smith

Conservation of Luck

Chapter One

I gave Wei my most intimidating beady-eyed stare. Poker just calls for a beady-eyed stare, doesn't it? It was working, too, because there were only three of us left in the game.

We were all sitting around a table in the family room of Wei's apartment. It had all the bachelor accoutrements, complete with a side-of-the-road couch, an empty-beer-can pyramid, and the latest cutting-edge flat screen TV and gaming system.

"Give me a minute, Ella." He glanced down at his cards and gulped. Wei was a wiry little guy, a grad student in computer engineering, aka a nerd. He did not do well under pressure. Was that a drop of sweat rolling down his cheek?

Ha. I smiled ever so slightly.

The window air conditioner chugga-chugged in the background.

I didn't need to look down at my cards. Full house, kings over fives.

"Come on, Wei!" Malik, Wei's roommate, said. "Bet or get off the pot, dude." Malik was an engineering physics grad student, so also a nerd.

I flashed a real smile at him. He was pretty hot for a nerd, with a football player's physique. I was figuring we might hook up later. After I won, of course.

Wei and I were the only ones left with any money and this hand was winner take all. We had an informal game once a week. Lately, the guys had been bitching about me winning too much. What can I say? I rock. And as a physics grad student myself I needed the money--so, what was I gonna do? Go easy on them? I don't think so.

Wei glanced at the time on his phone and said, "You can give me a minute. This is the last hand."

"Yeah, this is the last hand. Get on with it, already." Malik grinned at me. He must be thinking the same thing I was, namely, impending possible hookup. I grinned back. I was very hot for a nerd.

Pounding on the front door interrupted us. "Ella," a woman's voice said. "I know you're in there! Open this door!" I knew that voice.

Wei breathed a sigh of relief and carefully placed cards face down on the table. "I better go get that. It sounds super important." His tone of voice said it didn't sound super important. His tone of voice said he was avoiding losing a lot of money.

"It's not," I said. "Come back and finish the hand." I knew who it was, my best friend Crystal. She was in grad school for nursing and worked as a nurse's aide. Technically, I had asked her, begged her, to give me a ride into work tonight. I needed to get back to work at the lab.

He ignored me and answered the door. "Crystal? What's the emergency? Do you need Ella for something? I bet you do. Something important."

Crystal ignored him and stalked into the room, right over to me. "There you are!" She was short, with dark blonde hair and a cute upturned nose. When she'd been younger, she reminded me of an elf, but starting when we were about seventeen, she'd been steadily gaining weight. Now, she reminded me more of a soccer mom. She said between the two of us--her small and blonde, and me tall and dark--we covered all the bases.

"Can't this wait?" I said. "I'm about to win over two hundred dollars."

"No!" she said. "It can't wait. You made me swear, swear, to make sure you made it to the lab tonight by ten o'clock at the latest." She grabbed my cards out of my hand and threw them on the floor. Some of them landed face down, luckily. "You made me swear. Tomorrow is your Masters defense. May 31, 2030. You said it was your deadline!"

Ugh. She was right. That pressure on my chest wasn't the excitement of winning, it was dread about not being in the lab. I did need to finish my project. I only had like twenty-four hours to finish or I was screwed.

I looked down at the cards on the carpet. But I was about to win. Three kings. And two fives. There was no way Wei could beat that.

Crystal grabbed my arm and pulled me towards the door. "Come on."

I resisted.

"Sounds like you better go, Ella," Wei said. "Gosh, too bad."

"No," Malik said. "If she leaves, she forfeits. That's not fair."

Crystal grabbed for something in her purse. "Don't make me tase you."

I stared at her. "Seriously?"

"You're the one who gave me the taser," she said.

Technically, that was also true. Well, damn. She pulled on me again.

I let her lead me through the room, out the door, and into the hall. Outside the heat hit us like a ball-peen hammer.

"Bye, Ella. Good luck tomorrow, " Malik was saying when Wei slammed the door after us.

The cards and the money were calling to me, 'Ella, come back!'

But I made myself take a step away from the door. And then a second step.

Once we started walking down the hall, I felt a little better. I did need to finish my project tonight. If I didn't finish it, I would flunk out of grad school. That would be almost three years down the drain. There was that chest pressure again.

Crystal's mouth pressed into a thin line as we exited the apartment building and tramped across the parking lot. "You have a problem, Ella," she said as she unlocked her car.

Why had I blown off work when I needed to do it so badly?

"Did you investigate Gamblers Anonymous like I told you to?" she said as we pulled out.

"I love you, Crystal." We'd been friends since we were little kids. She was like a sister to me. "But you're wrong. I don't need Gamblers Anonymous. I'm not addicted to gambling." Frankly, I didn't think anyone could be addicted to gambling. The idea didn't even make any sense. It wasn't like it was a drug; it was nothing like coke or meth.

"So, it's totally normal that a twenty-five-year-old woman doesn't have money for a car or rent." She drove us towards my lab on campus.

"I have a lot of debt from student loans. Lots of people do," I said. "And Mom needs me. She'd be lost without me." I still lived with my mom; it had just been the two of us from the beginning.

Crystal flashed me a look that said she didn't believe me.

My stomach rumbled. My dinner had consisted of chips at Wei and Malik's place. We approached campus. "You can drop me here," I said, pointing at the convenience store on the corner. "I want to get a snack."

She pulled into a parking place.

I opened the door and hopped out.

"You are going into the lab now, right?" she asked.

"Yes. Thank you," I said. "Have I told you lately how awesome you are?"

"No." She may have thawed a degree or two.

"Well, you're very awesome," I said. "I totally owe you one." I'd have to put on my thinking cap to come up with an appropriate thank you. But later, after I'd successfully earned my Master's degree.

"Yeah, I am, and yeah, you do." She put the car in gear. "And stay away from those scratch tickets!" she called back as she drove away.

It was do or die time and so far, it looked like I might die. I sighed, examining my supposed quantum computer on the lab table.

My advisor Professor Smithson's lab was a fifty-foot by thirty-foot high-ceilinged room filled with bolted down old-school black lab tables. Over the last few years I'd piled a few of them pretty high with electronic components and computers and such.

Maybe I had bitten off more than I could chew. There were a few other q-computers in the world but they'd been created by large groups of experts.

Professor Smithson had warned me the project might be too big for a student. He said most Master's students got teaching jobs at the university rather than doing research, but I'd convinced him I could do it. I thought I could do it. I'd bet I could do it.

The machine should be working.

Why wasn't the damn thing working?

My cell rang. It was Mom. I stepped over and stood in front of one of the windows. "Unless you know why my qubits aren't working, I don't have time to talk to you right now," I said.

"I just called to see how things are going, Ella," she said. "I'm guessing not good."

She meant well but she didn't understand the pressure I was under. "No."

"So, will you be home at all tonight?"

"I'm not sure."

"What did you do for dinner?" she asked. "Should I leave something out for you?"

"No," I said. "I'll just grab something out of the vending machine here if I need it." I'd already eaten a questionable convenience store burrito and gotten a thirty-two-ounce cup of soda on my way into the lab. The soda sat here on my desk, next to my purse. It should last me all night if necessary.

"Okay, honey. I'm sure you'll figure it out."

"Thanks." Usually, I would share her confidence. But I was getting uncomfortably close to the wire--even for me.

"You're a brilliant young woman. I don't know where you get it from, you're nothing like me."

How many times had we had this conversation? She was a nurturing artist and my mysterious MIA dad was supposedly the good-with-numbers one. She was brilliant in her own way. But I was sick of telling her that. "Thanks, but, Mom, I'm busy."

Of course, I didn't know my dad so everything about him was a mystery. Mom said she updated him periodically about me and yet I never heard anything from him and we certainly never got any child support from him. Or birthday presents. Or Christmas presents. Or anything. So, basically, what I knew about him was he was an asshole.

"Okay," she said. "Good luck, not that you need it--"

"Thanks. Bye." I hung up and put my phone back in my purse. Geez. It was hot in here. You wouldn't think it would be almost a hundred degrees at 10:00 p.m. but there it was: Hello, global warming.

I took a drink and then opened the window over my desk and strode over to my equipment.

A breeze wafted across the room as I stared at my computer. It should be working. I'd used a scanning tunneling microscope to selectively remove hydrogen atoms on the surface of the silicon. Then, I'd added the doping gas. I peered at the small machine through the microscope. The acceptor atoms were at high density, in several layers. Bottom line: it was still silicon and it was superconducting.

I straightened and powered up the current again. On the monitoring computer, this time I noticed there was a blip of something that disappeared almost immediately. Ah ha. The info on the qubits was decaying too rapidly. My continuous measurements weren't correcting for this, as they should. I knew what the problem was: something was wrong with the readout resonator.

I got to work.

After I don't know how many hours, I fired everything up again and held my breath.

The monitoring computer registered eight qubits operating with no information decay. I jumped up. My lab stool clattered to the ground as it fell over. "Yes! It's working! It's working!"

I jumped up and down a little more. "Oh, yeah. Yay for me. I'm gonna graduate. Yeah, yeah. Hurray for me! I rock!" After a few minutes of this I felt a little sheepish. I righted my stool and sat down again.

"Okay, easy does it." I sent it a question: '1 + 1 = ?' Of course, q-computers were built for complicated calculations but they could do arithmetic too.

The quantum superpositions collapsed and I got back '2.'

"Yes!" I screamed and threw my fist into the air. "Yes, yes, yes! It works. It works. Master's degree, here I come!"

Then, I heard a sound from the doorway.

When I turned to look. that way, an older man wearing a security uniform was pointing a gun at me. "Freeze." I couldn't take my eyes off the gun. It looked ginormous.

I froze. "Uh, hi. Why are you pointing a gun at me?"

"What are you doing here?" he said. "Are you an intruder?

Are you here to steal something from the lab?" The gun, still pointing at me, shook. I felt my pulse ratchet up.

"Please calm down. I'm Ella Hote. I'm not an intruder. This is my lab. I'm a graduate student."

"Yeah, right." A bead of sweat rolled down his face. "What are you, like, eighteen years old? This isn't your lab." His color didn't look so good. His skin was sort of gray.

Still frozen, I said, "I'm twenty-four. And a half. But, are you all right, buddy?" He looked like he might collapse any second. "Do you want to sit down? Maybe you should sit down."

"You're just trying to get the jump on me." He waved the gun around and I felt sweat break out on my own face. "If this is your lab," he said, "show me your ID."

"Yes, sir. I'd be happy to do that. Whatever you want." I paused. "Can I un-freeze?"

"Yeah. But slowly."

Slowly un-freeze? A hysterical giggle almost escaped. "My ID is over there on my desk." I very slowly walked over to my desk, opened my purse and took out my wallet. I opened my wallet.

I heard a very loud pop, like a big firecracker going off as something zinged by my head. The window behind me shattered.

By instinct I crouched down. My heart hammered in my chest. This guy was going to kill me. How could he kill me when I just got my quantum computer to work? How could he kill me when I was about to get my Master's degree?

The glass stopped falling. I looked over at the guard.

He seemed confused. "Sorry," he said. His gun was still pointed my way. "I don't feel so good." He was having trouble catching his breath.

What was wrong with him? Clearly, something. "Are you sure you don't want to sit down?"

"ID!" he said.

Unfortunately, now, I had no idea where my wallet was. It wasn't in my purse. It wasn't on my desk. I looked around on the floor. Nope. "I can't find my wallet." I glanced out the broken window. Three stories down, I saw my purple wallet and assorted cards and IDs lying on the ground behind the bushes. "Uh, I think it's outside." Had I somehow thrown them out the window?

"That's it. I'm calling the cops." His shaky gun was still pointed at me.

I couldn't be arrested. I'd miss my Master's defense. I pulled my phone out of my purse and checked the time. Oh, no. My defense was scheduled for 10:00 a.m.--a mere four hours away. "Let me call Professor Smithson. It's his lab. He'll verify I work for him."

Right as I was about to dial his number, I heard a loud thunk. Scared another bullet might be coming, I jerked down and dropped my phone. Splash. It went right into my soda. "Shit."

In the meantime, the security guard had dropped the gun and was slumped against the doorway. "My arm hurts." He clutched his left arm against his chest.

I ran to him. "Do you have a cell?"

He nodded and fumbled at his shirt pocket.

I grabbed his cell and dialed 911.

At somewhere around 9:00 a.m. I arrived home in a taxi. Of course, I didn't have my wallet. I prayed Mom was still home. Since she was almost always late for work, odds were in my favor. "Just a moment, sir," I said to the cabbie. "I have to get your money from inside."

I ran up the stairs in front of our duplex and unlocked the front door. "Mom? Are you still home?" Our place was small and old, filled with furniture that was small and old--but it was our own.

"There you are, Ella," she said. "I was worried." Her concerned expression contrasted with her cheerful hand-made rainbow-colored teddy-bear scrubs. Even in her scrubs, Mom was beautiful with glossy dark hair, animated eyes, and luscious curves. She was proud of her appearance except for the fact that most people thought she was Mexican rather than Native American. People said I took after her.

"I'm sorry I worried you. I'll tell you what happened later. Can you pay the taxi driver?" I was already headed to the bathroom. I should have just enough time to shower, put on my suit and dash back to school in time for my defense.

"I don't think I have any cash," she said.

"I'm begging you, Mom," I called back to her. "I don't care

what you use: credit card, beer, sexual favors, please just take care of him."

I reached the bathroom, turned on the shower, and started stripping.

I came back out of the house about fifteen minutes later. Mom stood in front, still talking to the swarthy taxi driver. He looked like he'd just arrived from Iran or Turkey, all brown skin and black whiskers, with plenty of wavy black hair.

She giggled and tossed her hair. Correction, still flirting with the taxi driver. Her flirting abilities were legendary. Who do you think I learned from? I grinned, seeing her in her element.

"Actually, this is great," I said to the driver. "Can I get a ride to campus?"

The taxi driver inclined his head at Mom and said, "I already have a fare."

Mom smiled. "He offered to take me to the hospital. Such a nice man."

"I'm sure he is a nice man," I said. "But aren't you late for work, Mom?"

"Mom?" the driver said, smiling broadly. "Impossible. You must be her sister. You couldn't be old enough to be her mother." The cabbie clearly had flirting skills of his own.

Mom smiled some more and looked into his eyes.

I got into the taxi. "Can we please go? Please." I was already starting to sweat into my fresh clothes. It was going to be another scorcher.

The driver shrugged. "Whatever the lady desires." He stared at Mom.

"The lady desires to go." She gestured me to move over and scooted into the back seat next to me.

As we drove away, she asked, "Why didn't you come home last night?"

In the rear-view mirror, I could see the driver's eyebrows rise as he looked at me.

"Unfortunately, the security guard on duty last night in the building had a heart attack."

Mom raised her hand to her mouth. "Oh, no."

"I had to call an ambulance and I rode with him to the

286

hospital. And then I called his wife and waited until she got there. I guess he's going to be okay." I yawned. My lost sleep hadn't been for nothing.

"It sounds like he was very lucky you were there," Mom said. "Quick treatment makes a huge difference with heart attacks. We see it all the time in the ER."

"Do you usually work so late?" the driver asked me.

"No, not usually," I said, mind whirling. It was lucky for the guard that I was there. Probably any other night he would have collapsed and not been discovered for hours. Probably any other night he would have died. It was a sobering and sad thought.

When I came out of my reverie, traffic had crawled to a stop. What time was it? I didn't have my phone to check. Ugh. I needed to get a new phone. "What time is it?"

Mom glanced at her watch. "Nine forty-five. You're cutting it close, Ella."

"I see that." I craned my neck. No traffic was moving. We were already across the street from campus, a couple blocks from my building.

I opened the door and stood on the pavement. Traffic was at an absolute standstill. I leaned down and said into the taxi, "I'm gonna hoof it."

"Okay," Mom said as I closed the door. "Good luck!"

I started speedwalking towards campus.

Behind me I could faintly hear the taxi driver ask, "Good luck with what?"

Moving quickly but trying not to sweat too much on my suit, I passed several parked cars. And then I passed several crunched cars.

Moaning, bleeding people lay on the pavement. It was horrible. "Oh, God."

As I approached, an older woman whispered, "Help me, please." She was bleeding from her head and her leg twisted unnaturally underneath her.

"I will. My mom's a nurse. She's just back there. I'll go get her." I turned and started running.

I helped Mom triage. We enlisted some of the other commuters to apply pressure to bleeding wounds and to keep

287

the less-wounded but still scared people company until the ambulances arrived. Thank goodness none of the injuries were life-threatening.

And then I ran to my defense.

I got there, panting, at 10:40 a.m. The room was surprisingly empty. Oh no. Professor Smithson was there and a couple graduate students, but that was it. Professor Smithson looked just like you'd imagine the perfect grandfather to look. He always wore dapper suits and his full head of wavy pure-white hair was always perfectly groomed. I half expected him to take a pocket watch out of his vest and examine it. "Did I miss it?" I asked him. "Did you flunk me?"

Professor Smithson frowned. "No. Everyone's late for some reason." He looked closer at me. "Are you all right? Is that blood?"

I glanced down at my wrinkled bloody suit. "I'm okay. It's not my blood." I collapsed in a chair and tried to catch my breath. "There was a pretty bad car accident in front of campus."

"That's unfortunate," he said.

I nodded and sucked air into my lungs. "Especially for the people that were hurt."

When I finally got my breathing under control I stood up. "So, what's happening? Are we going to start? Can we without the rest of my committee?"

"I think we're going to have to wait for them," Professor Smithson said.

"I'm going to take a few minutes to go freshen up, then." I shuddered to think what I must look like.

As I walked past him, he touched my arm. "Ella, did you get it to work?" The look of concern in his eyes was how I always imagined a dad would look at his daughter. Of course Professor Smithson was old enough to be my grandfather, but still.

I nodded, throat suddenly full. "Yes. I got it to work." I smiled.

He smiled. "That's wonderful! I knew you could do it, Ella!" His praise was amazing. It washed over me like a warm wave. I'd never felt so good. Was this what it was like to have a proud father? My eyes felt full.

I tried to fix the moment in my memory. Remember this,

forever, Ella. He's proud of me.

We stood there for a few moments smiling until one of my other professors entered the room.

"Sorry!" Professor Perez said. "Are you waiting for me? There was a terrible traffic accident."

The moment was gone. "I'll be right back."

"No, Juan," Professor Smithson said. "Everyone else is late, too. We haven't started yet."

"Good." He rubbed his hands together. "I'm eager to put Ella through her paces."

I wasn't sure I could handle many more paces. So far, this whole day had been very challenging. I tried not to let my nerves take over as I raced down the hall to the restroom.